Andrei LIVADNY

The Curse of Rion Castle

The Neuro

BOOK TWO

MAGIC DOME BOOKS

The Curse of Rion Castle
The Neuro, Book # 2
Copyright © Andrei Livadny 2017
Cover Art © Vladimir Manyukhin 2017
English translation copyright ©
Irene Woodhead & Neil P. Mayhew 2017
Published by Magic Dome Books, 2017
All Rights Reserved
ISBN: 978-80-88231-31-8

TABLE OF CONTENTS:

CHAPTER ONE

A WARM STARRY night swept over the Toxic Moors.

Mere minutes had elapsed since Christa and Enea had faced each other in combat.

Reams of system messages flashed through my mental view,

Congratulations! You've activated the castle's stationary teleport!

Congratulations! You've activated the castle's safe respawn zone!

Congratulations! You've claimed ownership of Rion Castle!

You've received a new level!

New quest alert: Purge
Quest type: unique
Before dawn breaks, you need to purge the donjon of the spawn of the Dark.
Reward: By succeeding, you'll remove the ancient curse cast on the castle by enemy wizards. The castle control interface will be unblocked.

Wisps of mist floated in the moonlight. The ancient citadel dominated the island, its three defense levels masterfully cut into the towering cliffs. Rion Castle had suffered a lot during the century-old siege. Its walls were breached, its gate towers lying in heaps of collapsed stonework.

Time had completed what the enemy had begun. Autumnal storms had buried the inner yards in rotten leaves and broken tree branches which had eventually formed a fertile layer of top soil, offering root hold to thick woody vines which rambled up the castle walls, shrouding them in a green veil of oblivion.

I stood in the yard, facing the donjon. From now on, this was our clan seat. The heart of Rion Castle was cut in three precipitous peaks fashioned into towers. Their walls were lined with small fortified platforms built at several levels. Arrow-slit defense galleries and the tall vaulting windows of inner halls adorned the towering structures.

At a distance, strange calls echoed over the moors. Moonlight seeped over the ancient walls.

Rusty door hinges creaked. Zander, the mercenaries' commander, walked over to me and looked up, following my gaze.

"Alexatis, we're wasting our time," he said. "Don't you think we should be getting on with the purge? We only have seven hours left till sunrise. What are you waiting for?"

"I can't find anything about this ancient curse," I admitted as I watched a ghost's translucent outline appear from a breach in the wall, heading for a window above. "It's not in the Wiki. Forums don't mention it, either."

Shadows flashed past in the moonlight — probably a group of gargoyles moving from one defense platform to the next.

"Level thirty," Zander commented before the wall-nesting beasts could disappear from sight.

A weak light oozed through a row of arrowslits overhead. A few windows above them welled with a dull crimson glow.

"If this is in the quest you and Enea received, then you should be able to do it,"

Zander said confidently. "The night won't be boring, that's for sure."

He grinned in anticipation of combat. "Listen. You've got both the castle's stationary portal and its respawn point activated. I might bring in a few more men if you wish. Ten, maybe? What would you say to that?"

As I pondered over the state of my bank account, the others joined us. All but Platinus, that is. Our alchemist had stayed inside the donjon, rummaging through the mostly broken artifacts which littered the floor of the main hall. The majority of them were utterly useless — but still he'd managed to locate a quite decent wizard's staff which he'd immediately gifted to Enea to replace the one she'd broken during her fight with Christa.

Iskandar and Rodrigo, our two wizards, kept squinting curiously at the ancient item.

"Mind if we take a look?" they finally asked her.

"Sure," Enea replied matter-of-factly. She was still pale and tense from the recent combat. "I can't see its stats for some reason. Only question marks."

"How strange," Rodrigo agreed. "Look at the stone, it's gone completely dull."

"May I?" Iskandar took the staff from him but equally failed to bring it back to life. The weak spark which had initially glowed within the precious stone had already expired.

Iskandar shrugged. "How are you supposed to activate it? You sure our levels are high enough to use it?"

Togien shifted from one foot to the other, impatient. "Alexatis, what are we waiting for?"

"I'm trying to work out how to remove the curse."

"Don't overcomplicate things, man. The quest says we've got to purge the castle. And that's what we're gonna do! We'll mop the place up room by room. How difficult is that? We'll be done by the morning!"

Enea walked over to me.

The miniscule Alpha, her new Black Mantis pet, crawled out of her tresses and jumped over to her shoulder, then scurried down her arm until it reached her fingers. From there, he climbed onto the staff and scampered all the way to the top where he froze, studying the dead stone.

Funny critter. He sat there for some time, meditating, then scampered back down the staff.

"Alpha, you're hurting me!" Enea cried out. The little mantis had apparently pricked her fingertip.

Why would he do that? Why would a pet deal damage to its owner?

Blood from the wound trickled onto the staff which turned transparent, revealing what looked like a web of mummified blood vessels within. The bright drops of Enea's blood filtered inside and were immediately absorbed, filling and feeding the staff's shriveled capillaries.

A light flashed within the stone. Slowly at first, it began to pulsate faster and faster as if Enea's blood had breathed life back into it.

The Heart of a Hydra
Item type: A magic staff
Class: Relic
-50% to the Mental Energy expenditure required to cast a spell.
+10% to Physical Defense
+10% to mental defense
+10% to close-combat Damage
Effect: Aura of a Predator. Slows down or repels all non-Elemental enemies.
Restriction: only a rightful defender of Rion Castle

"You're one lucky girl," Rodrigo said in amazement, studying the item's stats. "But why Elemental? Isn't the Founders' magic based on Chaos?"

"You're the expert," Iskandar grinned sarcastically. "Enea, don't listen, he's just jealous. There's nothing we know for certain about the Founders or their magic, only rumors. No one has ever managed to study any of the ruins they left behind. In this respect, you and Alexatis have been really lucky."

"He's right," Rodrigo nodded. "Can you even imagine all the secrets these walls might harbor? Or the power of a clan smart enough to uncover them? Even I — I did hear about the ancient blood magic, of course, but I had no idea some of its artifacts had actually survived..."

"Right," Zander interrupted their discussion. 'Alexatis, what did you decide? Should I call in some reinforcements? Or do you think we can manage?"

Mechanically I glanced at my interface clock.

23.59.52

He had a point. It was midnight and we hadn't even started.

"Okay," I said. "We can use a few more men."

❋ ❋ ❋

DARKNESS FELL when least expected.

One moment the Moon illuminated the

donjon; the heavy sounds of the hydras' footsteps wading through the quagmire traveled far in the crystalline air. Then all the arrowslits and windows spewed out a viscous black fog which enveloped everything around us, wiping out the stars and damping all the sounds.

I stretched out my hand but couldn't see my own fingers.

"What's going on?" Platinus' angry voice came from inside. "Who turned off the lights?"

The earth shuddered underfoot.

"Get away from me!" a weak flash of light came from inside the donjon as Platinus, scared out of his mind, hurled one of his vials at some attacking force. I heard an angry growl but couldn't see any details in the darkness that flooded the air.

00.00

This was midnight by the Crystal Sphere's in-game time!

"Follow my voice!" Zander bellowed, failing to get to the teleport. "We need to stay close!"

The darkness shifted, its intangible depths stirring. A heavy wingbeat hit me with a sudden gust of wind. Something huge rushed past overhead. I heard a thumping sound and a weak cry, followed by the screeching of claws tearing through armor.

Togien. Warrior
Current status: Awaiting respawn.

Wheezing noises were followed by the rattling of swords. A yellowed shard of bone flew through the air, landing at my feet. The flash of a spell tore through the darkness.

Platinus. Sorcerer
Current status: Awaiting respawn.

The ancient curse cast over Rion Castle is active from midnight till dawn. It increases all respawn times tenfold and casts a Degeneration debuff on all respawned creatures, both players and NPCs, detracting 5 pt. from all stats for the duration of 5 hrs. with the exception of the Cohort of the Fallen.

* * *

"THEY'RE everywhere!" Iskandar shouted.

The viscous darkness stood between us. Even my Twilight Vision ability proved useless against it. The only way to find one's bearings was by focusing on the sounds — which too were spine-chilling. Masonry crumbling. Paving stones shifting with a screech.

A pair of bony hands grabbed at my shins. I sliced through the shriveled flesh, wrestling free of their grasp.

"Enea!" I shouted, leaping aside.

For a brief moment, a Cleansing Aura cast by Zander illuminated the entire area. The darkness shrank back, revealing a hair-raising view. About a dozen high-level warriors in rusty armor had surrounded the mercs. Pierced by a spear, Virgil's avatar was slowly vanishing. Tylor had sunk to one knee, his shield split, his sword broken, his life bar rapidly fading. His tag was absolutely crowded with debuff icons.

The earth shuddered again.

A cloud of ash rose into the air. Its particles were rapidly fusing, forming yet another tall outline.

A Fallen Legionnaire. Level 27

A rush of horror ran over me. I hurried to cast a spell before the enemy could complete his reincarnation. A roaring column of fire scorched through the darkness, scattering the ashes in the air.

I swung round. Behind me, Enea, Rodrigo and Iskandar were also surrounded. Still, the pulsating stone which topped the Staff of a Hydra prevented their enemies from getting too close. The staff's Aura of a Predator slowed the attackers' movements, saving the wizards from an imminent hand-to-hand.

Virgil. Warrior
Current status: Awaiting respawn

Tylor. Warrior
Current status: Awaiting respawn

The light expired.

Before the darkness could close over us, I grabbed a spear from the ground and hurled it at the nearest legionnaire in a desperate attempt to come to Zander's aid.

He was still going strong. The blade of his longsword tirelessly drew new combos in the air. Still, the thickening gloom had already begun to consume the dying glitter of the moonsilver weapon.

Rodrigo. Combat Wizard
Current status: Awaiting respawn

Iskandar. Combat Wizard
Current status: Awaiting respawn

Zander's icon in the group's interface

flashed red.

"Enea!" I shouted, trying to locate her in the pitch darkness. To no avail.

"Alex, I'm here! Help!"

A wall of fire rose to the sky, repelling the enemies' dark outlines.

I darted toward her. One of the legionnaires had already raised his spear, about to bury it in Enea's chest. Sensing my approach, he began to turn to face me. Too late. My sword sliced through his crumbling armor, extracting a hoarse scream from him.

Zander. Paladin
Current status: Awaiting respawn

This was a complete and utter wipeout.

The heaps of wind-driven fallen leaves began to smolder. Enea and I stood back to back. The undead legionnaires — there were five of them left — surrounded us. Our chances were minimal. My heart raced. I struggled to breathe.

The stench of death floated over the ground. To me, all this was perfectly real. The neuroimplant kept flooding my brain with the graphic images of our enemies' armor glinting in the dying flames, their visors oozing gloom. The dirt underfoot was mixed with fallen leaves and the shreds of burned flesh.

A bead of sweat dripped from my forehead, snaking down my cheek. I could feel Enea shiver. The legionnaires lingered, wary of the Aura of a Predator.

Fragments of thoughts flashed through my mind. I'd almost made the next level. I could take the risk. I had to attack them first.

"Keep healing me!" I shouted to Enea.

With my left hand I grabbed a spear lying in the smoldering grass and buried it in the nearest enemy's shield. The zombie swung round with the impact; the heavy spear shaft dipped, tracing a semicircle over the ground until it tripped up the feet of the legionnaire next to him. Trying to keep his balance, he opened up, allowing me to stab him with my sword. He recoiled and dropped his weapon, howling and clutching instinctively at his wound as if to stop the gushing of blood.

I swung round again. My sword's blade glinted through the gloom. Another enemy started making croaking noises.

I moved fast, giving it my all. The Aura of a Predator turned out to be one hell of a powerful debuff. The Staff of a Hydra slowed the enemies down, constricting their movements — but still the level gap worked in their favor. Two of them managed to get to me. Pain flooded my mind. I lost my footing before I could complete a new

---

attack. Blood trickled down my leg. A hefty blow from a rusty battle hammer had made my shoulder numb.

I somehow managed to block a new blow and stepped back, limping. Enea kept healing me non-stop but the flashes of the Minor Heal took too long to restore my health properly.

Still, I'd already smoked one of them. Four to go. The mercs had done a good job on them. Legionnaires didn't have Regeneration. Their life bars glowed crimson. All I had to do was finish them off. I could do that!

The tallest and strongest of them hurled his shield aside and lunged onto me. His oxidized sword whooshed through the air. I ducked just in time, slashing at his leg, then rolled over the ground toward the next one, stabbing him in the chest from below. His heavy body collapsed on top of me, pinning me to the ground, then crumbled to ashes.

A fireball roared past my shoulder. Another zombie went up in flames, torch-like, before he could finalize his attack. Still running, he took a few more steps and dissolved into a cloud of soot which slowly drifted to the ground.

Two left. This wasn't so bad, after all. Enea promptly ported out of another zombie's reach. A crossbow twanged in the dark. A heavy bolt pierced my armor and stuck deep in my ribs.

My life promptly plummeted, stopping at 10%. Blood gushed from the wound. My breathing seized. My vision swam. I couldn't expect an immediate heal as Enea's mental energy bar was dangerously close to zero while my sword kept siphoning my mana, feeding it to the glowing runes which allowed me to deal additional damage.

I struggled to remain standing. The Mortal Wound debuff I'd received with the crit prevented me from moving freely.

"Alex, the vial!" Enea cried out in desperation.

Impossible. My legs were weak, my fingers didn't obey me; the quick access slots in my interface blurred, then faded. My mind began to shut down.

I must have zoned out for a few seconds. A green flash exploded before my eyes. The pain released me. My every muscle filled with strength. My life and mental energy indicators soared, filling to the brim.

You've received a new level!

Still unbelieving that I'd somehow avoided going to my respawn point, I sprang to my feet and cast a look around.

Enea was nowhere to be seen. Two of the

surviving legionnaires stood with their backs to me, peering into the thick darkness.

One of them threw his hand in the air, pointing. "There!"

Still reeling from the shock, I unhesitantly lunged at them before they could disappear into the dark. I critted one (because a surprise attack almost always ends in a crit), then dodged the other one's blow by ducking under his battle hammer's path, slashed at his legs, then shrank aside and froze in place.

You've received a new level!

The darkness around me began to fall apart, disintegrating into separate wisps and revealing the dull pulsating glow of the gem topping the Staff of the Hydra.

"Enea!"

She turned round. With a weak cry, she rushed toward me and threw herself on my neck, pressing her body against mine, oblivious of everything around us. Her heart fluttered in her chest.

"Alex... you're alive..."

This wasn't like a game at all. The situation was too intense and poignant, too fragile, too real-life.

"It's all right. Don't get so worked up," I

stroked her hair. "You've saved me from respawning."

She sniffled. "No, I haven't. I just didn't know what to do. My hands shook so badly I spilled half the vial. I tried to heal you but it didn't work. Then those two bastards went for you. I ported without even looking. That orc just sat there stringing his crossbow. He stank like you can't imagine. His armor was all rusty. I was so jumpy I just hit him with Lightning."

"That's it! That's how I got the little bit of XP I needed!"[1]

"Really?" she ran her hand over my stubbly cheek. Embarrassed, she stepped back to pick up her staff from the ground. "So what are we going to do?"

Good question. I looked around. We'd done the first floor — or at least the outside of it. The darkness had shrunk upwards, swirling.

The little Black Mantis climbed out onto Enea's shoulder and cast a watchful eye around. Having noticed no danger, he began rearranging a disheveled lock of her hair. Cute beastie. He might grow up into a fearsome and devoted pet.

"Zander was right about one thing," I said. "A quest is always doable. If the curse can't be removed, they'd have simply rejected our castle

---

[1] As Enea and Alexatis are in a group, the XP they receive is divided evenly between them.

application."

"But there're only two of us left," Enea said anxiously. "The others won't be back till sunrise — and their debuffs will still be active!"

The trolls' heart-rending screams came from the tower's upper floors. It looked like the legionnaires killed everything in their path indiscriminately.

"I haven't found out anything about the curse," I said. "But now we have another lead to follow. Try to find what you can about the Cohort of the Fallen."

"Okay. Do you want us to stay here?"

"No. We're going upstairs. I want to see if the donjon is split into several locations."

"What's that gonna do for us?"

"If every floor is a separate location, then we just might be able to purge them all. Do you remember what I said to you about the game mechanics?"

A smile touched her lips. She must have remembered the pond, the toad and her first little triumph. "I see. Does that mean that Zander's level triggered the mobs' attack? Did you say they were adaptive?"

She was gradually learning to use the lingo. "Exactly. If these locations are adaptive, it means that the mobs too should be doable," I said, trying to cheer her up.

The recent fight with Christa had had a strange effect on her. Enea had grown quiet and unsmiling. Her impulsiveness was gone; a sudden fatigue had replaced her original excitement with the gameplay. She just wasn't used to it yet. Spending twenty-four hours sitting at the console surrounded by lifelike holograms could cause a serious mental overload in a newb.

* * *

"COME ON now," I drew Enea into the Resurrection Hall. According to the map, that was the name of the main hall of the donjon's first level.

It was dark. The lamps lining the walls had expired. Little purple lights floated over the teleport platform. I'd never managed to get to the control unit plastered with runes. Still, we didn't have the time. I'd have to leave all such experiments till morning.

The Heart of a Hydra cast its light onto the ancient walls. A narrow tunnel-like staircase snaked through the stonework, rising to the donjon's next level. The remnants of several portcullises, dilapidated and rusty, had blocked it once, preventing an attacking enemy from breaking through to the top floors.

Enea was busy looking it up online. Even though we'd received our first prompt, we still had to find out whether there was any mention of the Cohort in public access.

The thick layer of dust mixed with ashes felt springy underfoot. The darkness swirled high overhead. We'd have to enter it soon. In the meantime, I used Twilight Vision which highlighted the outlines of all objects which had been lying here since the times of the epic battle.

I picked up a good sturdy shield. The sword kept siphoning my mental energy. I didn't mind, really. It would be stupid to pass up the opportunity to deal some additional damage to the enemy. The narrow staircase, too, offered a decent chance of repelling any surprise attacks, as least long enough for Enea to cast her spells.

"Got it!" she exclaimed.

I was so glad to hear the excitement back in her voice. "Tell me. In a nutshell."

"I'd better read it. Here:

In days far gone, when the powers of Light and Dark had united against the followers of the Founder Gods, Rion Castle had become the last stronghold of the ancient religion, offering refuge to its remaining worshippers. Many a desperate year did the siege last. Many a time did the attackers attempt to storm the castle — all to no avail."

I interrupted her, "We know all this

already, don't we? What we need to find out is who the Fallen Legionnaires are."

She continued reading,

"The Cohort of the Chosen used to unite the strongest warriors, sorcerers and wizards amongst the Disciples. They didn't know defeat. Their arrival used to decide the outcome of the most desperate of battles. In the meantime, the dissent amongst the besiegers grew: you can't expect Light and Dark to coexist in peace. Soon it became pretty clear that the coalition was living its last days. Seeing that, the leader of the demons suggested launching one final offensive. Upon his orders, tunnels were dug through to the castle's underground dungeons. And as the battle reached its climax, hundreds of dark wizards sacrificed themselves to cast one last spell, shattering the cliffs in a desperate combined effort. The Cohort of the Chosen was sent to stop the assault..."

Enea stopped to catch her breath. I peered into the gloom. Up the slightly winding staircase, I could just see a door on a small landing.

"You all right?" I asked Enea without turning.

"Just out of breath," she said, gasping. The stone on top of her staff seemed to pulsate faster in synch with her rapid heartbeat. "I've installed a new VR system last night. I'm not quite used to it yet."

"So what about the Cohort? Did they manage to repel the demons' attack?"

"I don't think so. Here's what it says,

"Then the Higher Demons summoned a powerful control curse from the bowels of the earth. Only a few of the legionnaires managed to resist the spell while all others fell victim to dark magic and attacked their own from behind. The spell-bound warriors slaughtered the wizards before they could cast cleansing auras on them. And by doing so, they broke the solemn oath they had sworn to the Founders and became the Cohort of the Fallen."

"And the curse, what's that all about?"

"Every night the legionnaires return to relive that fateful night. Over and over again they betray their friends and storm the castle, killing everything in their path."

"Does that mean they're still formally under the demons' control?"

"Apparently not. Although the Cohort of the Fallen is listed under the Powers of the Dark, the legionnaires don't follow their orders. They simply pay for what they have wrought."

"You mean, they know what they're doing?"

"I think so, but they don't seem to be able to change anything," she offered.

I walked up the stairs and pushed the door. It creaked open, revealing a small room behind. It must have been an armory. The floor was littered with arrows and an occasional rusty sword. Halberds leaned against the wall. A few empty oil vats stood in the corner.

"Any ideas how we could lift the curse?" I asked her.

"Not yet," she admitted. "Can't think of anything at the moment. We might receive more prompts, you never know. In any case, I don't think we can just 'mop the place up room by room,' as Togien suggested. There're just too many of them."

"True," I said, exiting the room which held nothing of interest. The staircase led upward. Very soon we'd have to re-enter the darkness.

* * *

WE CONTINUED up the stairs. Soon the sticky darkness closed around us again, filled with mind-chilling whispers and whimpering.

The staff's light struggled to dispel the viscous gloom. It didn't cast long shadows any more, exuding a weak light around us.

"It's so cold here..."

I too was frozen to the bone. I didn't see where I was going anymore. The pressure on my mind kept growing.

"Alex," Enea said softly, "what is it between you and Christa?"

"Sorry, can we discuss it some other time? I'll tell you everything, I promise," I climbed up another stair and froze, listening in. I didn't hear anything suspicious.

"No, let's do it now," impatient jealous notes rang in her voice. "Why does this bitch always have to stand in our way?"

I turned to her in disbelief. What was wrong with her?

The staff's unsteady light sharpened her features. I didn't recognize the look in her eyes. I couldn't figure it out.

The Heart of a Hydra pulsated faster.

The staff's sharp end scratched the floor as she flung it up, pointing it at my chest.

She changed her grip on it, grasping the staff with both hands. So tense, so beautiful. So desirable.

What the hell had happened? The world seemed to have turned inside out. My most secret, most impossible dreams had suddenly resurfaced, escaping my self-control.

"Do you love her?"

Our locked gazes filled with pain. Our

emotions tensed up, sharpening to the point of insanity. One rash word, and there'd be no way back.

The runes on my sword glowed defiantly. Enea waited for me to answer. Still, the truth would kill her.

Once again our stares met. My forehead felt cold with sweat. My fingers closed around the hilt of my sword. My emotions were in overdrive, choking reason, drowning it in the depths of resurfacing desires.

"Alex, talk to me! I dropped everything and followed you like an idiot!"

In real life, moments like these are bound to end in either a desperate show of passion — or in a breakup. We both were like live wires devoid of reason.

Her lips shook. The daggers in her cold prickly glare pierced my heart but failed to dishearten my agonizing desire to possess what I couldn't have.

The darkness kept creeping up on us, enveloping us, disgorging faint shadowy outlines...

Enea saw them too. "Let's put an end to this!" she exhaled bitterly.

We struck out in synch.

Her staff's sharp tip missed my temple by a hair. My sword flashed through the gloom, piercing the clot of darkness just over her shoulder.

Clinging to each other, we watched the two shadowy silhouettes gain shape and detail, materializing. Two sorcerers clad in rotten tattered robes slumped to the ground behind our backs.

I could feel her heart flutter against mine.

My ears rang with the adrenaline rush.

The curse of Rion Castle had brushed our minds just to show us how deep and treacherous the emotional void could be. Its edge is all too easy to overstep; its abyss a long and hopeless drop.

"No," her hand touched my lips. "Don't say anything."

* * *

"STEP BACK," I croaked, sensing the cold's freezing approach.

We descended a dozen steps to the safety of the wall's curve and stopped by the armory's open door, just outside of the swirling darkness.

Enea was gasping, averting her embarrassed gaze.

I was seriously worried about her. Very. "Why would the castle's curse affect you so badly?"

She must have sensed the anxiety in my voice but not the reason for it. "Shouldn't it?"

I vividly imagined her in her VR room, surrounded by holograms. A player perceives the visuals and audio effects, plus an occasional input from the environment generator, allowing Enea to sense smells, temperature changes or the touch of a breeze. The tactile sensors allowed her to "feel" the objects around her. The shock membranes imitated the damage taken.

All of the above combined could build a rather believable immersive experience — but that was the extent of it! There was only one device which could affect a player's mind, triggering an uncontrollable surge of emotions.

The neuroimplant.

"What made you freak out like that?" I demanded.

"Alex, please! I don't know, do I? Just a momentary lapse. I couldn't think straight. I'm sorry, okay? To tell you the truth, I'm a bit tired. This new VR system is too powerful. I think that's what must have caused it."

"What, that new cutting-edge equipment? Could you describe it to me?"

What she said made me completely change my view of our technology levels. "Just a new-generation VR capsule. It's filled with special sensory gel. It comes with a feedback feature and resistance emulators. The immersion effect is just out of this world."

"That wouldn't explain how the curse could affect your brain! I'd like you to touch your right temple. Can you feel anything there?"

"Alex, please. Get a grip. What's wrong with you?"

I didn't reply, waiting for her to do it.

"Okay, okay," Enea touched her right temple. Or rather, her avatar repeated the movement she made in real life.

"And? Can you feel anything? Tell me!"

"I can feel something, yeah. A chip? So what?" she shrugged. "The sensory gel is absolutely stuffed with them."

"You need to log out — *now!*"

"Excuse me?" she stared closely in my eye. "Is this how you normally break up with someone? Couldn't think of anything better?"

A wave of heat rushed over me.

She didn't know! They'd used her! Without her consent! She too was part of the experiment!

"Alex? I'm waiting. Either you tell me what it's all about or I *will* leave this time," she sounded angry and upset.

"Let's go somewhere safe," I grabbed her hand and dragged her inside the armory, then closed the door shut behind us.

She perched on top of an upright barrel

and gave me a frowned look.

I forced the massive bolt bar shut and took a seat next to her. "Has anyone told you about neuroimplants?" I asked, struggling not to betray my emotional state.

"First time I hear about them."

"It's just a small gadget which processes all gaming events, then feeds them into the host's brain, allowing the player to experience virtual reality first hand."

"Bullshit. Impossible. The equipment I ordered is the latest thing. I consulted the experts. I wanted the best I could have. No one even mentioned something like that to me."

"Okay. Now I want you to do a quick online search. Have a look at the accident reports for March 18 this year."

She zoned out momentarily, then turned pale. "But that's *you*, isn't it? Alex? It says here you died in a road accident!"

"Not exactly. I survived. But I had to make a deal with the Infosystems. I didn't want to be reduced to a vegetable."

Breathless and visibly shaken, she hung on my every word.

"They suggested I take the risk and become a neuroimplant test subject. That allowed me to move to the Crystal Sphere."

"And your body?" she mouthed.

"It's still there, in the life support chamber. Attended by their medical staff."

Word by reluctant word, I was forced to tell her everything. About Christa's sudden decision to sell her Crystal Sphere account. About me locating her in the real world. And the rest of it...

"Jesus, Alex. I can't believe it."

"Whatever. Every word of it is true. I fear for your life, don't you understand? *I* have nothing to lose! I know the risks! But that duel with Christa could have killed you just with the shock of the pain! You need to log out! Please! You need to break contact with the implant! Call your father and tell him what you know now. I'm sure he'll find a way to protect you. This isn't a joke! You can die, as simple as that!"

"Why would they implant me with this thing?"

"No idea! They might have already finished fine-tuning it and are now busy pushing the test boundaries on the sly. Any feedback from unsuspecting users is priceless for the device developers."

Her pupils dilated, once again glinting with madness.

Her reaction was strange. She closed her eyes, stood up and began tapping the air with her fingers as if entering a code.

The battle chat window showed me what

she was seeing: the surge of a nasty-looking gelatinous goo and Enea's familiar body lying in it. The dull emergency light of the VR capsule was harsh on the eye. The other Enea kept pressing her hand to the chip stuck to her right temple to make sure it didn't drop and get lost in the gel.

She shook off her padded helmet which hung swaying on its thin cable. The picture I received through its projection visor blurred momentarily, surged with interference, then restored. I heard the hiss of the capsule's pneumatic lid as it rose sideways, opening.

She climbed out. Still, contrary to my expectations, she kept feeding me data!

Dozens of antigravity modules hovered around her, moving freely around the room. As far as I could remember, one such "Santa's helper" was more complex and pricey than a sports flybot.

They hurried to clean the girl up from the remaining bits of gel. Enea wrapped herself in a fluffy bathrobe and sank into a soft easy chair. And then-

Her avatar next to me opened her eyes.

What a shocking experiment. The battle chat window closed.

The dull light cast by the Staff of a Hydra danced on the tiny scales of Enea's unique armor, illuminating her face. The tiny Alpha climbed out of her hair and froze momentarily on her shoulder. With a sharp swing of his leg, he buried his venomous stinger in a tiny spider and swallowed him whole.

She didn't seem to have noticed. Looking me in the eye, she asked, "Can you feel everything? *Everything* everything?"

"I can."

Our eyes lit up with a rush of insane desire.

"Me too... It's not like it used to be. It's deeper... more intense," her lips timidly touched my cheek. "Alex, I'm not going anywhere," her whisper scorched my mind. "Don't even think about it..."

I buried my fingers in her hair. Our lips were touching softly. I was losing my mind.

"I'm not going," she whispered stubbornly between kisses.

"They'll find you, don't you understand?"

"I don't care. Whatever. I want to be with you..."

We couldn't draw ourselves away from each other. Tears ran down her cheeks. Her eyes glistened. Our nerves began to burn up.

* * *

CONGRATULATIONS! The darkness has retreated, unable to resist the new force which has just entered the Crystal Sphere!

You've successfully cleansed the second level of the donjon!
You've received a new level!
You've received Achievement: The Light of Passion
+1 to all stats whenever the person you love is with you.

We both startled.

"The developers must be spying on us," I said.

"Or it might be just the game engine reacting to the changes. It's adaptive, remember?" she clung to me, looking over the dusty, messy room. "This is crazy. It feels like a dream... but I don't want to wake up. What a shame I didn't know. I could have talked to Christa."

"She hates us."

"That's what you say. I'm pretty sure she's just a normal girl. She was probably so tired of all the pain... she must have been so lonely. She just happened to join the wrong crowd... and now she's freefalling."

"How do you know?"

"I'm a real-world girl too. You think I had it all delivered on a silver platter? I never knew my mother. My dad was too busy moving and shaking to take care of me. He shipped me off to a boarding school. The girls there were so spoiled you can't imagine. Such a bunch of sourpusses. Sorry, I don't even want to talk about it. Did you see the clock? We only have five hours left! I want my castle clean and filled with light! Come on now," she sprang up and pulled me by the hand. "We need to look for more prompts!"

"All right, all right. You can stay till morning. Don't argue. I know how these neuroimplants work. Once we complete the quest, you're going to log out and have a nice long sleep. That's an order."

"All right," she agreed. "As you say."

Very well. I had something else to do in the morning. It was about time Mr. Borisov and I had a talk. Seeing as he'd given me the summoning scroll, anyway...

* * *

OUTSIDE, the night was just starting to get a little lighter. I still couldn't see the Moon nor the stars.

The tiered ruins of ancient bastions rose

around us. The pitch blackness that used to envelop the castle now spiraled, swirling, high overhead.

I focused on the nearest of the platforms lining the donjon walls, about fifty feet above. It was formed by the cliff's natural ledge framed by stumps of collapsed masonry. This part of the donjon must have endured some devastating fire during the siege. We might still be able to locate the trebuchet positions on some of the little islands on the moors: they were the only weapons capable of hurling massive boulders to distances of five hundred feet and more.

Dark outlines appeared on the platform from a breach in the wall. Gradually their tags came into focus,

Fallen Warrior. Level 22
Fallen Sorcerer. Level 30
Fallen Guard. Level 25

The latter seemed the most dangerous of the three.

"What do we do?" Enea whispered.

"It looks like the legionnaires have spread all over the donjon. Do you think you could port us up to that platform?"

"Sure. The staff has enhanced my abilities really a lot."

"In that case, I want you to hit the guard with Lightning and port us straight away. Once that done, you should just stick to healing. Understand?"

She nodded.

"Are you ready?"

Lightning seared the air, critting the guard and shrinking his life bar in half.

I heard the recognizable popping sound of a teleport. Enea ported us both to the platform and buried the sharp end of her staff in the sorcerer's throat.

Its stone flashed, pulsating vigorously. The sorcerer's black blood hissed, darkening the staff, as the Heart of a Hydra erupted with crimson charges of energy. The sorcerer's tattered robes caught fire, dealing him additional damage.

I slashed through the warrior's armor, simultaneously casting Subzero with my left hand. The spell escaped my fingers with a flash, freezing the attacking guard solid before he could complete his assault.

My sword drew a well-practiced combo in the air. Wheezing, the warrior collapsed to one side. The guard's head tumbled away, leaving a bloody trail on the rock.

"Alpha, don't! You can't eat *that*!" Enea exclaimed. Her cheeks glowed from the fight, her eyes bright, her hair in disarray.

The Black Mantis — who'd grown quite a lot already — turned his triangular head in surprise but didn't dare disobey, shaking his spiky leg free of the tiny bit of dead flesh he'd managed to catch in flight.

The entrance to the tower was not far away. Still, having made sure that no more surprise attackers lurked around, I looked up at the next defense platform overhead. It was about thirty feet away, the wall around it virtually undamaged. No idea what awaited us there. Still, fighting our way through the donjon's inner halls swarming with the fallen defenders was out of the question. We wouldn't last long against them.

Enea's mana levels had already restored. She nodded to me, signaling she was ready to port us again.

"Wait," I clenched the sword's hilt, channeling my mental energy to the symbols lining the sword's blood groove. The runes along the top half of the blade began to glow.

My own mana took much longer to restore. I waited till the bar filled about 50%. "Off we go!"

Another popping sound. Darkness momentarily enveloped us, followed by a shaky torch light. A dull growl came from behind a helmet's lowered visor. A steel blade whooshed through the air.

I ducked. A poleaxe sank into the rocky

wall just above my head, striking off a cascade of sparks.

A burly orc clad in cargonite armor towered in front of me. His level was considerably higher than mine. Not good. The poleaxe looked like a toy in his enormous fists. His practiced movements betrayed an experienced warrior.

Darkness trailed after him over the rock debris, marking him as another victim of the ancient curse.

"Port yourself over there!" I pointed my sword at a fragment of destroyed stone bridge which must have connected two of the bastions. Supported by crumbling pillars, its middle vault still rose over the chasm way out of the enemy's reach.

In a short risky teleport Enea jumped onto it. She could now cast distance spells from the relative safety of the bridge.

I was alone against five of the Fallen. My chances of survival were negligible.

I chose a blood Elf whose level was the same as mine. Before attacking him, I sent a brief message to the battle chat,

Enea — the orc!
Got it!

A bolt of lightning seared through the

darkness, illuminating all around. In a cascade of sparks from his molten armor, the orc went sprawling to the ground. A large hole gaped in his breastplate, his clothes still smoldering. His angry roar shattered the silence.

Enea had invested all of her mental energy into this spell, the most powerful in her arsenal. It would take her several seconds to restore.

The agile Elf kept dodging my attacks with ease. His upper lip — apparently ripped during the battle for the castle and unable to heal since — rose in a disdainful sneer. Two more were stealing up on me from the side. My mana was taking too long to restore. I opened a quick access slot, equipping the shield.

The trailing darkness concealed the objects' true shapes. I could hear screams and the clanging of steel coming from the donjon as Rion Castle replayed the ancient tragedy as it had done every night ever since. If I failed to lift the curse, this castle would never become our home.

A smashed window frame went flying through the air, followed by a shower of broken stained glass. A gravely wounded knight tumbled out of the window and clattered to the ground in a heap. Immediately he jumped back to his feet and shouted, staggering and leaning onto his sword,

"Traitors!"

The Elf — who was on the brink of finishing me off — cut his attack short and lunged to one side, turning to the newcomer. "Helmud! Finally! Time to settle the score!"

Without hesitation, I hurried to the wounded knight's help as he began to retreat from the Elf's energetic attack. "Hold on!"

The exhausted knight struggled under pressure.

The orc was also coming for me now. The wound in his chest oozed darkness. I'd been wrong thinking that these locations weren't adaptive. The higher we climbed, the stronger the quest NPCs became.

Enea managed to cast Endurance on me, and not a moment too soon. A whack from the orc's poleaxe shattered my shield; I staggered but remained standing.

My life bar shrank about 10%. I didn't feel the pain yet. My blood was boiling with adrenaline. The neuroimplant kept adjusting the combat configuration non-stop. Throwing caution to the wind, I lunged at the orc, catching him in mid-swing as he opened up, raising his poleaxe for the final coup the grace.

My sword sliced through the metal, cutting deep into the putrid flesh.

The orc staggered and dropped to one knee. With a furious unintelligible growl, he attempted to scramble to his feet, losing strength. His hands refused to obey him; his tag sported a Mortal Wound debuff.

One down. I didn't have to worry about that one anymore. He was about to die a natural death.

I swung round. The knight was cornered with his back to the wall. His longsword had been broken. A shower of blows struck cascades of sparks from his armor.

A bolt of lightning pierced the attacking legionnaire. His body arced. I ducked under his halberd's trajectory in a desperate combo.

Black blood hissed on the rocks. A golden shimmer enveloped me. System messages flashed through my mental view, reporting a new level. The Elf swept the knight off his feet and buried his stiletto in a gap between his armor plates, extorting a wheezing scream from his victim.

A teleport popped open behind the Elf's back. He jumped to his feet and swung round.

The mortally wounded knight had helped us a lot. By putting up such a skillful and desperate fight he'd virtually nullified our enemies' hits.

Enea took a calculated risk and ported right into the thick of the melee. Her Aura of a Predator worked like a dream, slowing the attackers down and preventing them from promptly reacting to my attacks.

Soon the Elf collapsed to his side. Finally, an Ice Spear pinned the last of the cursed warriors to the wall.

I hurried toward the knight and proffered my hand to help him up. "Hold on! We'll heal you right now!"

He clenched my hand in his vice-like grip. His richly decorated armor was in tatters. All the engravings and filigree inserts covering it had grown dull; all the complex embossed patterns were buckled and deformed.

Enea cast a Minor Heal over him. The spell produced a spectacular show of flashes and surges of light, but that was about all.

"Won't work," the knight's muffled voice came from behind the visor. "The curse affects everyone."

"But you're not one of the Fallen, are you?"

"I'm Helmud — the knight who didn't submit to the demons' magic. Only my strength isn't worth much, I'm afraid. They," he pointed his broken sword at the bloodied bodies, "at least they don't remember what they did. But we remember everything. Every night we're trying to change the castle's fate. But we lose every time."

"Do you know how to remove the curse?"

"You can't," he slumped onto the collapsed remains of a battlement. "The curse is cast over the very souls of the Fallen."

"There must be something we can do!" I protested.

Helmud's life was rapidly dwindling, his muffled voice weaker with every passing moment. "Darkness has consumed their souls... The stone... its light.... can melt the darkness... the blood of a demon..."

In one last effort he unclenched his fist, offering me an oblong object made of some dull metal. A spasm ran through his body. He collapsed to one side and went quiet.

"What stone is he talking about?" Enea asked softly.

"No idea. You'd think there'd be a quest update, no?"

"What's that thing he gave you?"

I showed it to her: a cargonite locket on a chain.

Enea sighed. "How weird. I can't see its stats, only question marks. Same thing as with my staff," she gave the knight a long sad look. "I have a feeling we're missing something. We don't read deep enough into their prompts."

"Very well. Let's have a think. He made it clear enough that the Fallen hadn't possessed the power of spirit necessary to resist the demons' will. But prior to that, the legionnaires had confronted the Darks hundreds of times. What could have happened on that particular night?"

"I think we need to go back to the Resurrection Hall," Enea said. "That's where we received the quest, wasn't it? Do you remember those carvings on the walls? Could they be the answer?"

"Whatever," I agreed. "It's pretty clear we can't fight our way through here, anyway. We've only been confronted with the weakest of the Fallen — and we barely escaped with our lives."

● ● ●

THE MOMENT we entered the Resurrection Hall, the wall lamps went on again, their uneven light struggling with the darkness.

The walls here were indeed lined with images carved into the stone. Last time I hadn't had the chance to even notice them: everything had happened too quickly.

Enea took me by the hand. Our fingers interlinked. I may be thirty and counting in real life but now I felt like a young boy.

We walked along the walls, peering closely at the ancient carvings. Many of them had been eroded by time, some to the point where you couldn't even guess what they were supposed to depict.

"Look!" Enea's voice rang with excitement.

A scene in front of us must have portrayed some sort of ritual. It showed a long line of creatures of every imaginable race. A transparent rock towered at the picture's center. A warrior was kneeling on one knee in front of it.

"Now what would that mean?"

I peered at the runes. "This word here means *oath*," I pointed at the symbols I knew from my spell-casting practice. It was part of the Mortal Allegiance spell engraved on my sword.

"And this is supposed to be blood," Enea pointed at a tiny ruby mounted onto the engraving.

"The word next to it means *rock*," I added. "Which means... the oathing stone?"

"Exactly!" Enea hurried to check the spells she'd studied. "I think I can read these symbols. They mean *blood*."

"So if we tried to put it all together, it'll be... a warrior swearing an oath of allegiance and sealing it with his own blood?"

"Wait. I'll do a quick search."

"Try the *'oathing stone'* combination."

She nodded. "I got it! It's in some gamer guy's blog: *The Crystal Sphere Roadmap*. How interesting. He seems to mention certain plot lines which never made it to the game's release. The post is two years old."

"Can you read it to me, please? I don't have

the access. I can only use the in-game network."
"Right. Listen up:

Hi there,

The Crystal Sphere developers seem to be so confident about their pet project that they've just begun creating some long-term plot lines. Although I can't reveal my sources, there're rumors that the game's development might eventually bring us to the myth of the Founder Gods who supposedly used to control the whole of the Universe. A special update would then introduce a number of very interesting artifacts, including items made of cargonite: a special extra strong alloy whose secret is now lost.

Among new locations included in the planned update are some interesting ruins of quest castles which once used to belong to the Order of Disciples. According to my source, seizing the castles won't be easy because it involves completing complex quest chains which require the knowledge of the so-called "oathing stones"...

"Is that it?"
"Yeah. Most of the blog seems to have been deleted. There're only a few fragmented posts left."
"Okay. It sounds like the update he's

talking about has already been installed. Does the Wiki mention the oathing stone?"

"It does, but very little. Here, look," she forwarded me the link.

The Oathing Stone is a mythical and yet undiscovered blood-magic artifact supposedly built by the Founder Gods.

I did another search.

The Blood Magic is a lost teaching which creates a constant bond between an item and its owner. The Blood Magic lost its significance after the departure of the Founder Gods. Its artifacts are extremely rare and the consequences of using them can be unpredictable.

This looked like another dead end. I clenched the plain cargonite locket in my hand. The item was indeed dark with age.

The sunrise was almost upon us and we were as far from solving this mystery as ever.

The lamps lining the hall seemed to be dying. Some of them had already expired; others still oozed a dull weak glow. This place, too, was about to submit to the darkness.

"I have an idea," I clenched the locket in my hand. "Can you see this symbol?"

"It's the same one as the one on my staff," Enea replied. "Wish we knew what it meant."

"I wonder if it marks the item's owner as one of the castle's defenders. I think I'm gonna try and activate it."

"Not blood again! Aren't you afraid you might sign up for something you won't be able to fulfil? You have any idea what kind of forces we might end up serving?"

"I trust our little Alpha and his intuition. A pet can't hurt his owner — and still he stung you."

"All right, all right. Try it. I still can't see how it can help us."

"We'll soon find out. I told you I had an idea."

I used my sword to cut the tip of my index finger. A generous gush of blood darkened the ancient item, filling the indentations on its surface.

I waited.

The runes on my sword's blade flashed all at once, all of them. A wave of freezing cold swept over me, followed by a surge of heat. The central rune on top of the locket radiated a golden light, illuminating my face.

You've received an item: the Charm of the Sovereign (part of a set)

Restrictions: only the rightful owner of Rion Castle.

Effect: +10 to mana regeneration rate

+10% to attack strength

+10% to Stamina

The Shield of Reason (an ancient spell-like feature): +50% to the wearer's resistance to all mind-altering magic within Rion Castle limits.

The Charm's Aura:

The castle owner and all of his clan members receive +50% to resistance to mental attacks;

Each of the clan's allies in arms receives +5% to both physical and mental defense within a range of 60 ft. + 3 ft. per character's level.

He who has collected The Charm of the Sovereign, the Replication Ring and the Rune of Knowledge will receive the Ancient Legacy ability (+10% to Intellect, +10% to Learning Skills and +10% to Spirit).

"You all right?" Enea's voice betrayed concern.

"Yeah. Got some cool stat bonuses. And you? Did you manage to get some rest? We need to get moving. We have very little time left before sunrise."

"Where do you want us to go?"

"You'll see. It's a long story."

* * *

WE WALKED outside. The early morning air was considerably colder. The pitch-black fog had thickened; patches of frost glistened on the ground.

I turned toward the gate. "Get ready."

The moment we crossed the invisible line dividing the locations, the air grew warm. The dark fog dissolved, revealing the moon and stars.

"Alex, watch out! The Disciples!"

"I can see them," I raised my hand with the Charm in the air.

The ghosts lingered, undecided. They stopped their advance and began circling us, daring neither retreat nor approach.

Then the air filled with transparent clots of ectoplasm coming toward them from all directions. Holy cow! Some ability that was! Apparently, the three Disciple leaders could absorb the other ghosts' ethereal bodies, bringing their own levels up by imbibing the stats of all those undead wizards and sorcerers.

"Alex, we need to go now!"

"No. Wait."

"They're getting stronger!"

"They're not aggroing us for some reason, are they? Watch how they look at the charm!"

"You think they will help us?" Enea asked doubtfully.

"We'll soon find out."

Indeed, the creatures had completed their transformation. One of them floated closer, materializing as an old man with a long gray beard.

"Who are you?" he asked in a muffled voice.

"Can't you see?" I replied boldly.

"Neither the Charm of the Sovereign nor the Staff of a Hydra make you the castle's rightful owners. You're looters! You've had the audacity to disturb our brothers' ashes!"

"Very well. Try and kill me, then. Think you can do it?"

He did try — but an invisible force disrupted his spell, stopping him mid-word. The old man stammered and lowered his head, hunching, as if the burden was too much to bear.

"Let me go!" he croaked. "What do you want?"

"We've come to free this castle from the powers of the Dark. Sunrise is near but we're not strong enough to fight our way to the Oathing Stone!" I ad-libbed to check our theory.

"The castle's rightful owner would have used its teleport system in order to get there," once again his voice betrayed doubt and suspicion.

"It doesn't work, does it?"

"Oh," the old man paused, thinking. "We can't cross the gate. I wonder if someone removed the magic crystals?"

"You must have a few spares, surely!"

"They're all empty. Discharged. They're no good to you."

"Can't you charge them?"

"What, and channel our own strength into them?"

"Don't you want to finally rest in peace?"

He chuckled. "There's no peace in disembodiment."

"It's still better than being stuck in some old ruins."

He frowned, thinking. Finally he nodded. "We can give you the teleport crystals. We'll charge them for you. But if you fail... you'll regret it!" he threw a handful of crystals on the ground in front of him.

The ghosts' ethereal bodies disintegrated into transparent streams of energy which reached for the crystals, charging them up.

I bent down and picked up one of them.

You've received an item: a Minor Teleport Crystal

Charge: 100/100 (rechargeable)
You've received a new level!
Quest update alert: Purge
New task available: Activate the internal teleport system of Rion Castle
New task available: Find out which of the teleports leads to the Hall of Oaths

* * *

ONCE AGAIN did the Resurrection Hall lay in the dark dotted with the unsteady little flames lining its walls. The black fog seeped through the cracks in the crumbling stone, the bright glow of the resurrection point the only source of light in the room.

"Over there," I drew Enea in the direction of the stationary portal next to an ancient obelisk covered in runic symbols. We hurried toward it.

"How did you know the ghosts would help us?" she asked.

"I didn't. Not at first, anyway. But when they began syphoning other ghosts' energy, then I knew it."

"What do you mean, you knew it?"

"This is how games work. The reason why quest NPCs tend to have inordinately high levels is to make sure players can't smoke them just for fun."

"Didn't we kill some of them when we tried to get here?"

"We killed them in battle — which means they could still respawn soon afterwards. That's different. Secondly, we didn't have any quest items then. The moment we got them, the ghosts' levels grew accordingly. Which is actually a good idea on the part of the developers."

Panting, we finally reached the obelisk. I focused on the runes covering it while Enea caught her breath.

"I keep forgetting where I am," she admitted. "This feels like the only real world."

"You're taking it well," I said as I located a group of shallow slots in the rock whose shape seemed to fit the crystals. "When high-density holograms first appeared, that was something else, I tell you. In those days, that was state-of-the-art authenticity. Can you imagine I jumped out of my seat a few times trying to escape a monster? Cables flew everywhere!"

"You fleeing the battlefield? No way!"

"Fleeing from my own console, rather. Those were the days. Could you pass me the crystals, please?"

"There. Need help?"

"It's all right. You'd better check the portals' interface."

"How do I open it?"

"Just focus on the obelisk."

"Okay... oh yes, it works," her gaze glazed over. She fell silent, mouthing something.

I slid the remaining crystal into a slot, then joined her.

Oh wow. The interface was a jungle of buttons and drop-down menus, all in the Founders' language. Translation? — You could forget it.

"I'm lost," Enea said.

"It's all right. We'll sort it out in a moment. I want you to look for the symbols you know in the words *'stone'* and *'oath'*. Think you can find those combinations? I'll do the right half of the interface, you do the left."

"Okay."

After a few minutes of focused search through a multitude of inscriptions, we finally had the first result.

"Alex, I think I've got it. This word means *'an oath'*. But the symbols that precede it, I've no idea what they stand for."

Oh yes. It looked like my old language quest had acquired an unexpected urgency. "Let's have a look. Where is it? Can you highlight it?"

One of the buttons glowed green.

She seemed to be right. This looked like the only possible combination. Although I didn't recognize the first word in it, it was repeated on many other teleport control buttons. Could it mean "Hall"? Possibly.

"Are you ready?"

Enea nodded. Color drained from her face.

Congratulations! You've activated the internal teleport system of Rion Castle!
Chosen destination: Hall of Oaths.
Quest updated: Purge

* * *

WE PORTED to a balcony overhanging a huge oblong room. All of its walls were lined with high vaulted windows. Did that mean we'd reached the very top of the donjon?

The dawn was already upon us. We had very little time.

Statues of ancient heroes crowded the hall: full-size sculptures clad in tattered clothes and armor darkened with time. A freezing wind gushed in through the paneless window frames, tearing at the statues' clothing and jingling their weapons.

The doors leading to the hall had once been rammed open: the gaping entrance bristled with splintered wood.

Traces of a desperate fight were everywhere. The floor was littered with bloodied, disfigured bodies. Judging by their position, the Cohort of the Fallen had put up a fierce defense against those warriors and wizards who'd proved immune to the Dark magic.

The furious battle which re-enacted itself every night since. Still, for today it had already been over.

A few dark figures still ambled about the room. I focused on their tags. All of them were levels 200+.

"Here," Enea whispered, hiding behind the balcony's parapet. A wide staircase led down to the center of the hall where a desecrated oathing stone towered: a large transparent crystal which exuded a weak humming noise and harbored an opalescent clot of darkness.

Just above it, an emaciated demon floated in the bubble of Levitation aura. He was old and barely alive, his shriveled body covered in scars from a great many slashed wounds. Some of them were quite fresh and still oozing black blood, shedding an occasional droplet onto the Oathing Stone. The artifact absorbed it greedily, poisoning the souls and thoughts of all whose who once had shared their own blood with it as part of the sacred oath.

That was it! This was the curse of Rion Castle!

"The demon in on his last legs," Enea

whispered. "We can kill him."

"Wait," I watched the legionnaires ambling about the room. They would make quick work of us.

"Alex, but sunrise is near! I don't care if they kill us! At least we'll remove the curse!"

"Not necessarily. Can't you see that the demon's dying? They'll probably replace him with someone else in a moment. Wonder who that someone might be?"

She stared at me. "Christa? No way!"

"Why not? That could be the reason why she wasn't allowed to finish fighting you. She wasn't the one controlling the undead, that little was clear."

"But Christa is a *player*! They can't keep her here against her will!"

"But what if she volunteered? How do we know what kinds of quests demons receive? Maybe she thinks the reward is worth it?"

"But that's ridiculous. Alex? No one in their sane mind would agree to being tortured like this! Would you allow them to-"

We heard a commotion on the staircase. The five surviving legionnaires gathered together not far from the exit. They hadn't yet noticed us.

A warlock walked through the broken doorway. I knew him — I'd seen him the previous evening. He was followed by an armor-rattling group of liches dragging in a chained and struggling Christa. Enea had been right. Christa might have initially agreed to the task but once she'd realized what exactly was demanded of her, she must have had a change of heart.

The warlock wore a triumphant smirk. No wonder. He was level 70. He knew there was no one around who could challenge him or disrupt his plans.

The remaining undead followed in her wake. There weren't so many of them left! The legionnaires must have long lost their minds, killing anything that moved. The warlock's robes were in tatters, his retinue decimated.

Christa's eyes were filled with fear and incomprehension. "Let me go! I'm not doing it! I don't want to!"

"You've accepted the quest," the warlock said without even turning. "You agreed to its conditions. No one can change the destined path. Rion Castle will forever remain ours. Step aside!" he snapped at the five legionnaires.

Perfect timing. Only a few minutes left till sunrise.

"We're too late," Enea whispered.

"Not at all. Port us to the stone — *now!*"

---

* * *

THE POPPING SOUND of the teleport was akin to a clap of thunder.

The giant crystal didn't even budge when I collapsed on top of it. Still, the impact was enough to hurl the emaciated body of the demon through the air, his last drop of blood missing the stone and landing on the floor like a tiny bubbling smudge of ink.

"You? You survived?" the warlock threw his hand in the air, about to cast a spell. Enea sank the sharp end of her staff into the demon's bony chest.

His scream echoed from the walls. The warlock recoiled.

I hurried to drop to one knee. Blood magic! It was the only way to cleanse the stone and lift the curse.

My sword pierced the transparent crystal with ease and froze, reverberating. I closed my hands hard around the blade. Blood flowed down the defiantly glowing runes, streaking onto the stone, and was immediately absorbed by it, wiping away the darkness and rekindling light.

Howling, the sorcerer stepped back, recognizing his defeat. His magic bond with the crystal had been severed. The stone glowed brighter, its light illuminating every corner of the ancient hall, growing stronger and fiercer — and purer — with every passing moment.

The sorcerer wielded his staff in the air, pointing at me and Enea. "Kill them!"

Quest Alert: Purge. Quest completed!
You've lifted the curse from Rion Castle!

You've received a new level!

You've received a new ability: Blood Ties. From now on, your future is bound to that of Rion Castle. No matter where you are, once in every seven days you'll be allowed to instantly transport to the Castle.

You've received Achievement: Centurion. From now on, you'll be able to instantly summon any of the Cohort's legionnaires for the duration of 30 sec+3 sec. per level.
Cost: 100% of your complete Mental Energy capacity.

You've received a new ability: Legacy. From now on, you can control the ancient blood magic which exists in synergy with nature. The Founders' artifacts will reveal their secret properties to you alone.
Any acquired spells will be available 3 levels earlier than required.

-5% to Mental Energy required to cast a spell.

The Rion Castle interface has been unblocked.

Your Reputation with the Forces of the Dark has deteriorated.
Current Reputation status: Animosity

The system messages flashed past my mental view. We had only a few minutes left till sunrise.

The five legionnaires still stood between us and the hordes of the undead. These top-level warriors had already awoken from their thousand-year stupor, shaking off the haze of the ancient spell.

They charged at the undead at once, their merciless blows decimating the spawn of the dark.

By the time the first sunrays illuminated the hall, it was all over. Silence fell.

The five legionnaires crumbled to ashes.

A crystal screen appeared in the brightening skies,

A new force has arrived in our world!
Today Rion Castle has become the seat of

the Black Mantises clan!

All our previous achievements pale into insignificance in the face of this feat which has brought back to life one of the Founders' strongholds!

A new system message superimposed it in my mental view,

> _You've received Achievement: Exorcist._
> _+500 to Popularity_
> _+2 to Intellect_
> _+2 to Spirit_

> _New spell available: Exorcism. Deals 20 pt. damage with magic of Light to all creatures summoned by your enemy. Those of them whose levels don't exceed your own will be immediately removed and cannot be summoned for the next 60 min. Range: 100 ft._
> _All ghosts and spirits are instantly disembodied._
> _Cost: -10% of your complete Mental Energy capacity_
> _-10% of your complete Physical Energy capacity_
> _-10% of your hp._
> _The above stats revert to normal after 30 min._

Warning! If the attacker spirits' levels exceed your own by more than 5 levels, the probability of their disembodiment will drop to 80%, with a random chance of increasing the cost of casting Exorcism.

Warning! A frequent or incompetent use of ancient magic can kill the unskilled caster!

Enea let go of my hand and began walking amid the dead bodies, searching for Christa. She was still breathing. Her leathery wings spread listlessly on the floor. Her chest was heaving, her gaze dull with pain.

Enea crouched next to her, whispering something.

Christa struggled to focus, then gave a barely noticeable shake of her head.

Refusing to give up, Enea tried to cast a heal on her. That only made matters worse: the spell's golden aura brought blood bubbling to Christa's lips.

"Charity is a weakness..." she mouthed, forcing her head up. "You should remember that..."

Enea's eyes welled with tears. "That's the way I am."

"Don't feel sorry... for me..." a smile touched Christa's mangled lips. "This is a respawn... not death..."

Her body shuddered, convulsing, then went limp.

CHAPTER TWO

THE CRYSTAL SPHERE
RION CASTLE
THE DONJON'S OUTER WALLS

T HE MORNING turned out sunny, quiet and remarkably warm.

Enea and I walked out onto the balcony.

"Gosh, it's beautiful," she gasped.

A soft wind tousled her hair. Alpha the Mantis crept out onto her shoulder, looking curiously around.

The clouds seemed to be only an arm's reach away. A green expanse of woodland lay below, dotted with occasional gaps of glistening water and threaded with meandering streams.

I touched the wall. It felt cold and rough, the stonework cracked in places. The faded murals once adorning the masonry crumbled under my fingers.

Never mind. We'd restore Rion to its original glory.

I looked around me and congratulated myself on my initial choice. If the truth were known, the screenshots of the castle hadn't looked like much: just some old ruins lost amid the moors.

An impulse buy? You could say that. Still, I didn't regret one penny of it.

Packed with monsters, the surrounding quagmire offered excellent natural protection from any curious intruders. It might take our clan quite some time to find our feet.

I had zero experience in management, whatever that was supposed to mean here. Enea was the only person I could trust. The prospects of becoming a paper-pusher supervising the rebuilding of this behemoth didn't interest me in the slightest. My heart craved adventure.

"I'll be off, then?" Enea broke the drawn-out silence.

The pressure of the previous nerve-racking night released me. I didn't feel like talking. "Go get some sleep," I looked her in the eye. "And please speak to your father."

A smile touched her lips. "Leave that to me. I'm a big girl. How about you?"

"I might grab some sleep too. By then, the others will respawn."

We lingered, unwilling to say goodbye.

Enea took my hand. "I'll be back, I promise. Even if the implant doesn't work next time... I'll find a way to come back. Don't worry about me, okay?"

This conversation was quickly becoming awkward. So I just kissed her. "Go now. I'm not going anywhere."

Her avatar vanished.

Immediately I reached into my inventory for the scroll Mr. Borisov had given me. I tried to break the seal. As if! I pressed harder: to no avail.

Warning! You cannot use the scroll. Activation requirements are not met.

Oh really? Was it their way of letting me know the situation was still within the realms of gameplay?

"Leave it. You can't break the seal."

I swung round. Mr. Borisov stood behind me in a dark archway.

"Why did you call me? It's night in real life, by the way. I'm not some petty demon to run

---

your errands for you. I hope I'm making that clear."

He leaned over the parapet, taking in the scenery. "Beautiful."

My blood boiled. I was too worried about Enea to control my impulses. I took a swing and gave him a hearty thump.

My fist went through his avatar, punching the merlon behind him so hard that I grazed the skin on my knuckles.

You've been injured!

"Oh, do me a favor," Mr. Borisov gave me a squinted look. "It's not my fault that you're feeling grumpy. Go and smoke a few mobs, that might make you feel better."

"Why did you have to get Enea involved in your testing?"

He didn't even flinch, just pursed his lips and shook his head. "No one's done anything to her."

"She's got an implant!"

"Impossible. Wait a moment. I need to check something," he zoned out temporarily.

Soon he resurfaced.

"Any results?" I asked formally, forcing myself to stay calm.

"There's been a planned expansion of the

experiments. About a thousand devices have been built," he admitted grudgingly.

I pinned him down with my glare.

"Well, I'm sorry!" he snapped. "I may be a senior manager but I'm not God Almighty! Other departments don't report to me. Enea just happened to be among the target buyer group," he said, fiddling with the wedding ring on his finger. "Just an unfortunate coincidence. She shouldn't have been so darn pigheaded shopping for cutting edge technologies."

"I don't believe in coincidences."

"Neither do I. So I'll look into it. Just promise you won't do anything stupid, okay? I can tell you one thing: the implants are our future. They've already been fine-tuned. Stop glaring at me like that! Look at it from a different perspective. Enea seems to like you. Aren't you the lucky ones?"

"*Lucky*?"

"Of course. You're both young and living in a beautiful brave new world..."

"So you think it's normal forcing Enea to experience a full range of emotions?!"

"Alex, please. The implant can't force anyone to feel anything. All it does, it processes in-game events. You can't digitize love, I assure you! In actual fact, you should be worrying about a whole different set of problems."

"Which are?"

"Are you really so stupid?" he finally lost his patience. "Can't you see what you've gotten yourself into?"

Seeing my incomprehension, he began to explicate,

"In your desire to raise some Spectral Dust, you bought this ancient castle packed solid with Founders' artifacts. You've also removed the curse which has been keeping looters at bay. How long do you expect to keep it under wraps? Rumors spread fast. It won't be long until some opportunist or other wants to check if they can mug you for a couple of artifacts. The Moors are no place for lone players so they'll start making groups. And even a group can't make it here which means you should be expecting a well-trained raid. Say, fifty players, how about that?"

Oh. Never thought about it.

This Mr. Borisov seemed to be an expert in manipulation. He continued pressing on all the right points, pretending to change the subject,

"Think about it. All you have now is a bunch of ruins, no one to defend them, a handful of quests to complete and a bank loan. How are you going to juggle all that? Have you ever been a leader of a large group? You have any idea how to make an economically viable and battle-worthy clan?"

I shrugged. "Nothing money can't do."

"You're such a noob sometimes!" he snapped. "Okay, money is war's blood, I agree. So let's say you have a couple of million to spare. You think that's enough for all this?" he swept his hand over the magnificent ruins. "That might allow you to fix a few breaches in the walls and post some NPC guards, maybe. You sure you can hang on to what you've just claimed? You realize that tomorrow someone might come and try to do the same?"

I didn't say anything. He had a point. His harsh tone didn't offend me anymore.

"You'd better start thinking about how you can attract more players here," he continued. "But don't forget: what they need is adventure, a strong leader, a possibility to level up and a safe citadel. Do you see what I'm driving at? First of all, you'll need some suitable farming locations," he began unbending his fingers. "After that, you'll have to start looking for some dungeons and instances where your future clan members can practice raid tactics and farm unique items. The castle has to be rebuilt ASAP. It has to be populated, but *not* by NPCs alone. I'd say the optimal ratio of NPCs to players should be 50/50. I should hire some NPC vendors who could buy up any excess loot. Next," he'd run out of fingers and switched to his other hand, "the clan's raid groups should be constantly busy reconnoitering and mapping out the area, looking for any resource deposits and promising locations. The moors must be absolutely packed with unique ingredients, provided you know where to look for them. Such locations should be used regularly to ensure your crafters, herbalists and such can level up too."

He stopped abruptly, gazing at the misty horizon. "Rion is a truly unique place. You should be using this fact to your own advantage. You need to think of various ways of attracting more players. Once that's done, you might find you don't need major cash injections. Oh, and one more thing: this place is bound to become the center of all sorts of developments. You should be ready for surprises. The Crystal Sphere is a very young world full of potential. Here, lots of things are happening for the first time. Did you notice the sheer number of the unique achievements you've received?"

I nodded.

"So there you have it. At the moment, anyone can become a legend or fade into obscurity. Grab your chance. Claim your moment," he gave me an encouraging slap on the shoulder.

"What's gonna happen to Enea, then?"

"I'm sorry but I can't 'erase and rewind'. I

just don't know. It's up to her now. She might need to make some difficult decisions. Just please don't be such a killjoy. Just concentrate on the gameplay. This is what's vital at the moment. Leave the rest to me, okay? If Enea indeed reconsiders, we'll find a way to help her without her even knowing. I can promise you that. Agreed?"

"Okay, but what about her father?"

My question remained unanswered. Mr. Borisov's avatar had already vanished into thin air.

Oh great. He'd fed me a lot of promises, given me a pep talk and disappeared without actually telling me anything.

* * *

MY SLEEP was gone.

I had a long list of things to do, and every item on it was a priority. Still, I had to begin by unblocking the castle control interface.

The castle's holographic model unfolded in my mental view.

Rion Castle
Clan affiliation: the Black Mantises
Owner: Alexatis. Level 27. Neuro
Current status:
Defense, 2,137,964 pt.

Damage to the walls, 62%

Magic defense, 14,357 pt. Key elements missing from major runic chains. Source of power: not found

Attack potential: 137 pt (1 warrior)

Auras: not found

Passive shields: not found

The Element of Air: runic chain broken. Remaining runes: 12 out of 130

The Element of Water: runic chain broken. Remaining runes: 54 out of 130

The Element of Fire: runic chain broken. Remaining runes: 32 out of 130

The Element of Earth: runic chain broken. Remaining runes: 130 out of 130

The Element of Chaos: runic chain unfinished. The creation of the runic chain has been interrupted.

How weird. If the earth chain had all of its runes intact, why wasn't it working?

I focused on the message. A prompt popped up,

Requires an active source of power.

A glowing sphere formed around the castle's 3D model.

The castle's source of power (a Founders' artifact) couldn't be moved outside the indicated area.

The restoration of the existing runic chains is impossible. Power required: 10,000 pt. mana per minute.

Warning: the backup power source (the main accumulating crystal) is discharged. Currently only one defense function is being supported: the deflection of all incoming teleports. The remaining power is sufficient for 24 more days.

New quest alert: The Renaissance of Rion!

Find or recreate a source of magic power. The last known location of the old source of power is marked on your map.

Restore the runic chains in order to gain access to the Elements of Earth, Water, Fire and Air. Each element brings +250,000 pt. to the castle's passive shield and +100,000 to its attack potential.

Rebuild the castle's magic tower in order to gain access to spell scrolls and to be able to hire NPC wizards.

Rebuild the barracks in order to be able to hire NPC guards (warriors, level 50+).

Restore the training grounds in order to be able to hire NPC archers (levels 50+).

Restore the market and supply depots in order to gain access to trading activities.

Restore the surrounding villages in order to supply the castle with food stocks which in turn will attract new settlers.

Restore the inn, the tavern and the main square in order to attract travelers to the castle.

I opened the map. Now I could see twenty-four portals. I already knew that the castle's source of magic power could move through them randomly during an attack which prevented it from being seized or disabled by the enemy.

What I really didn't like was that the place marked as the source's last known location was situated high above the ground. If the enemy had indeed managed to disable the portals, the source of power could have simply tumbled down like a sack of potatoes from a great height and was now lying around somewhere in the brambles — or had even been swallowed up by the quagmire.

I didn't even look at the impressive lists of the materials and work force required to restore all the buildings and the outer walls. I simply didn't have the money.

At the moment, I focused on the map of the dungeons. There were three underground caves located right under the castle. Judging by the prompts, they must have been the ancient mines.

At the moment, they sported nothing but question marks.

They were our priority. I only had five days left to raise two cartfuls of Spectral Dust!

* * *

AN ICON lit up on my interface.

It was Zander back from his respawn point! I didn't expect him so early. Our respawn times must have reverted back to their original values.

Oh well. No peace for the wicked. I might have to grab some sleep some other time. I ported back to the Resurrection Hall.

Zander swung round to my teleport's pale flash. "Alexatis!" he looked worried and relieved at the same time.

"I'm okay," I shook his hand. "The curse is lifted!"

"Did you do it on your own?"

"Enea helped me. Still, there's plenty of work for everyone. Where're all the others?"

"They're on their way. A seven-hour respawn! What are they thinking about! Plus the debuff! It's a good job it didn't work. Sorry about the wipe, man."

"It won't affect your group's reputation," I hurried to add, cutting short any unwanted questions. "The quest was for me and Enea alone.

You were meant to be killed, anyway."

"You sure?"

"A hundred percent. You can't do anything with brute force here, trust me. So let's do it this way: we'll go down now, check the dungeons and see what mobs they have there. If we're up to it, we'll purge the dungeons and close the contract. Agreed? We'll count this morning as twenty-four hours. Enea and I promised an exclusive to the media," I swept my arm around the room, conjuring up the holographic footage of the castle walls engulfed in Infernal flames and hundreds of ancient warriors rising up from the quagmire. It looked impressive.

I could see that Zander appreciated my effort. The well-chosen camera angle allowed you to see the mercenaries taking the brunt of the battle.

"In addition to all this, I'll also give them the footage of our hydra encounter," I said. "The rest I'll keep under wraps for the time being."

"They'll start grilling me about the details."

"You've signed the non-disclosure agreement, haven't you?"

"I have indeed," Zander agreed, obviously relieved. He chuckled, looking at the hologram. "You have a good eye for images. I don't think many people will want to lay claim to the castle after seeing this. And it will definitely improve our

Reputation."

In the meantime, the other mercenaries had started to turn up, followed by Platinus and Togien. They showered me with questions.

"Is the interface working?" Platinus demanded. "Where's my lab? I'll need a smart NPC assistant, don't forget!"

"Can we have a look at the castle?" Rodrigo asked.

"This place is absolutely packed with scrap cargonite," Tylor said, choosing a couple of artifacts. "How much do you want for this?"

"Right, guys," I said. "No guided tours, I'm afraid. Nothing personal. At the moment, the castle and everything in it is classified information. We can do some trading in the evening when you receive your bonuses. Now we have work to do. We need to go down to the dungeons. Everyone. You too," I looked severely at Platinus.

"All right, all right," Togien boomed. "Show us where to go. What kind of dungeons are they?"

"There're some old mines located right under the main tower," I said. "We can't port there. We'll have to walk. The entrance is here in this hall. I need to warn you that we can't trust the old maps. The demons broke into the donjon from beneath by splitting the cliff's base. I need to know what it's like there now. Fancy doing that?"

"Why not?" Zander seemed to like the idea. "Let's go and take a look!"

The others cheered up too. Purging an ancient dungeon meant treasure, unique items and plenty of XP. No wonder: it had stood abandoned for over a thousand years!

* * *

THE RUSTY HOIST screeched. Heavy chains drew taut, lifting the rectangular slab of stone. It rose reluctantly, revealing a row of stairs leading down into the gloom. The gaping hole breathed cold and damp.

Our descent took forever. We checked every landing we happened upon. Most of them had three doors which must have once opened into ration depots. Over the past centuries, foodstuffs had crumbled to dust together with the bags that contained them; even the wooden crates had rotted away. The only mobs we met here were a few rats, skinny and weak.

"I thought this place would be packed with gold!" Togien grumbled.

I felt the familiar tingling sensation in my fingertips. There was a source of power somewhere below. I just hoped it wasn't another Altar of Chaos.

I immediately remembered my encounter with the Corporation workers. Altars of Chaos were in fact their tools meant to ward off players, preventing them from discovering the Corporation's secret passageways that connected the game with the real world.

Zander stopped and raised his hand. "Wait! This seems to be an entrance to a hall!"

Water glistened in the torch light. Was this the level of the bog? Already?

Disappointment washed over me. So much for our farming Spectral Dust! If the underground levels were indeed flooded, our little trading scheme with the Azure Mountain dwarves had just gone belly up.

"This is a water reservoir!" Zander announced, taking a few more steps down. "It must be their emergency supply. Look at these levers on the walls! They were probably used to pump the ground water up."

Virgil who was walking just behind him pointed at the mineral salt deposits lining the walls. "I don't think the pumps work anymore. The water level must have risen several times which means the floodgates are constantly open."

I lifted the torch higher, studying the steps. Their edges had apparently been worn by the passage of water. Virgil was right: this place was regularly flooded but equally rapidly drained. It looked like the flood waters gushed down the steps and disappeared in the fissure made by the demons.

We resumed our descent. The spiral staircase continued to bore into the castle's rocky foundations like a drill. Soon the surface of the walls began to change. They were covered in cracks and even occasional crevices that breathed cold and seeped water.

In the last twenty-four hours, I'd really had enough of the doom and gloom. I'd have loved nothing better that have a stroll in the sun. Still, there was nothing I could do about it at the moment.

"The mines I don't mind," Togien continued to grumble. "But you'd think they'd have some hoisting cages, wouldn't you? How were they supposed to transport the ore?"

"They used teleports," I said. "They don't work at the moment. The accumulating crystal is probably flat."

"Watch where you're going," Zander said. "Some steps are crumbling. Iskandar, I want you to bring up the rearguard. If someone trips up, you can cast Levitation on them."

Soon we reached another hall which looked more like a manmade cave, judging by the rough finish of its ceiling. The large stone floor tiles were listing, some of them tilted on their sides like ice ridges in the wake of deep fissures covering the floor.

Here I could finally see the gaping holes of the mining shafts topped with the rickety remains of hoisting cages. I recognized a rectangular block of stone amid the heaps of debris: a teleport platform, judging by the distinctive runic pattern.

"Great stuff," Togien said approvingly, following my gaze. "You think you can activate it?"

I could understand him. None of us felt like taking another hike all the way up.

"Not yet," I said. "I need some teleport stones. I've run out of mine."

Meanwhile, Zander approached one of the crevices and looked down. He cussed under his breath.

"What can you see there?" I asked.

"Nothing. It's all covered in Mist of War."

"There's no such ability in the Crystal Sphere," Iskandar said with confidence. "Nor spell. You sure that's what it is? Not some kind of smoke or fumes?"

"I wish," Zander stepped away from the fissure's edge which had begun to crumble under his weight. "Look for yourselves if you don't believe me."

Indeed, a gray haze swirled beneath,

concealing a treacherous drop. I could hear a far-off echoing sound ringing with metal, like a multitude of picks attacking rock.

"Togien, go check the cages."

He obeyed. The others waited patiently, casting curious glances at me and Zander. Platinus alone decided it was a good moment to show some initiative. He opened his robes and began studying the dozens of little pockets that covered the lining. Finally he fished out a vial containing some acid green liquid and offered it to me,

"Try to throw it down the crevice. It might help."

Remembering our woeful hydra encounter, I asked him, "Can you tell me how it works? You sure I won't lose levels for using this?"

He took offense. What was he like!

"Just read the label," he grumbled.

Last Chance Potion. Cleans the air of all traces of acids, poisons, dust, smoke and toxins. Indispensable for mine fires.

Okay. We might just as well try it. Climbing down through the thick haze didn't sound like a good idea.

"Zander, make sure I don't fall."

With his help I leaned down the crevice as

far as I could, dropped the vial and started counting.

Soon I heard the far-off sound of shattered glass. Immediately the gray haze began to disperse.

A large underground cavity lay below. Now I understood why the castle's interface had failed to offer accurate information. This must have once been a complex maze of caves connected by snaking tunnels. Now it didn't look anything like it, all thanks to the hordes of imps scurrying around!

For centuries they'd been mining ore and other resources here non-stop until they'd created a large underground hollow. All the caves and tunnels, including those dug during the storming of Rion — they had all disappeared, devoured by this enormous new location.

There were hundreds of imps working here. Luckily, their groups were small. I could also see plenty of prisoners. Dark obelisks, however, were few and far between — not enough to affect all the slaves quite a few of whom were chained; they looked exhausted and emaciated. Mining ore in the absence of strength or agility buffs is no joke!

A few groups were busy working at the center of the giant cave, away from its rocky walls. To my surprise, I noticed a few Dark conjurers among them.

I forwarded the video to the group network, activated my Observational Skills ability and sent a chat message to Zander, *Hold me tight!*

As I focused, lots of new details came into view. I studied the imps' tags, then those of their prisoners. The former were mainly workers levels 20 to 30. Very few warriors, which meant that Infernal creatures felt safe here. They'd been farming this location since time immemorial and weren't going to leave it any time soon.

The Imps may be greedy, shameless and mean creatures but they know their job, that's for sure. They're good at mining. As they worked, they left certain places untouched, creating crude stone columns which supported the ceiling.

This was a rather boring old cave of a quite unambitious design.

The prisoners were mainly humans. I didn't notice any orcs: only a few dwarves and even a kobold.

And who the hell was that?

A warlock?

Curiouser and curiouser. Level 50, not bad. He pranced around the cave as if the whole place belonged to him. What was he doing down there? He even had a retinue: a dozen liches and two dark casters, their levels slightly lower than his.

I just couldn't work them out. I could still sense the tingling in my fingertips. The source of magic power kept reminding me of its presence even though I couldn't locate it quite yet.

The warlock stopped and picked up a fragment of the broken vial. He cast a suspicious glance around but didn't look too alarmed: the broken pieces of the Last Chance Potion looked quite in keeping with the cave's grim insides.

He waited for an imp to scurry past, then grabbed him by the scruff of his neck, lifting the poor creature into the air. The imp squirmed under the warlock's freezing stare as the man asked him something but failed to receive a satisfactory reply. Irritated, the warlock flung the imp aside. The creature hit his head on a column, losing a few hp, then scrambled back to his feet and scurried away.

A nearby group of prisoners showed some interest in the incident. Two of them — an Elf and a Kobold shackled together — stopped hacking at the rock and focused their hateful glares on the Dark casters. The others — five emaciated peasants and three dwarves — slowed down, casting sideways glances at the scene.

Aha, finally! A burly orc clad in tattered leather armor appeared out of the cave's gloomy depths pushing a wheelbarrow. He must have dumped his load and was about to resume work.

His dull stare spoke volumes: the guy must have been here long enough to have lost all hope of ever getting out.

In the meantime, the warlock froze, leaning on his staff.

Was he casting a spell?

I stared at him intently, memorizing the way he mouthed the words. It's not often you get the chance to watch your enemy in action.

Wisps of dust began rising into the air, whirling together.

Got it! My Spell Interception ability hadn't failed me!

You've learned a new spell: The Veil.

Creates an obstructive haze concealing a selected area from prying eyes. The size of the area: 50x50x50 ft +2 ft. per caster's level.

Cost: 50% Mental Energy

Requires level 37

Dust billowed up, obscuring the view.

"Alexatis, get out of there," Zander and Tylor pulled me out of the crevice.

"What do we do now?" Zander asked.

"We might try to climb down and see if we can purge the cave," I said, giving Platinus an approving slap on the shoulder.

He beamed. The vials in his robes clinked softly.

"You think you might have some more of

those?" I asked him.

"Absolutely. But-"

"But what? Come on, spit it out."

"The ingredients are rare. And expensive. It's not called the Last Chance for nothing."

"That's not your problem. Remember what I promised? We'll get you a lab as soon as possible. Just wait."

I turned to Togien. "What do you think?"

"The cages are falling apart," he replied. "The machinery is all broken. But the shaft itself looks good. I've checked it. We can try and climb down here. The imps don't seem to use it."

"Good. I still don't understand why the conjurer raised dust again. Any ideas?"

"Simple," Rodrigo replied. "At least half the prisoners are free from the obelisks' control. The dust prevents them from banding together."

"For what purpose?" Iskandar said. "I don't think there's much chance of rioting down there. Each team of workers has a caster to heal the weak and cast control spells over the discontented. The dust only makes working harder."

"I know why he does it," I said.

All stares turned on me, quizzical. I gave them a brief run-down of the Cohort of the Fallen story. "Did you notice that the whole area around the old mine remains untouched? That's why the warlock had cast the Veil over it: to prevent any legionnaires from ambling around the dungeon aggroing the imps."

Iskandar didn't look convinced. "They must be hiding something here. I have a strange feeling about this place. I could bet all you want there's some crazy level-70 monster lurking at its center."

"You mean we're not strong enough to do it?" Zander asked.

"We could try," Iskandar replied. "Listen, Alexatis, fancy calling up an event? That could bring in more players from the city. The demons wouldn't like it!"

"Absolutely not," I said. "This dungeon is part of Rion Castle. We don't want strangers wandering around. No, I think we should try and do it ourselves. You get one-third of the loot but I get the pick of the artifacts. Zander?"

He nodded. "Sounds good to me. Can I have a word?"

* * *

"WHAT'S UP?" I asked him.

"Who's gonna be the raid leader?"

"Well, who do you think? You, of course. I don't have the experience."

He cheered up. "Excellent. Togien, Platinus,

come over here!"

The two approached.

"I need to know your abilities and available spells," he demanded. "What scrolls and elixirs do you have?"

As the raid leader, Zander was obliged to know everything each player could or couldn't do.

Togien didn't play hard to get. He owned an impressive supply of health elixirs. He specialized in tanking.

Zander checked his stats. "Good," he nodded. "You'll stay in one line with me. Platinus?"

The brief discourse that followed showed that Platinus was pretty useless as a sorcerer. His health was weak, his mana negligible, its regeneration rate slow. He didn't know any spells, either. His elixir stocks, however, boasted about fifty various potions.

"You will stay with Rodrigo and Iskandar," Zander gave him an encouraging wink. "Use your vials sparingly. No good wasting them on imps. But once we get to the dungeon boss, you can use some medium ones against him."

"Why medium?"

"Because if you happen to deal him more damage than Togien or myself, you'll pull aggro to yourself. Which will cause a wipe."

Platinus stared at him, uncomprehending.

Zander chuckled. "You don't know what a wipe is, do you? Look. The amount of aggro decides whom a monster will attack. If he considers you the most dangerous enemy, he'll ignore Togien and myself and go directly for you. Which in turn will cause a wipe, meaning we'll all be killed on the spot. Understood?"

Platinus gave a vigorous nod. Zander's instructions made him fidget nervously in anticipation of what was to come.

"Thanks, everyone," Zander said, dismissing them. Once we were alone again, he turned to me. "Alexatis, I'm not asking *you* any questions. Both you and your class are too special. If you don't want to tell me, I'll understand. You can just stay in the rear with Iskandar and Rodrigo."

Oh. I was the clan leader now, wasn't I? Even my abilities were classified information. That felt weird.

"Do you remember what happened to the hydras?" I asked him.

He grinned. "Mortal Allegiance! How could I ever forget!"

"At the moment it's the best I can do. But in order for it to work, I'll need constant heals and mana."

"Got it. If the going gets really tough, use it. We'll try to clear you a path to the boss, whatever he is."

"If push comes to shove, I have something to use, too."

"What's that?"

"I can summon a Fallen legionnaire for ninety seconds."

"What level?"

"Depends. But I might try and summon one particular character I have in mind. Also, if the boss starts summoning the Darks, I can cast Exorcism."

Zander raised a surprised eyebrow, "Why didn't you use it when we tried to storm the castle?"

"I couldn't. I only got it last night."

"I see. So let's do it this way. You stay in the rear with the wizards, right up until the final push. You'll be our strategic reserve. If the warriors need your help, I'll let you know. No stupid solo pranks. Deal?"

"Deal."

"Let's go get buffed, then. Pointless dragging it out. This is how we'll do it: we'll keep to the center of the cave, as far from the dark obelisks as possible. The warlock is our priority target. We might even get a glimpse of the boss if we're lucky."

"You think it's a good idea?"

"If we move from one obelisk to the next,

we'll get exhausted real fast. Some of my auras have as much as a ten minute cooldown. The warlock, however, can move randomly around the dungeon. Not a healthy scenario. So I suggest we smoke him first and then start purging the cave systematically. Oh, and one other thing. Do not use fire spells on the imps. It's either ice or mental damage."

"Why don't you have a proper healer in your group?"

"Couldn't find one," he replied. "Pointless hiring just any old quack. So we have to make do with scrolls, elixirs and my Paladin abilities."

* * *

THE TINGLING SENSATION in my fingertips was still there. A very nagging feeling. The invisible source of power had to be here somewhere.

Zander was calm. He knew what he'd gotten himself into. The dungeon was millennia old. No one had ever completed it before us. The imps here had to be nice and fat with plenty of treasures to drop. Our loot might exceed our wildest expectations. This I could tell by the ecstatic look in Rodrigo and Iskandar's eyes which glinted with anticipation.

Togien was restless and on edge. Armed with his battle axe and shield, he kept casting militant glances around him. Platinus was unusually quiet. He kept close to me, clutching yet another vial with a picture of some improbable monster on the label. Probably a generic image.

"What's that?" I asked him softly, trying not to disturb the wizards who were busy casting raid buffs.

You've received a mass blessing:
+50% to resistance to fire
+25% to Physical Defense
+25% to your Health quota
Duration: 30 min

You've received a mass blessing:
+20% to armor durability
+20% to close combat damage
+10% to all spell damage
+5% to your chances of dealing a critical hit
Duration: 30 min

"Cast Levitation!" Zander commanded, heading toward the gaping mouth of the ancient mine shaft.

"So what's that vial you've got in your hand?" I repeated.

Platinus turned pale. "Power of a Monster 2.0. If I drink it, my stats will go sky high for sixty seconds."

"Put it away. Didn't you hear what Zander's just said?"

"Why not? It's only sixty seconds! I might win the battle for you, you never know!"

"Right. Open the Wiki and look up 'aggro', now. How can you be so stupid? You can only use it if all of us get killed, understand? Better still, give it to me. Just to be on the safe side. Literally."

Reluctantly Platinus handed me the vial, then flung his robes open and reached for another one. This one had a large sign of the Red Cross on the label.

Levitation enveloped us, lifting us in the air, then placing us gently on the ground below.

The dust cloud concealed the ruins of the ancient mine, restricting visibility and gnawing at our life bars.

Zander cringed. "The demons are playing it safe. They've got a long-term DoT cast over the area. The legionnaires must have attacked them every night."

"Yeah," Virgil agreed. "Once they find out the curse has been removed, they might get cheeky. They might start pushing the envelope to see if they can conquer the upper levels."

My point entirely. We'd have to purge this place once and for all, otherwise we might have constant problems with them. Normally, dungeon mobs respawn regularly — or if they don't, a new set is generated for each group that enters the instance. But the fact that my quest was unique made Rion Castle an exception from the rule. Which meant that the imps might not respawn at all.

The dust cloud dissipated abruptly: a sure sign that it had been created by magic.

We inched forward until we reached the nearest tunnel which was swarming with imps busy hacking at the rock. There we met our first surprise. A junior conjurer: a filthy, ugly, hunched-up creature was sitting on a rock in the middle of a pool of bubbling slime, breathing in its toxic effluvia and murmuring something. Next to him stood a totem made of bones, topped with a tiny skull of some local rodent. Three blobs of darkness circled it incessantly, leaving a smoky trail in their wake.

I want my castle clean and filled with light, the warm memory of Enea's words touched my mind.

I could sense the growing pressure on my brain. My resistance to magic was quite good. The mercs had nothing to fear, either. But Togien and Platinus were in trouble. Both froze in place, their faces betraying fear and disgust.

"Zander?" I asked.

"I can feel it," he replied immediately. "The totem is trying to control us. I saw it happen before but never as powerful as this one. It requires one hell of a power source."

The conjurer fidgeted in place, casting suspicious glances around.

"Smoke the motherfucker," Togien's voice broke under the totem's mental pressure.

"One moment," Zander replied calmly. "Let the conjurer show us what he can do first. We can always use the logs for later reference."

"And what if the warlock arrives?" Platinus asked in a tense voice.

"Even better," Zander replied. "That would be a good pull."

We were still lurking within the dust veil. I could see Zander's logic. He was trying to work out whether the totems and junior conjurers made some sort of network. The mental pressure in itself was a useful albeit depressing tool responsible for the dungeon's somber atmosphere; still, we shouldn't forget that a magic network like this could also serve as a primitive alarm system, warning the others of any potential intruders.

Platinus' legs gave way under him. He crouched on the ground, whining and clutching his head. Togien's neck bulged with pulsating veins as he whispered dwarven protective spells

— apparently, with little success.

Zander wasn't in a hurry to cast his auras. He peered expectantly into the darkness.

Piles of rotting bones nearby emitted an unbearable stench. The cave which had looked so mysterious from above was in fact gruesome.

One of the piles of bones shifted.

I tensed up. Zander raised a commanding hand, gesturing to us to stay put.

This annoyed me. What was he waiting for?

Platinus promptly shut up. He sat on the ground swaying, staring nonsensically into space.

And there was the warlock coming!

The pile of bones shifted again. No, not bones. Dogs. Patches of matted hair clung to their skeletal frames. I couldn't look at their mangy heads.

Hell Hound. A Replicated Object. Level 30

Their tags made the blood freeze in my veins. But that wasn't all. The demons had a much worse surprise in store for any potential intruders.

The warlock stopped, mouthing something. I strained my eyes.

He uttered a few words in the ancient language. The blobs of darkness that were circling the totem now darted toward the dogs' lair. They enveloped it in an ashen haze which streaked down the creatures' bare ribs, penetrating their bodies and forming the outline of an enormous mythical creature.

Infernal Monster. A Replicated Object. Level 20.

You've learned a new spell: Object Replication
Class: unique, uncategorized. Part of the Founders' lost school of magic.
Mental Energy cost: varies, depending on the complexity of the replicated item/creature
Class restrictions: none
Requires:
Level 30
Intellect, 14
Willpower, 14

None of us had ever seen anything like it! I dreaded to even think how much mana it must have cost him to build an Infernal monster like that?

Zander's self-restraint had yielded fruit: they hadn't noticed us yet. The dust cloud kept gnawing at our hp but it was worth it simply to uncover the enemy's secret abilities. Iskandar was already busy analyzing the logs.

What happened next far exceeded the limits of our gaming experience. The monster, cobbled together with bits of flesh and bone, looked as if it was about to crumble apart. Its life bar barely glowed. Its movements were erratic — the thing may have looked scary but at the moment, it posed no threat to us whatsoever.

The warlock gulped down a mana vial. The totem began emitting more wisps of dark energy which headed for the man.

The warlock dropped to the ground, writhing in a pool of bubbling slime. He seemed to be having a fit. The imps abandoned their picks and tried to scamper to safety, apparently horror-stricken, but stopped dead in their tracks under the hounds' fiery glares.

The warlock resumed the spell.

I activated Spell Interception. Luckily, my Twilight Vision and Observational Skills allowed me to lip-read.

The imps nearest to the warlock exploded in a cascade of blood and gore, dissolving into clouds of crimson mist. An invisible force channeled them toward the monster, pumping him full of energy.

The creature's life bar quivered and began to grow.

You've learned a new spell: Dark

Regeneration

Class: unique, uncategorized. Part of the Founders' lost school of magic.

Mental Energy cost: varies, depending on the number of disembodied creatures and the amount of hp channeled toward the recipient

Class restrictions: none

Requires:

Level 30

Intellect, 13

Willpower, 13

"The legionnaires must have really put the fear of God into him," Zander said through his teeth. "Alexatis, if we survive this instance, I owe you."

"The spells can't be identified," Iskandar reported, suppressing his excitement. "This is the Founders' magic! The monster's damage can't be estimated! The hounds are under absolute negation with zero chance of a resist."

This was our analyst's verdict. Now Zander as the raid leader had to act upon it.

"Rodrigo, I want you to cast Negation. Iskandar, Alexatis, focus on the warlock. Togien, you need to aggro this creature. Try to last at least a minute if you can. Virgil, Tylor, you need to kill it. The warlock is mine. Don't bother with the imps. Let's do it!"

Zander lunged forward, leaving the safety of the dust cloud.

He must have decided to play it big from the start, attacking the warlock with the magic of Light.

The man wasn't easily scared. He raised his staff, building a wall of darkness between us. A Negation promptly cast by Rodrigo ripped the darkness to pieces.

Whining, the hounds tried to scamper away. Zander cast a 30-sec Silence over the warlock's retinue of liches. Unable to cast spells, they engaged in a hand-to-hand, much to the pleasure of Zander's moonsilver sword.

Obeying Zander's orders, Togien lunged onto the Infernal Monster. He gave it a well-calculated whack with his axe, pulling aggro to himself, then promptly recoiled, covering himself with his shield.

The monster reared up, showering Togien with blows.

The warlock tried to port out. As if! The Absolute Negation disrupted his spell while Zander's sword nullified his passive shields, forcing him into combat.

I pierced the warlock with two Ice Spears while Iskandar cast a generous dose of Subzero over every enemy.

Frozen to the knees, the warlock

whimpered and reached for the totem, clenching it with both hands.

A dull rumbling sound echoed throughout the cave.

The nearest imps — about fifty in total, including a dozen level-30 warriors — dropped whatever they were doing and assaulted Zander all at once.

The warlock was taking Zander's blows remarkably well. His life bar kept soaring. Suddenly his cloth robes disappeared, replaced by a suit of armor. Some ability that was! Talk about class switching! Even his name tag had transformed. Now Zander was fighting a Dark Knight!

Zander kept charging, performing combo after skillful combo — but now the two opponents were more or less equal.

Grunting under pressure, Togien kept pulling the monster's aggro to himself as Tylor and Virgil assaulted the creature from both sides, killing it with expert speed.

Things seemed to be working out in our favor... the problem was, the hounds were now coming back! Also, the imps were just too numerous.

I invested all of my mana into a hail of Ice Arrows, smoking the most brazen of them. Rodrigo cast the iridescent swirling spiral of

Mortal Cold over the shapeshifting warlock, slowing him down and allowing Zander to crit him. Still, at least ten of the warrior imps were already upon him, about to attack him from behind.

I was an idiot! I hurried to gulp a vial of mana as I sifted through my spells. You couldn't blame me, really: all my life I used to be a Warrior. What was my level now? 27, exactly.

I could now cast illusions, couldn't I?

Blessed be the sorcerer whose bag I'd found on my memorable first day in the Crystal Sphere!

I activated Legacy — which made all acquired spells available 3 levels earlier than required — and hurried to cast the 5-sec spell.

I tried to visualize a hydra as believably as I could in all its blood-curdling detail, complete with the clouds of acid mist escaping its many jaws. I also cast the Aura of Fear over it for good measure.

The screaming of the imps all but ruptured my eardrums.

The hydra I'd conjured up turned out to be twice its natural size. The sudden arrival of this bog monster had put things into perspective. Apparently, the imps were the cowards from hell — literally!

The workers scattered in all directions. The

warriors stopped dead in their tracks. One of them dropped his weapon; a few more turned gray with shame and fear when their loincloths suddenly became moist.

The hydra emitted a guttural hiss. Its twelve horror-spewing jaws were enough to impress even the hell hounds: the beasts stopped in their tracks and began backing off, growling.

To sum it up, the effect from my first illusion reinforced with the Aura of Fear had surpassed my wildest expectations.

Struggling out of their stupor, the imps began inching sideways toward the hydra, ignoring Zander entirely.

Virgil and Tylor emitted a triumphant yell as the Infernal Monster collapsed under their blows, crumbling to a heap of lifeless bones.

Staggering, an exhausted Togien stepped back as I continued to heal him non-stop.

Iskandar and Rodrigo kept the shapeshifting warlock under control. The desperate man fought to the last. He used his class-switching ability again, returning to his original form, then tried to escape using a teleport scroll. Zander caught him just in time, then performed a shattering coup de grace. With a heartrending scream, the warlock dissolved into a swirling cloud of ashes.

Zander swung round and nearly jumped

out of his skin at the sight of the hydra. It didn't take him long to see through my little trick though; he posted a grinning emoticon in the battle chat and got busy smoking imps.

Virgil and Tylor — who by then were done with the hounds — also joined the melee.

Iskandar and Rodrigo were busy restoring mana. I'd healed Togien completely. Finally I had a moment to take a look around.

Immediately I noticed Platinus crouching sneakily next to the pool of bubbling slime — which by now had completely defrosted — and trying to fill some vials with the filthy liquid.

Right, and what about the conjurer? Had he given us the slip? Apparently not. I could see a heap of old rags marking the place where he'd been smoked.

The only thing left was the totem grinning its weathered yellow fangs.

* * *

THE FIGHT was over. Zander cast a watchful look around, then sat down to meditate, restoring his health.

I was about to walk over to him when Tylor stopped me. "Wait a bit. He's busy performing a ritual. He's speeding up the cooldown times of the abilities he's just used."

Iskandar and Rodrigo were inspecting the totem discussing how best to neutralize it. I could tell by the slight quivering of the air around its tip that the artifact was still very much active.

We had no enemies left within a direct line of vision. Still, I was sure that further down the dungeon they had more surprises in store for us.

"Did you see that shapeshifter?" Togien asked. "What was that, some kind of multiclass?"

"He's only an NPC."

"Sure. Smart motherfucker. A real beast for his level. I wouldn't want to meet him in a one-on-one, that's for sure. These game developers have sick imaginations, whoever they are. I'd love to know what else they have in store for us here."

"Nothing wrong with that, is there?"

My inbox flashed with an incoming message. Sender: Enea. Status: Offline

She hadn't even bothered to log in. She knew I didn't have Internet access to reply, anyway.

Hi,

I couldn't sleep all night. First hot, then cold... I need to be with you. I know you're frowning now. Don't worry. I remember what I promised you. I need to see my father and take some security measures. But once I'm back... just you wait.

A shy emoticon clutching a heart was smiling at me.

"Alexatis?" Zander's hand lay on my shoulder. "What's this pensive look on your face?"

"Nothing," I closed the message. "It's personal."

"This is a quest dungeon, isn't it?"

"No. I didn't receive any quests if that's what you mean. I do have one related to the castle but I've no idea how to go about it yet. Haven't found any prompts, either."

"Mind telling me what it's about?"

"Why should I?" I really didn't feel like letting him in on the quest. Its conditions stated clearly that in order to regain its ancient glory, the castle needed the mysterious "source of magic power" allowing me to unblock most of the castle's unique functions.

"A warlock who can turn into a Dark Knight and who can materialize Infernal monsters... you can say what you want but this can't be just some game designer's whim," Zander replied. "He is a very complex character. He uses uncategorized magic. I understand your predicament but still, if there's anything at all you can tell me that might help us complete this dungeon, do it now."

"Okay. Read this," I send him a copy of the system message regarding the unknown "source of power" and added, pre-empting his question, "Don't ask me where it is. I just don't know."

"It has to be here somewhere," Zander said with confidence. "You sure you don't have any other quests involving this place?"

I shook my head.

"Good," he said. "It's okay. We can do it. Think you could spare some quest loot?"

"Unfortunately not. The quest bonuses unlock the castle's abilities, that's all. I'm not getting anything, only the XP."

"Hey, come over here!" Platinus called.

What a cheek! While our two wizards had been busy casting a tethering web of spells over the totem, this self-proclaimed alchemist had finished farming whatever ingredients he'd been farming and had sneaked up on the warlock's body, fully intending to check it for any loot. Luckily, he'd stopped just in time: there were several no-drop items in the lot.

We walked over to him.

"I only had a look! I didn't take anything! I just can't close the loot distribution window."

"Of course you can't. You'll make a fine master looter one day," Zander chuckled. "If there *is* such a thing as a master looter. Calm down now. I want you to read the items' stats to me. You're the only person who has access to them at the moment. Whatever you do, don't put them on!"

Platinus broke into a nervous sweat. "There's a bracelet, a ring and two runic tablets."

"I want you to focus on each of the items."

"Yes, of course," Platinus licked his dry lips. "Listen. *The Replication Ring. A Founders' artifact. Binds on pickup. -30% to the Mental Energy required to build items or living creatures using the Object Replication spell.*"

"Object Replication?" Iskandar asked in surprise. "Never heard of it!"

"It's probably some Founders' magic," Rodrigo suggested. "The logs don't say what spells the warlock used. There're no names, only question marks. They're listed as 'uncategorized'."

"I'm taking the ring."

"Alex, why would *you* need it, of all people?"

"We'll see. Next item?"

"*Bracelet of a Metamorph. A Founders' artifact. Effect 1: +5 to Agility. Effect 2: Allows the wearer to switch to a different character class with no decrease in levels. Duration: 10 minutes. The new class stats are assigned at random. Allows the characters with close links to the powers of nature to draw 10% of the mental energy of all surrounding creatures. Range: 100 ft.*"

"Yeah right. One of those useless wonderwaffles," Zander said, turning to the two wizards. "What do you think?"

Iskandar chuckled. "To do what, turn into a warrior? Might be useful... occasionally. But if that means lagging an extra set of gear around — I don't think so. Not worth it. Besides, what would I do with it? I don't have the necessary skills. Okay, so this thing might turn me into a warrior for ten minutes — then what? I don't know any blows. Or combos. Nah, I think I'd rather stick to my own class."

Rodrigo nodded. "Likewise. Trying to adapt to it is too much trouble."

"Still, that warlock fought well against me," Zander pointed out.

"Nobody argues with that. Still, you made quick work of him. The bracelet didn't really help him, did it?"

Zander grinned. "Yeah, right. Had there been two of them, they'd have made quick work of *me*. So what did you decide? Who takes the bracelet? Togien, fancy turning into a wizard in your spare time?"

The dwarf cringed and shook his head.

"Alexatis?"

"I'll take it. Platinus, what's next?"

"*A runic tablet. A Founders' artifact. +5% to a random characteristic.*"

"Shit. Is it a no-drop again?"

"No, it's not."

"Good," Zander cheered up. "That means we can pass it around and experiment. Or even auction it off if necessary. Alexatis?"

"Sounds good," I agreed. "The other tablet will remain in the clan's treasury."

"Deal," Zander seemed pleased. No wonder: we'd only just entered the dungeon and already we had four unique items.

"There're also seven hundred gold coins, some rare alchemic ingredients and two scrolls... with hidden stats."

"Give the scrolls to me," I said. "You can keep the ingredients. Zander will have all the gold and other precious metals in his safekeeping. Once the raid is over, we'll sit down and share it out properly."

No one objected.

Although I wasn't yet going to use the two spells I'd learned from the warlock — Dark Regeneration and Object Replication, — the ring which added 30% Mental Energy to cast the latter was a great acquisition for the future.

The Bracelet of a Metamorph was still an unknown entity. Still, it was a perfect match for my class.

"Now, everyone," Zander commanded. "We need to check the area. There must be some treasure stashes here. Don't go too far! Whatever you do, keep within the view of the others. Have you insulated the totem?"

"We have," Rodrigo replied. "I'd love to take it back with us to study it. Still, it's too powerful, the bastard. It keeps syphoning magic from somewhere."

"We'll sort it out on our way back," Zander decided. "You have five minutes to collect the loot. Alexatis and I will back you up."

The others wandered off in search of any treasure chests and stashes.

CHAPTER THREE

I T DIDN'T TAKE them long to collect the loot. Togien with his Dwarven instinct for hidden treasures had indeed excelled. Platinus was busy studying the cave's meager vegetation, collecting herbs and taking samples of the bubbling pools of toxic slime.

"Alexatis? There's someone to see you," Rodrigo's voice resounded in the voice chat.

"Who's that?"

"Some prisoners."

"Send them here."

A small group of NPCs appeared out of the dark. An orc, a kobold, an Elf, two humans (both peasants, judging by their humble attire) and three dwarves.

Their name tags were in full view. The two peasants were neutral to us; all the others, friendly.

"Master!" the kobold approached me ignoring Zander entirely and clumsily dropped to one knee. "Allow us to follow you!"

The Elf followed suit. The dwarves chose to keep a safe distance. The orc, however, stepped forward, joining the ranks of our newfound volunteers.

"I want to fight!" he growled.

All three were a sorry sight: emaciated, their gear long broken. Their tattered clothes offered no clue of what they might have been in the past.

Their name tags, however, proved more helpful:

Highr. Kobold. Level 30. A Warrior
Arwan. Light Elf. Level 32. A Hunter
Dahvr. Orc. Level 35. A Warrior.

Their hp bars were frozen at 25%. The prolonged captivity, hard work and meager food had resulted in permanent debuffs.

They wouldn't be much good in battle, would they? Zander too looked skeptical.

"I understand you want to show your appreciation but you aren't strong enough to fight!"

"Our desire is enough!" the orc growled.

"We'd rather you tell us something about the dungeon," Zander said.

The kneeling prisoners ignored his comment entirely. "We're warriors," the kobold said. "Our ancestors served Rion's original owners. Heal us, Master, and let us fight for you!"

What, to remove permanent debuffs? They didn't want much, did they?

The Elf looked up sharply at me. "I can keep three arrows in flight! Give me my strength back, and you won't regret it!"

Their trust in my powers was probably based on all the legends about what the Order of Disciples could do. But I wasn't one of them, unfortunately.

"Would you like to stay in the castle?" I asked.

"Yes, Master!"

I had the first inkling of an idea. I needed to check it. My reputation was at stake though: if I failed, it could give rise to all sorts of unpleasant rumors.

I took the Charm of the Sovereign from around my neck and clenched it in my hand, feeling its microscopic spikes dig into my skin.

My closed fist glowed with a warm weak light. My life bar quivered and began to shrink.

"Do you swear your allegiance to me, the rightful owner and defender of Rion Castle?"

"We do!" three voices replied as one.

The charm's light grew stronger, enveloping the three kneeling figures in its glimmering golden haze.

The world stood still.

"The Aura of the Sovereign!" Arwan gasped.

The orc, the kobold and the Elf scooped the golden shimmer and poured it over their gaunt faces. Their life bars began to grow. The debuff icons disappeared from their tags!

The peasants and the dwarves had apparently regretted their indecision. Too late: the golden shimmer had already expired, triggering a new chain of system messages in my interface:

You've received a new level!
You've received a new level!

You have new ability and main characteristic points available!

By using the Legacy ability, you've unlocked a new effect of the Charm of the Sovereign: Aura of the Sovereign. Allows one-off removal of any debuffs cast on your loyal supporters.
Cooldown: 24 hours

Cost: varies, depending on the required effort.

Warning! You've lost 25% hp. Required restoration time: 10 min. For the next 60 minutes, your Life will take 15% longer to restore.

Apparently, everything had its price. Quite a hefty price in my case. The drop in my health had brought it dangerously close to the pain threshold.

Never mind. I could take it. But the effect it had produced! The mercs stood motionless, casting wary glances at me. The orc, the kobold and the Elf, however, looked more hopeful.

I reached into my inventory for the chitin bow I'd procured while farming the insects and handed it to Arwan. "Take it. We count on you."

I had nothing to offer to the warriors. Zander came to my rescue. He rummaged through his own inventory and produced a couple of items he obviously could part with for the raid's sake.

The kobold got a halberd. Zander seemed to have a decent knowledge of other classes and races' needs. The orc received a heavy scimitar.

All three perked up, beaming.

When Rodrigo and Iskandar recovered from the shock, they cast two buffs on them to compensate for the absence of proper armor: Stamina and Skin of Stone. Platinus fished out a few of his healing potions and shared the vials between the volunteers.

Nice miracle work! Zander PM'd me.

Get away with you, I replied. *That's nothing compared to what you paladins can do,* I added, trying to do him justice. *Your abilities aren't as costly, either. I just decided to give the artifact a quick check.*

Your health is really down. Is it normal?

It's okay. It'll come back up.

Togien walked over to me. "Alex, these guys," he pointed at the dwarves, "would like to join too."

I checked their tags for any debuffs. None. Their levels were good. Sturdy guys.

"Very well," I replied. "Find them some weapons and bring them under your command."

Three more, I PM'd Zander.

That I can see, he replied without enthusiasm, apparently not too thrilled to see his well-choreographed team growing barnacles. "Togien, tell the dwarves to keep close to you."

The peasants maintained a wary distance.

"And you — who are you? Where are you from?"

"We're from around here," one of them replied. "We're not warriors, we're farmers. We fish and work the land for a living."

"You should wait for us here."

"Oh no! The demons will catch us again."

"Can't you hide somewhere?"

"Can we follow you instead? There're plenty of our folk still left over there," the farmer pointed to the gaping depths of the cave. "The demons captured at least a hundred. We can't wait to pay them in kind."

"Very well. You can follow us if you want," I said, ignoring Zander's unhappy stare. Farmers from around here... that was interesting. I hadn't seen any villages or farms around. They'd probably been long destroyed, in which case a hundred hard-working NPCs might come in handy. We could find a safe little island nearby and allow them to settle in and build their lives back up. The Crystal Sphere's economy was one of its cornerstones. It would be downright stupid not to take advantage of this opportunity. Besides, the Renaissance of Rion quest required the restoration of the villages around it.

In the meantime, Togien had come up with some weapons for the dwarves: a poleaxe and two battle hammers. Had he lugged them around all this time? Why? I might actually ask him when the moment was right.

"Fall in," Zander commanded, casting watchful glances around. The warlock's death could have had the most unpredictable consequences; but at the moment, the area looked safe.

He gave us a brief run-down of our responsibilities. Rodrigo and Iskandar rebuffed us using a new scheme: they cast passive shields on the entire group, increasing our resistance to the element of Fire as well as mental and physical damage.

Zander wasn't using any of his abilities quite yet. "We need information about this dungeon," he gave the prisoners an inquisitive look.

The dwarves shrugged. They'd only got here recently. The farmers hurried to tell us what they knew about the dark obelisks. But it was the orc who offered the most valuable intel.

"There's a road nearby. We use it to take the ore to a large crack in the ground. We load the ore into cages and lower it down."

"We?"

"Yeah. The slaves, I mean. We can't escape from here, can we? There's no exit to the surface here. I know," he touched the scar on his face as if still smarting from the memory. "There's a bridge across it, guarded by demons. They're not very strong but there're quite a few of them. Twenty or so, I think. They won't let anyone cross to the other side. Even the imps aren't allowed there."

"And this warlock, have you seen him often?" Zander asked.

"Oh yes. He's well-known here. Constantly sneaking around. He checked every mine at least twice a day."

"Why?"

"He needed the artifacts. Sometimes the ore veins take us to small caves. That's where we used to find them. Old scrolls, weird objects... Usually cargonite tablets covered in ancient writings.

Zander and I exchanged glances. He motioned me aside.

"What do you say?" he laid a heavy gauntleted hand on my shoulder. "I should make a quick dash to the bridge. We can use the surprise factor, smoke the guards and cross to the other side before they know what's hit them. I have a funny feeling that's where all the cool stuff begins!"

I could understand him. Mercenaries are interested in loot and unique items — definitely not the kind of spoils a handful of emaciated slaves can offer. Our fight with the warlock had made it pretty clear that the demons weren't interested in farming ore. This was only a by-product of whatever they searched these caves for.

The imps had been hacking at these rocks for centuries in the hope of finding a meager ore vein or even a Founders' artifact — which happened much less frequently. The demons must have realized their value and would do anything to lay their hands on them. Even if the odds of finding a crumbling scroll containing an ancient spell were probably once in a century, apparently it was worth the risks, the costs and the trouble.

Zander's eyes glinted with impatience. Our paths might actually begin to part over this. The single runic tablet he'd received from the warlock had magnified both the range and effect of his auras. The only other way he could do it was by getting at least ten more levels.

I too realized the artifacts' value. Still, I couldn't approve of his plan. "We keep on farming," I said firmly. "We purge the dungeon and free the prisoners. That'll allow us to level up a bit by the time we reach the bridge."

"Whatever," he chose not to argue, suppressing his disappointment. At his level, he didn't get any XP for farming imps. Still, our agreement still held, forcing him to keep his ambitions in check.

* * *

THE CAVE was enveloped in darkness. Some of the crude columns supporting the ceiling were speckled with tiny luminescent stones whose weak glow tried to disperse the gloom.

I focused on one of the stones, habitually expecting the mind expander to offer a prompt. By now, I took its immediate reactions for granted. As part of the neuroimplant, the mind expander could read some of the stronger mental images, then conduct its own search in all available databases.

Snow Obsidian. A rare variety of volcanic glass. Magic properties: none

How strange. What was causing it to glow, then?

"Togien, take a look," I pointed at the faint blue aura. "Seen this before?"

He peered at the stones and nodded. "Volcanic glass."

"Why is it glowing?"

"No idea! Normally it shouldn't," he sounded interested. "Look closely. See that tiny spot at the center? It's like a little flame," Togien expertly picked out a few stones the size and shape of a pigeon egg. "This is weird. They keep glowing! Wonder if this is some kind of transformed matter?"

"You think they're affected by the dark obelisk?"

"They must be. What else do you suggest?"

I tried to take one of the stones from him. An unbearable heat burned my fingers. Instinctively I jerked my hand away, dropping the stone on the rocks. With a flash, the volcanic glass broke.

Rodrigo and Iskandar swung round. "Which one of you broke a mana vial?"

They didn't even notice the stone's shattered fragments which had already turned gray and lifeless. The air around them, however, felt electrified.

Platinus who'd been watching me all this time gave me a wink. "I did," he told the wizards. "Sorry about that."

They seemed happy with the explanation.

Platinus inched closer to me. "Is that transformed matter?" he mouthed. "Can I have some for my experiments?"

"Maybe."

"Thanks. I won't say a word!" he assured me in a whisper. "Why is it a secret?"

"The mercs don't need to know about Spectral Dust."

"Got it."

Togien, however, tensed up. "Alexatis? What the hell is going on here?"

I really wasn't in the mood. I'd been up and running for almost forty-eight hours. The credibility of my experience was beginning to get to me. Bouts of pain surged through me regularly — the price I was now paying for my recent use of the Charm of the Sovereign — but I had to grin and bear it. I couldn't explain it to anyone. They were here for an adrenaline rush, impatient to push themselves to the limit and milk this dungeon for every drop of gold, loot and XP it had to offer.

I had to worry about other things. I was desperate for a second wind. Exhaustion had made me snappy and irritable: not the best of qualities for a raid member.

I had the implant to thank for all this. It made me sense the danger coming from the cave: the beastly vibes emitted by some evil force, dark and viscous as tar, its freezing-cold waves washing over my mind.

"May I have the stone, please?"

Togien handed me the glowing rock. I squeezed it in my hand.

Its initial effect felt like an electric shock. I shuddered in an agonizing spasm which was soon replaced by a wave of warmth coursing through my veins, from my hands to my elbows and further up, sending goosebumps up my spine and making my whole body erupt in perspiration.

The stone's aura licking my clenched fingers began to weaken as if it had shared all of its accumulated energy with me.

My head cleared. "Give me another one!"

Casting wary glances at me, Togien reached into his inventory.

This time it didn't hurt. I felt much better. The sneaky ideas of Zander's potential betrayal had disappeared from my mind. Now I could see him and his group for what they truly were: they valued their reputation too much to be tempted by an extra handful of artifacts.

The stone's glow expired.

Your Synergy ability has grown 1 level!
You've learned a new skill: Energy Transfer
From now on, you can use any fragment of transformed matter to accumulate physical, mental or vital energy.

The message took my breath away. Few sorcerers could boast this level of expertise! The Neuro development branch was indeed full of surprises.

You've activated a fragment of transformed

matter.

Select the type and percentage of the energy you would like it to accumulate.

Selection accepted.

Type: vital energy

Rate: 1% per sec

Time left till full charge: 1 hr. 13 min

I knew how I would use the charged stones. I had those empty slots on my sword's hilt, didn't I? The stones fit them perfectly.

* * *

THE DUNGEON appeared deserted — treacherously so. Too busy with all the latest developments, I hadn't even noticed the darkness creep up on us, thick and sticky. I struggled to breathe in the air permeated with dust.

Zander stopped and raised a warning hand.

The echoes of many steel tools assaulting the rock merged into a monotonous clatter. This sounded like a large imp group at work. Zander stepped back, simultaneously issuing orders to change our formation,

"Wizards, take the flanks. The warriors will cover you. Togien, you stay with me. Alexatis, stay in the rear with the newbs in case the demons break through. Arwan, come over here!"

Reluctantly the Elf glanced at me, awaiting my orders. I nodded.

Zander handed him a quiverful of arrows from his own supplies. "The conjurer and the totem," he said. "Think you can do it?"

Without answering, Arwan pulled the bowstring taut.

"Iskandar, I want you to cast Wind. Gently! I don't want it to alarm them."

We formed an arrowhead: Zander and Togien in front, the wizards behind them with Virgil and Tylor flanking them. Me, Platinus, the orc, the kobold and the three dwarves in the rear. The peasants were cowering in a fissure way behind.

A light breeze touched my face — more like a draft, really, which are quite common in underground caves. It blew the clouds of dust aside, revealing about fifty worker imps and a couple of dozen prisoners controlled by a dark obelisk. The group was lined up along the cave wall, monotonously hacking at it. The only untouched slab of rock emitted a faint glow. This must have been the dark spirit's temporary abode.

There were two totems here, with a conjurer posted next to each. The demons' levels were mainly 25 to 30: quite doable. Which in turn meant that the spirit's level was at least 35.

Five warriors strode to and fro behind the workers' backs.

"They've got a cheek, really," Virgil commented. "You can tell they've got no one to keep them on their toes."

Zander took in the setup. "Wizards, wait for Arwan to finish up, then begin casting blanket damage. Togien, you start pulling aggro while I try to get to the obelisk.

The sheer number of spread-out targets didn't seem to faze Arwan. Without saying a word, he deftly raised his bow and loosed off two arrows, then swung round and loosed off two more.

The guy was a born sniper, I thought as I watched both conjurers bite the dust. Two crits out of two! He did an equally spectacular job with the totems, their bony structures crumbling to the ground.

Zander lunged forward. Togien used his class ability to increase the level of danger emitted by him. The imps beelined for him, furious, ignoring everything else around.

Iskandar and Rodrigo attacked simultaneously. Pools of acid materialized in the imps' way, dealing repeated damage, followed by a flurry of Subzero which slowed up the more brazen ones.

Arwan didn't stop there. Standing behind Togien, he kept loosing off arrows. Only three of the warrior imps made it to Togien, their lives dangerously close to zero.

Both the orc and the kobold shifted from one foot to the other, impatient to join in the melee — but by then, they had no potential enemies left: our wizards had already smoked all of the workers.

The dark obelisk, however, proved a hard kill. Time and time again Zander hacked at it with his longsword but only dented the surface. The cornered spirit shrank deeper into the rock, only responding with occasional debuffs and gradually weakening Zander's auras by reaching them with its tendrils of darkness.

Once the imps ceased to be a threat, Tylor and Virgil hurried to his aid. Still, their blows couldn't do any serious damage without ruining their weapons' durability. The dark creature put up a good fight. The spectral glow enveloping the rock began to thicken, forming vague outlines conjoined by magic: skulls baring their teeth, fragments of spines, bony arms reaching out for you... Wisps of darkness trailed behind the ghosts identical to those left by the legionnaires. At least twenty of them circled the air, accelerating into the attack.

They lunged at our warriors. Zander left

the obelisk alone, stepped back and cast Expulsion.

The cave filled with mournful howling as the spell's beaming light scorched the darkness, destroying the summoned ghosts. The dark spirit, however, stayed intact in the safety of its rocky shelter.

Togien produced a pickaxe from his inventory. He spat on his hands for a better grip, ran up to the rock and began swinging at it strong and fast.

I watched his damage stats.

Not good. Togien may be a Master in Mining but even he had trouble handling transformed matter. His every blow only removed 20 pt. of the rock's durability while the haze of Infernal darkness enveloping it promptly restored the damage.

Even worse: the trapped spirit had regained control of the prisoners, making them pick up their weapons in preparation for a counterattack.

We might end up having to fight with potential allies before we could resume our attacks on the rock!

That wasn't the way to do it.

I waved to Rodrigo and Iskandar, motioning them to stop. Accompanied by the orc and the kobold, I made a dash for the obelisk, splashing through the hissing pools of acid still streaked with frost.

As I ran, I glanced over the NPC prisoners' name tags. Much to my surprise, one of them turned out to be a player in dusty but still sturdy cloth gear. A cleric? He was straining to overcome the obelisk's dark charms, shaking his head and mouthing something, stubbornly trying to cast a spell.

Some willpower the guy had! I watched in awe as he resisted the spirit's pressure on his mind.

"Zander, stop wasting your abilities!" I shouted, noticing him readying his hands to cast Cleanse.

Grudgingly he obeyed.

Counting each pace, I ran past the obelisk. The distance seemed enough for my purposes. The spell's range could affect both the obelisk and the prisoners enslaved by it.

Casting Exorcism required 8 sec. concentration. Never before had I cast a spell without previous practice. Needless to say, I was nervous — especially because the prisoners armed with whatever they could find were already heading for me, rattling their shackles.

I took my time enunciating the words of the spell.

Done it.

If I was expecting some spectacular visual

effects, I was wrong.

A thick, dull silence hung in the cave.

The prisoners stopped. A fine web of cracks ran over the obelisk, oozing ectoplasm. Its green droplets hissed, evaporating, leaving deep dents in the rock.

The spectral haze began to rise toward the cave's ceiling, condensing to form a face distorted with fury.

An otherworldly whisper entered my mind, "I'll remember you."

* * *

YOU'VE RECEIVED a new level!
You have new abilities available!

I breathed slow and deep. Pain was scorching my mind. I was so weak it felt like I would never move again. My mental, physical and vital energy bars all hovered at 30%. The spirit's level had been considerably higher than mine — and now I was paying the price.

"You okay?" Zander looked seriously worried.

"That's what this spell does to a caster."

"I can't see any debuffs. Why isn't your life growing?"

I wasn't going to explain the mechanism to

him. Zander must have realized it as he stopped asking questions.

Iskandar walked over to me. "You think auras might help?"

"Maybe. Something to bring up health capacity and regeneration rate."

A gentle soft light enveloped me. The pain subsided but I was still weak.

"This is a ten-minute buff," Iskandar said. "I'll cast it again when it expires."

"Thanks, man," I perched myself on a flat rock. "Togien, I want you to mark the obelisk," I said, trying to sound matter-of-factly.

In any case, I'd had my dose of ancient spells for the day. I looked around. Arwan stood nearby, busy explaining something to the group of liberated prisoners. "Arwan, I need to talk to their cleric."

The only player in the NPC group confidently walked over to me. Nickname: Raoul. Level: 27.

"Thanks for your help," he said, brushing the dust off his clothes.

"How did you get here?"

"I was doing some leveling near Agrion when those Darks captured me."

I couldn't believe my ears. "Not players, surely?"

"Nope. NPCs," he cringed. "They needed a

healer! Wretched savages. They cast control on me and ported me out. I don't remember very well. There was this ravine we had to cross..."

"Why didn't you provoke them? They might have smoked you. You could have started a fight or something. "

"I didn't want to lose my gear," he admitted. "I had no idea where I was or where I might respawn. Also, I hoped it was just a plot line. They said there was an ogre in need of a heal. If I did that, they said, they'd make it worth my while. But I received no quest message. I thought it strange."

"And? Did you heal him?"

Raoul heaved a sigh. "Impossible. Level fifty-three, five thousand hp, how are you supposed to heal *that*? He'd gotten caught in a rockfall. Broken every bone in his body. Was squirming and screaming like you can't imagine. A Grand Master in Mining, can you believe the irony? His Regeneration ability wouldn't let him die. They used him as some sort of tunneling machine."

I made a mental note. Despite their rather questionable intellectual skills, ogres can be quite useful — like, when one needs to storm an enemy castle. And I was pretty sure you could come to some arrangement with them.

"I tried to do what I could for twenty-four

hours," Raoul went on. "They couldn't keep me for any longer. So I just logged out and went to bed. The next day I logged in — and I was back here! Shackled to the rock, pick in hand, with imps all around me!"

"Your bind point must have been changed."

"Exactly. Some bug this is. Every time I log in, I get back here. I wrote to Support but they never replied. I thought I might have to create another char and start all over again. Luckily, you came."

"You can stay with us if you want," I suggested.

His eyes lit up. "I'd love to! I need to settle a few scores now. I've got plenty of time — I've lost my job because of these Dark bastards!"

"Why, did you fail a quest because of this?"

"Not here. A real-world job," he admitted reluctantly. "I missed a few days at work trying to get out of here. And had I lost my char, I'd have had nothing left at all. This way at least I could use the game money."

"You have a family?"

"No."

"Any idea where you are?"

He shrugged. "I only got the local map working."

"These are the Toxic Moors."

"No shit! How am I supposed to get out of

here? Are we right under the moors now?"

"Ever heard of Rion Castle?"

"I think so. Some kind of old ruin. The Ravens were going to purge it and claim it, I think. From what I heard, it's packed with artifacts. They were going to call up a raid but it didn't work out for some reason."

"Rion Castle is right above us. I'm its new owner," I said to duly impress him. No point trying to conceal from him what everybody already knew. Firstly, because our group could use a healer. And secondly, because this Raoul definitely wasn't as simple as he looked. His gear was quite mediocre. It definitely hadn't been worth him staying in slavery. Which could only mean that he must have had some cool character-boosting items in his inventory.

Raoul widened his eyes in surprise. "No way! So you're the clan leader?"

"Ever heard of the Black Mantises?"

"Nah. I spent all last week here, I told you. You're cool, man! I saw you squeeze that spirit out of the rock!"

Zander walked over to us. "We've found three chests: two with gold and one with cargonite. About thirty grand in total. The imps weren't exactly poor. We also found four more rune tablets same as before, with random stat boosts."

Raoul listened to it, spellbound. I had to strike while the iron was hot. "So would you like to join us?"

"May I?" he asked, suddenly doubtful, so generous my invitation must have sounded after Zander's announcement.

"You most surely can," I said, "if you don't mind sharing your local map with us."

"Not a problem," he said, forwarding it to me.

"Zander, can you send him an invite?"

Zander chuckled. "You've got the whole lot of them waiting."

* * *

THE PRISONERS were gaunt and emaciated. About twenty of them were farmers; they were already casting greedy glances around the cave in search of anything worth pilfering in recompense for their years of slavery. I told them to join the others in the rear and stay put.

I was left with five Elves, three dwarves and two tall warriors of some unknown race.

"Master," Arwan dropped on one knee, speaking for everybody. "Please allow us to join you."

"You want to join the battle?"

"We want to join *you*. For good."

I looked questioningly at the dwarves.

"For good," they echoed.

"And you," I turned to the sinewy warriors, "where are you from?"

"We're Arhats, the Guards of Gloom. Our home is in the desert behind the Azure Mountains. My name is Kray."

"I am Ikhtar," the other added.

"The Guards of Gloom?"

"That's what we've always been called. Darkness is everywhere, even under the desert sun. We are the warriors fighting the spawn of the Dark."

"How did they manage to capture *you*?"

Kray frowned. "In battle, you can never tell. We all swore to serve the one who delivers us from slavery."

"We did," the dwarves nodded, fingering their shaggy beards streaked with dust.

"Very well. You're in," I said, ignoring Zander's silent disapproval. "Found any weapons?" I asked him.

"Only some cargonite," he replied. "Two very weird spears," he showed me a naginata-like weapon, "and five swords with unreadable stats and low durability."

I looked over the ex-prisoners. "Any of you know how to use polearms?"

"We do," the two Guards of Gloom stepped

forward.

"We can fight with our picks," the dwarves hurried to assure me.

"Okay. Then you," I looked at the Elves, "will take the swords."

Their faces lit up. What a shame Enea wasn't with me now. She would have appreciated this moment of unbridled joy.

"How susceptible are you to the power of totems and Dark Obelisks?" I asked the two warriors.

"Alas," Kray lowered his head. "Their power is overwhelming. It's the only reason we found ourselves in slavery."

Zander butted in via the group chat.

Alexatis, are you nuts giving cargonite artifacts to NPCs? I can buy them from you!

Don't worry, I replied. *You'll get your share of the loot. But first we must purge the caves — and to do this, we need all the help we can get.*

By then both Kray and Ikhtar had already had their naginatas at the ready. The Elves — who were generally much more resistant to mental attacks — looked at me expectantly: even despite their natural 10% resistance, the obelisk had managed to keep them under its control. I had to give Arwan his due: his killing of the dark conjurers at such a dangerously close distance must have demanded every bit of willpower he could muster.

"Now listen to me," I said to the two Guards of Gloom. "The only way I can protect you is if you join my clan and stay in the castle."

The two eagerly nodded.

The Elves held a whispered discussion between themselves. They weren't any less eager to join us in battle — but still I thought I'd caught the word "family" in their arguments.

Finally Arwan seemed to have snapped at the others, using a language I didn't know. He raised his head sharply, looking at me,

"We're joining the clan!"

The dwarves took much longer to make up their minds. Two of those we'd just liberated stepped aside; the remaining four joined our ranks.

Both the orc and the kobold, however, joined us unhesitantly. Duly impressed by the healing they'd received, they were impatient to wreak their revenge on the Darks.

Joining the clan was quite straightforward. I had a special tab in my interface which looked pretty self-explanatory, even though I was yet to work out some of its functions.

One by one, I highlighted the icons of the

---

two Guards of Gloom, selecting them, and activated the "*Join*" button.

Got it!

New tabs sprang up in the clan interface: Reputation quests, leveling, etc., etc.

I repeated the procedure several times, adding the Elves, the dwarves, the orc and the kobold.

This was what I finally had:

Alexatis. Level 30. Neuro. Current status: Online

Enea. Level 27. Battle Wizard. Current status: Offline

Platinus. Level 18. Sorcerer. Current status: Online

Our names were followed by those of the NPCs. They had no status report: they were constantly online by definition.

I highlighted the entire list and focused my gaze on the Charm of the Sovereign icon, activating it.

A cascade of pale light erupted, enveloping the ex-prisoners in its silvery shimmer. When it finally expired, each of the new clan members had a 50% resistance to mental attacks icon next to their names.

Phew. It had worked. If the truth were

known, I hadn't even been sure whether the 50%
thing was applicable to NPCs.

Raoul watched the scene, suitably
impressed. "Can I join your clan too?"

"You can. But we might need to run a
quick check on you later."

"That's not a problem. I wasn't expelled
from other clans, if that's what you mean. No
Reputation penalties. Nothing on my PK counter.
My char isn't the best for solo leveling anyway.
And you've just saved it."

"All right," I selected him and activated the
Join button, casting the Charm of the Sovereign
aura over him too.

Excellent. We had a cleric!

New clan quest alert: Turf Wars!
In order to neutralize the constant threat of
a Dark invasion, you need to purge the dungeons
of Rion Castle from the spawn of the Inferno.

Reward: +1 to the clan's level
+1000 to the clan's Reputation

Unhesitantly I pressed *Accept.*

* * *

RION CASTLE
SUBTERRANEAN DUNGEONS

BEFORE MOVING on, Zander and I needed to discuss our next steps.

We studied the map I'd received from Raoul. His constant tribulations and logout attempts had allowed him to map out most of the dungeon as apparently, login locations were randomized enough to land him at five more mines manned by large imp groups. The road to the ravine was also marked on the map.

Judging by what we'd already learned, dark obelisks were the biggest threat for us. And if we moved quickly, then I wouldn't be able to use Exorcism: the price would be too high.

"I suggest we lure them out," Zander said, applying the coordinate grid to the map and performing the calculations. "Here," he inserted a place marker, "this is where we need to be. This spot falls equidistant to the five obelisks, just out of their respective reach. Or do you think the spirits can leave the obelisks in order to get to us?"

"They might," I replied. "If the imps don't beat them to it. Five groups, that's at least two hundred mobs and possibly ten conjurers."

"Their numbers are irrelevant. This is a

perfect position, look. The cliffs form natural defenses with only three potential access routes. And we have plenty of warriors to defend them. Virgil can tank, that's three tanks in total. The wizards will cast blanket spells."

"You really think they'll let us take up this position?"

"Nope. We'll *port* there. I have the coordinates."

"We can't. There're too many of us. A standard teleport won't do it."

"Maybe not," he reached into his inventory and produced a Mass Teleport scroll.

This was one hell of a rare spell. I didn't even know you could copy it to a scroll.

"So what do you think?" he said. "How about teaching the Darks a lesson?"

I had nothing to say to that. Now that we had a cleric, our raid's survivability had soared. And if I could destroy all five Obelisks with just one Exorcism, so much the better.

"Very well," I said. "Do it."

Casting frequent glances at the map, Zander began plotting the positions, serrying our ranks as tight as he could to avoid any teleport accidents.

His efforts resulted in three groups. Zander, Togien and Virgil were the tanks. The dwarves, the orc and the Elves were our damagers — not that they'd have to do much in the upcoming melee. The wizards were our main weapon: their job was to smoke as many enemies as they could before we even reached the chosen position.

The kobold and the two Guards of Gloom formed a reserve defense circle around the formation's center, protecting Platinus, Raoul, Rodrigo, Iskandar and myself.

"You have two minutes to cast buffs!" Zander commanded.

In addition to our Skin of Stone, Stamina, Knee-Jerk Reactions and Resistance to Fire, Raoul also cast a Minor Regeneration and Health of a Giant.

"Get set!"

Zander took his place in the formation, pulled out the scroll, entered the coordinates, then touched them.

* * *

FOR A SPLIT second I didn't know where I was.

The kobold's hot wheezy breath seared my cheek.

We stood in a thick cloud of dust surrounded by the clattering of tools, creaking of hoists and groaning of prisoners.

The imps' five main mines formed a wide

arch in the ever-widening cave.

We'd been ported to a small platform already cleared of all debris, surrounded by towering cliffs and banks of slag and depleted ore. The place looked very much like an archeological site littered with old pegs and lengths of string once used to divide it into a grid.

These first impressions were immediately gone. I sensed a soft push to my back as our wizards cast Levitation, rising over the cliffs and heaped debris.

The clattering of the tools died away, replaced by monosyllabic exclamations of surprise promptly replaced by fury.

"Serry the ranks!" Zander commanded.

A flash of light illuminated the cave as a Heavenly Shield unfolded around us, protecting us from the conjurers' attacks. Blobs of darkness clashed impotently against it, exploding on impact. Arwan expertly climbed a large heap of slag and struck back, downing a few dark casters with a hail of arrows.

A hundred throats hollered their fury.

Imps poured onto us from every direction. Overtaking the workers, warrior imps hurried first. Wisps of darkness trailed in their wake as Dark Obelisks tried to reach us with their mental magic.

Still, Zander's calculations had been spot

on. The ashen wisps of darkness drooped and dissolved, unable to get to us.

Arwan's tireless shooting made the imps squirm in frustration. More and more conjurers cowering behind the prisoners' backs dropped to the rocky ground stained with their black blood, wheezing in their last agony.

Hovering in the air, Rodrigo and Iskandar hung back to back and began rotating slowly, mouthing a desperate spell.

Their joint effort softened the cave's rocky floor, turning it into a treacherous quagmire. About fifty mobs fell into the viscous substance which was rapidly solidifying, turning back into stone. The creatures shrieked, trying to get out while struggling against the flow of the crowd which was trampling them to death.

Raoul kept casting Recovery non-stop. Our wizards' mental energy bars momentarily emptied, then filled halfway up again.

The narrow passages between the cliffs seethed with fighting. The demons were so numerous that they crowded each other out, forcing some of them to climb the cliffs in an attempt to get to us.

Arwan kicked a few of them out of his way but still was forced to retreat as more and more imps shinnied up the cliffs, ignoring the passages. Their ability to scale heights had instantly ruined Zander's well-conceived plan. About a hundred mobs were fast approaching us from above and were about to shower down on our heads.

Three spirals of Mortal Cold reached out for the enemy's avant-garde, followed by acid rain.

Now try to pour some liquid nitrogen over a rock and then sprinkle it with acid: you'll see what I mean!

The cliffs shattered, raising vortices of swirling acid. The demons screamed, frost-bitten and burned with acid, as they dropped to their death.

Our wizards had given it their all. As they gulped down elixirs, Raoul hurried to cast another heal over everyone.

Zander, Virgil and Togien held the passages like one man. Their warriors hacked at the enemy with grim determination, smoking demons by the dozen.

The kobold growled his protest: he hadn't yet had a chance to show himself. Both Guards of Gloom froze next to me, calmly awaiting orders.

I was busy maintaining the Levitation Aura to keep Rodrigo and Iskandar afloat.

In the meantime, the demons' numbers had swelled. Reinforcements kept flooding in. Apparently, there were a few more groups working nearby, not marked on Raoul's map.

"Watch out! Sling shooters!" Zander shouted.

A volley of rocks showered our positions. I barely managed to cast a Stamina over the two wizards. Overcome by the pressure of the battle, Rodrigo cast Chain Lightning, decimating the enemy. Blind with rage, the imps redoubled their efforts, scaling the rocks toward us.

"Retreat!" Zander's voice thundered overhead, saving us from immediate defeat. "Form a circle! Second row, raise your shields above your heads!"

Iskandar and Rodrigo squirmed on the ground under the barrage of rocks. Raoul hurried to their help, saving both from certain death.

The situation was getting worse by the second. Although we still held our ground, our resources weren't limitless. The imps were just too numerous — and we were too busy fighting back to deal any damage.

The kobold exchanged glances with the Guards of Gloom. "Can we?" he growled, addressing me. "Our time has come!"

The imps were almost upon us, climbing the banks of dead bodies. The warriors of the front line struggled under the pressure. The Elves couldn't fight back as they were busy holding the shields over their heads, covering me and the wizards from the torrent of rocks.

Our main task — to aggro the obelisks and lure the spirits out to be exorcised — remained unfulfilled. I just didn't see any other way.

"Do it!" I said, then turned to Arwan, "Form steps with your shields!"

The Elves didn't have to be told twice.

As it turned out, the kobold didn't need steps. He crouched on his hind legs, leaning on his tail, then uncoiled his lithe body, springing over the warriors' heads and landing on the nearest cliff. His halberd whooshed through the air, clearing a path in the demonic ranks.

The two Guards of Gloom followed in his wake with remarkable agility. Their naginatas drew the blurred outlines of almost imperceptible combos in the air.

The long ancient pole weapons hit the enemy with terrible precision. The two warriors' silhouettes were reduced to a slurry of shadows. I was almost sure they were using Combat Trance — one of their race's unique abilities — but how long would they be able to keep it up?

Zander immediately saw that the tide was turning. "Iskandar, bring my aggro up! Rodrigo, shut down those slingers!"

Rocks continued to shower the shields like hailstones.

The imps froze, undecided. Zander's aggro began pulling them in, distracting them from the bleeding kobold and the exhausted Guards of Gloom.

"Relieve the front line!" Zander kept snapping orders while fighting off demonic hordes.

The dwarves stepped back, completely worn out. Virgil and Tylor gulped more potions. Raoul was taking care of the orc whose life was deep in the red. The Elves who were yet to join the battle hurried to Zander's aid.

Bleeding profusely but alive, the kobold and the two Guards of Gloom finally fought back to us. Raoul promptly cast a healing aura over them. The guy definitely knew what he was doing.

In the meantime, Iskandar and Rodrigo had managed to choke the slingers' positions in toxic fog. The imps' shooting stopped, their triumphant squeaking replaced by croaks of agony.

I was so fed up with all the system messages flickering before my eyes that I minimized them all.

"The spirits!" one of the Elves pointed.

Finally! They just couldn't stay inside their dark obelisks any longer! By now, the imps' ranks had shrunk: those still left were mainly uncoordinated workers with decimated life bars who doggedly kept re-entering the battle in small groups with no hope of winning.

Arwan had smoked all the conjurers a long time ago. Their totems had collapsed, fractured by the Elves' arrows. Bound to their obelisks, the spirits hovered at a distance, too far from the demons to control them.

"Serry the ranks!" Zander snapped. "Alexatis, your turn!"

He didn't need to tell me. Throughout the battle, I'd tried to go easy on my abilities, awaiting this very moment.

"They're coming!" Zander took his place in the formation. "I've got Expulsion back. You want me to use it?"

"No point. It won't work against them."

The spirits had already left their rocky dwellings and were now approaching us, their outlines shimmering with grayish-blue auras. I checked my interface. Thanks to all the XP the raid had earned during the melee, I was now level 35. Excellent. That would make casting Exorcism far less costly.

The spirits advanced warily. There was nothing around they could use as shelter. Their translucent bodies were mere clots of darkness veined with crimson. Not a very pretty sight.

They weren't in a hurry to attack. Not that they needed to: each of them had at least a hundred ghosts under their command.

Still keeping a respectful distance, the spirits encircled us and froze, hovering in the air. They must have sensed we were up to something.

Their subtle whispers didn't affect us. The Shield of Reason emitted by the Charm of the Sovereign boosted our resistance to all mind-altering magic, preventing the spirits from casting control on us.

The ghosts charged upon us, oozing gloom.

They were still out of my range. Oh well, I'd have to do it in two stages, then. Never mind. I'd survive. I could do it!

As the ghosts were trying to force their way through Zander's and Raoul's defense auras, I cast the first Exorcism.

A vociferous groan echoed through the cave.

The ghosts vanished. Just like that. They weren't resummonable, either. The spirits too had received one hell of a debuff.

Instinctively they attacked. By killing hundreds of ghosts, I had generated tons of aggro, leaving them no choice.

My lips turned cold. My fingers twitched with tension. My life had plummeted, leaving me with virtually no mana. Exorcism took eight seconds to cast. If I failed the second one, I wouldn't get another chance.

My head swam. I was losing concentration.

Was I strong enough to cast it again?

But yes! The potion! Power of a Monster 2.0! What was it Platinus had said? All stats would soar to the sky?

I gulped the obnoxious drink, sensing my body fill with inhuman strength.

"Alexatis! Whatcha waitin' for?"

Zander did cast Expulsion, after all. Not that it hurt the spirits in any shape or form, but at least it bought me a couple of extra seconds.

The spirits reached for each other, merging together, joining forces in order to forever imprison our raid in a silent cocoon devoid of time and space.

The air around us shifted, thickening. Even the unflinching faces of the two Guards of Gloom betrayed instinctive fear.

The moments felt like an eternity. Finally, the last word of the ancient spell fell from my lips.

The spirits wailed. The spell ripped through their bodies, twisting them into tight swirls of darkness which flew in all directions, breathing fire, then fell apart, showering the ground with clouds of ash.

Silence prevailed. The far-off echo of a rockfall arose and died in the dungeon's depths.

CHAPTER FOUR

THE CRYSTAL SPHERE
THE DUNGEONS OF RION CASTLE

WHILE THE MERCS collected the loot, I was having a quick recovery break, sitting nearby watching all the bustle.

This wasn't really the right time to do it, but I simply had to sort out my new stats and abilities. I had lots of points available so I thought I'd better invest them now before I had to face the great unknown again.

I'd already realized that in order to use the Founders' ancient magic, I had to invest in Intellect, Stamina and Spirit. Strength and Agility could also use a little boost, considering my class' potential as a Warrior.

The killing of several hundred ghosts and five dark obelisk spirits had earned me two more levels. Raid leveling was definitely the thing to do. Together with the racial bonus (+1 pt. every 5 levels), I had in total 16 stat points available plus 19 more to invest into abilities. Also, the Exorcist achievement I'd received for lifting the curse had added another 2 points to both Spirit and Intellect.

Very well, then. Let's have a look.

As I distributed the points, I kept three objectives in mind: first, how best to fit the requirements of the spells I'd learned, secondly, to raise my Health quota and thirdly, to boost my Warrior abilities.

This is what I finally had:

Alexatis. Level 37. Neuro

Life, 242,5/242,5 (Stamina, 190 + Gear, 32.5 + the Charm of the Sovereign bonus, 22)

Physical Energy, 135/135 (Strength, 120 + current abilities and the gear bonus, 15)

Mental Energy, 248/248 (Intellect, 180 + current abilities and the gear bonus, 68)

Physical Defense, 275 (Scaly Armor, 210 + Agility bonus, 65)

Physical Attack, 91.3 (Mysterious Sword at 50% Durability, 25 pt. + Strength, 13 + the gear bonus, 2 + Intense Training, 6 + character level, 37 + the Charm of the Sovereign bonus, 8.3)

Mental Defense, 89% (Self-Control + Spirit + the gear bonus = the Charm of the Sovereign bonus)

Elemental Defense, 20% (Spirit and the Scaly Breastplate)

Mental Attack, 97.9 (spells studied, 50 + Unity of Schools, 2 + character level, 37 + the Charm of the Sovereign bonus, 8.9)

Mental Energy Regeneration, 18.34 pt./sec (Spirit divided by 2 + 0,84 bonus from Synergy, Power of Reason and Self-Control + the Charm of the Sovereign bonus, 10)

Strength, 13.5 (Secret Knowledge, 12+1 + the gear bonus, 0.5)

Intellect, 24.8 (Secret Knowledge, 18+1+the gear bonus, 0.8+the ring, 3+the Exorcist bonus, 2)

Agility, 13 (the gear bonus, 12+1)

Stamina, 22.5 (19 + the underwear kit bonus, 1.5 + the Charm of the Sovereign bonus, 2)

Spirit, 15 (13 + the Exorcist bonus, 2)

Main Professions, Require activation

Achievements:

Celebrated Pioneer
A map-making app available

Clan Founder
+ 1,000 to Popularity, +1 to all Reputations

Exorcist
+2 to Intellect, +2 to Spirit

Centurion
Allows you to instantly summon any of the Cohort's legionnaires

The Light of Passion
+1 to all stats whenever the person you love is with you

The Neuro Development Branch:

Secret Knowledge, 1:
Observational Skills, 1
Spell Interception, 1
Unity of Schools, 1
Acquisition of Blows and Combos, 1
Reflex Optimization, 1
Unity of Origin, 1
Legacy, 1. *Not activated. Requires level 45*

Evolution, 1:
Intense Training, 3
Pain Threshold, 5
Synergy, 2
Crit, 3. *Not activated. Requires level 45*

Power of Reason, 1:
Insight, 1
Self-Control, 4
Enhanced Perception, 1
Energy Transfer, 1. *Not activated. Requires level 45.*

Legacy:
From now on, you can control the ancient blood magic which exists in synergy with nature.

The Founders' artifacts will reveal their secret properties to you alone.

Any acquired spells will be available 3 levels earlier than required.

-5% to Mental Energy required to cast a spell.

Crit:

+10% to your chances of dealing a critical hit. +5% to your chances of dealing damage with the Element of Chaos in a successful (i.e., not blocked by the enemy) attack. Every new level of the ability adds +3% to your chances of dealing elemental damage.

Energy Transfer:

You've learned to accumulate the surrounding Elements' energy in order to transfer it to stones or charge up magic scrolls. Every new level of the ability adds +5% to both energy accumulation and energy transfer rates.

Once I did eight more levels, I would have access to three more abilities. Which why I was very cautious in distributing the available points. Three of them I invested into Crit; the rest I set aside, reluctant to part with them quite yet.

"Alexatis, you okay?" Zander asked, eyeing the Guards of Gloom. The two warriors had ignored the abundance of loot and chosen to guard my peace instead. They hovered nearby, shooing off everyone who attempted to approach me with a question or a request.

"I'm fine, thanks," I replied.

"Your life has dropped a lot," he commented.

"It's okay. It'll be back in a few minutes. I told you these ancient spells come with price tags attached. You'd better tell me how many more prisoners you've liberated."

"Over a hundred. Seventy-six farmers, the rest are Elves, dwarves and three more orcs. I'm sure they're gonna ask you if they can join the clan."

I grinned. "Is that Arwan doing his sales pitch?"

"Not at all. After everything they've just seen, I'd be surprised if they didn't. I would."

"No one's stopping you."

"Unfortunately, I can't. I have my own route," he forwarded me the list of loot. "This is indeed a virgin dungeon. A player's dream."

The list was indeed impressive. A hundred grand gold — yesterday I couldn't have even dreamt of ever having so much money! Thirty-five cargonite items. Armor, weapons and rune tablets.

Scrap cargonite (mainly fragments of

unidentified items) was listed separately — all two hundred pounds of it!

"And this is what the spirits dropped," Zander reached into his inventory, producing a handful of jewelry and five charged teleport crystals. That was a nice surprise. Now I could activate the dungeon portal.

All the jewelry — about a dozen rings, chains and bracelets — were relic items of unknown origin. There were two ways of identifying them: I could either convoke several Masters in Jewelry, Archeology and Enchantment to see what they had to say — or I could find out their purpose by just trying them on.

The latter option was less time-consuming but definitely not as safe. The artifacts might possess some concealed stat preventing me from removing them. They could even be cursed for all that I knew — after all, they used to belong to malignant spirits.

"I'm going to add them to the clan's treasury," I finally said.

"That's fine with me," Zander agreed. Then he added, noticing that my life had already restored, "So? Should we go and check on your new recruits?"

* * *

ZANDER HAD BEEN right. All of the ex-prisoners asked my permission to join the clan.

I remembered my morning conversation with Mr. Borisov and his contemptuous disregard for NPCs. I didn't subscribe to it at all.

Firstly, unlike guards, vendors, workers and other hired toons, the liberated prisoners were self-sufficient characters in their own right with well-developed identities and even personalities. Secondly, they could move freely between locations, accumulate XP, level up, receive new abilities and actively participate in the clan's life.

Thirdly, they weren't likely to log out just because they were tired, or had a family emergency, or had to get up early to go to work. Like myself, these were local denizens — which might prove a crucial factor in a number of situations.

Having said that, they couldn't really replace Enea, Togien or Platinus.

With my silent permission, Zander did a quick evaluation of the new clan members' levels and specializations, meticulously checked their weapons and gear and divided them into squads.

"Alexatis! We need to get going!" he reminded me.

In total, we now had four orcs, twenty-seven Elves, fifteen dwarves, a kobold and two Guards of Gloom.

We sent all the farmers to the old mines deep in the rear. The demons were highly unlikely to venture anywhere near them out of old habit, too scared to bump into legionnaires.

Soon our clan's combat section was lined up, ready to be buffed.

Raoul, Iskandar and Rodrigo strode along their ranks casting long-term buffs on the greenhorns.

Zander gave them one last check. "Platinus, hand them out some of your healing potions. One each."

We had to be economical with our supplies. I had indeed hoped to procure some reinforcements down here — but I'd had no idea they'd be so many!

"Alexatis?" Zander turned to me. "Mind saying something to them?"

Rhetoric had never been my forte. Neither was clan leadership. I might have some catching up to do before I could become a half-decent clan leader.

"I don't think they need a pep talk," I said, seeing the burning desire for vengeance in their eyes.

"Off we go, then," Zander concluded.

"Pointless dragging it out. We've lost too much time as it is. You have any idea how many imps we've smoked? The moment they start arriving at their respawn point, the Darks will start to panic. I don't think their respawn point is around here."

"Where, then?"

"In one of the otherworldly planes."

"How do you know?"

"Gut feeling," he joked.

The raid got under way. Our every step brought us closer to the mysterious crevice.

The four orcs were pushing wheelbarrows piled high with ore. The creaking of the ungreased wheels drowned out the rustle of footsteps and the clanging of weapons while the cave echoes distorted sounds even more, camouflaging our approach.

Soon the outline of the bridge loomed out of the dark. Unnoticed, the orcs turned off toward the hoisting cages.

In the uneven light of the torches, the crevice oozed subterranean gases.

About twenty demons guarded the bridge, all of them level-30 Warriors. Five liches hovered over the rocks, holding magic staffs.

"Archers ready!"

Zander, Virgil and Tylor broke into a run. The bridge was narrow enough for them to block the guards, taking the first blows upon themselves.

The demons tensed up, sensing danger. Finally seeing the three warriors lunging at them, they reached for their weapons.

Bowstrings began twanging. A barrage of arrows showered the demons' rear ranks. A natural bank of heaped-up dead bodies arose, preventing the front ones' retreat.

Rodrigo and Iskandar challenged the liches. The flashing of their spells dispersed the gloom. Defense auras flared up; ashes rose up into the air.

Our orcs whipped out the swords secreted within their wheelbarrows and assaulted the hoisting cages, slicing through the cables, then pushed them into the crevice.

Our attack proved so sudden, powerful and well-coordinated that it was over before we knew it. In less than a minute, the bridge was ours.

Zander crossed to the other side first, took a look around and waved to us to follow.

❋ ❋ ❋

I PAUSED on the bridge and looked down. Darkness swirled about a hundred feet below, concealing the bottom of the crevice. Its cracked walls threatened to collapse.

I really didn't like the prospect of having

demons as neighbors. A lot of Infernal creatures had wings so nothing really prevented them from invading these caves again. The imps were unlikely to leave us alone, either. What could I do to block this breach between worlds? No idea.

"The Element of Earth might do it," Rodrigo suggested. He paused, about to add something, but apparently reconsidered and walked away, shaking his head.

Easy for him to say! Elemental control required the kind of power and specialization I at my current level couldn't even hope to attain.

"Alexatis!" Zander called me, peering at something.

The entire raid had already lined up on the other side of the precipice. The orcs took their places, grinning. The Elven archers who'd been instrumental in our lightning victory remained on their guard, wary and alert.

Once I crossed the bridge, the prickling sensation in my fingertips grew stronger. Now I could clearly make out a weak shining light filtering through the gloom.

"This is the final part of the dungeon," Zander said, seemingly uncomfortable. "This light... and no mobs around... This doesn't look good."

"Check your mana regeneration rate," I told him.

"You're right. It's grown," he said, surprised. "How did you know?"

"What you see up ahead is an Altar of Chaos. Do you remember when Enea brought you to rescue me from a dungeon? There was an altar there, right? That's one of those."

"Yes, I remember, sort of. I never got close enough to see it."

"Good for you. These ancient places of power have only one thing going for them: they speed up mana regeneration provided you're within their range. But don't even think about touching one! That would be pushing your luck."

"Why? Is it so bad?"

"It's Chaos, you see. You just can't tell. You might lose several levels. Or it might strip you of an ability."

"Random effects?"

"Exactly. Luck of the draw."

"I'd love to know what the demons farm here," Zander said, peering into the gloom. "Can you feel a cold draft blowing?"

"Can I ever!"

"You know, don't you, that it's the game's way of warning you?"

"Warning me against what?"

"All sorts of things. Say, you're walking through a forest where a high-level mob is lurking. That's when the temperature drops like this," he explained.

"Are you sure?"

"You can bet your life on it. I've been through it plenty of times."

"Does that mean that's where the dungeon boss is?"

"Well, what do you think? Or did you expect us to enter the cave, collect all the loot and happily go home?"

"So what do you suggest?"

"At the very least, we need to have a look at it. We can leave most of the raid here. We'll only need the wizards and the cleric: this fast mana regeneration thing might save our bacon, you never know. How's your sword?"

"Still... er... still *hungry*."

"In this case we should get closer to the altar and buff you to your ears. How many runes should light up for the sword to work?"

"A whole sequence. Its length doesn't matter."

"Got it," Zander swung round. "Raoul, I want you to come with us. Arwan, your group will cover us. You can open fire at your discretion but not before we engage. Understood?"

The Elf nodded.

"Platinus, have you got any powerful elixirs left?"

"Only a couple of Disintegration Potions,"

he replied.

"I need them," Zander took the vials, then cast a frowned look over the kobold and the two Guards of Gloom. "Where d'you think *you*'re going?"

"We're not leaving Alexatis," Kray said firmly.

Zander gave them a studying look. "Very well. As long as you keep to the rear. No one should try to get in front of me. Is that clear?"

They nodded curtly.

"Let's go see that source of power, then," Zander ordered. "Then we'll decide what to do."

* * *

WE LEFT THE BULK of the raid by the bridge. The Elves and the warriors followed us in pairs: one archer, one warrior.

Zander walked first, followed by Virgil and Tylor.

A faint trail snaked around the cliffs. The cave's walls began to close in on us. Strangely enough, here the cold draft was considerably weaker.

Finally, the rocky walls closed overhead, forming the entrance to a small cave.

We entered.

There it was. Another Altar of Chaos.

A dull aura enveloped the ancient place of power which emitted the already-familiar weak humming noise.

Zander looked around the cave, sizing up the potential combat site. The place wasn't too big. Some collapsed stone structure lay in a heap by the opposite wall. The Altar of Chaos rose in the center. The surrounding walls were lined with gaping doorways into small rooms scantily lit with tiny little flames.

The cave seemed deserted. The silence began to get on my nerves.

"Arwan, I want you to post your archers by the entrance. Alexatis, are you ready?"

"One moment," I replied, studying a standalone cliff which must have been crudely fashioned into the semblance of a four-sided column. "Take a look at this. There's a locked door here."

Zander walked over to me and frowned at the sight.

Several thick heavy chains which oozed heat were wrapped around the column, securing a slab of stone which concealed what appeared to be a doorway. The makeshift door was covered in a complex pattern of runes.

I focused on it. No prompts popped up.

"Never mind," I said. "We can sort it out later."

I walked back to the altar. My head was swimming from its emissions. My muscles began to twitch.

I clenched the sword handle, feeling the little spikes dig into my skin, triggering the sword's ancient magic. My mental, physical and vital energy bars promptly shrank.

Following Zander's instructions, Raoul began healing me. Rodrigo cast Stamina on me; Iskandar added a buff increasing physical energy capacity. But even with this powerful backup I could barely stand on my feet. An agonizing pain surged through me, then subsided. I could taste blood in my mouth.

I'd have loved to know what was behind the closed door. Was it even worth the risk?

None of the group had any idea of what I was experiencing.

The Mortal Allegiance runic sequence running down my sword's blade began to glow. It was almost two-thirds full when I heard the familiar squeaky little voice,

"Don't you dare feed here! This is all mine!"

I struggled to turn my head to the sound.

A translucent figure appeared out of the altar's glow.

This wasn't a demon. An old man, rather. His blurred name tag slowly came into view. I peered at the words distorted by surges of interference,

Dietrich. A Reaper.

No level, no race, no specialization, nothing.

He was dressed in some tattered old rags. Why would a ghost need clothes, anyway? Where would he even get them from? This worn gray jacket definitely looked familiar.

I peered at the frayed sleeve patch,

Infosystems Corporation
Defective Mobs Squad

A cold shiver ran down my spine.

Zander didn't seem to notice him. The others, too, just stood there matter-of-factly. Was I the only one who could see him?

"I can't use them," the old man eyed me greedily. "They're dummies. Empty shells. Not like *you.*"

"What do you want?"

He smacked his lips. "I want your neurograms."

"Are you nuts? You really think I'll give them to you?"

The frail ghost was no threat to me. If

anything, I was curious.

"That's what *he* thought," Dietrich stroked his sleeve patch. "*He* was real. Like you. He was strong. I couldn't take all of his memories. I need more. I need knowledge, experiences... I need feelings."

His insane glare was burning a hole in me. I immediately remembered the two Corporation workers I'd seen next to the other Altar of Chaos. Hadn't they mentioned some convict they'd used to test the neuroimplant prototype? His name was Dietrich-something too.

"Zander, we've got a ghost in here!"

"Where do you see it?" Zander looked around himself, then shrugged. "There's nothing here."

Just as he'd said it, the slab of stone shuddered within its fiery chains. Someone or something was trying to break out.

"They've found me!" Dietrich wailed in impotent rage. "They've found me!"

He leaned sharply toward me. "It's you! You've brought them here! There's too little of me yet... but I'll be growing! And that's when I'll come for you! You'd better watch out! I'll come for you!"

He shrank back and disappeared into the altar's glow.

Now the slab of stone was jumping in its rocky frame. The fiery chains were about to snap under the pressure of the unknown force which was trying to break free.

"You're stupid," the fading voice echoed in my mind. "They're using you. They'll drain you dry and leave you to die. *I* know!"

The voice died away, disappearing into depths unknown.

Zander froze in front of the column, ready to face the new danger. Still, it looked like we had even bigger problems now.

The ruins in the back of the cave shifted. A lithe shadow darted in the torches' uneven light.

Reguar. Arch Demon. Level 70. A Reaper.
Status: Dietrich's slave and protector

The creature's tag was fiery red.

* * *

"EVERYONE, get back!" Zander shouted.

A thunderous rockfall drowned out his voice. The ceiling caved in, dropping huge chunks of rock. Clouds of dust filled the place. I heard a pitiful cry as one of the Elves was crushed to death.

We didn't seem to have a hope in hell. Still, Zander decided to risk it. He stepped forward to meet the monster.

The Reguar's black hide had an olive sheen to it. His body was covered in scar-like runic inscriptions. I couldn't see them properly in the glow of the creature's fiery shield which coursed over his outline. He was clad in a scanty loincloth.

He was over ten feet tall, all muscle and furious rage.

"Diiiietrich!" his roar rolled over the cave, crumbling the rock debris and settling the clouds of dust. "Diiiiietrich!! Where are youuuuu? Where are my neuuuuuurograms? I want to reeeeeeeeap!"

In a lightning move, he grabbed Zander, then flung him aside. "A dummy!" he roared his disappointment.

Virgil and Tylor rushed to Zander's rescue.

We had nothing to lose. The entrance to the cave had collapsed. The only way out was through getting ourselves killed: a few seconds' work for a level-70 monster.

Even the dream world of the Crystal Sphere had its own dead-ends, literally. And this wasn't even a game scenario.

"I want to reeeeap!" the Reguar thundered, crushing the remains of the stone structure in the corner. His muscles were taut like steel cables. He swept the two warriors off their feet and smashed them against the altar, stripping them of virtually all hp.

"Dummies!" he roared in disappointment.

Raoul kept casting Mass Healing non-stop. It was only thanks to him we were still alive.

Anger flooded over me. "Shut your mouth!" I yelled.

"A *Neuro*?" the Reguar swung round to me. "A *Neuro*... Yes, you are! I can feel it! You're a Neuuuuuuuuuro!"

At that moment, the runic sequence on my sword blade had finally kicked in. The last of the Mortal Allegiance symbols sprang to life and sent a thin flow of energy down the blood groove, activating the spell.

"Come here, you bastard," Zander growled, taking a swing. The demon flung him aside and barged toward me. He wasn't interested in other players' avatars. He could sense only one living being here, or rather he could sense my neuromatrix — all the others were, in his view, just worthless empty shells.

The Elves showered him with arrows.

Pointless. The damage was minimal. Ignoring the threat, he continued toward me, his fiery stare focused on the only piece of human flesh in the cave.

He walked past the crude column, leaving it behind him still shuddering under the throes of the unknown force. The chains securing the stone door were now white-hot, melting before my very eyes, until finally they snapped.

The massive slab of stone covered in fiery magic writings thudded to the ground.

Despite the absence of names in their tags, I recognized the newcomers straight away.

These were Corporation workers. That's it, you son of a bitch! Prepare to die!

A slashing blow from a worker's sword sliced through the Reguar's back, halving his life, while a magic attack extinguished his fiery shield, simultaneously activating the cave boss' special abilities.

The demon roared his fury. Single-use portals opened all along the cave's perimeter. Their depths glowed crimson, letting out freshly-made golems. Dripping with thick red magma, the golems staggered toward their master, leaving molten footprints in the rock floor.

Pressed against the Altar, Virgil and Tylor kept receiving repeated damage. Their tags were chock full of some unidentified debuffs. The golden healing spiral rotated among them as the ancient place of power kept changing its effects chaotically, healing the warriors, then stripping them of their strength.

Zander lifted himself to one knee and leaned against his sword, struggling to his feet.

The Elves kept a low profile for the

moment, saving arrows and waiting for the signal. Rodrigo and Iskandar, where were they?

Obeying the order, the kobold and the two Guards of Gloom stayed next to me, covering my back. No idea what had happened to Platinus.

The floor shuddered underfoot.

The thick fog of toxic gases was consuming the cave. The portals had expired. The golems' crimson outlines glowed through the smoke; they continued their advance, dropping pieces of hardened lava.

The Reguar had lost all interest in me. He now had a much more dangerous quarry to hunt. The Corporate wizard in his gray robes swung round, drawing a circle with his hand. With a sharp hiss, ice met with fire, turning the golems into frozen statues which then exploded, torn apart by the rapid change of temperature, and collapsed in a heap of steaming slag.

You've just witnessed the casting of Antagonism spell!

For your information: You cannot learn restricted-use spells.

The Reguar's life shrank another 30%.

That was the end of him, surely.

As if! The Reguar's next actions betrayed remarkably quick thinking totally uncharacteristic of an NPC.

Instead of wasting his remaining abilities on furious but futile attacks, the demon acted out of the box. Ignoring his scripts, he went berserk.

He leaned forward, grabbed at the altar with both his hands and ripped the altar from its pedestal, then hurled it at the portal column.

The glow of the Corporate teleport flared up momentarily, then expired. A fine web of cracks ran over the column; it stood for another moment, then collapsed in a heap of rock debris.

"Neuuuuuuros!"

The demon's two powerful arms pierced the workers' avatars with remarkable ease.

Normally, they would have disappeared, leaving behind two lonely bundles of the players' gear sitting on the floor. But the game kept glitching.

A blissful smile distorted the demon's features.

He hadn't regenerated, no. His life was still deep in the red. What happened next was absolutely unthinkable.

The two workers — the wizard and the warrior — were thrashing about on the floor, convulsing in death throes. Roaring with laughter, the Reguar lifted both in the air. The workers' bodies seemed to leak whiffs of blueish gray smoke which the demon imbibed greedily.

Mechanically I focused on the prompt,

You are watching the process of identity matrices disintegration with their following consumption by the new host body.

"Did you see those visuals?" Raoul's tense voice awoke me from my stupor. "That was a nasty way to go!"

"Who were they?" Platinus asked hoarsely.

"Those were mob hunters. Apparently, the Corporation hires some elite players to locate and eliminate any glitchy mobs."

A shiver ran down my spine. Didn't anyone realize the sinister significance of what had just happened? Did they still think this too was gameplay?

Unlike them, I knew the name of the "defective" mob's next victim. No points for guessing.

I was the only Neuro left.

I looked around me in search of a potential escape route.

The portal had shut down.

The altar had been reduced to a luminous lump of rapidly metamorphing matter.

The entrance to the cave was blocked with large chunks of rock, with Elves lurking behind them.

Both Virgil and Tylor were unconscious. They appeared dead but for some reason, their avatars hadn't vanished as they should have.

Iskandar and Rodrigo sat sprawled on the floor, immobilized by a Curse of Stone.

Zander was still trying to scramble to his feet. His movements were sluggish and uncoordinated. The blow must have damaged his equilibrium.

I was shaking with an adrenaline rush. I desperately wanted to live. "Arwan! Aim for his eyes!"

Bowstrings began snapping. With a roar, the demon swung toward me. The mob hunters' bodies slumped lifelessly to the floor.

His movements jerky and disjointed, the demon ripped the arrows out of his bleeding eye sockets. Not that it helped him. I could clearly see the icon of the Blindness debuff hovering over his head.

I lunged forward, escaping an erratic swing of his arm, and dragged my sword across his belly, ripping it open.

Black blood gushed out.

You've dealt a critical hit!
You've cast a curse: Mortal Allegiance!
You've received an Achievement: Mad Valor,

for attacking an enemy whose level is twice as high as your own.

As if that made any difference.

The damage I'd dealt him was miniscule. The scars covering his body were in fact protective spells tattooed deep into his skin. I was too weak to harm him.

The Mortal Allegiance had only managed to slow him down a little.

"Everybody! He's our main target! Raoul, can't you remove the debuffs off the wizards? Watch his movements! He's blind! Try to duck his blows!"

The kobold and the two Guards of Gloom assaulted the monster with abandon. Their long polearms were perfect for this kind of combat. The Elves continued shooting, aiming at the demon's most vulnerable parts. With a resolute shake of his head, Zander clung to the wall and scrambled to his feet.

Rodrigo and Iskandar came round.

The demon struck out blindly. My three warriors circled him, ducking his blows. Zander had finally perked up a little and joined in the attack. Slowly but surely, we were frittering the demon's hp away.

Finally the wizards joined in too, illuminating the cave with the flashes of spells.

My blood boiled with adrenaline. The absolute realism of the experience had wiped away my leaden fatigue.

"Watch out!" Zander shouted. "He's got ten percent life left!"

He was right. Now the demon was about to use his last and probably the most powerful of his abilities.

The monster froze, enveloped in a murky protective aura. He began to grow, transforming into his combat shape which was ever larger and stronger, his body a giant knot of muscle.

A cloud of acid mist escaped his jaws, filling the cave.

I was choking. My lungs were about to explode. Holding my breath, I squeezed my eyes shut from the caustic fumes.

The demon was now blindly crushing the rocks. He had nothing to lose. Now that his bulk took up half the available space in the cave, it was only a question of time until he got to us.

A vial shattered on the rocks nearby.

"Last chance!" Platinus yelled triumphantly, then screamed, ducking a blow.

Our alchemist was too good for words. Now that we were all pushed to our limits, I was beginning to realize how priceless each of my team was.

Once the acid had stopped assaulting my

eyes, I resumed my attack with renewed vigor.

The wizards, Raoul and the archers retreated to the walls. The demon may have transformed into a spiky Infernal beast, but it hadn't helped his blindness. His eyes were still studded with the feathery fletches of the arrows; his crushing blows were inaccurate and uncoordinated.

Still, now he appeared to have one hell of a powerful armor. Our combined attacks couldn't make a dent in it.

"Keep going! We're nearly there!" Zander shouted. Still, each of his sword blows stripped the creature of a meager 20 to 30 hp. Mine couldn't even do that. The kobold's halberd and the naginatas of the two Guards of Gloom dealt 10 pt. damage each. That way we were going to poke at the mob's armored hide till the cows come home.

I had one last trump card left. I'd been saving it for a desperate moment like this. And it looked like now was the time to use it.

I leapt aside, dodging a blow. The demon's spiky fist crashed into the wall, causing a small rockfall. I waited for it to subside, then clenched the Charm of the Sovereign and started reciting the summoning spell.

I concentrated, trying to visualize the summoned creature as best I could.

It worked. A whirl of tiny flames raised by the Centurion spell parted, releasing the figure of Helmud the Knight.

His eyes focused on the demon's combat incarnation. "You godless spawn of Satan!"

He lunged at the monster. The demon's life dropped promptly; a Mortal Wound debuff added to his stats. Not that it helped Helmut a lot: a spell unknown to me had disembodied the knight on the spot.

"Alexatis, step back!" Zander shouted. "Leave him alone! He'll die now, anyway!"

Leave him alone? I don't think so!

I assaulted the monster again. He reared up, about to lash out at me in one final crushing effort.

I had to finish him off. Nobody else could do it.

A crit!

A fading scream echoed from the walls, replaced by deafening silence.

The demon's still-twitching heart swayed on the tip of my sword. It constricted one last time, spewing a squirt of black blood, then stopped.

My head swam. I couldn't think straight.

Someone forced me aside. The demon's enormous bulk came crashing down. His many wounds began to fester whiffs of blueish gray smoke.

I shook. Those were his victims' neurograms! For a while they hung in the air, forming a haze which then shifted and headed for us, reaching out to the Elves, the kobold, the two Guards of Gloom...

* * *

SYSTEM MESSAGES flashed incessantly through my mental view. I struggled to skim through the more important ones,

Quest alert: Turf Wars. Quest completed!
+1 to the clan's level (+5% to any of the clan groups' actions, +3% to any of the castle buildings' Durability when restored or built anew)
+1,000 to the clan's Reputation

You've received Achievement: Demon Slayer (+10% to any damage dealt to the forces of Inferno)

You've received Achievement: The First Amongst Equals:
+10,000 to your Experience awarded for completing a unique dungeon;
+10,000 to your Experience for dealing a critical hit to an enemy whose level is twice that of yours.

For your information: The Administration of the Crystal Sphere highly appreciates your role in the dispensing of a defective mob. They would like to offer you a further +5% to all Experience received, on the condition that you do not disclose any information regarding this incident.

You've received Achievement: Acclaimed Leader. Your influence on other players will keep growing with every new level.

You've received a new level!
You've received a new level!
You've received a new level!

I sat there completely drained, trying to restore.

"Alexatis, I've just spoken to Togien," Zander disrupted my meditation. "His dwarves are already busy clearing the rockfall. They might be here in thirty minutes or so."

I'd never seen him look so grim. "Okay, so what's the bad news?"

"The Darks are stirring. The dwarves reported some gargoyles which had appeared from the crevice, flown over it, then turned back. It looks like Virgil and Tylor's avatars are screwed. They just won't disappear. I think I've lost my old group," Zander glanced at Iskandar and Rodrigo who were cowering by the wall, looking more than absent.

"What happened to those two?" I asked.

"Please don't ask. Their stats are okay. No debuffs, nothing. I don't think it was the Curse of Stone that the demon cast on them. This is probably some uncategorized spell."

Platinus walked over to us. I gave him a bear hug.

He looked embarrassed. "I've run out of potions," he told me.

"That's all right. You can always make new ones," I said. "Once we're back, we'll set up a lab for you. I might even get you a few apprentices. From now on, you're our Head Alchemist. You can experiment all you want."

He beamed.

"Hurry up," Zander said. "We need to check the demon's body before it disappears."

The arch demon's corpse took up almost all of the cave. His combat avatar hadn't transformed back. Segments of the creature's unique natural armor bristled with spikes.

"Arwan, come here for a moment."

The Elf obeyed. His head was still shaking with shock. He'd received quite a few neurograms. All of the NPCs had gotten more than their fair share while the players — Zander, Platinus, Iskandar and Rodrigo — hadn't received any. I could only wonder about any potential consequences.

"Are there any Masters in Flaying among you?" I asked him.

Arwan cringed from the stench. "We'll find someone."

Zander touched the demon's body, activating the loot distribution window. "Not much," he reported. "Two cargonite vambraces and some kind of gadget. It looks like Dwarven craft."

"Can you read their stats?"

"Okay. Now... *the Vambrace of Retribution. Item type: Relic. Part of a set. Requires level 50. Restrictions: Only Paladin. Effect: deflects 30% incoming damage back on the enemy when worn on the blocking arm.*"

"Is it a no drop?"

"No, it's not," he sounded suitably impressed.

"What else?"

"*A Vambrace of Regeneration. Item type: Relic. Part of a set. Requires level 50. Restrictions: Only Paladin. Effect: +10% to the hp regeneration rate in combat. 5% to the wearer's chances of restoring his or her Health after receiving a critical hit.*"

I could tell he was itching to have both. Still, with these kinds of decisions one should never rush. These were unique items. I might have some Paladins joining my clan at a later date, too. "Okay. What about the gadget?"

"I really can't tell."

"Oh, do me a favor."

"Seriously. It has no stats, only question marks. It's a sphere about a couple of feet in diameter, covered in runes. Oh. I think I do know what some of them mean."

"Can you translate?"

"It says, *a Citadel*. That's the best I can do. Listen, how about I swap my share of raid loot for these vambraces? Provided I can keep the rune as well."

"But how about your group members?"

"I'll sort them out. It's not your problem, anyway."

"Are you sure?"

He maintained a moody silence, awaiting my decision.

No wonder. Between the aura-boosting rune, the ten-percent regeneration, the chance of receiving a full heal and the thirty percent of incoming damage deflected back on the enemy, his leveling would be a dream.

And what would I get in return?

All of the gold, weapons and cargonite we'd farmed, plus thirteen runes, the fragment of the Altar of Chaos and the mysterious spherical gadget. "Don't you want to discuss it with Iskandar and Rodrigo first?"

"No, I don't. I told you I'd sort it out."

"Very well. You can have them. And the rune. Now can I have the sphere, please?"

My inventory promptly became one item richer.

* * *

NO MATTER how long I stared at the sphere, it remained blank. No prompts, nothing.

I'd managed to work out, by scientific trial and error, that the cargonite segments of the sphere could move independent of each other, changing the runes' respective positions — but that didn't seem to serve any purpose.

Never mind. It still remained a valuable item. I might have to find out the runes' meaning before investigating any further.

I replaced the sphere in my inventory and headed for one of the small adjacent caves. There used to be four of them in total but at the moment, this was the only one free from rockfalls.

Never mind. We had plenty of time to get to the rest if needs be.

I entered the cave. A torch cast a dim light on a table laid with neat rows of stone and cargonite tablets covered in ancient writings. A stack of yellow parchment scrolls, some of them sealed, was heaped up nearby.

I took screenshots of the scene just in case, then collected the precious loot. This must have been the dwelling of the warlock. That's how he must have gotten his uncategorized spells and unique abilities — by studying the Founders' magic.

I seemed to have a moment to spare. The Elves were busy flaying the demon's body and removing the armor plates while the dwarves were still trying to hack through the rockfall to us. I could afford to turn my attention to riskier experiments.

I cast a glance at the kobold and the two Guards of Gloom who kept following me around like a bad smell. "Mind stepping back for a sec, guys?"

"Why?" the kobold growled. "Are we in your way?"

He pointed at the molten part of the wall from where the golems had appeared. "What if the portal starts working again?"

"It won't. Please."

Reluctantly they obeyed.

I approached the still-metamorphing fragment of the Altar and focused.

Manifestation of Chaos

Item type: Relic
The number of elements controlled: 4
Interaction rate: 50% (requires boosting components)
Effects when used: random (requires stabilizing components)

For your information: in order to use a Manifestation of Chaos, you must possess Level 5 in both Synergy and Enhanced Perception

This was really bad timing! I did have some available points to invest into both — but then again, once I made level 45, that would open a new development branch. I really didn't feel like wasting my precious strategic reserve on the developers' whim.

But what could I do with this, eh, manifestation? Should I put it into my inventory? Not a healthy idea, really. But leaving it here would be equally imprudent.

The best thing would be not to touch the damned thing at all — but the news of the new Infernal visitors left me with no choice. Following the gargoyles' recon mission, the main forces of the Dark were bound to arrive — possibly, temporarily forcing us out of their dungeons.

I bent down and picked up a rotting spade handle lying on the floor. Gingerly I used it to touch the altar.

It reacted in the most unexpected way. The old wood exploded in flames.

You've successfully attempted to gain control over the Fifth Element
Status: control granted.
Interaction rate: 2%. In order to increase your energy intake, you need to move the Altar closer to sources of live energy.

That was quite spectacular.

Exclamations of fear and surprise came from everywhere. The Elves stopped working, staring at me. Each of them had lost 2% life — while my hp numbers had grown considerably.

What the hell was this thing? What would happen if I did take it outside — would it syphon all life out of all living objects?

This little experiment had given me a lot of food for thought. There was no way I was gifting it to the Darks. This thing was way too dangerous. They could use it to bring untold suffering to our world.

I opened my interface. Unflinchingly I invested the necessary number of points into both Synergy and Enhanced Perception, then focused on the fragment of the altar again.

It began to vibrate, glowing brighter. It

---

seemed to transform faster, too.

My head swam momentarily. When I refocused, I saw a new message in my interface:

A new unique ability unblocked: Elemental Control.

For your information: in order to interact with the elements, you're required to use one of the Founders' artifacts built for that purpose. Direct interaction is available from level 10.

Requirements:
Intellect, 25
Willpower, 25

But this wasn't a Founders' artifact, surely? I was probably not thinking straight, what with the stress and exhaustion. Never mind. Let's do it again.

I focused on the altar.

Manifestation of Chaos
Item type: Relic

Aha! Its name had become clickable!

I swiped it with a smooth motion of my eyes. A drop-down menu appeared,

Create a new Altar of Chaos (unavailable at your current ability level)

Install a stabilizing component

Boost your interaction rate with the Element of Fire: currently unavailable. The boosting runic sequence is broken.

Boost your interaction rate with the Element of Air: currently unavailable. The boosting runic sequence is broken.

Boost your interaction rate with the Element of Water: currently unavailable. The boosting runic sequence is broken.

Boost your interaction rate with the Element of Earth: requires the installation of a stabilizing component

Create an interaction link with the Element of Chaos; currently unavailable. The boosting runic sequence incomplete.

Create an interaction link with the realm of Nature: currently unavailable. The boosting runic sequence not found.

I pressed the *Install a stabilizing component* button.

The mysterious sphere promptly

disappeared from my inventory and materialized outside, encasing the luminous fragment of the altar. The sphere's runic segments shifted and started falling into sequences. One of them lit up, glowing from the inside.

Congratulations! You've restored the source of magic power of Rion Castle!

You've activated the runic sequence of the Element of Earth!
+250,000 to the castle's passive shield
+100,000 to the castle's attack potential

Quest update alert: The Renaissance of Rion!

You've received a new level!

Warily I touched the sphere. It was cold. Still, how was I supposed to transport it? I tried to place it in my inventory. As if!

Unauthorized operation

Would you like to activate the teleport system: Yes/No

I clicked *Yes*, then waited with bated

breath. It's not every day you get to build an artifact of this caliber.

The sphere blinked, disappearing in the blue flash of a teleport. A moment later, the ground shuddered underfoot.

"Alexatis must have a contract with the gods of Earth," Togien's voice came from a tunnel which now gaped open behind me. "The rocks just parted! What kind of magic was that?"

A torchlight dispelled the tunnel's gloom, followed by Togien himself. "You all right? You can come out now! It's safe! Only..." Togien's gaze betrayed fear and confusion. "The sides of the crevice have come together. It's completely gone! Can you imagine? All you can see is the wooden framework poking out! Alexatis, did you do that?"

CHAPTER FIVE

THE CRYSTAL SPHERE
RION CASTLE

W E PORTED out into the castle's first defense level. The sun was about to set, its warm rays still drenching the ground.

The peasants crowded nearby, looking lost and fearful. They'd had their fair share of grief. The clan's combat section lined up in the central square to receive their orders.

"I'm gonna log out now," Zander said, giving me a hearty handshake. "You know where to find me if you need me."

"Nothing from Virgil and Tylor?"

"No. I'll try to contact them IRL now."

We bade our farewells. Neither Rodrigo nor Iskandar had even bothered to say goodbye. All three disappeared instantly which was perfectly normal. You don't notice things like that in a game.

Togien didn't look too eager to stay, either. Not that I minded. He had his work cut out for him for the next few days.

Raoul, however, wasn't in a hurry to leave. He needed to change his bind point and check if it worked correctly this time.

"Can you wait till I sort out everyone?" I asked him.

The cleric nodded. "How are you gonna house them all?"

Good question. All the newcomers needed beds, food, some rest and new tasks to keep them occupied. Last thing I wanted was for them to idle about the castle.

I looked around me. The place lay in ruins. A long time ago, the first defense level had been nicely built up with streets, shops, taverns and even a market. Now it was a wasteland overgrown with weeds.

All eyes were on me. I could physically sense them. The newcomers watched me expectantly, apparently waiting for their clan leader to work his magic and turn the surrounding desolation into a bustling town.

I made up my mind. "I want to talk to your elders."

Back in the dungeon, I'd noticed that peasants seemed to belong to several groups. They were all men: apparently, the demons who'd kidnapped them weren't interested in women or children.

Five peasants approached me.

"How long have you been in captivity?" I asked them. "Where are you from? How far are your villages?"

"Have a look at this, sir," a scrawny man in torn dusty clothes offered me a well-used piece of leather. I unfolded it. A rough map of the area was clumsily scratched into the leather, looking more like a child's drawing. I could make out the castle and a smattering of tiny isles around it, some of them linked together by man-made paths.

I peered at the villages' names: Hinterwall, Chaffinch Creek, Owl's Valley, New Forest and Anglers Corner. They were spread out at more or less the same distance from the castle: about two hours' walk as the crow flies.

"There's no sun underground. No idea how long we've been here," the man whose name was Quieton gave me a heavy look. "You think you could help us get home? Our wives and children probably think we're dead."

"It's getting late," I said.

"It's all right! We know the area, don't we?" he scratched his beard. "We saw some boats by the shore."

"They're all rotten!" exclaimed Smarty — a young, lanky and very freckled kid clad in tattered leather armor. He threw his hands up in protest, "You touch them and they fall apart! Do you want us to become fish food?"

I wanted to ask Platinus if he had any ideas but stopped just in time. I kept forgetting this wasn't the real world.

I immediately thought about the siege tower abandoned in the vicinity hundreds of years ago. Its wood remained as hard and as sturdy as ever. Wasn't there some spell cast on it?

Did I have something similar, by any chance?

I opened the *Uncategorized Spells and Abilities* tab. Immediately I saw what I was looking for:

Object Replication
Level, 1
Allows you to create items and devices using existing or imaginary templates and source materials.

Successful frequent use of Object Replication allows you to level it up, opening new possibilities.

"Right," I said unhesitantly, "let's go see those boats of yours." Leaving the farmers here to sleep rough wasn't going to improve my popularity.

We'd run out of mana vials a long time ago. Still, I'd managed to collect about a dozen fully charged Snow Obsidians back in the cave. They'd have to suffice.

We walked through a large breach in the castle wall onto the high river bank. Rotten wooden steps led down to a small stone pier. The untroubled waters were tinted with the crimson of the sunset. About a dozen waterlogged boats were moored by rusty chains.

They didn't interest me. I walked over to the large fishing longboats lying alongside them. Although equally waterlogged, they looked sturdy and spacious enough.

A small crowd of onlookers lined the bank behind my back. Curious Elves, dwarves and orcs joined the farmers, eager to see what I was going to do.

I pulled a fully charged Obsidian out of my inventory and clenched it hard in my hand, praying I wouldn't faint in front of my new vassals. I then focused on the steps, visualizing them as strong and brand new.

Soundlessly I mouthed the Object Replication spell. To say I was nervous would be an understatement. My plan was too crazy even for a fantasy world. I had no idea how the spell might work. This was uncategorized magic. Did I have enough energy and concentration to complete what I'd started?

The undergrowth rustled in windless air. An uprooted pine tree bobbing in the water nearby suddenly rose into the air and exploded, forming a cloud of wooden dust.

My mana bar shrank dangerously — but by then, the Obsidian I was clenching in my hand had already begun to release its centuries-old energy.

The cloud of dust reached out for the steps and was immediately absorbed by the woodwork. The steps and the balustrade changed color to a lighter shade. They now looked freshly built.

I had to show everyone a good example. I was just about to mount the staircase I'd so ingeniously restored when the kobold beat me to it. In one long leap his lithe body landed on the top step. Before I could react, he'd run the entire length of it. Once down, he tilted his head toward us and growled,

"Behold the Power of the Founder Gods!

Even I was suitably impressed — let alone

the NPCs who'd just been witness to this new manifestation of the ancient force that had been feeding their legends.

"You can come down now," I told the farmers. "I want you to drag the longboats onto the shore."

I didn't have to say it twice. Everybody got to work. Soon all five longboats were sitting on the narrow strip of dry land overhung by the cliffs.

In the next half-hour, I'd used up all of the Obsidians I had. The XP bar next to the Object Replication icon was already one-third full. My head had begun to ache. Still, it was worth it: by then, a small fleet of boats capable of taking at least a hundred people was rocking on the waves by the shore. Even though I hadn't built a single new item, it didn't really matter. The farmers' stares filled with wary admiration said it all: the castle had just regained part of its ancient influence. Rumors of tonight's miracle were going to spread, growing all sorts of implausible details. At this initial stage, the castle could definitely use this kind of unofficial publicity.

"Go back to your families," I took the chance to laud an appropriate send-off speech. "From now on, your dwellings are under my clan's protection. If any of you desire to come back and bring your families along, or start a new settlement nearby, I'm fine with that. Tell your village elders that the Dark reign is over!"

Quieton and Smarty jumped back into the water and waded toward me. "Thank you, Alexatis. We'll never forget it."

"I'll be back!" Smarty added. "I'll go see my family and come back to join you. I'd rather be a warrior!"

The boats set off. Twilight fell. Torchlight glistened in the dark waters surrounding Rion Castle.

I climbed the stairs back up and lingered, watching the boats' lights which by now had parted, each taking its own route.

"Let's go back to the donjon," I told the warriors. "Time to set up camp."

* * *

TOGIEN AND PLATINUS had already logged out with the promise of coming back early next morning.

The only player still left was Raoul.

As we climbed toward the third defense level, I checked the auction. It was the only marketplace available in this part of the Crystal Sphere.

I ran a quick search. It didn't take me long to locate what I was looking for:

A Large Raid Tent
Sleeps: 20
Price: 1,000 gold

A Minor Camping Site
Sleeps: 50
Price: 5,000 gold

A Camp Ration
Contains: potions, food (meat, bread and cheese), water (buffed)
Price: 8 gold

Excellent. I chose the Minor Camping Site. We could always use one in the future. Unlike the Large Raid Tent, it had the added bonus of allowing me to billet warriors of antagonistic races separately.

Food was more of a problem. The rations were pricey to say the least. Still, tonight I had to make an exception, considering the late hour and the prisoners' sorry state. Starting from tomorrow, I'd have to think about proper food deliveries.

I too could barely stand on my feet. I definitely wasn't going to wander about the castle in search of sleeping facilities. I wasn't even sure there were any. In our situation, a hearty serving of bread and cheese, a swig of water and a warm sleeping bag in a perfectly safe, mopped-up location seemed like the best choice.

"Arwan," I said once I completed the transaction, "know how to put up a tent?"

The Elf shook his head. "I can build a treehouse real quick," he offered.

"I see," I said. "Raoul, come over here," I leaned forward and began lining up the packets on the ground. "I want you to show the others how to put up a tent. Here they are, as well as some food and water. Help them to set up camp right by the entrance to the donjon. I'll go and reset the respawn point. I'll PM you once I'm done."

"Sure," he nodded. Apparently, he wasn't new to virtual camping.

As he taught the NPCs to use players' equipment, I returned to the Resurrection Hall and opened the respawn point tab.

The mercenaries had already removed theirs. Excellent. The only users left on the list were Enea, Togien, Platinus and myself.

I opened a new tab and listed all the NPCs. The interface promptly offered another surprise: moving an NPC respawn point cost five gold each.

It was a good job I had the money!

If the truth were known, I wasn't enjoying my new managerial functions at all. I might need to hire some assistants, otherwise, I'll be busy all day sorting out and following up on a plethora of vital albeit petty issues.

I switched to the teleport tab, then PM'd Raoul,

How's it going?

We've set up camp already. I've distributed the rations. The Elves are happy. The dwarves are grumpy as usual. The orcs have refused to sleep in tents point blank.

It's all right. I'll sort them out. You can move your respawn point to the Resurrection Hall now. Know how to do it?

Sure! Thanks! Can I try it now?

Be my guest.

I got busy changing the portals' settings, restricting access to the dungeons and declining all incoming teleports.

A dull green flash in the respawn zone announced Raoul's arrival. He looked thoroughly pleased with himself.

"It worked! It worked! I can keep my char!"

"Excellent. Go and get some sleep now. Tomorrow we'll discuss your future position in the clan."

"Sure! Thanks! See ya!"

He logged out, disappearing into thin air. I stayed for a while, completing my work, then walked out.

The place was bathed in moonlight. Our small camp was still bustling with life as everyone celebrated their newfound freedom.

I walked over to the orcs' leader who was sitting by the campfire with three others. "Davre, what's up? Why don't you want to sleep in the tents?"

"Not our thing."

"And what if we need to go on a raid?"

That got him interested. "A raid? Where to?"

"Discipline is for everyone," I replied. "If everybody starts setting their own rules, we're not going anywhere. With due respect to your customs, do they say anything about your not sleeping in tents?"

"I don't think so."

"That's sorted, then. You'd better get used to it. No more sleeping rough."

"And how about the castle?"

"We'll restore the barracks as soon as we can. There, everyone will have a room for him or herself."

"What, like a prison cell?"

"Sorry, but if you want to stay, you'll have to get used to creature comforts. Trust me, they're not as awful as you might think."

"Can't we build ourselves a cave? A nice big one! With a large fire that never goes out!"

And a nice big pile of rotting bones, I added mentally. Still, I didn't want to appear too soft on my first day. "No caves within the castle's limits," I said firmly. "Your men take first watch. The Elves will replace you."

He growled his understanding, nodded and returned to the fire.

My tent was at the very center of the camp. You could easily tell it by the clan's banner that topped it. The two Guards of Gloom stood a solemn watch by the entrance, the blades of their naginatas glistening dimly in the moonlight.

I found Arwan, "I want you to choose the watch. You'll relieve the orcs in two hours' time. In the morning, we'll form hunting parties."

"Yes, leader!"

That's it. Enough for today. Time to catch a few Zs.

I turned to the Guards of Gloom, "You aren't going to stand here all night, are you? There's no need for that. Go and get some rest."

"We're not tired."

"Very well. Suit yourselves."

I was too exhausted to argue. They were

NPCs, after all. Me, I was only human.

* * *

I'D HAD A GREAT sleep.

You're well-rested and full of energy. Effect: Vigor. +2% to the XP received for the next 6 hrs. - 2% to your Mental and Physical Energy expenditure for the next 6 hrs.

I had a quick breakfast, then threw the tent's flap aside and strode out.

The sun was almost overhead. The kobold (who must have relieved the two Guards of Gloom) growled a greeting.

The camp was empty. No sentries were posted on the castle walls. For a moment, I stood there speechless. Had my valiant army deserted?

I turned to the kobold, "Report."

"The Elves have gone hunting," he replied. "Master Togien arrived and took the dwarves down the caves with him. The orcs caught three thieves."

"What, local farmers?"

"Moor goblins," he growled his contempt. "They tried to get to the donjon. Davre wanted to hack them down but Master Platinus told him to bind them hand and foot and lock them up."

"Where is he?"

"He arrived two hours ago. He's gone to the Moors now."

A shiver ran down my spine. "What, alone?"

"The orcs wanted to go with him. Master Platinus said he needed some herbs to make some magic wine for tonight's party."

"A *party*. And what are we supposed to celebrate, may I ask?"

"Rion Castle Day!" the kobold replied unhesitantly. "The farmers came back with boatfuls of food. They asked me to tell you about them but I didn't want them to disturb you. They'll be back tonight."

Holy Jesus. How long had I slept? "Any sentries posted on the walls?"

He nodded at the lush green of the vines shrouding the old fortifications. "Arwan's snipers. You can't really see them."

"Did you get some rest?"

"I don't need it, do I?"

"Why, not at all?"

"I can stay awake for a week. I only need food and drink once a month."

"Go and get some food. That's an order. Where did the orcs lock up those thieves?"

"I'll show you," he said and headed for a nearby tower.

Its entrance was blocked by a huge

boulder. The kobold pushed it effortlessly aside.

"They're here," he nodded. "Go and skin them alive if you wish."

"I'll take care of them," I said.

I walked in. The tower's only room was bathed in shadows streaked with the dusty sunrays bursting in through the narrow arrowslits.

The floor was littered with the rotten fragments of collapsed roof beams. Three scrawny green-skinned creatures cowered behind them. On seeing me, they attempted to shrink back even further but the chains used by the orcs proved too heavy for them to move.

I perched myself on top of a wooden crate. "Where are you from?"

Ignoring my question, they glared back at me, their eyes filled with fear and hatred. They hadn't asked me for mercy. Then again, they probably couldn't speak our language. Having said that... one of the prisoners was a level-31 shaman. Quite powerful, apparently. A necklace of hydra's fangs hung around his neck. All three wore loincloths. Their weapons — old gnarly clubs — lay by the wall out of their reach.

"Did you hear the question? Who are you and what did you need in my castle?"

Without lowering his gaze, the shaman tried to sit up. Rattling his chains, he rolled to one side and forced himself up.

"We don't need scrap metal," he mumbled with a toothless mouth. "We've come to claim what's ours. If you don't give it to us, the spirits of the moors will be angry with you."

Aha. This sounded like the inklings of a dialogue. And potentially, also a quest. "I didn't take anything from you."

"You didn't. The Legionnaires did. They stole our totem!"

"Can you give me more details?"

I heard a rustling noise behind me. The shaman's eyes opened wide with fear.

I swung round. The two Guards of Gloom stood behind me.

Kray gave the shaman a long look. "Spawn of the Dark," he snapped. "You should never turn your back on him. Ever. He is clever and treacherous."

The shaman cringed, apparently not too happy with the characteristic. "You want war?"

"Why, do we have a motive?" I replied.

"We want our totem back! Give it to us, or I'll bring thousands of our brethren to your walls!"

I didn't like his attitude at all. Still, I tried to remain calm. "Your totem, what does it look like? Where did you see it last?"

"You'll know it when you see it! It's made of

Khmor wood which wriggles as if it's alive. Give it to us and we'll leave! If you don't, it's war!"

"Stop threatening me. Tell me everything as it was. Remove his shackles!"

Reluctantly Ikhtar obeyed. Kray pressed the blade of his naginata to the shaman's throat, "Sit still."

"Kray, please don't," I said. "I can take care of myself."

He stepped back, as watchful as ever.

The shaman lived up to Kray's apprehensions. The moment he was freed of his fetters, he cast me an evil eye and attempted to recite a spell.

Before Ikhtar could react to such cheeky behavior, I disrupted the spell by gently punching the shaman between the eyes, stripping him of a few hp. "If you can't have a civilized conversation, you'll have to stay chained, I'm afraid. Your brethren are more than welcome to come here. From what I heard, you took the Darks' side during the siege. And you know what? I can't remember seeing a single goblin prisoner in the dungeons below."

His face fell. "Wait! Yes, you're right! Our ancestors did fight the Disciples. But that's not our fault! We've come to claim what's rightfully ours!"

"So are you gonna talk or do we continue to

waste our time?"

"It's the ex-shaman's fault, the one we had before me," he began tearfully. "He took the totem and some warriors and left for the castle. We never heard from them again. And we can't go on without the totem, you see. Life is just too bad. No frogs to hunt. All the fish has gone to other places. Hydras keep attacking us. Please help us!"

New quest available: Troublesome Neighbors.
Quest class: Unique
Find the ancient totem lost by the Moor Goblins, then decide what to do with it.
Reward: varies depending on your decision
Deadline: 30 days
Decline penalty: immediate war with Moor Goblin tribes

"Very well," I said, much to the two Guards' astonishment. "I'll let you know if we find it. I'll tell my warriors to release you now. Go back home and warn everyone: whoever trespasses on our lands will be sent to his ancestors' afterlife pastures."

"You're too weak! The castle is destroyed!"

Oh well. You can't change a goblin's cheeky nature. "You wanna try?"

"No," the shaman realized his faux pas. "Not now."

"That's it, then. When my men find the totem, we'll contact you. Kray, get them out of here."

* * *

"WHY DID YOU let them go?" the Guards demanded. They had no idea I'd received a new quest.

"Think. Are we prepared to go to war?"

Kray shrugged.

"Some tribes don't understand nice," Ikhtar agreed. "They only appreciate power."

"How do you know? Have you dealt with Moor Goblins before?"

"Goblins are goblins. It doesn't matter where they live. They're scheming and spiteful."

"I'll remember that."

That was it, then. I had to find the totem and decide what to do with it. Can't be too difficult. Judging by the item's description, you couldn't really miss it.

I opened the clan chat. "Togien? How's it going?"

"Okay," he replied. "We're busy with the first obelisk. My Master level is going up. Which is a good thing because my Profession could use some growing. Thanks for inviting us."

"You need anything?"

"No, it's fine."

"Any Dark visitors? Should I send you some warriors just in case?"

"Nah. We can manage."

"Okay. Keep me posted."

Good. Things seemed to be moving. This one obelisk could garner us two cartfuls of Spectral Dust. Having said that, where was Platinus? This wasn't the right moment to make celebratory arrangements, really.

No messages from Enea.

I raised my head to study the donjon's three precipitous towers. Restoring them required some thought. Dozens of floors; hundreds of rooms. I needed to inspect them all. The castle's 3D model only gave a very vague idea of its structure. Also, most of its halls, rooms and galleries were highlighted either red or orange.

I had to collect all the available artifacts before all else. But where was I supposed to store them? The unfinished quest prevented me from accessing the Armory.

I filtered out all the damaged areas. That left me with a few tiny bits of the donjon highlighted in green plus two large zones which appeared to be intact. Both were situated at the same height about a hundred feet from the ground between the west and the east towers. According to the prompt, that's where the Disciples used to live: the personal dwellings of all the warriors and wizards privy to the Order's top secrets.

I'd love to take a peek at them. Judging by the fact that their walls remained unbreached, this area must have been the defenders' priority. The Disciples must have held these rooms long after the rest of the castle had fallen.

* * *

WE USED teleports to get to the donjon's tenth level, about halfway to the top.

A long circular corridor seemed to lose itself in the gloom. Cobwebs clung to the walls, interweaving with the tattered remains of tapestries still hanging from the ceiling.

The two Guards of Gloom froze next to me, tense and alert. They didn't seem to be comfortable in closed spaces like these.

The silence was unnaturally thick. The air was stale.

In places, the walls were still lined with rusty torch holders.

My feet sank into a thick layer of dust. This place should be safe. The castle was my property, after all. Still, I couldn't shake off the feeling of

---

danger.

Kray produced a torch and a tinderbox. I motioned him to wait.

First, I wanted to see how the castle control interface worked. Now that the source of power was working, I couldn't understand why some of the donjon's basic functions remains inactive. It made no sense. You'd think my arrival should have caused this corridor to be lit up, the same way as the Resurrection Hall was.

Ikhtar reached out to push some cobwebs out of his way and promptly jerked his hand back. "It stings! This place is a trap!"

I hurried to open the castle control tab. I really should have studied it before venturing anywhere on my own.

Found it.

Magic traps and protection veils. Can be installed in areas vulnerable to enemy penetration. Can also be used to restrict access to certain vital areas.

In order to navigate the traps, it is advised to use personal magic items (i.e., rings).

Aha. I highlighted the entire level in my interface, then clicked on *Show and disable all defense apparatus*.

The map erupted in a multitude of red

dots. Every door here had been charmed; the entire floor, walls and ceiling were covered in crimson spots. The portal area seemed to be the only safe place around.

As I clicked *Disable*, most of the red magic seals blinked and went out. The cobwebs, however, stayed put.

"Don't move," I told the two warriors before studying more prompts.

Predatory Cobweb
Item type: trap
Warning! Uncontrollable growth of the item detected! The item cannot be disabled.

Shame. I didn't want to resort to radical measures.

A wall of fire rolled over the corridor, sweeping away the cobwebs and lighting the few remaining torches. An unsteady glow illuminated the rocky walls. A draft of air ruffled the smoldering tapestries, sucking the whiffs of smoke into rusty air vents mounted on the ceiling.

Before the fire could spread, I cast Ice, disabling the traps and completely ruining the tapestries. The floor was covered in melting slush. This probably hadn't been a good idea, after all.

The doors lining the corridor's outer wall creaked ajar.

Kray leaned his weight against one of them, forcing it open.

So! Those Disciples didn't live so badly!

If I expected to see a row of humble monastic dwellings, I couldn't have been more wrong. This "cell" consisted of two spacious rooms with large vaulted windows, their dainty furnishings virtually undamaged — probably thanks to some ancient durability spells. The ornate draperies had preserved most of their original color.

Still, you could tell this room used to belong to a warrior. Both the armor stand and the weapon rack were empty. The disarrayed bedclothes had rotted away.

A large ancient book lay open on the table. I chose not to touch its yellow pages for fear of them crumbling to dust.

Talking about dust, there was plenty of that everywhere. The window panes were intact — probably, thanks to the castle's defense shield which had remained active even after its defeat.

I peered at the book's open pages. They were covered in sketches of a very interesting combo performed with two short swords. I needed to see Platinus about this book. He should know of some chemicals that could be used to restore aged paper.

* * *

IT TOOK US several hours to inspect that one level. The corridor was lined with fifty rooms. Excellent. I could already see them housing my most important clan members.

I reopened the castle interface and checked the list of characters available for hire.

First of all, I would need a majordomo to control and coordinate NPC staff.

The hire tab was equipped with sliders allowing you to set each particular character's stats and abilities.

I really had to look into it now. This was getting a bit urgent.

To search for a suitable character, please enter the characteristics you require. If your requirements disagree with characters' standard settings (i.e., you need a troll with a high IQ), you can create a character from scratch. Please note that this will considerably increase the hire cost.

Very well. I could try, I suppose.

I moved the sliders, maxing out Intellect, Thriftiness and Managerial Skills.

Oops. This, for some reason, had blocked all the other sliders. Had I used all the available points? Very well, let's see the result first. I could cancel my choice any time, anyway.

I pressed *Preview*.

A new tab opened. A holographic image stared back at me: a highly intelligent fiery-eyed demonic creature.

Okay. Let's do it again.

I slid Intellect down to 7. Ditto for Managerial Skills: that would leave my future butler some potential for professional growth. Strength... don't need it... let's leave it *by default*. Wisdom... now that's interesting. If he ignored his master's hasty order to make sure that the said master didn't repent at leisure — would that be wise of him? Very well. Five points is good enough.

Agility: by default. Good Looks: by default. Thriftiness: five points. I didn't want to create a stingy little hoarder who'd have a hard time parting with every rusty nail. Logistics: eight points. This is an important feature indeed.

The rest of the stats got blocked again.

Okay, what have we got now?

A Blood Elf. Tall and blond, his green gaze betraying millennial wisdom. Age... three hundred-plus.

Name: Lethmiel.

Why not? I could try, couldn't I? Hire cost: 5,000 gold. Salary: 500 gold a month.

Quite pricey but then again, the castle needed a lot of running around. My majordomo had his work cut out for him. I should really have invested a few points into his Constitution.

I definitely liked the result. I knew that Blood Elves had a leaning to magic. Their ancestors used to serve the powers of the Dark — but by now they'd left their gloomy past way behind them.

I pressed *Hire.*

A cascade of golden light poured down from above, forming an Elven outline which gained shape and detail. Lethmiel spread his shoulders, coming to life. His piercing gaze focused on me; he lowered his head and uttered a few words in an ancient Elven language.

Noticing that I didn't understand him, he immediately switched to common speech,

"I'm at your service, Sir. I've arrived as soon as I received your invitation."

"You can call me Alex."

"I'm yet to deserve such familiarity," he replied with dignity. "What can I do for you?"

"You can start by hiring new staff," I replied. "You decide how many we need. Their primary task is to inspect the castle including the outer fortifications, and to collect all weapons, gear, scrolls, books and cargonite items they find. They can be stored temporarily here," I forwarded

him the castle map and the internal portals'
coordinates.

"How much can I spend?"

"A thousand gold to begin with. If a
hundred workers isn't enough, let me know."

"May I offer a word of advice?"

"Please do."

"If you hire common workers, they might
do more harm than good. Allow me to contact the
experts, Sir. They will collect and store all the
valuables, then promptly forget about it."

"Why, do they receive a memory wipe?"

"They don't need to. The experts I mean
aren't interested in the castle nor its artifacts."

His gaze betrayed an unusual craving. I'd
heard about this particular trait of Blood Elves
before. For them, magic was a physical need akin
to thirst or hunger. Unfortunately, they were
forced to suppress it too often.

"I know how you feel," I said.

"You don't. I can sense the presence of an
ancient power. But I'll do as you say," he lowered
his head. "May I use a microscopic bit of the
power for communications?"

"Absolutely. Please report any unusual
findings ASAP. Don't touch any time-damaged
scrolls or manuscripts. I'll ask Master Platinus to
make a special sealant to fix them."

"There are also some spells that can do

that."

That sounded interesting. "How long do they last?"

"Where, here? In Rion Castle where every rock oozes power? They will last forever!"

His gaze warmed up: he'd managed to talk the castle's owner into using some magic, after all!

"Very well. In that case, I'd like you to choose a room to use as a library. What else do you need?"

"A few Magic Eyes. Ten might be enough. We'll use them to inspect the inaccessible areas, especially those blocked by rockfalls. Once we're done, you can use them for surveillance purposes."

A Magic Eye? I'd never heard anything about them.

I checked the auction. *No results found.* Which meant it wasn't an item.

"Very well," I said. "If you can make them, please do. But only for emergencies."

"As you say, Sir."

Kray's voice disrupted our conversation. "There's a strange door here!"

"I'm coming," I called back. "Lethmiel, I want you to choose a room as your office and make a list of everything you might need. Then get on with the hiring. I expect you to report to me tonight. Ah, one more thing! If, by any chance, you find a totem made of Khmor wood, call me."

"I'll do as you say."

* * *

THE TWO GUARDS of Gloom were awaiting me by the teleport pad.

They had been right. This wasn't one of the room doors which lined the outside of the circular corridor. This looked more like some secret passage.

You had to give the two warriors their due: you couldn't see anything there. The two massive blocks of stone were identical to those next to them. You had to be really observant to notice a wafer-thin gap between them and the rest of the wall. The only thing that could attract a sharp eye was a shallow oval depression in one of the blocks.

No trace of any opening mechanisms around. Should I try and force the door open? Somehow I didn't think I could.

An impatient excitement flooded over me. What could be in there? Some secret storage? Or another arsenal?

I checked the map.

Indeed, a large round room was supposed

to be here — with no entrance to it marked anywhere.

So how were we supposed to get in? Could it be an illusion? The stone blocks looked and felt perfectly real. No prompts appeared: apparently, the rightful owner of Rion Castle was supposed to know how to get in. Even the Guards of Gloom stepped back deferentially, as if expecting me to do something.

The small depression in the stone was the only clue I had to go on. It looked the right size to lay something small into it... small... like a charm? *The* charm?

I had no other option, anyway. I removed the Charm of the Sovereign from my neck and pressed it to the stone. It fit perfectly.

With a screech, the door halves shuddered, raising faint clouds of dust. The two slabs of stone jerked forward, then began to open.

I stepped in first.

Torches lit up around me, illuminating a very, very weird place.

This wasn't a storeroom. Nor a hall. This actually looked like a vast cave.

Now why would they build a dungeon in the very heart of the castle, mere feet away from the elite Disciple warriors' quarters?

The floor here was uneven, the walls rough. The torchlight was too weak to dispel the shadows: the center of the cave was bathed in gloom.

Never mind. Let's see what we've got here.

I pulled out one of the torches and stepped in.

The silence was deafening. The rustling of my footsteps echoed weakly from the walls. Every few steps I kept coming across large boulders covered in dents and notches.

A dull metallic shape glistened in the torchlight. I looked up at an enormous armor-clad figure. What a giant! Twenty feet tall at least. His intact armor glowed purple. I couldn't see the creature's face behind the closed visor of his helmet. One gauntleted hand was clutching a halberd, the other a longsword. What an unusual choice of weapons.

I stopped, peering at the creature.

Cargonite Golem.

Class: Relic. Made by ancient Master craftsmen. One of a kind.

The giant towered over the top stair of a spiral staircase.

How many more mysteries did this castle have in store for us? Even more importantly, why couldn't I see the secret rooms in my interface?

Wasn't I supposed to have access to them as the castle's new owner?

Apparently not. The castle's builders had probably never entertained the idea of the castle ever changing hands. I may have bought its physical bricks and mortar, but it would take me some time to restore the place to its original glory by unraveling all its hidden mysteries. Step by tentative step, I had to prove my right to be called the new owner of Rion Castle.

All this had flashed through my mind as I studied the golem. It didn't move. No further prompts came up: no level, nothing. The centuries of oblivion must have reduced it to a lifeless statue.

Very well, then. Down we go! I was dying to find out where the spiral staircase might take us.

I stepped forward. A gentle rustling sound echoed around me, rapidly growing to a roar.

The statue stirred. The giant lowered his head.

A shining light escaped the visor's eyeslits as if the golem had opened his eyes, sensing my presence.

"Defend yourself!" a voice roared inside him.

Before I could move, a prompt popped up over his head, flashing with rapidly changing numbers,

Cargonite Golem
Class: Relic
Level, 240... 200... 150... 70... 50... 41..

This son of a bitch was adaptive! He could level down just to make sure he didn't swat me like a fly!

His halberd whooshed horizontally through the air while his sword came down onto me. I managed to dodge the blow. The golem's choice of weapons combined with his sheer height and the length of his arms gave him a definite advantage, on one condition: he had to keep the enemy literally at arm's length.

I ducked behind the nearest boulder, then somersaulted toward his feet, closing the distance. I had no intention of getting killed in my own castle.

Excellent. His halberd couldn't get to me anymore. I only had the sword to take care of.

Twice I attacked him, dealing him a decent amount of damage, until the golem's life shrank about 30%.

But he had a surprise ability, didn't he?

The giant flung the halberd aside, then buried his clenched fist in the stone floor.

The floor shuddered. The shock wave knocked me off my feet. I received a stun debuff which momentarily disabled me, preventing me from promptly jumping back to my feet.

The sword's blade pierced my chest.

My mind exploded with agonizing pain.

* * *

"ALEXATIS!" Raoul's cheerful greeting trailed away in surprise. "Whassup? Have you been killed or something?"

I struggled through the spongy, resistant green glow. It felt like surfacing from the oceanic depths. I was angry and jittery.

A portal flashed open, disgorging Kray and Ikhtar. Both looked anxious. Seeing me, they lowered their guilty heads. "We tried to follow you! But we couldn't! Some force just didn't let us in!"

"That's all right," I said, overcoming the numbing deadly cold in my chest. "Raoul, I want you to come with me. You too, both of you. I also need Arwan. Find him and tell him to come ASAP."

All my items and gear were intact, which was strange to say the least. Ditto for XP, even though I was bound to have lost some for being killed by an NPC.

Arwan came running.

"To the portal," I ordered, hastily creating a new group.

"Alexatis, what's going on?" Raoul demanded. "What's wrong with you?"

We ported to the circular corridor. This time the stone doors opened as soon as I touched the charm hanging around my neck.

"I want you to listen very carefully," I said. "I've no idea what this room is. Inside, there's a cargonite golem. A relic. He guards a staircase that leads to the floor below. He's armed with a sword and a halberd. When he loses 33% life, he activates an Earthshaker ability, punching the floor to knock you off your feet and casting a 10-sec debuff on you. We need to smoke him. I can't do it solo. We must work as a group."

This time the invisible protection veil let all of us through.

The torches lit up. The golem was still active. He ambled about, making the floor shudder with his footsteps.

"Alexatis, look," Raoul pointed at the weapon racks. "I wonder if this is a practice room?"

That made sense. Smart boy. I'd never even thought about it. I'd been too sidetracked by the mystery of it all.

"So you're back, aren't you?" the voice thundered. "Well done! You've learned your lesson! A leader should never act alone! Let's do it!"

I barely managed to grab a shield with rather decent damage absorption stats.

The range of his Earthshaker was 30 feet plus 2% per level — over fifty feet in total.

I shook my head. How did I know that? Was it my mind expander dropping helpful hints? I had to check the logs to see if they reflected the neuroimplant's activity.

Somehow I doubted it. Still, I made a mental note of the tip, telling the two Guards of Gloom to attack from the flanks leaving the cleric and the Elf in the rear. I calculated the distance to the golem and nodded to Arwan, ordering him to open fire.

Arwan didn't let us down. He loosed off five arrows in rapid succession, stripping the golem of 33% life in order to activate his Earthshaker ability.

The floor shuddered, raising stone dust within a radius of 50-plus feet. This just showed me the importance of having a competent clan analyst. I really needed to start looking for one in the nearest future.

In the meantime, Raoul cast a Stamina buff on the group, adding 25% to our resistance to physical damage. He then created a source of magic light right under the cave's ceiling which allowed us to see the golem pick up his halberd.

A circular slashing blow from something

like this would make quick work of our warriors.

Holding the shield in front of me, I stepped forward. Obeying my orders, the two Guards of Gloom were expertly flanking the golem, keeping a safe distance without aggroing him.

I blocked the halberd's shattering blow with my shield, dodged the sword attack, then immediately counterattacked, focusing the golem's attention on myself.

He was one powerful bastard. He'd very nearly knocked the crap out of me. My left arm had gone numb. The shield's durability had dropped to 50%. Still, I managed to get to him again.

The Guards of Gloom crept up on him from the rear and assaulted him with lightning combos, bringing his life down another 33% and triggering his next ability.

"Watch out!" I yelled, hearing a sequence of snapping clicks as if hundreds of little slots had opened in the golem's body.

The next moment he showered us with a barrage of crossbow bolts.

My shield's durability dropped to zero. The sharp steel arrowheads pierced its wood, pinning the shield to my left arm and preventing me from discarding the now-encumbering item.

Crying out in pain, I ripped through the leather straps and hurled the shield aside studded with crossbow bolts like a porcupine. A warm healing wave washed over me, closing my wounds and removing the Bleeding debuff.

Raoul had taken cover behind a dented rock ledge. Arwan was fine too: he'd kept a safe distance way out of the crossbow bolts' range.

I attacked the golem again, stubbornly drawing aggro to myself. I couldn't see the Guards of Gloom anywhere. Had he smoked them?

No, he hadn't. Both had promptly dropped down on hearing my warning, so they were both in one piece.

My successful attack seemed to have driven the golem berserk. His halberd drew circles in the air, crushing through nearby cliffs. It took all of my reaction and agility to escape his murderous attack, increasing the distance between us.

I couldn't get anywhere near him now. A new fiery icon appeared in his tag: Inexhaustible Strength. This must have been his last surprise ability as by now his life was deep in the red.

"Arwan, slow him down!"

The Elf lingered longer than usual, taking aim. His arrows hit a barely noticeable gap in the golem's shoulder armor. With a screech, the creature began to slow down.

"Finish him off!" I shouted, lunging at him.

The golem's arms had weakened considerably. His deadly halberd listed to the floor, hitting it in a cascade of sparks and leaving a deep furrow in the stone tiles.

He was on his last legs, literally.

Kray dealt the final blow, detecting the golem's vulnerable spot and burying his naginata in the back of his neck.

A wailing scream echoed through the cave.

A golden glow enveloped us. We all received new levels. My system messages were even more interesting:

Hidden quest alert: Victorious Spirit. Quest completed!
You've proven your right to leadership.

You've gained control over the Cargonite Golem

You've gained access to the Disciples' combat practice room

You've gained access to the clan's reserve storeroom.

Reserve storeroom? How cool was that? Could it be on the floor below, down that spiral staircase?

"Alexatis, I got a new level and an achievement," Raoul told me, beaming. "This is my first achievement in the Crystal Sphere! How totally awesome! It wasn't even that difficult, after all!"

"We've got new levels too," the two Guards of Gloom didn't try to conceal their pride at the fact.

"Great job," I told them. "You've done good. Arwan, where are you?"

"I'm here," he stood nearby, peering at something. "Hey, look what I've found," he hurried toward us, holding an unusual-looking bow and three quiverfuls of arrows.

"Mind if I take a look?" I said.

Bow of a Marksman Archer
Class: relic
Made by ancient Master craftsmen
Permanent effect: +2 to Agility, +10% to attack strength, +25% to range.

This looked like a remarkably light and easy to use weapon. The arrows too deserved a mention. They came in three types: the armor-piercing ones with cargonite arrowheads, the flaming ones treated with some alchemic concoction unknown to me, and some with a 5-sec paralyzing effect, with a Paralysis spell cast over them.

"They're yours," I handed them to Arwan. "You've proved worthy of them."

The Elf turned pale with emotion. "Sir, I didn't even dare hope-"

I still couldn't get used to them constantly "sirring" me. I'd never had to deal with NPC clan members before.

This small act of generosity seemed to receive everyone's approval. Arwan beamed. Kray and Ikhtar's gazes betrayed respect. Raoul grinned and gave me a thumbs-up, then slapped Arwan's shoulder.

"Right," I said. "Now go have a look around."

I walked over to the fallen giant surrounded by rock debris.

I focused, peering at him.

Cargonite Golem
Class: Relic
Status: Awaiting orders
Durability: 99%
Status of accumulating crystal: Charged. Charge: 15%.
Available modes: Standby, Bodyguard, Property Protection, Site Protection, Patrolling, Practice Combat, Escort
To activate Practice Combat mode, please

---

enter the desired aggression level (unprovoked attack, provoked attack, passive aggressive defense).

Warning! The Golem is powered by the castle's source of power. Please make sure his accumulating crystal is fully charged before taking the golem out of the castle limits. The crystal's charge is enough for ten minutes of autonomy.

Shame. He was no good in a raid. And even within the castle's walls using him wouldn't be that easy.

It was probably best to leave him here in the practice room. We could use a good sparring partner.

I began fiddling with his options until I managed to put him on charge, then activated the Site Protection mode.

CHAPTER SIX

THE RESERVE STOREROOM hadn't lived up to my expectations.

I walked down the spiral staircase. A glowing defense veil let me through. I found myself in a large room all done up in light-green marble, with a disabled teleport pad at its center. The room's ceiling was decorated with large inserts of transparent crystal exuding a soft light.

Weapon racks and armor stands made of sturdy wood lined the floor. Some still bore name plates.

And that was the extent of it. The century-long siege had exhausted all of the castle's resources. This wasn't the right place to look for unique armor sets and precious weapons: I'd have more luck searching for them amidst the ruins marking the places of fierce street fighting. I just hoped I could still retrieve some of the artifacts.

Neither the teleport nor the storage room itself were marked on either the floor plan or the castle's 3D model. That left little doubt to the fact that the castle was permeated by a complex web of secret rooms connected with teleports available only to a chosen few. What I found strange was that apparently, I didn't yet belong to their number.

Reluctantly I activated my map-making app. It looked like I'd have to find and investigate secret locations myself and make my own map of them, for my own personal use.

A broken accumulating crystal lay on the marble tiles next to the teleport pad.

"Raoul, everything okay?" I bent down to pick up the crystal fragments. Each of them contained a pulsating charge of energy. Transformed matter.

"I wanted to come down but the veil won't let me through," Raoul replied. "It may look like some glowing air but the moment you touch it, it turns rock hard. Your two bodyguards here are a bit restless."

"I'm coming now."

I was dying to find out where the teleport might take me. What a shame I didn't have any charged crystals with me. I made a mental note to always carry a few around. This secret portal system was bound to resurface in other places too.

As I walked back up, I checked the auction. Oh. Depending on their size and capacity, accumulating crystals could cost anything from 25,000 to a 100,000 gold.

In the light of this, Mr. Borisov's dismissal of "major cash injections" began to sound rather questionable. I'd love to know who made accumulating crystals.

My mind expander helpfully kicked in and did a quick online search, then offered me the result,

Requirements for building an accumulating crystal:

A fragment of transformed matter of a required size;

A Jeweler (level: Renowned Master or above)

A Sorcerer in possession of level 30+ Item Enchantment ability

They didn't want much, did they? Okay, I might actually have enough of the transformed matter lying around. But as for Renowned Jewelers, this part of the world had a definite shortage of them. From what I'd heard, there were some qualified masters making crystal armor and stat-boosting stones on some of the Yonder Isles. That was a good month's trip from here — and even then, to the best of my knowledge, there were no sea routes laid there yet. All the items available at auction were either rare archeological finds or loot dropped by top-level mobs.

Wait up. How about I talk to Lethmiel? He's over three hundred years old, for crissakes! He must have done his fair share of traveling, surely?

The magic defense veil let me obediently through.

The Cargonite Golem was already at full charge. He slowly turned his head this way and that, keeping a watchful eye on Raoul who was busy collecting some stuff by the entrance.

"Can you make it a bit lighter here?" I asked him.

"Alexatis, I've found some very interesting moss!" he replied, totally consumed by his discovery.

"Raoul, please, I need some light."

"In a moment!"

The crystal inserts overhead lit up, emitting a bright powerful glow.

"How did you do it?" I asked. "Is it a spell?"

"It's an ability I have. All magic sources of light switch on in my presence, dealing minor damage to all creatures of the Dark."

"What do you need the moss for?"

"I decided to study Alchemy," Raoul replied. "You can never have too many elixirs. A cave like this right in the middle of the castle, isn't it awesome? I've already found some very rare fungi. When I see Platinus I'll ask him to ID them for me. I can't do it myself for some reason."

I looked around me. The size of this "practice room" was indeed impressive. The huge boulders littering the floor weren't cemented down so you could use Levitation to move them around, creating dungeon models. A large flat strip of level ground nearby must have served as an obstacle course: it had all sorts of practice elements as well as several training dummies.

According to my clock, it was already half past three. I needed a break and a bite to eat, really. I still had to inspect the surviving floor of the east tower, the one that used to billet the Disciple wizards.

* * *

THE MOMENT I thought about food, Lethmiel contacted me. "Sir, Master Platinus is back."

"And?"

"He made some wine using ancient recipes. The lunch is served on one of the main tower's conarps. I've marked it on your map."

"Good. I'm coming now," I said without specifying what the hell a *conarp* was. "You gonna join us?"

"I have too many things to do, Sir."

"You could use a break. There's something I need to talk to you about."

"Yes, Sir."

I dismissed Arwan and both Guards of Gloom. Raoul declined my invitation, too busy inspecting the castle's secrets. I could understand him. Players rarely buff themselves with food unless absolutely necessary.

I located Lethmiel's marker on my map and ported to the central tower.

A long succession of lush halls took me to an open terrace overhanging the tower and ringed with a crenellated parapet. The castle's architecture was in fact quite peculiar. The builders had cut the defense structures into the peaking cliffs, using the cliff ledges as natural fortification platforms.

So that's what the ancient word meant: *Conarp*, a cliff ledge. I might need to remember that.

The air was warm and windless. In the past, the platform must have been used as a catapult position to control the approaches to the castle. The view from here was awesome: all three defense levels lay below me in full view.

I could see the farmers unload food supplies from their longboats. Gradually, the castle was beginning to bustle with life again. Elven hunters had already returned with bountiful game; the workers hired by Lethmiel had already cleared the water well and were now busy freeing the inner yards from vines.

Togien joined us, looking utterly pleased. Apparently, leveling Mining was working well for him.

The table was laid for six. Lethmiel shrugged in response to my quizzical stare: what if I wanted to invite some guests?

"How are the Moors doing?" I asked, taking my place on a high-backed chair. Comfortable it was not.

Platinus pointed at two tall wicker bottles. "Ancient recipe. Instant ageing. I've made three more barrels of it for the party but not as good as this one."

"Okay. We'll sample it now. Just please

keep in mind that we need spectral dust more than we need wine at the moment. We need it in industrial quantities."

"Of course. I've also farmed some ingredients to make my Disintegration Potion. But where do you want me to make it? I have no lab!"

"You'll have it today," I assured him.

Lethmiel poured out the wine, then took his place at the table. Admittedly, he looked more aristocratic than all of us put together.

We took our time over our meal. Recently, I'd had my fair share of camp rations so now I was enjoying the excellent wine, the food, the view and the company. What a shame Enea wasn't with me! I hadn't heard from her since.

"Lethmiel, who cooked the food?" I asked.

"I hired some kitchen hands," he replied. "The castle staff is now kept to a minimum as you asked."

"Have they begun inspecting the rooms?"

"They have indeed. They started from the lower floors and moved up. Plenty of items but virtually nothing really valuable yet."

I paused. "If I may ask you... Have you ever been to the Yonder Isles?"

Lethmiel nodded. "I was lucky to be born at the time when the Founders' portals still worked," he explained willingly. "When I was young, no one called them the Yonder Isles. They were right at the heart of it — an amazing city, the epicenter of crafts and trading, built on the archipelago's many isles connected by bridges. Over the centuries, however, the ancient power dwindled to nothing, rendering portal travel impossible. Trade collapsed. Finally, a big earthquake destroyed most of the city. To the best of my knowledge, the isles are now home to some primitive tribes who've long forgotten their ancestors' glory. There are a few jewelers' settlements there, however, who've preserved their ancient secrets."

"Aren't there any new trade routes?"

"The sea is treacherous there. Lots of powerful storms. Sea monsters attack ships, too."

"There must be some old maps of the Isles, surely!" I said.

He nodded. "There are indeed. Unfortunately, they're no good."

"Can't one use the map to enter the coordinates into a teleport scroll?"

"Unfortunately not. Scrolls have range limits."

"That's not true," I said. "I know nothing about any range limits."

"Okay, let me put it this way. A wizard strong enough to create and charge a scroll capable of transporting a person thousands of miles hasn't been born yet. But even if the entire wizards' guild joined forces in order to create such a scroll, it would still be too risky. The old maps aren't very accurate. Where firm ground once stood, now the waves are licking around. A lucky traveler might find him or herself ported to an island inhabited by unspeakable monsters prowling the ancient city ruins."

"Does that mean that without the Disciples' portal system the world split apart?" Platinus asked.

"Unfortunately," Lethmiel admitted. "The Savage Lands never used to be a problem for travelers. Now they're forced to hack their way through virgin forests inhabited by monsters. It's like this everywhere."

Togien nodded and rose from his seat. "I'm off, if you don't mind. Time to use my pick. I want to put in another couple hours' work."

"Sure. We won't stay much longer, either. We need to find Platinus a nice room for his lab."

Togien left. Platinus — who didn't enjoy digital food much, either — wandered off to check out some plants in the cracks between the crenels.

"Alexatis, mind if I take a look around?" he asked. "You never know, the wind might have blown some rare plant seeds here.

I nodded. He darted off looking definitely

much happier with his new life compared to his boring old Agrion stretch.

"Why all this talk about the Yonder Isles?" Lethmiel cast me a sharp look. "Are you going to travel there?"

"In fact, I am. Not because I want to," I admitted, laying the fragments of the broken crystal onto the table. "This."

He perked up. "Transformed matter? May I?"

"Be my guest. How many teleport pads are there in the castle?"

"Nine hundred and three," he replied mechanically without taking his gaze off the tiny clusters of energy lurking within each fragment.

"How many of them working?"

"Seventy-two."

"Now you understand? The Isles are the home to the only surviving community of Master jewelers capable of shaping fragments of transformed matter into crystals," I heaved a sigh. "Some eight hundred crystals! The mind boggles. No idea how I'm going to pay for them. And I'll still have to have them charged."

"Do we have enough transformed matter?" Lethmiel's voice betrayed a sudden agitation.

"Oh yes, we do."

"But that changes everything!" his eyes changed their color from a soft emerald to an acid green. "Traveling to the Yonder Isles is too risky! Even if we hire a sturdy ship and a convoy, we might not make it. Think of all the sea monsters, the storms and especially human greed..."

"But I need more teleport crystals. The castle is too big for us. We can't control it without being able to port instantly around."

"I couldn't agree with you more!" he said passionately. "But if you'll allow me to speak my mind..."

"Please do."

"The Founders' legacy is virtually unstudied," he tried to compose himself. "My people have spent centuries researching its mysteries, piecing the ancient wisdom together crumb by tentative crumb. This legacy triggered wars the kind of which the modern world has never seen. Whoever manages to decipher the ancient knowledge will rule the world."

"Got it. What's your point?"

He paused, looking me in the eye. "You're a Neuro, aren't you?"

Oh. What an interesting conversation. Now how would he know that? NPCs can't see players' stats. They have their own ideas of leveling, abilities, characteristics and whatnot.

"There's a legend that claims that all living beings share the same origin," the Elf continued, apparently acknowledging my right to remain silent. "This quite agrees with our information. From time to time, there's a Neuro born into this world, regardless of race. You can't tell the difference just by looking at them. What makes them special is their natural aptitude for the Founders' magic."

"What makes you think I'm one of them?"

He suppressed a smile. "The castle walls have eyes and ears too. The Elves of Light told us how you'd disembodied the dark spirits in the dungeons below. Last night you helped the farmers by rebuilding their boats for them. That's at least two ancient spells you've used, which is impossible for a mere mortal!"

Uh oh. Rumors spread fast here. "Very well. Let's presume I'm a Neuro possessing some ancient magic. How would that help us restore the teleports?"

"You can create things," he passionately assured me.

"Can I really? What does that make me, a god or something?"

"No. One can't turn a rock into a living being. But to shape an item using an existing sample — you can most surely do that. If I may suggest, it's much easier to facet a crystal than to rebuild a rotten boat! All you'll have to do is *remove* all extra stuff. You don't even have to do it artistically: you don't need to be the proverbial sculptor liberating a statue trapped within the block of marble."

He had a point.

Lethmiel's eyes burned with agitation. His fingers shook as he pieced together the broken crystal. A whispered spell fell from his lips, binding the fragments. Now the crystal looked whole albeit still cracked.

"Should I send someone to see Master Togien?" Lethmiel asked. "We'll need a piece of the dark obelisk he's working on."

"*We*'ll need?" I repeated, taken aback.

"Sorry, Sir. I apologize for my indiscretion. I'm too nervous."

He was definitely keeping something back from me. Was he waiting till I could prove my power?

I saw no point in playing hard to get. Mr. Borisov had been right: I couldn't keep my identity under wraps for much longer.

"We don't need Master Togien," I said, reaching into the inventory for the obelisk fragment and laying it on the table amid the bowlfuls of delicious food.

The fragment was opaque. It seemed covered in some sort of murky veil constantly trying to solidify its surface.

The Elf tensed up. His fingers twitched as if trying to grab the item. He jerked his hand away, overcoming the urge.

How strong was the Blood Elves' memory of their servitude to the Dark forces! This was an ingrained, challenging legacy which promised supreme power without revealing its cost, harboring countless temptations.

As he was struggling to overcome his dark urge, I inconspicuously slid the Replication Ring on my finger. I should have used it last night instead of wasting the precious obsidian. "Let's do it," I said.

My voice awoke Lethmiel from his trance. For him, the Founders' magic was a sacred mystery lying outside the realm of logic. For me, however, it was infinitely easier. The moment I focused on the crystal, its 3D model appeared in my mental view.

Using my eye movements, I shifted it around until I placed it inside the fragment of transformed matter.

That was it. Now all I had to do was use the Replication Matrix spell to, as he'd eloquently put it, "liberate the statue trapped within a block of marble".

Slowly and unhurriedly I uttered the spell.

The murky veil surrounding the dark obelisk fragment seemed to have thickened. My mental energy bar began to shrink. My regeneration rate was still too low.

I struggled to maintain concentration. After three seconds, the outline of the 3D model began glowing. The surface of the obelisk fragment in front of us erupted in a fine net of cracks.

An explosion thundered, showering everything around in cascades of broken stone. A light cloud of spectral dust rose into the air, settling onto the finely served table.

Lethmiel's cheek twitched as one of the fragments grazed him. Blood trickled down his chin.

I enunciated the last word of the spell. The gray crystal turned transparent. A tiny fiery dot glowed at its center.

Lethmiel sneezed. "Apologies, my lord!"

My lord? Oh wow. My status, whatever it was supposed to mean to the Blood Elves, seemed to have considerably elevated in his eyes.

"Hey, what're you up to?" Platinus' voice came from behind me. "You can't breathe in Spectral Dust, it's not good for you! That was some explosion, I tell you!"

Lethmiel sneezed again.

"Drink this, quick," Platinus offered him a vial.

A teleport flashed open inside the castle building. The two Guards of Gloom ran out onto the terrace, followed by Arwan and the kobold.

My makeshift rapid response team had

reacted admirably to the emergency. I motioned them to stay put: no harm done.

The finished crystal lay before us amid a bunch of smashed tableware. It looked like the spitting image of the real thing.

Lethmiel wiped his weeping eyes and nodded gratefully to Platinus. "I do appreciate your help."

He then reached out without actually touching the crystal and froze.

Was he casting a spell? No way!

He wasn't. His lips didn't move. Still, the crystal began to glow from the inside.

Lethmiel heaved a labored breath. "That's it. Excuse me, my lord. I couldn't help myself. I should have warned you."

I couldn't believe it. "Did you just enchant it?"

"This is a modest ability of mine, one I've taken all my life to develop. I can only perform it once a day. Oh... I'm sorry, I need to sit down."

"You sure you're okay?"

"Enchanting is very strength-consuming. I'm not young anymore," he picked up a wine goblet powdered with a fine layer of Spectral Dust. Its intricate silver had turned black; a purple film had formed on top of the wine.

"Give it here," Platinus took the goblet from him and poured the wine into an empty vial. "I'm

---

sure it's some new poison!" he announced with all the gusto of a born researcher. "Or a potion with some interesting properties," he added, opening his inventory and squirreling away everything tainted by the transformed matter: the food, the wine and the tableware. He used a special brush to collect every speck of Spectral Dust and every crumb of the stone's fragments.

By the end of his manipulations, there was only one item left lying on the table:

Magic Crystal
Made by a Neuro
Properties: unknown
Purpose: Unknown
Requires activation

I packed it into my inventory, then decided to finish off what I'd started.

I relieved the kobold and the Guards of Gloom, ordering them to check the outer walls and set up sentry posts wherever they thought fit. None of the three warriors would be any good where I was supposed to go. The east tower — or rather, one particular floor of it that used to billet the Disciple wizards — was well protected against brute force, be it cargonite or cold steel.

I opened the chat. "Raoul, where are you?"

"I've found myself a room. Chambermaids

are gorgeous here. I'm helping them dust my place," he chuckled. "Did you hire them?"

"Quit loafing about. Time to get back to work. I've sent you a map marker."

"Coming."

Almost straight away, a teleport flashed open. Raoul walked over to me and cast me a questioning eye.

"We're going to check out the east tower," I explained. "But first, could you please give Lethmiel a heal."

As Raoul cast healings and blessings on the Elf, I turned to Platinus and lowered my voice, "What do you think is going to happen if you make a potion with Spectral Dust and drench arrowheads in it?"

"I can try," he replied softly. "I've no idea how it might work though. One thing I can tell you: I wouldn't want to eat a rabbit killed with one of those."

Which set me thinking. Transformed matter had proven to be an even more valuable resource than I'd originally thought. It looked like our deal with the dwarves was actually a bargain for them. I had to make good on my initial promise but I definitely wasn't going to enter into any more deals with them. I had to go careful with our strategic supply — at least until we knew more about the unique substance and its properties.

"Off we go," I said. "Lethmiel, you're coming with us."

* * *

THE EAST TOWER was bathed in gloom and silence. The floor plan here was entirely different from that of the donjon's west wing: the teleport had delivered us to an enormous vaulted hall.

The darkness was filled with weird crackling and humming noises. Our footsteps raised clouds of fine dust, revealing the complex ornamental design of the tiled floor.

"Mind your step," Lethmiel warned us. "I suggest we have a good look around first."

"Raoul, could you please sort out the lighting," I said. "Lethmiel, whassup? What got your alarm bells ringing?"

"It's the tile pattern. I can see some geometric figures but also some floral designs. And here," he pointed under his feet, "are some Elemental symbols."

"Do you think they're traps?"

"I don't know," he shook his head, peering at the complex pattern of entwined lines. "They could be. Or it might be a floor scheme for performing certain complex rituals."

"I think it's the latter," Platinus echoed.

"Somehow I don't think the Disciples used to walk here in zigzags."

He leaped over onto a tile covered with a pattern depicting a coil pipe and a test tube.

Nothing happened.

He heaved a sigh. "Shame."

"Wait! Don't move!" suddenly I knew how to check the patterns' purpose. "Lethmiel, would you please step onto that tile with a plant motif? Raoul, where's our light?"

"Sorry. My ability doesn't seem to work here."

"Never mind. Can you see the tile to your right covered in healing symbols?"

"How do you know?" he sounded doubtful. "I've never seen those symbols before."

"Just do as I say, will you? Think you can jump over onto it?"

"Well, whatever."

That still left us with the tiles marked with the four Elements: Water, Fire, Earth and Air. The tile design seemed to lead toward one large tile at the room's center.

"I don't think my racial identity allows me to claim the role of a druid," Lethmiel said. "Also, I can't see the sign of Chaos anywhere. We must be missing something. If this structure is indeed a defense mechanism against invaders, then the idea seems too simple."

He had a point. Still, I'd received no prompts: the castle interface seemed to be testing my limits. The floor plan showed no active traps at all here.

Just to be sure, I clicked the *Show and Disable All Defense Apparatus* button.

Nothing changed. Could it be that the complex pattern of ancient magic had lost its potency over the centuries of oblivion? In the absence of a source of power, that was more than likely.

I really didn't feel like getting killed again. Two respawns are a bit too much for one day. Still, just standing there peering into the darkness wasn't an option, either.

"I can see some ash and bones here!" Platinus exclaimed.

"What's the symbol like?"

"As far as I know, this is Fire."

Everybody else stirred, looking watchfully around them.

"Someone's drowned here!" Raoul announced.

"Can you see the sign of Water on the tile?"

"Nope. It's blank. Covered in water, actually, yeah. A Moor Goblin is lying right in the middle with his eyes popping out as if he's just drowned."

"There's one over there, too!" Lethmiel

exclaimed. "It's too far to see him properly but I think he was turned to stone!"

I could see one now, too: some remains of a creature which must have been torn to pieces by a powerful storm.

The others went quiet, waiting for me to do something.

Should I have come here on my own? What if there was no secret passage here, after all? The hall might be perfectly safe for me but deadly for any strangers.

"I want you to go back to the teleport pad," I said.

"Why?" Raoul asked.

"Because it's a safe zone," I pointed at the blank tiles surrounding the portal.

"So how do we cross the hall?"

"I think I have to do it on my own."

Platinus frowned. "How do you know? Your landlord status didn't help you much against that golem, did it?"

"I might still try."

"Okay," Raoul handed me the torch. "You do what you want. I'm gonna heal you."

* * *

BRACING MYSELF, I began walking toward the center of the hall. The tiles formed a concentric pattern which might mean that all the really cool stuff was located at the hall's center.

A pillar of fire roared up unexpectedly, singeing me and showering me with sparks and embers.

My life dropped somewhat but the effects of both the Charm of the Sovereign and my armor set bonus (+10% to Elemental protection) managed to keep it within safe limits.

Raoul got so scared that he hurried to cast a heal on me. The moment the spell's aura touched me, my hp dropped to 50%, triggering an acute pain. The heat promptly scorched the skin on my hands, covering it with bursting blisters.

"Stop it!" I yelled.

"You'll burn to death!" Raoul shouted.

"Stop *now*!"

"All right, all right!" he interrupted the next spell he was casting.

Slowly but surely, my life began to climb naturally back.

I chose to grin and bear the scorching fire, inching toward the room's center.

A gust of freezing wind assaulted me next, putting out the flames and enveloping me in unbearable cold. My teeth were chattering. My armor was covered in fancy frost flowers. Clouds of misty breath escaped my mouth.

I kept going. A dozen feet or so further on,

an almighty ocean swell rolled over me.

I managed to take in one last gulp of frosty air and kept walking against the water pressure until my lungs protested, sending cascades of tiny bubbles out of my nostrils up toward the non-existing water surface.

I began to choke and splutter. My life bar kept shrinking in leaps and bounds.

Then the water was gone.

Breathing fitfully, I stepped on the next tile.

My feet sank deep into jellified rock. My physical energy counter began spinning as now every step demanded all the strength I could muster.

I was almost there.

When I finally made it to the center, I had virtually no life left.

The round tile at the center kept metamorphing: sometimes gushing fire, then freezing, now clenching my feet in its rocky embrace only to open up as a bottomless whirlpool.

Chaos, the forefather of the Elements, didn't deal me any damage; but suddenly a new icon sprang up in my interface: a countdown timer.

What was I supposed to do?!

I racked my brains for a solution, all the while burning, drowning, freezing and turning to stone, until finally I knew what it was. The answer was so simple I should have known it straight away. Frozen into the solidified rock for the umpteenth time, I finally saw it: a shallow oval depression at the center of the tile.

Overcoming the deadly cold, I pulled the Charm of the Sovereign from my neck and waited for the water to subside. Just as the timer counted the last clicks, I laid the artifact into the depression.

The Elemental metamorphosis stopped.

An unknown force pushed me up to the surface, leaving me exhausted and breathless on the flat stone devoid of any patterns.

A multitude of crystal lamps in cargonite mountings lit up all around the hall, dispelling the gloomy veil and revealing dozens of doors that lined the room's walls, all of them ajar.

Hall of the Elements: access granted!

The magic depository of Rion Castle: access granted!

Please enter the names of the beneficiaries to be granted access to the living quarters, the Hall of the Elements, the enchantment rooms, the spell plane and the chemical lab.

The familiar screeching sound of stone blocks moving around echoed around me. I promptly shrank back. The central tile dropped, transforming into a spiral staircase which led to the floor below.

Enough adventures for one day.

I hurried to add the names of Platinus, Raoul and Lethmiel to the beneficiaries' list. "You can come here now," I called them. "You're good with the system."

Lethmiel ran up to me first and helped me back to my feet. "Your resistance to the Elements is impressive, my lord!"

"Can I heal you *now*?" Raoul asked, casting puzzled glances at me. He knew nothing about neuroimplants and was probably asking himself what I was doing, sitting lifeless on the floor with no debuffs to show for it. Why wouldn't I just spring back to my feet and hurry on to face more adventures? Life in the red, big deal. Experienced players were known to smoke mobs while literally expiring themselves.

A warm healing wave wiped away the pain, filling my aching muscles with a new energy.

I promptly sprang to my feet. I didn't want to overcomplicate things for him, potentially triggering unwanted questions. "You have a look around. I'll just check what's down there."

"Can I come with you?" Raoul asked.

"If you wish. Provided the magic veil lets you through. I haven't worked out how to switch it off yet."

"I'll try. I'd love to know what's down there. Plats, you coming with us?"

"No, thanks," Platinus waved his offer away. "I'm fine here. The lab must be here somewhere, I can feel it! You sure there're no more traps?"

I shrugged. My map didn't show any. "Lethmiel, are you coming? Or would you prefer to stay here as well?"

"I'd rather come with you if I may."

"Off we go, then," I said, leading the way down the spiral staircase.

Ten or so stairs down, we came across a protective veil. You could confuse it for a stream of hot air rising up, slightly distorting the outlines of the objects behind it. But when you touched it, it felt harder than rock.

"Won't it let *you* through?" Raoul asked, anxious.

"Wait a sec," I peered at the obstacle, trying to trigger its interface or at least a prompt. Nothing.

Now why would a defense mechanism identical to the one in the Practice Hall fail to recognize me?

"We need a wizard," Raoul concluded.

"That's me. I'm multiclass, don't forget."

"Then why won't it let you through?"

So impatient! I opened the castle control tab. The decision had to be pretty simple. Problem was, I hadn't had enough time to study all the menus.

Got it. Protection veils came in two types: regular and reinforced. The latter had their own access system. Apparently, the names of those granted access had to be entered into the spell that created it!

Was this the end of the line, then? "Lethmiel, did you ever come across this type of protection spell?"

"Oh, yes. I've traveled a lot and studied the ancient ruins."

"The names of those granted passage here were apparently entered into the spell that created the veil. Any idea how to rectify it?"

"Oh! Admittedly, I once came across something very similar. This is the oldest branch of magic imaginable. You don't see it at all these days!"

"Cut the crap, will you?"

"In order to get through, we wrote our names on the obstacle."

"Did it work?"

"To a degree, yes. I survived. But the warriors who accompanied me were consumed by flames. I'd venture a guess that it has something to do with one's race."

"Very well. Let's try it."

I touched the veil and drew my name in fiery letters which flared up, then disappeared, consumed by the flowing air currents.

"I don't think I feel like coming," Raoul took a step back. "I'm gonna check on Platinus."

Fair enough. After all his recent tribulations and login problems, his character was too important to him.

"Lethmiel?"

This one needed no encouragement. The ancient magic was calling his name. Unhesitantly he touched the veil and wrote his name which too flared up, consumed by the currents of power.

I held my breath and stepped in.

* * *

"IT'S DARK," Lethmiel commented.

He lit up a torch. A multitude of crystal lamps all around us reflected its uneven light.

We were standing in the doorway to a large hemispheric room lined with massive bookcases. A library?

An empty one, unfortunately. All the books and scrolls once kept here were now gone. Slowly Lethmiel walked between two rows of desks still preserving the dusty outlines of disintegrated manuscripts.

"I don't understand," I struggled to suppress disappointment. "Okay, so they could have used up all the scrolls while defending the castle. But that still doesn't explain the absence of books. Where are they?"

"Turned to dust, I suppose," the Elf replied. "Some knowledge can be too dangerous to pass on."

"You don't mean the Disciples could have destroyed it themselves?"

"Unfortunately, I can't think of any other explanation. I can sense the influence of the ancient power. The manuscripts crumbled to dust. We can't help that. But at least we can replenish the shelves! There are lots of books being found in castle rooms. I'll make sure they're handled with care. I will be allowed to come here, won't I?"

"Of course. Seeing as the magic veil has already let you through."

"In that case, I'll personally take care of all the manuscripts. Would you like to test the crystal you created?"

"Why, have you discovered a portal?"

"I have indeed," he began moving the massive carved desks and chairs around until he cleared a small area. "The accumulating crystal is broken — on purpose, I suppose. Barbaric as it may seem, drastic times demanded drastic measures."

I crouched next to the portal, studying the socket.

The crystal I'd built with Lethmiel's magic help seemed to fit it perfectly, both in shape and in size. Question was, would it work?

I clicked it into the socket. The ancient symbols encircling it flashed momentarily, then expired.

"Didn't work," Lethmiel commented sadly.

"Wait," I focused on the item. I could see new data!

Universal Accumulating Crystal
Capacity: 10,000 pt. mana
Status: activated. Requires charging.

For your information: The use of dark transformed matter in the making of the item hinders the charging process, adding 50% to the charging time, and may result in 10% losses of the accumulated power.

You can use the accumulating crystal in: 13 hrs.

"Lethmiel, do you know of *light* transformed matter?"

"Absolutely. Ancient temples worshipping Mother Nature and the Elements use a source of power different from this one. But there, the creation of transformed matter can take millennia. Why?"

"You see, this crystal is made using *dark* transformed matter. That's why it has problems charging and staying charged."

"Shame. It's normal, come to think of it. Does that mean we can't use the portal?"

"Yes, but only in thirteen hours."

"That's all right. We can wait. If I may offer my opinion, my lord, seeking for sources of light transformed matter isn't really worth it. What you need to do is use the power of the Elements because it's the one closest to the original Chaos. From what I heard, transformed matter comes in many kinds and can be farmed in all sorts of places. Inside volcanoes, for instance. At the bottom of the ocean, too, because water pressure can transform certain minerals. Also, elemental spirits often possess some truly unique resources provided you can talk them into parting with them."

"Right. Let's go upstairs, then."

I can't say I was happy. I was too used to receiving rewards for any effort. Then again, who was I to complain? Over a hundred surviving rooms, the Hall of the Elements, a library and a Practice Room guarded by a Cargonite Golem! Not bad for one day.

* * *

UPSTAIRS in the Hall of the Elements, Raoul and Platinus were already waiting for us, impatient.

"Alexatis, I've found the lab!" Platinus announced. "The entrance is blocked! We need that thing you wear around your neck!"

Aha, so they'd worked it out, then. I really should be more careful in the future. I had to find some useless cargonite trinket and put it around my neck: let them think it's the magic master key.

It's not that I was paranoid or something. I just shouldn't be constantly flashing the unique artifact.

"Okay then," I said. "Let's have a look."

They pointed at one of the doors defended by the same kind of protective veil we'd just seen.

Behind me, Lethmiel seemed to be listening intently to something only he could hear. He then uttered a few Elven phrases without really addressing anyone.

I turned to him. "What's up?"

"The castle seems to be restoring its old power! Magic veils have just sprung up everywhere. Workers report auras blocking their way which then turn rock hard upon touch. One thing I don't understand: why do they all belong to the element of Earth?"

He was dead right there. The castle was supposed to be protected by all four Elements. What he didn't know was the damage to their runic sequences: Earth was the only one still active. Still, I wasn't going to tell him that. They could be my clanmates and all that, but I'd better keep a few things to myself for the time being.

Lethmiel patiently awaited my verdict. Still, he had to take care of the practicalities seeing as the restoration works had all but stopped. "We might need to adjust the access," he offered.

I had to reopen my interface and try to make some sense of it. I had no one to delegate it to. I had to do everything myself.

Switching the protection off completely wouldn't be wise, even though we'd already lost three workers who'd tried too hard to force their way through the magic veil and had been turned to stone as a result.

I opened the castle's 3D model. Lots of new markers flickered before my eyes. In addition to all the active portals, floor plans were now marked with thousands of doors which had suddenly acquired magic properties. Lots of corridors now bore the symbols of magic protection. The markers came in every shade of color from pale green to acid red.

"I need some time to look into it," I told Lethmiel. "I might need your help."

His eyes glistened with curiosity. "What exactly would you like me to do?"

"We need to make some rings — or maybe bracelets — that could serve as keys. How many workers do we have now?"

"Fifty cargonite collectors, not to mention the cooks and the castle staff," he replied, then added apologetically, "I'm sorry but my abilities don't include bulk enchanting skills. Mass production never interested me."

"Platinus? You any good at mass enchanting?"

"I seem to have a development branch that does it," the alchemist replied.

"Never used, I suppose?"

"It's level 1 by default. Hey, wait a sec! I don't want to level up Sorcerer! I need to study Alchemy!"

"Cool down, will ya? Alchemy is a profession. What kind of stats does it require?"

"Mainly Intellect. Oh, and also Spirit."

"And how about Sorcerer?"

"Intellect, Spirit and Stamina."

"See? You can have it both ways, can't you?"

"I suppose so. They have to be leveled up separately."

We stopped by the lab's door. I wasn't in a hurry to disable the veil.

"Please don't drag it out," Platinus begged. "I can't wait to see it."

"Think you can help me with mass enchanting?"

"All right, all right," he grumbled. "You can take poor Platinus and split him into ten, if you have to."

"Sorry dude, but I can't help it. You're the only person I can trust with the job. Making Rings of Access isn't for everyone!"

He was obviously flattered by my version of the truth. "Okay," he said, perking up. "But promise you'll help me with the development branch!"

"Absolutely," I touched the veil, inscribing our nicknames on it. "In you go."

The magic veil obediently let us through. Still, this method was too time-consuming. I couldn't spend my days rushing around the castle doing it for all and sundry. Which was why I needed a bunch of enchanted rings.

Platinus stepped in and froze, transfixed.

Me, I couldn't care less. All those cobwebbed test tubes and coil pipes crowding the dusty tables didn't impress me in the slightest. Not so Platinus: the moment he saw the complex system of interconnected ancient vessels, he began shaking with emotion. Reverentially he blew the dust off some of the equipment, then darted for the shelves lined with millennia-old vials.

He read a few labels and sank onto the nearest stool. A new debuff appeared over his head: *Confusion.* He'd just cast it on himself!

"You okay?" an alarmed Raoul hurried to cast Vigor on him.

"Yeah... I just need a breather... Alexatis, you can't even imagine... this is... these are..."

"It's okay, Plats, take it easy. This is your lab now, just as I promised. But first you need to help me make the rings."

"Anything! We should start now!"

"First I need to have a look at this development branch of yours."

"Not a problem," he zoned out, studying his own interface, then forwarded me the data.

Okay, let's take a look.

So! He'd jumped twenty levels since he'd joined the raid! Excellent. I checked the development branch. I didn't want his char to level up unevenly.

Platinus had three specializations: Magic, Illusion Casting and Enchanting. Somehow I didn't think he was going to bother with Illusion Casting. Now Magic was different: you just couldn't ignore it. It had lots of spells and yet-inactive abilities for enemy control.

Okay. What did Mass Enchantment

require? Oh wow. Level 25! Plus five more spells he had to learn to gain access to the required slot.

"Have you ever tried to enchant your potions?" I asked him.

"No. Why?"

With the help of my mind expander, I did a quick research of the relevant manuals, copied the most important information, then sent him the link to the resulting article.

"Oh wow," he said, skimming it. "I knew nothing about this ability. How cool!"

"If you go down this route, you won't be able to level up Magic or Illusion Casting until you reach level 50," I said.

"That's not a problem," he dismissed my warning, impressed by this new possibility.

"In that case, here's the tutorial. It'll show you how to distribute the available XP points. Just follow the scheme. I'm going to buy you the spells you need. Your job is to learn them."

"Not a problem! One question: is there any difference between item and potion enchanting?"

"You'll have a new ability in a moment: *Choice of Treatment*. It's allow you to choose what to enchant: the potion or the vial it comes in."

"Sure!"

Raoul stood nearby casting envious glances at Platinus. That was a good lesson for him, actually. The clan alchemist had just received a bunch of privileges: a unique lab, a rush through levels and some free spells.

Very well. If that prompted Raoul to think in the right direction, that would only be a good thing.

＊ ＊ ＊

IT TOOK US over an hour to make all the rings. Both Platinus and I had gained another level while experimenting. I'd used Object Replication to create rather plain-looking items (if you forget the materials they were made of) while Platinus enchanted them, inserting a magic marker into each. The latter we'd procured by combing through the castle's security logs.

Apparently, the castle's passive shields were all set to Paranoid mode configured by the Disciples during the siege. I hadn't changed it. I was quite happy with the status quo at the moment. The only people who could walk freely around the castle were a few trusted clanmates as well as the rapid-response security teams I was going to create within the next few days. The danger of a Dark invasion was still too imminent; Moor Goblins too were a threat to be reckoned with. I was almost sure they'd try to infiltrate the donjon... in which case they were in for a few nasty surprises.

"All done!" Platinus wiped the sweat from his brow. Item enchanting demanded a lot of concentration. He wasn't quite up to it yet.

I scooped up a handful of rings and gave them to Lethmiel, then forwarded him the castle's 3D magic model with all the multi-colored protection barriers and their activation zones marked on it.

"The rings are set to grant access to the markers from green to orange," I told him. "Each ring binds on equip. It can neither be removed nor lost. This is yours, with full access to all castle rooms. Raoul — take yours. All the zones you have access to are marked on the map."

"Thanks," Raoul said, apparently pleased with his access level. "You won't regret it."

"I need to hand these rings out, then," Lethmiel headed for the portal pad and disappeared in a flash of light.

"How about you?" I asked the others. "You gonna log out? Or would you like to stay? It looks like we might have an impromptu party in a moment."

"I need to take a look around the lab," Platinus said, impatient to get rid of us.

"Very well. You?"

"I'd rather log out, if you don't mind," Raoul replied. "I'll be back in the morning," his voice trailed away, bleak and cheerless.

We left our alchemist to sort out his relic equipment and walked out into the Hall of the Elements.

I motioned Raoul to stop for a moment. "You have problems?"

"That's all right."

"I'm serious. Is there anything I can do for you?"

He faltered, then admitted, "I have a few debts to pay off."

"How much?"

"Seven hundred credits. For me, it's lot. It's not a bank loan. I borrowed it from some guys I know."

"Why didn't you tell me?"

"You really think I'd have asked you for money the moment I joined the clan? You just don't do that."

"I know. Still, you helped us purge the dungeon. You can use your share of the loot, that's for sure. You have a way of converting in-game currency?"

"Yeah," his bleak stare glinted with curiosity.

"What's the exchange rate at the moment?"

"One to ten," he replied in surprise. "As if you didn't know!"

"Sorry, I've been too busy just lately. I've just transferred you eight thousand gold."

"But there's no way I earned so much! If the truth were known, I should pay *you* for rescuing my char."

"We'll sort it out," I proffered him my hand. "Log back in as soon as you've put your affairs in order."

I didn't need to ask twice. Raoul gave me a hearty handshake, then logged out.

CHAPTER SEVEN

THE CRYSTAL SPHERE
THE OUTER WALLS OF RION CASTLE

J'D MANAGED to complete the walls inspection before nightfall.

In the light of everything that had happened, we had to decide which fortifications needed restoring first.

Togien had tagged along. To my surprise, he also had the profession of Builder.

"Why would you need it?" I asked.

He shrugged. "Use your head. Gwain and I, we work down the mines, right? If the framework got rotten or if the brickwork is loose, who's gonna take care of that? Unless you want the mine to come down on you, of course."

Aha. That explained it. "Fancy an experiment?"

"Why not? What do you want me to do?"

"I'd like you to check your logs and see how much XP you received for a cubic meter of bricklaying."

"Wait a sec. Aha, found it. A hundred XP per cube."

"How much do you need to make the next profession level? Which one do you currently have?"

"Level 9 in Bricklaying and 7 in Carpentry."

"Can you check Bricklaying for me?"

"Let's have a look... I need.... yes, I need to lay another five and a half cube for my next level."

I pointed at a fragment of brick wall destroyed by a hefty trebuchet ball. "What do you think they used as cement?"

He studied the split blocks of stone. "No idea. Can't see anything. Couldn't they have built the castle with magic?"

"In which case the stones have to stick together automatically, right? How do you normally lay bricks?"

"I use my Lime Mortar ability."

"Fancy giving it a try?"

"You have to be joking! There's no way I can lift any of those! You need someone with a

100 pt. Strength to do that!"

"And now?" I cast Levitation, raising a massive rectangular block of stone in the air.

Togien promptly pushed the block into place and lingered over it, mouthing a spell. Having finished, he pressed the stone down.

It worked! A thin white layer of cement materialized momentarily below it, then disappeared. The stone looked one with the rest of the wall.

"How about XP, did you get any?"

"Sure," he forwarded me a system message,

You've restored a fragment of ancient stonework!

+100 XP to your current Profession level.

"Oh wow," Togien looked lost. "Five more stones like this and I'll make another level!"

I was more than happy with the result too. "So? Do you think we could invite some bricklayers over here?"

"At this rate of leveling? They'll be lining up from here to Agrion City!"

"I'd love to know more about this Magic Stonework," I said, focusing on the wall.

The wall is in a state of disrepair. In order to gain access to its characteristics, please restore

---

the wall first.

I didn't even notice night fall. I got the celebrations under way, then found Lethmiel and asked him to speak to the village elders for me. Then I ported to the main tower.

The terrace where we'd dined earlier offered a great view of the castle and its grounds.

I could hear music playing in the inner yard. Torches cast an uneven light over the cobblestones. Fires were piled high; even from here I could smell the aroma of the finest Elven spices on the roasting meat.

I leaned against the low parapet and gazed at the tall flames dissolving in cascades of sparks.

The celebration was now in full swing. I was never one to rise above the occasion but tonight for some reason I didn't feel like joining the whirl of a pre-programmed party. If only Enea were here with me! Still, she hadn't resurfaced yet.

Mechanically I peered at the crowd, searching for Arwan, the kobold and the two Guards of Gloom.

There they were, joined at the hip as usual. An Elf and a kobold drinking together! True, human players were known to make stranger bedmates — but NPCs? They lived by their racial differences.

I had a funny feeling I knew what all four had in common. All of them had received their share of neurograms back in the underground dungeon.

I really needed to keep an eye on them. Had the fragments of human identities taken root within them? If so, I needed to know any potential outcomes of this reluctant "upgrade".

Lots of questions, not enough answers — worse still, no one to provide them. Who was Dietrich? What had prompted him to use the Altars of Chaos as portals? How had his pet demon gotten hold of neurograms? Who had sealed the service entry which allowed Corporation workers access to the world of the Crystal Sphere? Was all this part of the planned experiment — or had it gone completely awry?

Somehow I didn't think I could expect clear-cut, truthful answers from anyone. All I could do was keep an eye on the situation, piecing together whatever information I could lay my hands on. Or should I go back to the other Altar of Chaos (seeing as I knew about it anyway) and try to have a heart-to-heart with this Dietrich creature?

The moon rose over the moors. Something caught my eye: a weak glint moving down one of the creeks in the faint moonlight.

"Lethmiel?" I mouthed.

Yes, my lord, his voice echoed through my mind.

Have you got a Magic Eye ready?

I've got two.

Could you hand me over the access?

Yes, my lord. Is anything wrong?

That's what I'm trying to find out. I'd like you to contact the Elves and tell them to take up their positions on the walls.

A new icon appeared in my interface.

I activated it. A brief vertigo overcame me as the Eye began its course high above the castle. It took me some mental adjustment in order to stabilize the picture and focus the magic energy on the area I was interested in.

Darkness parted. The creek waters glistened silver in the moonlight. The dark outline of a large, crudely made raft flowed soundlessly with the current. And another one. A whole fleet of them.

Now who might that be? Some NPC

fishermen from a moorside village?

Somehow I didn't think so. I needed to find out who our nighttime visitors were and how they found their way here.

Maintaining concentration, I forced the Magic Eye to move down a notch.

Moor Goblins. Now I could clearly see their squat stocky figures sloppily camouflaged with heaps of rotting algae. There were at least fifty of them per raft, not counting the shamans who were circling their totems while muttering something.

So they'd decided to attack us, despite the agreement we'd achieved earlier this morning?

The castle was virtually defenseless. I was so struck by the thought that I very nearly lost control of the Eye just as the goblin fleet turned toward the castle.

Quest Update: Troublesome Neighbors
You must repel the goblins' surprise attack.

I tried to estimate their approximate numbers. Bad news: there were at least three hundred of them there. The rafts moved downstream expertly, apparently controlled by experienced pilots.

If they continued at this speed, they'd land on Rion Isle in twenty minutes — while all I had was a motley group of NPC ex-prisoners and about a hundred farmers who'd arrived to celebrate with us.

Clenching my teeth, I peered at the attackers' tags. Levels 30 to 50!

We couldn't hold the castle on our own. The only solution I could think of was investing every bit of the money I'd just farmed in the underground dungeon into hiring some castle guards ASAP.

I switched the eye to Patrol mode and opened the castle control interface.

Impossible. The hire rates were out of this world. The best I could do was either fifty archers or a hundred foot soldiers. And because the castle's restoration wasn't complete, the highest permitted level of the guards was 39.

Okay. I could hire the foot soldiers. I had twenty archers of my own. That might be enough to deter the enemy for a while. Having said that, it was probably easier to surrender all the inner courts and hold out inside the towers.

I had but a few minutes to make a decision. The goblin fleet was already approaching the delta's passages. Soon it would be within the direct proximity of the castle. One might think they'd land straight away. They had two access routes: either via the pier (the stairs to which I'd so helpfully repaired) or through the ruins of the barbican where the shore was the flattest.

Foot soldiers or archers?

I leafed through the interface tabs, all the while realizing I had to interrupt the party and order the Elves onto the walls, but I simply didn't have the time to do it all! Lesson learned: my very first experience in castle defense command had already put things into prospective, and... and my archers needed more arrows. The hired NPCs only had a quiverful each. Time to check the armory.

Nothing in there.

By then, the first raft had already cleared the creek. Five more followed, approaching the shore. They began falling into a formation.

That's it, then. I had to hire foot soldiers.

I pressed the button. It glowed red.

Operation denied.
The enemy is within sight of your sentries.

The system message hit me like a ton of bricks. Very clever, Alexatis. You should have stepped on the gas when you had the chance!

The music stopped. Alarmed voices resounded under the donjon's walls.

The Elven avant-garde must have spotted the enemy and raised an alarm. And I knew the question they should be asking themselves: where was their wretched clan leader and what did he think he was doing?

I was here — admittedly, pretty clueless about how to repel the surprise attack. The only thing I could think of was activating the castle's magic defenses. Until now, I hadn't even got the chance to look into it. I simply hadn't had the time.

I opened the magic defense tab. The source of power had already charged the surviving runic sequence to about 25%. And what was this? How interesting... It might actually work... provided I acted upon it *now*.

"Lethmiel, get the golem out onto the shore!"

Without closing the interface, I whipped out a teleport scroll from my inventory, focused on a distant spot within my direct line of vision and broke the seal.

I found myself on the shore surrounded by the Elves busy stringing their bows and taking up their positions along the steep bank.

"Don't shoot!"

My spectacular arrival at the scene had suitably impressed the already-desperate farmers, earned me a few respectful glances from the archers and triggered an outburst of malicious fury in the enemy lines. Not bothering to hide anymore, the goblin warriors sprang to their feet, shaking their weapons and bellowing their battle cries.

Runic sequence activated: the Element of Earth

Warning! You're about to use 25,000 pt. of the Castle's attack potential. Restoring it might take up to 72 hours. Are you sure you want to proceed?

The Elves froze at their positions, awaiting my command. I stood alone on the steep shore. Goblins raged below. Their rafts had already crossed the channel of fast-flowing water at the center of the delta and were now within bowshot.

A cargo portal flashed open behind me. The farmers screamed in fear. The whole shore shook under the golem's shattering gait.

But even that was nothing compared to the power of Earth.

It came as a faint whiff of cool breeze which wrapped itself around me, filling me with the kind of primal strength I'd never thought I had. A destructive ancient force entered me, coursing my veins, suppressing whatever human traits I still had and turning me into a blind vehicle of Elemental power.

Mechanically I glanced over the waves. The water rippled under my gaze. A low roaring sound came from the moors. The steep bank began crumbling, showering the water below with pebbles.

My gaze alighted on the first raft. The roaring sound seemed to grow stronger as it approached from the moors. Hydras' petrified screams were followed by desperate howling as moor creatures sensed the looming catastrophe.

I focused on the enemy.

The goblins promptly shut up and began rowing hard toward the shore.

My eye pupils dilated. The earth began to tremble. Sharp squelching sounds came from the moors. I was struggling to control the Earth's fury.

So I let go.

With a heartrending rumble, sharp cliffs erupted from the water, piercing its surface sideways. Splintered wood flew everywhere. The ropes binding the rafts together began to snap. One of the cliffs pierced a raft and lifted it high in the air; a few more disintegrated into a chaos of wooden debris. The remaining craft were sucked under by whirlpools filled with the bursting bubbles of marsh gas.

A few goblin survivors desperately tried to swim to the shore but my Elven archers quickly discouraged them.

The current sped up, frothing and sweeping the flotsam out of sight past the jagged line of cliffs which were already cracking and crumbling as they sank. Fearsome underwater monsters added to the chaos, finishing off any goblin survivors.

Finally, the crushing elemental force released my mind. My vision blurred. My muscles slackened. The two Guards of Gloom jumped to my rescue: their strong hands supported me inconspicuously while the kobold growled at the curious farmers and Elves, keeping them at a respectful distance while I gulped a quick vial.

My vision cleared. My muscles quivered.

Lethmiel was fussing around me. "You can't do things like that on your own, my lord!"

The Cargonite Golem walked over to the water's edge and slowly turned his head as his fiery glare searched the seething waters for any surviving enemy.

Cheers came from every direction. I stood there torn by mixed feelings: the joy of my lightning victory tainted by the guilt of my momentary lapse of judgment. My procrastination might have cost us dearly.

Quest update: Troublesome Neighbors!
You must find out what prompted the Moor

Goblins to attack you.

It could wait till next morning. Now I needed to restore. This impromptu show of channeling Elemental forces had completely drained me. I felt ravenous. I headed for the nearest fire with a still roasting rabbit turning over it when Lethmiel stopped me,

"The dinner is served in your rooms, my lord," he said matter-of-factly. "I've taken the liberty of getting two chambers ready for you. Would you like to teleport there?"

"Aren't I supposed to stay and celebrate our victory?"

"Not necessarily, my lord. Familiarity breeds contempt. If I may advise, it might be better not to tone down the impression you've just made."

"Very well. As you say."

* * *

IT WAS ALMOST midnight when I had my late candlelit dinner. The magic lamps were barely glowing as all of the available power was being used to recharge the castle's attack potential and to support the now utterly useless magic veils that had switched on in the castle's destroyed areas.

I really should have gotten some sleep but I knew I couldn't. So many things had happened in one day that I just couldn't take it all in.

I couldn't sleep, no. Also, there was something else I still had to do.

I picked up a stack of parchments, a quill and an inkwell, then traveled the castle's portal system to get to the Hall of the Elements.

My fingertips began to prickle.

I walked around the hall for a while, stopping on a tile or other and listening to my sensations.

Found it.

Predictably, the tile was marked with the symbol of the Earth. On top of protecting the castle, the only surviving runic sequence also served as a potent power focus.

I sat on the floor cross-legged, placed the parchment sheets onto a flat piece of wood and began laboriously copying to them the more energy-consuming albeit necessary spells. You never knew when they might come in handy.

Exorcism, Object Replication, Dark Regeneration, Mass Teleport, Teleport Coordinates...

This time I decided not to charge them as I risked dropping dead from exhaustion. I had a better idea. Once I'd copied all the spells, I left the sheets neatly stacked on the tile bearing the sign of Earth.

I'd come back here in the morning and see whether it had worked or not. Did the Hall of the Elements have the energy necessary to charge scrolls?

I took another sheet and wrote on it in large letters (for Platinus, Raoul and Lethmiel),

Do Not Touch!

Then I went back and spent the next ten minutes in bed trying to sleep. I couldn't. With a sigh I got up and walked out onto the balcony.

The stained-glass room door closed silently behind me. The party was long over. The yard was silent, the dying fires barely glowing. The alarmed night calls of moor creatures and the heavy gait of the golem whom I'd set to Patrol mode were the only sounds disturbing the night.

A faint whiff of wild violets touched the warm, heavy air.

I swung round. Behind the stained-glass door, the candles on the table shed transparent tears which rolled down the fancy candlesticks.

The little flames swayed as if disturbed by a faint breeze.

Noiselessly I opened the door. The aroma was stronger here. "Enea?"

The candles cast an uneven light upon her

face.

"Alex!" she draped her arms around my neck, gazing unblinkingly into my eyes. "I'm back."

"But the implant?"

"I've got it. Properly this time. I had a falling-out with Dad. Let's not talk about him, please."

A cold shiver ran down my spine. "Was it Mr. Borisov who helped you?"

She pressed her face to my shoulder. The smell of her hair tickling my cheek was driving me crazy.

"What difference does it make?" she whispered. "I've made my choice. I'm back to be with you."

* * *

I AWOKE in the morning to the quiet sound of melodious chiming.

Eleven o'clock already! My interface was flashing with several missed calls and the To-Do List icon.

Enea was nowhere around.

I sat up. I can't have dreamed her up. Dawn had already broken when she'd fallen asleep in my arms.

Lethmiel was serving breakfast on a small

side table. "She told me not to wake you up, my lord," he half-turned to me. "She asked me to forward you this marker."

The castle map flashed with an emerald dot located on one of the destroyed floors.

"Have you met her?" I asked.

"I met her already last night," he replied calmly. "Who else could have given her a magic access ring to ensure she could pass through the protection veils? Your lady is as beautiful as a forest dryad..."

"Why would she want to go there?"

"She didn't tell me."

"Okay. What else have I missed?"

"We have two wizards asking your permission to come here. Apparently, there was a breaking news story in the Crystal Daily News this morning reporting your crushing victory over the goblins. We've received over two hundred new clan applications. I would suggest you introduce some kind of vetting for the applicants. Fame has the tendency of attracting all types..." he fell into a meaningful silence.

"How did they get hold of the video?!"

"That's what I was asking myself too so I spoke to Arwan this morning. He sent out his scouts who discovered a spy lurking on one of the isles. According to him, the video is legit. He demands to see you referring to some 'exclusive story agreement' that Lady Enea apparently promised him."

I immediately remembered the sleazy Daily News reporter. "His name isn't Sciatant, by any chance?"

"Exactly!"

"You've locked him up, I hope?"

"He's in chains. The orcs are guarding him. A very brazen individual, if you ask me. He started mocking his guards claiming he could disappear in an hour's time. Can you imagine? We had to cast a Curse of Stone on him just to shut him up."

Pointless taking him to task for unauthorized use of magic. One thing I couldn't understand: how had this seedy paparazzo managed to get here? I needed to have a heart-to-heart with him about it.

"Your breakfast," Lethmiel reminded me.

"Thanks. I'll look into the clan applications. What about those two wizards?"

"Their names are Iskandar and Rodrigo. I never met them before so I can't advise."

"You can allow them limited access to Floor One of the donjon. I'll have a talk with them once I sort all this out."

"Yes, my lord."

He left. I splashed some water on my face, equipped my gear, ignored my breakfast and ported directly to the donjon's destroyed floor.

* * *

AFTER the early-morning rain, the ruins felt damp and gloomy.

A rat squeaked in the echoing silence.

"Alpha, give me a break!" Enea's voice resounded in the dark. "I told you to get the *rat*! Forget spiders! You're big enough now! Are you afraid of it? You be careful or I might change your name to Omega! Which is not a-"

She didn't finish. I heard a rustling sound followed by a thump. Another desperate squeak echoed from the walls.

"So you see? You can do it! Now another one — but please find it yourself! I'm not going to highlight targets for you anymore!"

I walked toward the voice. There they were, all present and correct. Enea was sitting on a big barrel with her legs tucked under her. A closer inspection revealed about a dozen rats cowering amid the debris. Alpha the Black Mantis froze in combat stance at the center of the desolation. He'd grown a lot. The scales of his chitinous armor glowed with a healthy sheen.

I checked his stats. So! Level 9! He must have acquired his first abilities already. Unfortunately, Enea was the only one capable of seeing them.

"Aha," I said. "Enjoying a bit of leveling?"

She smiled but stayed seated. Was she afraid of the rats?

Enea must have read it in my gaze. She shrugged. "If you wanna kiss me, come and do it yourself."

Alpha cast an annoyed glance at us.

"Keep working," she whispered to him, draping her arms around me.

I slid the bracelet onto her wrist.

"It's beautiful," she said, admiring the fine silverwork of ancient symbols against the purple glow of cargonite. The item looked like a great work of jewelry indeed. "A Bracelet of a Metamorph?" she looked up at me askance, awaiting a further explanation.

"You wanted a multiclass, remember?"

"I did," she said with a mischievous glint in her eye. "How can I do that? Do I need to apply to the admins?"

"All you need to do is install a certain macro, then touch the bracelet."

"You're a magician!"

"I'm a Neuro," I forwarded her the data. "Have you got it?"

"Yeah... I'm installing it... done it. Nothing's changed."

"Take this," I reached into my inventory for

two more items: a light but sturdy shield made of dragon hide and an elegant one-handed sword made of enchanted cargonite. Both items had been discovered on one of the upper floors of the east tower. Judging by the dainty runic script covering the sword, I wouldn't be surprised if this fine example of the Founders' weaponry had been the prototype for Elven swords.

"Alex, but I'm not a warrior! I don't even know how to use these things!"

"You'll have to learn," I replied in earnest. "How do you feel when your mana is at zero with no vials to bring it back up and the enemy keeps on coming?"

"I feel lost," she admitted. "I just don't know what to do in those situations. Now I'm curious. What can this bracelet do?"

"It allows you to briefly switch your class with a fifteen-minute cooldown."

"But what about my armor?" forgetting about the rats, she ported to the center of the room. Sunrays poured down through the breaches in the walls, illuminating her shapely form.

"That's the whole thing," I said. "Thanks to Master Jurg you don't need it yet. The set he made is brilliant against physical damage. You wanna try?"

"It feels scary... yes, actually I do," she

burst out laughing, trying on the shield and weighing up the light sword that seemed to have been made for her hand. "You're full of surprises, you! I just hope you won't make me sweat in the practice room."

"Oh yes, I will."

"No!" she tried to fake fear but the pimples on her cheeks refused to comply. "Can we try now?"

She touched the bracelet. The name tag over her head blinked, changing class. The Staff of a Hydra automatically disappeared within her inventory.

Awkwardly she raised the sword and the shield, stepping toward me. I rolled over toward her, ducked under her sword blade and sprang to my feet, slapping her unprotected upper arm. She shrieked. I stood up and took her in my arms.

She threw her head back, laughing. "Is this what you call practice?"

"Your hold on the shield is wrong. And you forgot the sword completely. Let's do it again. Watch me."

"Okay. I'm afraid I might hurt you."

"We'll see."

I let her go and stepped back a few paces, then repeated my "surprise attack".

This time my hand slapped the shield.

Before I could roll back, I received a quite tangible blow to my legs and collapsed in a heap, breaking a few rotten planks and raising a cloud of dust.

"Alpha!" Enea exclaimed.

"He's right," I scrambled back to my feet and brushed off my clothes, watching the mantis warily approach me sideways. "You shouldn't be angry with him. A pet is obliged to defend you in any situation. What you should do is change my status to Friend."

Alpha stopped but kept watching my every move. He was level 11 already! He'd purged the room of all the rats!

"What did he just use to bring me down?" I asked Enea.

"He has this ability called a Disabling Blow... Ouch!"

The bracelet's effect had expired. Both the sword and the shield went into Enea's inventory. The Staff of a Hydra reappeared in her hands.

"Let's go now," I said. "You'll be practicing with the Cargonite Golem. That's what he's meant for. As soon as we sort out all the pressing issues, we'll go on vacation, you and I."

"Where to?"

"We could go camping to the Savage Lands. How about that? We could do a bit of leveling, cook on a campfire and bathe in forest lakes."

She seemed to like the idea. Her face brightened. "That would be great. Where are we going now?"

"Rodrigo and Iskandar are here. They want to talk. Also, we have an old reporter friend of ours that we've locked up. He somehow managed to sneak in here and film last night's defeat of the goblin raid. We also have a lot of new clan applications from both warriors and wizards. We need to come up with some kind of a test for them, like an entry exam. Also, we have the missing runic sequences to find. Last night Togien and I saw some stones cemented into the walls with runes inscribed into them. We only have one runic sequence working so we need to restore the other three. This is what's urgent. Tomorrow we'll have enough Spectral Dust to go visit the dwarves again. We also need to decide who we need to hire to restore the castle walls. Lots of things to do."

"Too much for the two of us."

"Don't forget Lethmiel. He's a good manager and a very interesting guy."

"Still we need more people to help us. I know. I've been researching clan management while waiting for my in-mode capsule to be installed."

She nodded to Alpha. With her permission, he happily flitted up her shoulder. He was way too big to lurk in her hair now.

We continued discussing clan affairs while walking to the portal.

"We'll need some players to head the clan's combat section," Enea continued. "A few trustworthy mid-rank warriors and wizards."

"Question is, where are we supposed to find them? I actually have an idea about the combat section. I'll tell you at lunch. But how we're going to staff all the other sections, I just don't know..."

* * *

WE PORTED to the Resurrection Hall.

It had already been cleaned up: the floor swept, the debris removed, the artifacts collected and put away. The walls had been washed of the centuries' worth of cobwebs and grime. A few tables and easy chairs from the upper floors had been set up in a corner, forming some sort of leisure zone.

Several rows of chests were lined up next to the respawn point, ready to receive the players' backup gear sets.

Iskandar and Rodrigo sat at a table, their faces grim.

"Hi there," I said.

Both beamed. "Alexatis! Enea!"

I pulled out a chair for Enea. I loved doing that sort of thing for her. Her return had added a new touch to my life: something indescribably beautiful that held the promise of a better future. We kept catching glances and touching each other, the growing desire burning us up from the inside.

I shook off the momentary obsession. The two wizards must have had a good reason to come to see me here. "Now. What's up?"

"Our group is gone," Iskandar replied. "Virgil and Tylor seem to have botched their characters."

"How about Zander?"

"He's gone nuts."

I remembered the paladin's weird behavior immediately after our Dietrich encounter. "Did he rip you off or something?"

"Oh no. He paid us in full. But then it got weird. He dumped the group, just like that. Apparently, he's gone solo. We met him last night at the market in Agrion: he walked right past us as if he didn't even see us. He's level 72 already."

"I'm not surprised. The bracers and the runic tablet I gave him have enhanced his Paladin abilities giving him a considerable advantage over any NPCs within a two or three day walk. He must be on his way to the Top 100."

"He's already made it," Rodrigo said. "But

that's not why we came here."

"What can we do for you?" Enea asked.

"We're looking for a temp job while we're putting a new group together," Iskandar said bluntly. "We can't earn money without warriors."

"Or should I say, we don't feel like joining any dubious raid or party we might come across," Rodrigo corrected him. "Earning a pittance doing one-off jobs isn't an option, either."

"Do I understand that money is the only thing that keeps you in the Crystal Sphere?" I asked. "No interest in the gameplay at all?"

"We've done it all, man," Iskandar replied. "Interest alone doesn't cut it. Yes, we're in it for the money. Anything we can earn in the real world is peanuts compared to what we can make here."

Enea and I exchanged glances.

Was she thinking the same thing as I was?

I didn't say anything. She smiled, taking over from me, "We have a counter-proposition for you."

"To join your clan," Rodrigo chuckled knowingly.

She cheerily ignored the sarcasm in his voice. "We have a few commanding positions open. Some of them are quite interesting."

"Like what?" Iskandar leaned forward, curious. He seemed to like Enea as a person, especially seeing how expertly she's just ironed out a potentially sensitive situation.

"Well," her eyeballs twitched as she zoned out, pretending she was scrolling through a non-existent list for the right contract, "how about the clan's combat section? You'd be in charge of other wizards during raids. It would be your job to screen any new clan applicants and assign them to groups. Or," she blinked as if leafing through imaginary pages, "we have the position of the Keeper of the Wizards Tower still open. His responsibilities include the teaching position in the Mastery School we're about to open once the Wizards Tower is restored. But if you find that too difficult — because not everyone enjoys public speaking — I could offer you the position of clan librarian. We have a whole archive of unique manuscripts containing the precious crumbs of the Founders' magic which absolutely have to be decrypted and preserved. Also, we have-"

I just sat there admiring her panache. She was doing a faultless job, describing a whole plethora of secondary tasks I'd never had the time to think about; the tasks that had been marring my inner vision as the yet unsurmountable problems which we couldn't tackle with our current numbers.

Rodrigo rubbed his chin.

Enea's comeback had been a great addition to our clan. I was a warrior; admittedly I could handle an arch demon or channel an Elemental force but I was no good at negotiating with experienced players like these.

She, however, immediately knew how to approach them. Nobody trusts mercs; they're not the most popular bunch of people. Few treat them as friends which is a great shame. Every person has his or her own philosophy and convictions, as well as a few cherished but yet unattainable dreams. Of stability, for instance. Or of their own hard-earned top place in the gaming community.

A vagabond mercenary or an arch mage in charge of the Wizards Guild of Rion Castle? This was a no-brainer. A soldier of fortune hired to cut throats for someone else's advantage or a legendary commander of the Black Mantises' combat section?

"There're certain drawbacks, too," Enea added calmly. "You should be aware of them."

The two wizards looked admittedly lost, as if some magic door to a worldful of opportunities had just slammed shut in their faces. "What's the catch?"

"There's no catch. Rather an agreement. Rion Castle is a very special place. The Founders' legacy. There is a certain blood magic artifact —

the Oathing Stone — which was central to the curse we've just removed. We've purged it from evil. All new clan members must seal their oaths with a drop of their own blood. The Cohort of the Fallen is a good example of what might happen to a traitor."

"In other words, once you join you can't quit?" Rodrigo asked, fidgeting.

"Oh yes, you can. You can always quit if you want to. You can also be expelled for a number of serious offences. The Oathing Stone guards the clan against traitors alone. Alex and I decided not to make a secret of it. All new applicants will receive a fact sheet of the Oathing Stone's properties. That will allow them to make an informed choice."

Rodrigo and Iskandar exchanged glances. "All this sounds very interesting. Can we think about it?"

Enea flashed them a smile. "Absolutely. These kinds of decisions can't be made lightly. Still, we don't seem to have much time. The goblins might not be the only ones crazy enough to challenge these walls."

"Actually," Rodrigo interrupted her, still fidgeting, "Alexatis, can you tell me now? It *was* an uncategorized spell, wasn't it? We couldn't believe our eyes watching that video! To command Earth the way you did, you had to be level 100 at least!"

"You'll know it when the time is right," I said. "We'll be awaiting your decision."

"Very well," Iskandar gave me a hearty handshake, then turned to Enea. "Say, tomorrow morning?"

She flashed them another smile. "Absolutely."

* * *

THE PAIR OF WIZARDS headed toward the portal, closely watched by the two Guards of Gloom. They were on sentry duty today: I had been forced to post them here to guard our "strategic facility" if I wanted to get a few moments of privacy in Enea's company.

"The reporter is probably waiting for us," I said. "The Curse of Stone must have already expired."

"Alex, please don't be too hard on him. If you think about it, everything he did was in our interest. The camera angle was fantastic. I couldn't have chosen a better one myself."

"Did you see it?"

"What do you think? By the way, you really can't see the castle on the video, only a dark outline in the background. They mainly filmed the goblins. They must have set up the camera on some isle behind their backs."

"How did I look?"

"Like yourself but *very* impressive. A powerful uncategorized wizard, a real clan leader. And the golem behind your back! He was awesome! This place was a mess, wasn't it? And I missed it!" she hooked her arm through mine. "Let's finish whatever we have to do first. I still have the wizards' contracts to prepare."

"You think they'll be back?"

"A hundred percent. They're both good guys and excellent wizards. We couldn't have found better ones if we'd tried. Actually, I meant to ask you. Do you have any old friends here, someone you know really well? It would be great to completely staff the clan's combat section with good commanders before we go back to see the dwarves."

I gave it some thought. I used to know this guy... we'd started out together back in Middle Earth. He was a good sort and excellent warrior. I knew him in real life too: he actually used to live next door. He was a perfect candidate. Problem was, I'd lost contact with him over a year ago just as Christa and I had begun tackling that complex plot line.

I'd love to know where he was now. Considering the fact that the Crystal Sphere had been aggressively devouring other game worlds ever since, it stood to reason he might have ended up here.

Should I try and look for him? Why not? I still remembered his nickname: I knew he'd bought it with the intention of never changing it.

My mind expander kicked in, helpfully entering a search term:

Archibald_2020

Got him! Excellent. I typed off a quick message hoping for a prompt reply.

It came within a few seconds:

Archibald_2020 has blocked your message.

Excuse me? WTF? So we hadn't seen each other for a couple of years, so what? Why blacklist me?

Never mind. No skin off my nose.

As I closed the message, I glimpsed the flashing of the map icon.

How interesting. Apparently, my Pioneer achievement allowed me to pinpoint a message sender's location provided it was situated in the vicinity of a public teleport.

The map opened on an unknown region predictably clouded by the Mist of War. I noticed a small gap in it and zoomed in. A village called Idyll.

A smattering of cottages and a stream on the forest edge. And what's this marker?

Archibald_2020

The marker was green. How weird. Red dots grouped all around it.

Now I knew it. My friend was in trouble. He probably had all incoming messages blocked by an enemy app to prevent their victim from contacting anyone.

What now? This Idyll, where was it?

I zoomed out. It wasn't that far from Agrion, actually. I'd never been there before.

"Enea, you think you can handle the reporter without me?"

"Absolutely. Something happened?"

"I found an old friend. He's in a village near Agrion. Not far from the portal. My map-making app located him."

"Can you ask him to join us?"

"I don't think so. He seems to be in trouble."

"Can't I come with you, then?"

"No, you can't," I gave her a peck on the cheek. "In any case, the place must be crawling with guards already. I'll take my rapid response team just in case."

"Alex, please take me with you!"

"And how about the reporter? We can't keep

him for more than twenty-four hours. Please talk to him. I won't be long."

"All right," she said reluctantly. "Is it because of my implant?"

"Also," I admitted. I didn't want to lie to her. "Tonight we'll go to the practice hall and find out both your pain threshold and combat feedback. I'm sorry but I'm not risking it. We should do some practice and analyze your logs first."

"Okay," she heaved a sigh, apparently realizing she couldn't outtalk me on this one.

"*Arwan and Highr, full combat alert,*" I began issuing orders via the castle network. "*Davre, Enea is on her way to you. Until I'm back, she's your responsibility.*"

The orc growled his understanding.

The two Guards of Gloom happily vacated their post. It was no fun guarding the portal knowing that the Castle defenses deflected all the incoming teleports anyway. Their standard NPC characters seemed to be growing more complex. It was as if they had developed a different worldview after the neurogram incident.

The kobold and the Elf came in running in full combat gear. Ten seconds — excellent result!

The kobold looked at me unblinkingly. He appeared perfectly calm.

Arwan squinted at me, "How many?"

"Ten, probably more. I only have a tiny bit of

the map available, just the area by the teleport."

"Are they strong?"

"No idea," I admitted. "We'll have to go and see for ourselves. Come on now! On the double!"

* * *

THE TELEPORT disgorged us onto a quiet dirty side lane under a cold drizzling rain.

A scruffy cat darted away from us. The nearby gardens erupted in fierce barking. A gust of wind swayed a still-burning streetlamp, rattling a faded *Tavern* sign.

The number of the red dots had grown. So many! Thirty at least!

A bowstring snapped. A body thumped to the dirty ground.

"Robbers," Arwan explained, loosing off another arrow. "All clear!"

"Stay put," I glanced at the map. The red dots kept changing positions quickly. Mounted riders, most likely. "Highr, you too! Don't let them near the tavern!"

With a decisive nod, the kobold took a better grip of his halberd. The Elf had already disappeared in the wet thicket of a nearby hedge.

I bared my sword and stepped toward the tavern. The two robbers were lying on the ground by the porch with arrows in their throats.

They were NPCs. An illegal local gang courtesy of some idle hacker with too much time on his hands.

I kicked the door open and walked in.

The tavern was empty. All the tables and benches lay in disorderly heaps along the walls, swept away in the heat of the fight. The place looked like it had been hit by a tornado.

A portal's iridescent entryway shimmered at the center of the room. Archibald's marker hovered directly over it.

The floor around the portal was littered with the robbers' bodies. Archibald had done a good job.

Kray leaped over an upended table and landed on top of someone.

A robber. The fight had left him much the worse for wear. His life was barely glowing.

I peered at his stats. *Level 30. Gang member. Gang leader: Mossy Yorm.*

Never heard of him. A portal set up inside a tavern wasn't normal, either. Its mouth breathed cold.

Quest Alert: Old Friend!
Quest type: Unique
You must find out what happened to Archibald
Reward: varies
New quest available: A Helping Hand!

Quest type: Regular

Mossy Yorm's gang terrorizes local villages. You must eliminate it.

Reward: 1,000 gold from the city treasury

Your Reputation with the denizens of Agrion and nearby villages will improve considerably.

I turned to the captured robber. "Who's Mossy Yorm?"

He grinned. "You really wanna know? Take the portal, then."

The kobold's growl reached us from the outside, followed by the neighing of a scared horse and a series of high-pitched screams of pain.

Of course. They couldn't close the portal before they transported all the loot they'd collected from the nearby villages. The gang's lair had to be far enough from here — most likely, in the mountains. Still, somehow the gangsters seemed to always know the location of the guard patrols which allowed them to sneak out before the city guards could join forces and repel an attack.

I had no idea where the portal might take us. We had to do it in two stages. First we'd complete the Helping Hand quest and only then hurry to save my old friend.

I opened the battle chat. "Enea? Change of plans. I need all the orcs and the Elves. I need you to arrange their transfer to the public portal located in the village of Idyll." I forwarded her the data.

"Got it. Sciatant and I are coming too."

"Ah, so you two are buddies now?"

No matter how worried I was about her, it wouldn't be a good idea to chaperone her around too much, denying her all the best (and most dangerous) adventures and basically ruining the game for her. She wouldn't understand. She might even take offence.

"We seem to have some mutual interests," she replied. "Mossy Yorm and his men have been terrorizing the area for over six months now. The Daily News offer a live broadcast of the event, provided we can hold the portal and teleport to Mossy Yorm's lair. Even the Ravens couldn't do that."

"Did they fail the quest?"

"They did. A few members of their assault group did make it to the other side. No one has ever heard from them since."

"Were they players?"

"Yes. Sciatant thinks the admins must have deleted their accounts for some reason."

"I don't think so. If they suspected foul play, they would have deleted the quest and disbanded the NPC gang. What worries me is the illegal communication jammer."

Enea paused. "We'll be with you in ten minutes," she finally reported.

"Why so long?"

"I've called Raoul, Platinus and Togien. Lethmiel is busy working on the clan's logo. We need to send in a combat group of players. No NPCs. Talking of which... Take a look at Arwan, Highr, Davre and the Guards of Gloom. Can you explain why they're not marked as NPCs anymore?"

"You don't mean it!"

"Didn't you notice?"

"No I didn't. But I think I know the answer. Can Sciatant hear us?"

"No. I've blocked his access for the time being."

"Excellent. For all it may concern, they're not NPCs. They're fellow players and legitimate clan members. That's all for now. Hurry up!"

"Lethmiel is asking if he can come too."

"Tell him to forget it. Who's gonna guard the castle — his kitchen boys?"

"He says he might be able to keep the portal open with the help of a few Snow Obsidians provided you have them. He can set the Cargonite Golem to wall-guarding mode."

I had to think fast. "Okay. Tell him he can come."

"Shall I bring Iskandar and Rodrigo?"

"Please. Provided they too wear the clan logo. Hurry up. I'm going in. Time to pay those robbing bastards a visit."

"Alex, don't!"

"Why not?"

"The moment you go in, the portal will close. Just stay put until we arrive."

"Very well. Will do. Hurry!"

CHAPTER EIGHT

E VENTS SEEMED to have taken a fast and unexpected turn.

I left the Guards of Gloom by the mysterious portal and walked outside.

The rain kept drizzling. Three more bodies lay in the dirt: the gangsters' patrol.

"Did you catch the horses?"

Arwan nodded. A born hunter and warrior, he definitely knew what he was doing. He wasn't the kind of guy to make mistakes or overlook things. Had he not tethered the horses, they could have returned to the gangsters without their riders, alarming them to our presence.

I turned to the kobold. "Highr, what're you doing in the middle of the street?"

He promptly dove into the nearest hedge.

The public portal sprang to life, disgorging Iskandar and Rodrigo.

"Come over here!"

They ran up to me. I took a moment to clue them in. "Consider this a one-off job. We can discuss the terms later. Now I want you to set up some protection so that no one can see the portal work."

Iskandar looked intrigued. "Thanks for thinking about us. You can find trouble anywhere, can't you?" he added, grinning, while Rodrigo got busy casting a magic veil on the crossroads. Now no one could see us deploy our assault group.

"This is a city quest. You can't ignore it. They might cut down your Reputation."

"Is that it?"

"I was looking for a friend. They've kidnapped him. Ever heard of a Mossy Yorm?"

"Who hasn't? No one has ever seen the man though. From what I heard, he's a player gone nuts. A complete scumbag. His character is a troll. How low can you sink to play as an ogre?"

"I see. That's why no one has seen him. I remember reading that the Crystal Sphere welcomes all the mythologies, even the most ancient ones."

"What's that got to do with it?"

"What, the Norse myths? Don't you remember that a troll turns to stone when exposed to sunlight? Which means he can only rob people at nighttime and leaves his gangsters to do the job during daylight hours."

"Yeah right," Iskandar sounded skeptical. "I also heard that trolls are stupid. But this one was smart enough to cast a portal! And not just any old portal! From what I heard, using it strips you of your levels."

"Temporarily? Or permanently?"

He shrugged. "No idea. There's no one to ask. No one has been back to tell the tale."

"That's weird," I replied, watching the road. "Players can't die. You can't even keep them in captivity for longer than twenty-four hours."

"Listen, Alexatis. After I saw that arch demon screw up Virgil and Tylor's chars, I'm not sure of anything anymore. But you're right: the legend of a hardcore nutcase player can't be just a groundless rumor. I think someone must have lost their char and decided to make a fresh start. Just a theory."

The arrival of my clan's assault group interrupted our discourse.

* * *

THE CRYSTAL SPHERE is a young world. Here, a thirty-strong squad is a power to be reckoned with. Especially when all of its warriors and archers are clad in cargonite. The unique armor doesn't hinder your movements; it's light so it can be used by a variety of classes. I could see that even our cleric hadn't refused the additional protection of a gorgeous set of armor.

Enea and I had our scaly armor on. Sciatant immediately got to work. Admittedly, he knew what he was doing, using short-range teleports to find the best camera angles for his live broadcast.

The clapping of hooves and the neighing of horses sounded at a distance.

Arwan promptly deployed the archers to their positions. The first quest wasn't a problem. Even a less numerous group of players could have tackled it.

The kobold returned from a recon mission, reporting a group of about twenty riders moving toward us. They were those who'd been left behind to guard the cart piled up with all the loot. In an agricultural backwater a good day's hike away from the nearest city, they definitely felt strong enough to harass helpless villagers. You could tell this wasn't their first time. Their behavior betrayed considerable experience.

Sciatant got restless. Without knowing my plan, he couldn't choose the best camera angle. Finally, he gave up and scurried toward me.

"Could you please give me a hint of what to expect?""

"Nothing really," I replied. "My archers will kill the riders. That's the extent of it."

"That's not good enough!" Sciatant protested. "Can't you punish them using some uncategorized magic? Just think how awesome it's gonna look!"

"Ridiculous, more like."

"Excuse me?"

"It's ridiculous. It's like taking a sledgehammer to crack a nut. I haven't come here to show off. But you can go with us through that portal if you wish. That's going to be an exclusive to end 'em all! Provided Mossy Yorm does exist, of course."

He gulped. Blood drained from his face. "I'm coming," he managed. "Yes, absolutely."

* * *

THE GANG WAS a piece of cake. Predictably, Sciatant cringed: our brief melee definitely wasn't headline material. Our twenty Elven archers made quick work of the robbers, leaving nothing to do for the orcs.

Farmers who'd been cowering in their cottages poured out into the street, showering us with gratitude. This was a typical end to a run-of-the-mill quest for an average group of five to seven players.

"Now!" I said. "The Elves are porting back to the castle. Davre, same applies to your orcs — but you're staying."

We had to act fast before the portal closed. I called up Lethmiel and handed him two fragments of dark matter. I had no Snow Obsidian left. "Will this do?"

"Yes, I think so. With this I might last about five minutes."

"We don't need so much. The moment we cross, you can let the portal close. We have scrolls with Rion Castle's coordinates when we need to port back."

"Alexatis, wait," Sciatant came running. "I understand you can't let me go first. That's normal. But could you please turn the camera on and stream the video to me?"

"Absolutely."

He beamed. "I love your confidence!"

I kept forgetting about this "live coverage" thing. And what if we failed?

We walked back into the tavern. Lethmiel was already sitting on the floor cross-legged, his arms spread wide, clutching a fragment of transformed matter in each hand.

I peered at the portal.

A new system message popped up,

Warning! You're about to enter an advanced-level location.

Please think again. If you're not sure you can do it please turn back.

Warning! The Crystal Sphere administration can't guarantee your character's safety should you decide to enter the portal.

I chuckled. This Mossy Yorm wasn't stupid, whoever he was. Was he trying to scare everyone away — or did he mean to lure them in?

Archibald's marker was still hovering over the portal. My old friend was on the other side — and he seemed to be okay for the time being: the green color of the marker meant he was still alive.

"Kray, Ikhtar, you go in first. Davre, Togien and Highr, you follow. Enea, Arwan and myself after you. Iskandar, Rodrigo, Raoul and Sciatant in the rear."

My decision was based on my group's combat potential. We had no idea where the portal would take us. It could be some cliffbound canyon in which case the two Guards of Gloom could use their Combat Trance ability to mop up

---

any enemy force, clearing a landing zone for the rest of us.

"Cameras on?" Sciatant reminded.

I didn't bother to reply. The battle chat was on, streaming pictures from Kray and Ikhtar's eyeshots directly to me.

In the meantime, Raoul and the wizards had finished casting raid buffs on us. We were ready.

"In we go!"

The two Guards of Gloom disappeared within the portal's iridescent glow.

I had no visuals from them! The portal blocked *all* communications!

"This is outrageous!" Sciatant exclaimed.

The portal flashed again, swallowing the three warriors. Concerned, I turned to Lethmiel. Still maintaining the portal, he was mouthing something, staring unblinkingly at Enea.

A whirl of autumnal leaves rose in her wake, then disappeared, absorbed by her avatar. A new buff — Forest Nymph — added to her stats.

We stepped in. Cold flames enveloped us momentarily, followed by the sound of molten ice drops and the pitter-patter of pebbles showering to the ground.

We stood in a narrow snowed-in mountain gorge.

The zigzagging strip of the sky was barely seen high overhead. The surrounding cliffs oozed water which froze in mid-flow, forming ice clusters which resembled solidified waterfalls.

At a distance, a barely discernible arch marked the entrance to some ancient structure.

Our levels remained intact. The reports of the portal's magic power must have been greatly exaggerated.

We hurried to regroup. Togien raised his shield in front of himself and stepped forward. His battle hammer festooned with lightning made threatening crackling sounds.

Sciatant exited the portal last. Contrary to our expectations, the portal didn't shut down. Apparently, Lethmiel wasn't the only person maintaining it.

I waited, second by excruciating second.

Lethmiel must have already stopped maintaining it.

Silence. The portal was still there.

"We advance slowly," I ordered. Davre, you stay by the portal."

The arch in front was topped by two large statues hewn from white limestone. I had a bad feeling about them. Two humanoid creatures stared at us, their faces cracked, parts of them missing. I couldn't quite make out their features. They had three-digit hands. Their gear looked strange: it was neither armor nor regular clothing. Long snakes arched over their shoulders, reaching from their backs and sinking into their chests. I'd never seen anything like it.

"These are the Founders!" Sciatant exclaimed, visibly shocked.

"Are you sure?" I asked him.

"A hundred percent. There was an ancient temple discovered recently which was preserved better than most. It's packed with statues identical to these."

Walking in formation, we warily approached the arch.

"I can't get the streaming function working," Sciatant complained.

"You can still record it," Togien quipped.

Rodrigo stopped, peering at something. He brushed away a thin layer of snow, revealing a big lump of ice.

A player's avatar was frozen within the ice waterfall. He was emaciated and gearless.

"This is a Raven guy," Rodrigo said softly. "I met him a few times."

Where the hell were we? I checked the map-making app. The main map opened, showing a small island, its precipitous rocky shores surrounded by icebergs.

I tried to scroll the map to the nearest continent but couldn't. The island was surrounded by the Mist of War.

"Look, another player," Raoul's voice broke. "No gear. That's against the rules, isn't it?"

Sciatant ported to a rocky platform above and took a look around. "There're dozens of them here!"

He paused, observing the coastline. "The island is small, surrounded by the ocean. No vegetation... Alexatis! My Agrion bind point is gone!"

"So is mine," Iskandar agreed.

Enea nodded, too.

A new message appeared in my interface,

Your resurrection point is not available.
New Quest Alert: Survival

Brief and totally incomprehensible.

Our group stopped in its tracks. The portal behind us was making crackling noises. The entrance to the mysterious structure gaped before us.

I checked the scrolls. Rion Castle's coordinates had disappeared from them.

The only logical thing to do would be to admit our defeat and go back. However, I could still see Archibald's green marker on my map. He was somewhere within the ancient building.

"Group, return!" I shouted. "I'm staying!"

"But, Alexatis-"

"Do it! The portal is the only way out of here!"

"But what if it shuts down?" Enea exclaimed. "What's gonna happen to you?"

"My Blood Ties ability isn't blocked. I can use it to get back to Rion. You can't. The teleport scrolls are ruined!"

No one moved.

"Go!" I shouted. "Davre! What are you playing at? In you go, *now*!"

Reluctantly the orc walked back to the portal and tried to step into it. An invisible force pushed him back out.

* * *

AFTER A FEW MORE futile attempts to port, it became clear that the island wasn't going to release us easily.

It was cold. Big fluffy snowflakes descended from the sky. We peered at the large transparent ice clusters, discerning players' figures within. So many of them. You could tell that some of them hadn't been on the island that long: the ice didn't cover them completely.

"Do players disappear often in the Crystal Sphere?" I asked Sciatant.

"It can happen," he admitted. "Normally,

the admins apologize and recompense the loss of characters to the players."

"That's not what I asked. Does it happen often?"

"Not that I'm aware of. I only know of two such cases. One was during the recent Spectral Dust farming fever when an Agrion dungeon turned into a trap due to server overload. Players would enter it and disappear without a trace. The second one was the Ravens' recent attempt to complete the Helping Hand quest. They lost five clan members."

"Did they reappear?"

"No idea. I've never heard about this island, either. What are we going to do?"

"We have to go in," I said. "There's no other way. We'll have to pay Mossy Yorm a visit."

Togien entered the structure first and froze, casting watchful glances around him.

We followed him into a long rectangular room. Three holes in the ceiling were casting pillars of daylight onto three small platforms. A petrified troll stood motionless on one of them.

Was it Mossy Yorm?

"Is he going to come alive after sunset?" Enea whispered to me.

"I don't think so. Can you see the moss growing on the stones? It creeps right up his leg. There're no bones lying around. No treasures, no

---

loot."

"So whose gang is it?"

"We'll soon find out."

Warily Togien advanced, walking down the center of the hall. The two Guards of Gloom slid along the walls, shadowlike.

Once we reached the troll, I motioned the raid to stop and tilted my head up to study the statue.

A ladder was leaned to the troll's back. A makeshift plank platform had been rigged up under the hall's ceiling, housing hoists, rusty chains and other machinery.

A primitive but quite clever contraption. If you climbed the ladder and pulled the levers, you could in theory close the hole in the ceiling, shutting down the light. Would the troll come alive then?

"Does the sun ever set here?" Enea asked.

Good question. The moss overgrowing the troll's leg was indeed undamaged. And he could only come back to life in the dark.

"Legends tell of only one place where the sun never leaves its zenith," Kray replied. "It's the Lost Island, the Founders' last refuge. But no one knows where it is."

"Arwan, would you climb up and take up a position there," I said. "And while you're at it, will you please check the mechanisms and see if they still work?"

Effortlessly the Elf began the risky ascent.

"You sure you want to bring Mossy Yorm to life?" Enea whispered anxiously. "You really think it's a good idea?"

"I don't know yet. We need to check, anyway. It's too quiet here. The gang has been active for six months already. This place should be packed with loot."

"Unless it gets sold straight away," Sciatant pointed out.

"By whom — the NPCs?"

"By a player who's made his lair here."

That made sense. It explained a lot of things.

We heard a soft popping sound. Simultaneously, a fireball made of entangled lightning appeared at the far end of the hall.

"The portal's shut down," Davre reported.

This was a no-brainer. The portal's shutdown must have triggered the arrival of the lightning ball. The only thing left to work out was how to reactivate the portal.

Further on, we discovered a few more bodies lying on the floor, robbed naked.

"Why are they all so skinny?" Enea asked.

"The Crystal Sphere pays great attention to detail," Sciatant replied, filming non-stop. "If you want to cast a spell, you have to memorize and actually recite it. And those players who think they can go without food soon notice that their physical energy levels drop and their avatars develop a gaunt expression."

Enea shook her head in surprise. "Why would they do that?"

"To boost the game's economy. Not many players would bother cooking but they still need at least one meal a day. So they buy their food. Now multiply a few silver by the number of registered users, and the result might surprise you."

"Does that mean that these are the avatars of players who just dumped them here when they realized they couldn't get out?"

"Apparently," Sciatant agreed. "Can't see any other explanation."

"This location is glitchy," Togien grumbled.

"No, it's not," Sciatant replied. "Locations like this one do exist. Whoever manages to complete them without dying receives something truly special."

"I think someone has already done it," I said. "So now they're using their new advantages."

"Doing what?"

"Luring players here and robbing them."

"Why would he need the Mossy Yorm story, then?"

"To draw more players to the place by triggering quest generation. Whoever tried to complete the "gangster quest" consequently lost their chars. But if the player skulking within this location has already completed it himself, it makes it perfectly legitimate. The admins see no reason to interfere."

"No reason?" Enea repeated. "I thought you weren't allowed to kill other players?"

Sciatant smiled. "That depends. Had I been the one who'd discovered this location, my karma would still be positive."

"How would you do that?" Togien chuckled skeptically, casting him a sideways glance.

"I think that his victims died from cold, hunger and desperation," Sciatant replied. "The location's owner visits it, say, once a week to collect the loot. And if one of the trapped players attacks him, then it's self-defense, isn't it?"

"That's awful," Enea said. "How can one be so cynical?"

Sciatant shrugged. "We all have our little money-making schemes."

"Has everybody received the Survival quest?" I interrupted him.

"Yeah," Togien grumbled. "Question is, how do you want us to do it? The only enemy I can see is the stone troll. Any ideas why they would need this machinery for his activation?"

"I'd say it's in case the portal lets in a large group like ours," Iskandar suggested. "We can last a week, can't we? I always have some food and elixirs on me. We can also use spells to start a fire."

I really wasn't looking forward to the prospect of spending a week or two away from the castle, unable to handle any potential emergencies. Also, Enea's and my authenticity levels could become a problem.

"Excuse me!" Togien protested. "I'm not spending a week stuck behind the console waiting for that scumbag to come and collect his loot!"

"You have other options?" Raoul said. "Dude, we're trapped here."

"Let's have a look around first," I said, "and see if we can find my friend. Arwan, are the hoists working?"

"They are but I need someone to help me. You need to turn two levers at once."

"Davre, go and help him. If we need to unpetrify the troll, I'll let you know. In the meantime, I'd like you to block the mechanism somehow to make sure nobody else can use it."

As I spoke, Sciatant was busy filming the emaciated ice-bound bodies with a dramatic running commentary,

"So here we are, trapped on this tiny island

surrounded by icebergs. Still, Alexatis and his beautiful advisor Enea don't lose heart. Our clan leader definitely has more aces up his sleeve!"

Ignoring his pretentious soliloquy, I motioned the others to follow me.

* * *

THE FIRST HALL ended in a corridor cut into the rock.

According to the map, it led to a cave with Archibald's marker hovering over it.

And there he was, my old friend, doing something totally out of character for him. This level-43 warrior was busy bashing a slab of stone with a rusty hammer.

"Hi Arch," I said. "Have you decided to level up Mining?"

He swung round, promptly changing his gear set. Now an armor-clad knight towered before us, clenching a two-handed sword. "Alex! What are you doing here?"

I wasn't surprised he'd recognized me: after all, my avatar was based on my real-life appearance. "Believe it or not, I'm here to rescue you."

"Yeah right! But anyway! Oh man, it's so good to see you!"

He sheathed his sword behind his back,

lifted his visor and scooped me unceremoniously into his steely hug.

"Watch out!" I managed. "You're squashing me!"

The two Guards of Gloom watched us anxiously, ready to leap to my aid.

Archibald had become one with his role. Having released me, he knelt on one knee before Enea, paying tribute to my lady's beauty. Today she looked lovelier than ever, even when she frowned.

I peered at her stats,

+10 to Charm
+10 to Loveliness

This was Lethmiel and his Forest Nymph buff at work!

I decided to stop Arch's ham acting. "You know this is a trap, don't you?"

"Is it?" he asked without taking his eyes off Enea. "Why, what's the problem?"

"We need to talk."

"Wait a sec," he finally focused on my stats. "A *clan leader*? No way! You have a clan?!"

I nodded. "And a castle. These are my clanmates," I introduced Enea and the others to him. "Now tell me how you got here!"

"By pure accident. I was having dinner in

the inn when all of a sudden I heard a terrible noise. All the tables and benches just flew against the walls. When I looked up there was a portal open right in the middle of the room."

"Did you see the robbers come out of it?" Togien interrupted him impatiently.

"Oh no, man. The robbers were hiding in the woods near the village. I'd seen them on my way to the inn but thought I'd deal with them after dinner."

"We saw three dead robbers lying by the portal."

"That's right. They came in from the street, so I killed them. They had a cheek, really!"

"Did you see anybody else enter the portal?"

"Don't remember seeing anyone. But I did. I was curious. All communications cut off straight away. I really didn't notice. I was too busy walking around this place. I saw the frozen bodies and the two Founder statues. Then I knew it. The fake dead bodies didn't bother me. It takes more than that to freak *me* out. But the entrance... You know I like to do a bit of reading when I can't sleep at night? These days I study *The Crystal Sphere and Its Mythology* — highly entertaining! Quite an eye-opener, too. It was written by the scriptwriters — which means there's a location for every legend mentioned in it."

"So where do you think we are?"

"This is the Temple of Oblivion on the Lost Island," Archibald replied confidently.

"And what's under that slab of stone?"

"Treasures like you can't imagine, man!"

"I see. Now listen to me. The frozen bodies you saw are the actual players' avatars. There's no way back from here. The portal has closed. This is hardcore, man. A no-respawn location. You have any supplies on you?"

"A couple of health elixirs and a bit of bread."

"That's exactly the kind of player this trap targets. How long do you think you can last without food?"

"Don't know. I never tried. From what I heard, five days is tops. After that, strength, agility and stamina drop to critical. Also, old wounds might begin to bleed."

"We'd better start thinking about how to get out of here," I said.

The Old Friend quest was still active. I might have found Archibald but we still had to survive.

"The place is empty," Togien said. "No artifacts, nothing. Whoever those bastards are, they still have to reactivate the portal and control it somehow. What if there are indeed treasures hidden under this stone?"

"Archibald, could you please tell us more about this Temple?" Enea asked. "We can't access the Wiki. You're our only hope."

"There's a legend," Archibald eagerly began, "which says that when the Founder Gods got fed up with their new creation, many of them left the Crystal Sphere, weakening the pantheon. That's when the powers of Light and Dark came into being, giving rise to new religions. The Founders didn't interfere. Gradually, their control over this world began to dwindle. Still, the ancient artifacts preserved their original powers. People began hunting for them, starting wars and destroying whole cities, razing temples and great citadels to the ground. Their incompetent use of the artifacts led to the portal system malfunctions. That's when our world broke down into isolated regions and fell into degradation. No one has seen the Founders ever since. According to the legend, they took their last refuge in the Temple of Oblivion on the Lost Island where time is slowed down. One day spent here is equal to several years. Did you notice that the sun barely moves in the sky? According to another legend, when the sun finally begins to decline over the Lost Island, it will usher the fall of all our civilizations, inviting the Era of Black Sun: the millennia of never-ending cold and darkness."

Togien shivered.

"This is a nice legend," Enea said, having listened to Archibald's story. "I'm sure it has some grains of truth to it. I especially like the idea of a different time flow. We can't leave the castle unsupervised. The sooner we get out of here the better."

"How about the treasure?" Togien asked.

"We need to find a way out first. We can always come back for that later."

"I don't think so!" Raoul exclaimed. "If this is indeed a unique Founder location, we might not be able to come back. Don't you realize how lucky we are? Normally, to get to a location like this, you need to complete dozens if not hundreds of quest chains!"

"So how can you explain it?" Enea asked, busy thinking about something.

"Easy!" Raoul said. "Some lucky player must have got here by accident. He smoked the troll and discovered one of the Founders' last teleports. He probably even had no idea of all these legends and things. He decided to use the opportunity by making agreements with some of the local gangs, then porting there. The gangs would rob villages pretending they arrived by portal; the local authorities would alert everyone and issue quests targeting the mysterious portal. Whoever accepts the quest will end up here, losing all their gear which costs a lot of money these days."

"Sounds logical," I agreed. "I suggest we accept it as a working theory."

"To tell you the truth, this Black Sun legend is common among many of the Crystal Sphere nations," Togien said.

"This is true," the two Guards of Gloom agreed.

"We'll deal with all the legends at some later date," I said firmly. "What's really important is the fact that someone's already managed to work out how to control the portal. Which means we can do it, too."

"This troll must be here for a reason," Togien said. "I suggest we bring him back to life and smoke him."

I opened the group chat. "Arwan, I'd like you to take a good look at the hole in the ceiling. What can you tell me about it?"

"It's been made using magic, that's for sure," the Elf replied. "The edges are smooth as if molten by fire."

"And what can you say about the hoists and other machinery?"

"They look pretty new. The chains are rusty though."

"Very well. Keep your eyes peeled," I turned to the group. "Did you hear that?"

"Does that mean that our 'lucky player' is a wizard?"

"Most likely. A quite advanced one, too. He needed some powerful spells to cut a hole in the rock and expose the troll to the sunlight."

"He didn't do it straight away," Archibald said. "Did you see there were three holes?"

"My point entirely," Togien grumbled. "We need to bring the troll back to life and smoke him. He must be the location boss. He's sure to drop some unique item or other. Wonder if that might be the key to the portal?"

Enea laughed. The cold hadn't dampened her optimism. "Guys, you're so predictable. You just don't miss a chance to rattle your sabers, do you?"

Togien frowned. "What do *you* suggest?"

"I suggest we speak to him."

"Trolls are too dumb."

"Well, a troll who lives in a Founders temple just might happen to be special," Enea insisted.

Archibald looked interested. "How do you want to talk to him?"

She flashed him an enigmatic smile. "I have an idea. Should we go and see if it works?"

I nodded. We weren't in a hurry to study the lightning ball or try and break the slab of stone supposedly concealing the treasure. Based on my previous gaming experience, I could safely say that not every mob should be slaughtered on sight. Some unique locations harbored quest NPCs which might make you regret attacking them before having spoken to them.

❋ ❋ ❋

THE PETRIFIED TROLL looked menacing. The club he was clutching in his hands must have weighed a good 250 pounds.

If he attacked us, smoking him would be a problem. I told everyone to take up their combat positions just in case.

In the meantime, Enea was busy discussing something with Davre and Arwan. Both nodded and reached for the hoist handles.

"On your guard!" I commanded. "If he aggroes us, we kill him!"

The rusty machinery creaked, pulling the chains taut. The plank platform shifted slightly toward the hole in the ceiling, casting a shadow over the troll's face and his weapon arm.

"Enough!" Enea commanded.

Archibald and I were flanking her, ready to cover her with our shields and take a blow should things go wrong.

The troll's face erupted in a web of fine cracks. Stone dust showered to the floor. His eyelids quivered.

Mossy Yorm opened his eyes. He tried to straighten his back — and failed: the rest of his body was still entrapped by the sunlight.

The ancient walls shuddered with his angry roar.

Enea stepped fearlessly toward him, "Hello, Mossy Yorm!"

"Who is it?" the troll growled, struggling to move. His gaze searched for Enea. Raising clouds of dust, he forced his hand to move — but before he could raise his club, his stare softened. "Hello to you too, Forest Nymph!"

"I'd like to talk to you, that's all. We won't hurt you."

The troll attempted to move his head to look around him as far as his stiff neck allowed. A cloud of mist escaped his jaws. His eyebrows were dusted with frost. "Yorm is cold... He's freezing."

"We'll start a fire in a minute. But look," Enea pointed at an old fire site surrounded by a circle of rocks, "there's no wood around here. How did you manage to keep the fire going? Also, isn't firelight harmful to you the way the sunlight is?"

"The wood?" he frowned, trying to remember. "Yorm used to go to the forest. The old, dead forest. Yorm took big trees. He broke them and put them on the fire. The fire is warm. It's good and kind. Are you frozen too? Forest Nymphs don't like cold."

"How did you get to that dead forest?"

"Yorm used this," he tried to turn around but couldn't. "I can't remember. Yorm took this thing... It's hot and round."

"Do you mean this?" Enea signaled to Iskandar who promptly cast Levitation, lifting the lightning ball and moving it within the troll's line of vision.

"Yes!" he roared, relieved. "Yorm used this! Yorm took this in his hands and thought about the forest!"

"Is it so easy? You think I could do it?"

"It's hot," the troll warned her. "You need the glove. A bad wizard found Yorm in the dead forest. He followed Yorm and stole the glove from him."

"Do you know where he hides it?"

"The bad wizard is hiding in the treasury. Set me free, O Forest Nymph, so I can break his head!"

"Do you promise not to hurt my friends?"

"Oh, you beautiful, delicate Nymph! Yorm isn't angry with you! Yorm is angry with the wizard! Yorm was having an afternoon nap when the bad wizard sneaked in here. He let the sunlight into Yorm's cozy dark cave!"

"And if we get rid of the light, will you help us defeat the bad wizard?"

"Oh, yes!" the troll rolled his eyes in his sockets. "Yorm doesn't want to be a rock anymore! Yorm's blood is cold!"

"How did you get here?" Enea asked.

I could see that she was taking the chance to find out more about the location. Admittedly, she was good at it. Then again, Lethmiel's Forest Nymph buff must have played its part in it too.

"Yorm has always been here!" the troll growled. "The God gave him the glove and told him to guard his treasure! The God told Yorm how to find food and firewood. He wanted Yorm to be warm and happy!"

"The God? Founder God? Will he be back, do you know?"

"Yorm doesn't know. The God has been away a while. Set me free, O Nymph! Your friends will be Yorm's friends!"

"Very well. Just please don't forget what you've just promised me."

"Yorm doesn't hurt beautiful nymphs! Yorm's word is stronger than rock! Yorm is hungry! But first Yorm will break the bad wizard's head!"

Enea cast me a questioning look. I nodded.

"Arwan, Davre! Shut off the light!"

Sciatant who'd been hanging about filming

all the while hurried to scamper out of reach and switched to a long shot, running a non-stop commentary,

"This is truly incredible! Enea's charms proved irresistible for the soft-hearted troll! Now we're about to see the revival of this legendary creature that used to know our Founder Gods!"

The sunlight faded.

With a thunderous sigh, Mossy Yorm straightened his back.

Now I could see his stats: his level 100 and the icon of the Skin of Stone buff next to it.

The realization stunned me. What kind of wizard was that, capable of defeating this monster? And what were our chances against him?

"Break my head, you said? Be my guest," a calm, sarcastic voice came from the back of the temple.

* * *

THE WIZARD.

My Twilight Vision ability allowed me to see his stats. Level 102. Name: Scorp.

He didn't look too impressive. He wore some tattered robes with cargonite roundels stitched on them every which way. The Founder's Glove enveloped his right hand in its iridescent aura. In his other hand he held the Staff of Oblivion, very ancient and very intricate.

Yorm growled, indignant. I wanted to shout "Regroup!" and couldn't. The words froze in my throat. Still, my Neuro abilities had already registered an almost-instant casting of a spell,

You've intercepted a spell: Muteness

I couldn't move my lips at all. They felt duct-taped. The troll's growling had stopped, too. None of our wizards had been fast enough to prevent the attack.

The spell seemed to have affected Scorp too. Apparently, there was no resistance against it. His mouth had completely disappeared from his face.

The next moment, his staff cast a Curse of Stone over us.

I became blind and deaf. Now I knew what Mossy Yorm must have felt. My body had turned to stone.

It hurt a lot. It was scary.

The thin stone crust covering my eyes began to crack and crumble. I could see our enemy now. He was walking through our petrified ranks, his lips curved in a disdainful sneer. Yes, I could see his mouth as the 10-sec Muteness had already expired.

He stopped and knocked the tip of his staff on Sciatant's head, removing the fragile stone crust. "Are you filming? Good. You'll be the last to die."

With this promise, he turned to the troll. "What's that now?" he asked him, shaking his head. "What's with all the head-breaking nonsense? You've been standing here nice and quiet, and now what? You think I've been wasting my time in here? I don't need to bash any more holes in the ceiling. I can just pulverize you, you idiot. This glove — it's not just for portal control."

Slowly he ran his gloved hand over Yorm's stone skin, leaving a trail of deep fiery scars.

You've just witnessed the effect of a lost ancient spell.
Name of spell: Disintegration.
Type: Advanced Founders' magic

My interface was still working. This so-called wizard had a problem. Quite a few problems, even. And he was blissfully unaware of them.

Firstly, blanket spells are exactly what they're called: they're flat. Which meant that Arwan and Davre on their plank platform overhead were perfectly safe from the effects of this remarkably strong and long-lasting Curse of

---

Stone.

Secondly, I'd already added Mossy Yorm to our raid. With allied NPCs, you don't need to ask their permission to do so. Which meant that he too was now affected by the aura of my Charm of the Sovereign which improved his resistance while decreasing the duration of the debuff.

Thirdly, we were considerably more numerous.

Unfortunately for him, Scorp knew the exact duration of his spell. He decided to use this time to rub more salt in our wounds.

He stopped by Enea, studying her unmoving features, then raised his gloved hand. "The lady's so beautiful. Would be a shame to kill you. So I won't. I'll just add a few final touches to your pretty face."

His fiery fingers reached out for her.

My blood boiled. The debuff icon disappeared from my interface.

Congratulations! Overcome by emotional pressure, you've successfully deactivated the effects of the Curse of Stone!

You've received +10% to Resistance to all types of magic!

"Leave her alone."

The wizard swung round. He raised his

staff and swept me off my feet in a lazy, negligent motion. That's the power of a level gap for you.

Immediately a fiery arrow sank into the back of his head, compliments of Arwan. Admittedly it dealt the wizard no more damage than a mosquito bite.

Growling, Davre jumped off the platform onto the floor.

I struggled back to my feet.

The wizard watched us sarcastically, playing with his staff as he waited for more desperate moves. He seemed to find it highly amusing.

With another sweep of his staff, he enveloped us in a cloud of silvery haze.

You've been struck by the Staff of Oblivion!
-90% to Strength, Agility, Stamina, Intellect and Spirit.

I'd known that sooner or later I might have to tackle a much stronger enemy. Which is why I'd come prepared.

Weak as a kitten, I struggled to break the seal on the Exorcism scroll I'd made for exactly such an occasion.

The wizard stopped in surprise, duly impressed by the effect. An uncategorized spell that had canceled all his debuffs in one fell sweep! He wasn't happy.

His lips curved in a smirk. "We're strong, aren't we? But you shouldn't think a couple of scrolls can change anything."

"Don't you touch the Nymph!" the unpetrified Yorm swung his club, bringing it down on the wizard's skull. "Don't you dare go near her!"

The troll invested all his fury into his next blow. A stun and a crit! The wizard's hp dropped to zero.

He collapsed to the floor. However, the next moment he sprang back to his feet. His Life bar was already 100% full!

"Everybody, target him!" I shouted. "Raoul, wake up! Keep healing us!"

Yorm took another swing with his club. It hit an empty space as the wizard had already ported out of his reach, targeting Rodrigo and Iskandar as his most dangerous opponents. Now that he knew what the troll was capable of, he wasn't going to repeat his mistake.

His Staff of Oblivion glowed, enveloped in flames. The wizard was definitely good with two-handed weapons. Judging by his pose, he was about to deal a circular blow. Both Rodrigo and Iskandar were doomed.

"Watch out!"

Combat spells might not hurt him. But

passive ones — those that dealt no damage — were bound to work.

I cast Levitation. The wizard lost footing in full swing, shooting up to the ceiling, his fiery staff hitting the rocks overhead and showering us with red-hot stone fragments.

Excellent. "Keep him dangling!"

The wizard wriggled in mid-air, trying to reach for a vial and gulp its contents. He finally dropped to the floor, losing about 10% life.

He had become immune to Levitation.

Shouting something, he lunged at me. The two Guards of Gloom swung their naginatas, aiming for his legs, but their shiny weapons disintegrated, shattered by the magic shield which absorbed the damage.

I managed to dodge the blow. The staff left a glowing scar on a column next to me. Scorp's gloved hand brushed against Yorm's chest, forcing him to recoil. He ported out of Yorm's reach just in time.

Enea loosed a bolt of lightning at him. Another -2% life, excellent. Iskandar and Rodrigo joined her. Between the three of them, they shrank his hp 30%.

The wizard ported again. Archibald's shield exploded in a cascade of fragments like a pane of glass. Raoul promptly cast a heal on him. Archibald rolled over the floor, dodging the touch of the fiery glove.

Three bolts of lightning sank into the wizard simultaneously.

"Alpha, don't!" Enea screamed.

The little black mantis sprang off her shoulder and lunged at the enemy.

No! He'd get himself killed! He was only level 11!

"Yes!" Scorp jeered. "Send them all! Let's have some fun!"

Ignoring the mantis, he ported again and hit Yorm twice real hard.

The troll roared in furious agony. He may have been strong but agility wasn't his forte.

"Come on, let's rock and roll!" the wizard guffawed. He seemed to be enjoying the fight, cock sure of his own invincibility. His life was already back at 100%. He seemed to syphon mana non-stop from some source unknown to me. He had nothing to fear.

By now, Yorm was pretty much useless. The blow from the Founder's Glove had lodged his life firmly in the red. Raoul was trying to heal him but it took too much time. He wasn't strong enough to restore Yorm's health.

I could see where this was all going. Scorp would exhaust us, making us waste all of our mana, then knock us off one by one.

An Ice Spear sank into Yorm's chest. The

troll staggered. He was dying!

I had no choice. I gulped a mana vial and began casting a new spell.

The words escaped my lips in clouds of ashen breath. My chest was frozen inside. As I focused on the wizard, I glimpsed Yorm's bulk sinking slowly to the floor.

Target selected.
Spell selected: Dark Regeneration

The wizard choked on his own sarcastic jeer. He screamed. His eyes seemed to pop out of their sockets.

Because I hadn't attacked him, none of his defenses had worked. This time the ancient uncategorized spell spared me all the gory effects. The wizard's life bar emptied. A bolt of pitch-black lightning escaped his body, hitting the troll.

The wizard's empty robes dropped to the floor. His glove and his staff stopped glowing.

Mossy Yorm's body arched on the floor, convulsing. His life bar filled 50%.

* * *

I COULDN'T STOP shaking. My chest was empty and cold. I faked nonchalance, trying not to betray what the dark spell had just cost me.

"Oh wow," Archibald looked suitably impressed. "You're something, man, I tell you! Why didn't you do that straight away?"

I didn't reply. Enea and Raoul were busy healing me. The use of uncategorized magic depletes your physical, mental and vital energy. No idea whether I'd ever be strong enough to use it without any detrimental damage to myself.

Enea laced her arms around me. "Alex," she looked me in the eye, "Are you all right?"

Her gaze melted the block of ice wedged in my chest. "I'm fine."

Togien walked over to us, casting wary glances at the troll. "Alexatis, that was Dark Regeneration, right? You sure Yorm won't go amok? Did he receive just the wizard's life or also his identity?"

Good question. I just hoped that Scorp's identity had disintegrated. Not because he was so tough that he'd very nearly killed us, oh no. I had no problems with that. He'd put up a good fight. But his business ethic... there I wasn't so sure. The guy definitely had some sociopathic tendencies.

Yorm seemed to be coming round. His health was restoring. There was no malice in his stare. Nothing seemed to have changed in him.

"Do you mind?" I asked him, picking up the staff and the glove. Those were dangerous items that required some serious studying.

"Help yourself," the troll grumbled.

"How are you going to fetch the wood, then?"

"Yorm is ashamed. Yorm let the Gods down. He failed to save the Temple. Yorm will leave."

"You can't leave your post, surely!"

"*You* saved the Temple," he told me in earnest. "This is your job now!"

Enea laughed. "I don't think so. I'm afraid it's still your job. But," she gave him an enigmatic smile, "if you give us the glove you can come to our castle. Do you like the moors?"

Yorm looked interested. "Food?"

"Are you a cannibal?"

"Sometimes," he admitted. "When there's nothing else to eat."

"Have you ever tried hydra meat?"

"No. Is it good?"

"Let's do it this way," I offered. "You can come and catch a few hydras so you can decide whether you like them or not. If you do, you can come at night to get some food and firewood. On one condition. You can't touch human beings! Agreed?"

Yorm nodded. "The treasure!" he suddenly perked up, remembering. "We must go and look!"

It appeared like our unintended but deadly

foray was nearing a happy end.

Three more messages appeared in my interface,

Quest alert: Survival. Quest completed!
You've received a new level!

Quest alert: Old Friend. Quest completed!

* * *

WE TOOK a short rocky tunnel to the cave where we had discovered Archibald to begin with.

The slab of stone he'd been hacking at lay shifted to one side. A weak light escaped from within.

Enea and I walked down the stairs first, stopping in the doorway of what appeared to be a rather small room.

A library.

There were hundreds of ancient books here. That's what the treasure was.

Before leaving, the Founders had used the Temple of Oblivion as a secret stash for their knowledge.

I was probably the only person here who realized the true value of the yellowed manuscripts. The others looked pretty disappointed, even Sciatant.

I took one of the books in my hands, brushed off the centuries-old dust and began leafing through it.

All the entries in it were made in the Founders' language. I couldn't read them.

But if Scorp could do it, so could I.

I closed the book and took a look around the room. Aha. On one of the desks I saw several sheets of parchment, a quill and an inkwell. These must have belonged to Scorp. He must have tried to decipher the ancient writings, in which case...

Enea walked over to me and peered over my shoulder. "What's this you've found now? You're all shaky again. Are you cold?"

"This is the Founders' alphabet," I whispered, struggling to conceal my agitation so as not to attract Sciatant's attention.

"And what are those marks next to the letters?"

"I think it's their phonetic transcription."

"You're right," she admitted. "Did the wizard do that?"

"I don't think so. Look, the ink is the same color. The notes are just as ancient!"

"Wait up. Look, there're more parchments here. A whole stack of them! Look at these words — some of them are already translated! Oh, Alex. This is a *dictionary*. It's not complete but still..."

Quest update alert: The Mystery of The Ancient Manuscripts!

Using the words you already know, enter them into the dictionary, then try to translate several books, filling in the blanks by guessing the meaning of the missing words.

CHAPTER NINE

W E GOT BACK to Rion late the following night.

Lethmiel had been at his wits' ends, desperate to hear from us. I gave him a friendly slap on the shoulder, then told him about the Temple of Oblivion, explaining the different time flow phenomenon.

"Thank you so much for the Forest Nymph buff," Enea gave the old Elf a peck on the cheek. "There was a moment when it actually saved us all!"

"You're worthy of it, my lady," he replied,

impassively courteous.

"I'd like you to meet Archibald," I motioned the warrior to approach. "I just hope he decides to join us."

Iskandar and Rodrigo walked over to us. "We most certainly will," both said unhesitantly. "It would have been stupid to have said 'no' after everything we'd just seen. When and where do we swear in?"

"We're not in a hurry," I said. "Tomorrow we have a trading expedition to see some dwarves. When we have enough new members, then we'll hold the ceremony. I'd like you to join in in the screening of some of the applicants: all the monks, wizards, clerics and sorcerers. Once Sciatant makes his footage public, we can expect a new wave of interest in us. You think you can do that?"

Both looked happy with the task. "Absolutely!"

"Then you should begin interviewing new applicants starting tomorrow morning."

We had so many things that demanded immediate attention!

"Archibald, I'd like you to stay," I said. "Enea and I would like to ask you to head up the clan's combat section. You could start screening all the warrior applicants."

"What, just like that?"

"We don't have much time. You understand, don't you, that we need to capitalize on all the hype. But we can't just accept all and sundry."

He nodded. "Very well. I could stay for a bit, I suppose. I've done this kind of thing before. I can start tomorrow morning. You don't have a room, by any chance, where I could leave my avatar? I have to log out now. I didn't sleep at all last night."

"Lethmiel will show you your room."

The Elf promptly found him some lodgings but wasn't in a hurry to take him there. He lingered expectantly nearby.

"Any news?" I asked him.

"The crystal we built is fully charged. The portal's activated. I didn't dare test it on my own. But you're tired now. Should we leave it till morning?"

"No, let's do it now."

Enea whispered something to her pet. Reluctantly Alpha climbed inside her hood to sulk. Our brave mantis was grounded: his fearless attack on a wizard ninety levels higher than his own could have very easily gotten him killed.

I told the two Guards of Gloom to accompany us. One never knew where the portal might take us.

We ported to the Hall of the Elements, crossed the magic veil and entered the library. It wasn't so empty anymore: whatever books and scrolls we'd already discovered in the castle lay open on the desks.

The portal emitted a steady glow. No idea where it led.

Hadn't we had enough adventures for one day?

With that thought, I stepped onto the stone platform.

Reality rippled around me, submerging me into a soundless darkness. The air was stale here. The strand of a cobweb touched my face.

A dull flash revealed the outlines of a smith's forge, stacks of cargonite bars, several vise benches, a few weapon racks and wooden dummies.

"Light it up," I said.

Lethmiel cast a cold fireball and sent it hovering under the ceiling.

"A smithy?" Enea looked around herself in surprise. "How strange. Why would anyone want to connect a library to a smithy?"

"Probably because the smithy was used by wizards," Lethmiel said, pointing at an ancient manuscript.

I read the title aloud, "*Weapon Enchantment Manual*".

"This is priceless! And here, look," Enea bent down and picked up some loose pages scattered all over the floor, "someone has tried to burn them! Alex, take a look! This is also a manual!"

I peered at the pages. The fragile yellowed scraps of parchment were covered in faded drawings and inscriptions in the Founders' language.

I could understand a few simple words. *Cargonite, metal, fire...* the rest was unintelligible. I saw a few more familiar symbols and tried to read the word... *water*!

"Lethmiel, we need to collect all the pages. Can you do that?"

"Of course. I think they're part of the same book. The pages are numbered."

I bent down and picked up a leather book spine embossed with a single word:

Cargonite

Quest update: The Secret Alloy!
Collect the manuscript pages and show the resulting book to Master Jung.

"I'm afraid we'll have to collect the pages now," I said. "Can you help me?"

Soon we came across the book cover, too. I

took pictures of every page we found, just in case.

"This looks like a guide to cargonite alloys," Lethmiel said, studying the drawings. "Ah, here's Spectral Dust!" he pointed at the picture of a blacksmith pouring some powder into water. "I wonder if they used it to change a hardened metal's properties?"

"I think I know of a blacksmith who might look into it," I said. "But first we need to copy all the pages."

"I'll take care of that," Lethmiel said. "Should we leave the manuscript in the library?"

"Definitely," I said.

Kray came over to us. "Our naginatas are broken, sir. Can we have new ones?"

I looked at the weapon stands. They held five one-handed swords, three halberds and seven naginatas: the exact copies of the ones we'd found in the dungeon.

I saw no reason to say no. Both warriors had proven their worth in battle; both were damn good with polearms. "Sure. Help yourselves."

"Thirty-two pages, according to the page count," Enea set the book cover over the stack of fire-licked sheets. Her voice betrayed the exhaustion of a challenging day. "I think we've found them all."

"That's it, then. Dinner time," I said, drawing a line under the day's adventures.

"Lethmiel, I'd like you to hire a few calligraphers to copy the book. Oh, and will you please cast some spell on the pages to make sure they stay together. I need a copy of the book by tomorrow morning."

* * *

SHAFTS OF MORNING light filled the room.

Enea was still asleep. Gingerly I freed my arm from under her head and got up. I splashed some water on my face, picked up a coffee cup from a tray and walked out onto the balcony. The chef hired by Lethmiel knew what he was doing. Once I'd explained to him what I needed, he'd spent some quality time experimenting with various ingredients until he got the coffee to taste and smell just right.

I looked forward to the new day.

The warm morning breeze felt fresh on my face. A fishermen's boat approached the pier. An Elf squad was guarding three sturdy carts while some workers loaded them with cratefuls of Spectral Dust.

I pulled yesterday's book out of the inventory and began leafing through it. Nice surprise for Master Jurg. Even though we hadn't translated it yet, the drawings themselves were pretty clear: this indeed was a manual on making cargonite alloys.

The air in front of me thickened, forming a thin haze that served as a backdrop for a fiery message,

Dimian the shop owner has arrived.

Lethmiel was true to himself. The guy used every opportunity to practice magic. In this respect, he was very similar to Platinus who'd already made the necessary quantity of Spectral Dust and left for the Toxic Moors, having cadged a squad of orc guards for himself. He'd be gone all day now, farming rare ingredients.

Time to wake Enea up. It was going to be a busy day. I also had an idea about the castle restoration. It was actually Lethmiel's unusual behavior and his passion for ancient magic practices that had given me the thought.

"Hi," I heard.

She was already awake and enjoying this world, taking in her own freedom and our happiness. Like a mischievous little girl, she ignored the doors and microported everywhere in fast, decisive bursts.

Her lips touched mine. "Where's my coffee?"

"On the table. No, please don't port! You'll splash it all over yourself. I'll fetch it."

As if! Before I could blink, she was already back with her coffee, a cheerful glint in her eye. Alpha clung to her shoulder, casting wary glances around. He didn't look happy with all this porting about.

"I want a hug and a story! How's everything going?" he demanded, beaming with joy.

"Dimian's just arrived. He's waiting in the Resurrection Hall. Platinus took the orcs and left for the Moors."

"Did you hear the racket last night?"

"No. What happened?"

"Yorm decided to come and fetch his wood," she laughed. "I had to get up and close the window. The hydras were screaming like you can't imagine."

The clan control tab in my interface blinked. It was Iskandar and Rodrigo logging in. Archibald arrived next.

I opened the voice chat. "Lethmiel, are you ready to receive new applicants?"

"Yes, my lord. There's plenty of food to go around. We've set up camp not far from the ruins of the barbican. Sir Archibald suggested using it as a training ground. He'd like to hold a tournament among the applicants. It can start as early as lunchtime."

"Good," I opened the information tab. Oh wow. We had over three hundred applicants already, impatient to join the fabled Black Mantises. Not bad for a start. "No news about the Moor Goblins' totem?"

"Not yet," Lethmiel replied. "Then again, we've only inspected less than half of the donjon. But we did discover another floor with perfectly intact rooms we can use as dormitories. They're not as big as those of the Disciples but still they're better than tents or inn rooms. Our workers are busy cleaning them up now."

"How many people do you think you can put up there?"

"At least two hundred."

"Excellent! Get on with it. We'll be off to the Azure Mountains in a minute."

Enea sipped her coffee, listening to our conversation. I contacted Archibald,

"Hi, Arch. How do you plan to select new members? What are your rejection criteria?"

"Hi, man. I'm not going to reject anyone."

"So what's this tournament for, then?"

"I want to see what they can do. It'll be an elimination game. Based on the results, I'll form the officer cadre and groups of other ranks. If everything works out as I think it will, you can expect the first Toxic Moor raid within a few days."

"But why do you want to accept everyone?"

"Because those who won't like it will quit

anyway. You'll see. We need to set up a thirty-day trial period. That way we'll have well-knit combat groups in time for the swearing-in ceremony. By the way, we will need perks, the more the better. Not that I'm going to spoil them but we absolutely need to reward those who deserve it. Oh, and one more thing. You need to hire some merchants and change their settings so that they get a better selection and prices than the city shops. Think you can do that?"

"Absolutely," I said. "Today it'll be done."

"Perfect. Keep me posted. Come and see the tournament when you can, both of you. It's a very empowering sight, I tell you."

"I will, but don't expect us before lunchtime."

"Okey dokey."

While I discussed a few last-moment details with Iskandar and Rodrigo, Enea finished her coffee and got dressed. "I'm ready."

"How about breakfast?"

"We can have it downstairs. I'd like to see Dimian. We never discussed the final terms of the deal."

"Okay. That'll give us the chance to take a squint at the applicants. Iskandar and Rodrigo will cast a guest portal in a moment."

"Yes, but how are we going to keep it running?"

"I'll switch it over to the castle's power source."

"In that case, put your arms around me and hold on tight!"

* * *

THE NEXT MOMENT, we found ourselves in the Resurrection Hall.

The brief teleport had taken my breath away. Enea was full of surprises. This was neither a mischievous prank nor her joyful abuse of a brave new world's capabilities: Enea was using every opportunity to level up, purposefully and cool-headedly.

Our arrival remained unnoticed. The hall was now brightly lit and decorated with the clan's logos. The precious stones that studded the ancient wall carvings glinted in the lamplight. The guest portal worked nonstop, disgorging new players. Their reactions were identical: that of shocked amazement. The majestic castle was a far cry from Agrion. The Cargonite Golem rendered them speechless: he stood frozen at the entrance to the inner court, following every visitor with his fiery glare.

As we walked toward Dimian sitting at one of the tables, I noticed a considerable amount of female warriors among the applicants.

"Good morning, Dimian!" Enea gave him a hug.

"It may be good to some but not to me," he replied.

I took a seat opposite him. "Why, what happened?"

"The guild wants a piece of me. They threatened to expel me. Even the gold I paid them didn't help. Too many ill-wishers."

"And if they do expel you, what's gonna happen then?"

"I won't be able to do any trade, will I? I'll have to become a traveling peddler!"

He looked really distraught. He even ignored his food. Enea and I, however, attacked our breakfast with gusto. We were both hungry.

"Does that mean that you can't keep your shop if you're not a guild member?" I asked.

"I'll have no right to," he corrected me.

"What is it they want from you?" Enea asked.

"They want the portal coordinates and a monopoly to the Spectral Dust trade."

"A what?"

"You heard," Dimian helped himself to some wine and took a sip. "They told me to bring all the Spectral Dust to the Guild."

"What kind of price are they offering? Any good?"

"As if!" he made a helpless gesture. "No idea what I'm going to do now."

"Close up shop, pack your goods and move over here," Enea suggested.

"What, just like that?" Dimian hiccupped with anxiety. "Who do I pay the taxes then? And where do I apply for the trade permit?"

"The castle is mine. We're a clan. I decide who can trade here."

"That's all good but... you won't want to have problems with the guild. They might jack up their prices, and then what are you gonna do? You've got one hell of a place here. They'll charge you a fortune for every rusty nail you might need."

"Nails are not a problem," I said. "We can make them here. But you're right: I'm not looking forward to having problems with the guild. Enea? What do you think?"

"I think that Dimian doesn't have any Spectral Dust. *You* do. You're the one trading with the dwarves."

"I knew it!" Dimian groaned. "You've ruined me!"

"Not if you move over here," she repeated. "I'll sort it out with the guild. You'll still be a member. You'll still pay your taxes to them. And as for your loss, we'll have to pay you a compensation, won't we?"

"How much?"

"It's up to you. How much do you need to build a shop here and stock it?"

"You want me to tell you now?"

"Why not? You have the time until we finish our breakfast," Enea gave me an inconspicuous wink. "Would you like to become the clan's official trade representative?"

Dimian turned pale. A clan's trade representative! This was a position that opened lots of doors. "Yes, please," he croaked, forgetting all about compensation.

"In that case, let's do it this way. Go to the second defense level and choose a place for your shop. Then give it a good think. How much money do you need? Do you know of a smart shop assistant? Or are you going to serve customers yourself?"

"I don't think I can. It's not a job for a trade representative."

"Do we have an agreement, then?"

"Will I get another piece of parchment like the one you gave me? I can't remember what it's called now but I do know that I need it."

"We'll write one especially for you, sealed and everything. And all the vendors who might come here in the future will be under your control. Just promise not to charge us too much for rusty nails," she added with a deadpan face.

"I won't, the Gods of Light my witness!"

She turned to me with a mischievous glint in her eye. "Alexatis?"

"Well... I suppose we could make Dimian our trade representative. He can open the first shop in Rion Castle. On one condition. You must promise me to buy your goods at prices slightly higher than those in the city, and sell them slightly cheaper. Think you can do that?"

"Absolutely!" he beamed. "Easy!"

"Then go and find a place for your shop."

"How many floors can I have?"

"Two. You'll have the shop and your office downstairs and your family's personal quarters upstairs."

"But how about my town house?"

"You can keep it. You need to hire a shop assistant to help you in there. We'll use it to sell any surplus rare items."

"What kind of items?"

"Hydra skins. Rare herbs and potions. That sort of thing."

"How about cargonite? In Agrion they say you've got loads here."

"Forget cargonite. It's a strategic resource. None of it is for sale — not at the moment, anyway."

* * *

ENEA AND I finished our breakfast and walked out into the inner court. The flood of new applicants had already thinned out. Now we could hear their voices coming from the barbican beyond the outer wall.

Arwan came running toward us. "All done! All the crates are loaded and fastened. I've checked it myself. Here," he handed me a book. "Lethmiel asked me to give you this."

It was a copy of the manuscript we'd found the night before. I packed it away in my inventory.

Then I gave the carts a thorough check. Everything looked fine.

The two Guards of Gloom were guarding our precious cargo. They were coming with us. We were also taking twenty Elves: archers as well as warriors. Togien had declined my invitation saying he had urgent things to take care of. Still, I had a funny feeling he simply didn't like other dwarves that much.

Iskandar and Rodrigo marched past us, taking a column of wannabe wizards, clerics and sorcerers to the barbican. They must have made an arrangement with Archibald about holding some group fights. Rion Castle was coming back to life. If it continued like this, Enea and I might be back from the Azure Mountains just in time for our first tournament.

"Serry ranks!"

The group teleport scroll I'd made in the Hall of the Elements worked like a dream. The next moment we found ourselves back in the Azure Mountains at the already-familiar rock plateau: a safe location whose coordinates I'd double-checked earlier. We'd reinforced the carts and fitted out the horses' eyes with blinkers to make sure they didn't bolt.

Arwan was in charge of his Elf group. Enea and I took a wary look around, remembering the earlier attack. This time the place looked deserted. The wooded mountain slopes were ablaze with autumnal crimson. The air was cold and clear.

The Elven avant-garde disappeared up ahead. The flank guards took up their positions. I signaled to advance.

Unhurriedly we moved off. The Twin Watch Ravine was literally just around the corner. The dwarves weren't going to meet us: Mychior and I had made an agreement to keep the date and time of the new delivery under wraps.

The two Guards of Gloom in the rear looked around them with a reserved awe. Desert dwellers, they'd never been in the mountains before. The cargonite blades of their naginatas glistened weakly in the frail sunlight.

Aha, there were the long fire streaks by the roadside, followed by the circles of scorched grass and several large boulders cleft by the heat.

Enea took my hand. Our fingers interlaced. I couldn't believe that it had only been a few days since we'd been here, forced to fight an unequal battle. So many things had happened in this last week that it felt like a lifetime.

The stocky figure of Mychior hovered by the entrance to the ravine, pretending he was taking a stroll enjoying the views. Still, I knew he'd come here to meet us. He just couldn't help himself, could he?

"Hi," Enea waved her hand.

I was happy to see him too. I needed to talk to him in private before all hell broke loose.

In the meantime, our caravan had crossed the border of the trade post. Now we were safe. Enea and I lingered at the foot of the giant rock statues.

I shook the dwarf's calloused hand. "Everything okay?"

Mychior nodded. "I received your message. What do you want to talk to me about? What can possibly be more important than this?" his gaze followed the cartfuls of Spectral Dust so precious to the dwarves.

"I need some experienced masons and

stone carvers familiar with Elemental runic sequences."

Mychior squinted at me, nibbling at a blade of grass and casting glances at the cargonite naginatas of the Guards of Gloom. "How experienced?"

"Very. The best you have."

"Sorry, Alexatis. I don't think you have enough gold to pay for their services. No offence. You need Grand Masters."

"Not everything in life can be measured in gold," I said calmly. "There're other values too."

He gave me a condescending grin. "Like what?"

"Like skill. Such a master will get the opportunity to level up while turning his apprentices into a legendary-level group of experts."

He didn't look too surprised. "Rumor has it you've bought an old castle. So what? You can hire some farmers to rebuild its walls. Anyone with a trowel can do that."

"Possible. I'll tell you more: a group of farmers can even kill a monster with pitchforks. But what do they gain from it? Now if the said monster is slain by a lone warrior, the latter might become a legendary hero. See my point? How long has it been since the Grand Masters of your people created a seminal masterpiece?"

He fingered his beard. "I can't remember. Everything worth making has already been made."

"In which case you can give them a message from me. Tell them I know how to get the title of Ultimate Master."

The shock rendered him catatonic.

Finally, he looked up at me, "I need to know who you're interested in."

His tone had changed radically. He must have grasped the situation fully now. These kinds of promises weren't made lightly.

"Explain yourself," I said.

"An Ultimate Master will bring eternal glory to his kinsmen. We have many celebrated dynasties, and each has its own Grand Master."

"It's up to you," I said. "I'm pretty sure they'll pay a lot of money to the middleman who'll grace their house with such an offer. On one condition."

"Say it."

"I need three of them."

"Are you sure? Three Ultimate Masters?"

"Yes. And their apprentices will become masters in their own right."

"Oh. How is it possible? Please, Alexatis. You're not exaggerating, are you? Because if you are, my position as a middleman will cost me very, very dearly."

"It's all right. Let's do it this way. I can take one of the Grand Masters with me so he can get a look at the castle and decide for himself."

"Very well. But it might take a bit of time. You think you can wait until tonight?"

"Sure. Enea and I have other things to do here."

"Agreed. I'll find a Grand Master for you. Just please don't let me down!"

* * *

IT HADN'T TAKEN us long to exchange all the Spectral Dust to gold ingots (which was the agreement I'd made with the dwarves). The dwarves bought it all up in bulk. We didn't even need to unload the carts: there were two cartfuls of painstakingly packed bales of gold waiting for us under the lean-to. All we had to do was unharness the horses and put them in the other carts.

I gave detailed instructions to Arwan, then relieved the Guards of Gloom. Neither Enea nor I needed any bodyguards.

I wrote a quick message to Archibald, apologizing for not being able to make it in time for the tournament. Not today. I also a sent a note to Lethmiel, asking him to prepare quarters for the dwarves.

"That's it," I said, handing Arwan the mass teleport scroll. "Off you go. We should be back by nighttime."

Arwan beamed, proud of his mission. It wasn't every day that he was entrusted with the task of breaking a teleport seal and taking a caravan of gold back to Rion Castle. A mundane job for a human player, this was an honor and big responsibility for an NPC.

Portals started popping, raising swirls of dust.

"That's it," I said when Arwan's marker reappeared on the map. "They're back in the castle. Shall we go and speak to Master Jung?"

Enea smiled. "Why, you want to poach him too?"

I smiled back at her, taking her hand. "I don't think he'll agree. But we can try."

We walked out of the Twin Watch Ravine and followed the winding road lined with boulders for a while, then turned off onto a disused mountain trail.

The day was bright, the skies clear. Fine threads of cobwebs hung in the sun-drenched air. River rapids roared nearby.

The foothill was overgrown with brambles. I could see the lone cliff and the old pine tree on top of which I had landed while laying the tentative route to this part of the world.

Enea set Alpha free for a bit of leveling. The brambles were crawling with petty mobs which could become welcome pray for a level-11 Black Mantis.

"I wonder if Master Jurg could make *him* some armor," I said.

Alpha disappeared in the brambles which soon filled with the sounds of a fight, followed by a stifled scream of some local critter.

"He's still growing. We won't get the size right," Enea replied, drawing me toward the precipitous drop. Together we stood there admiring the river's swift flow as it took its crystalline waters to places yet unknown. "Jeez, it's beautiful."

She could say that. These woods were well and truly untrodden.

I took her in my arms. She laced her arms around my neck. Her lips clung to mine.

We stood there on the very edge of a chasm, unable to draw ourselves apart.

"Let's step back," she finally whispered. "I'm a bit dizzy."

A pine branch shifted, releasing a swift shadow that darted toward us.

A large spotted feline slewed to a halt a few steps away from us.

Mountain Lynx. Level 22

It stared forlornly at us. The word "pet" was gone from its name tag.

"Sarah?" I asked, still unsure.

The lynx walked over to me and rubbed her forehead against my knee. Then she lifted her head. The hopelessness in that gaze was heart-wrenching.

She'd recognized me. But the girl, her owner, where was she? A pet can't get lost, it's against the rules. Had something happened to Kimberly (because that was the name of the young Drow, one of the two I'd met during my first time here), the lynx wouldn't have been able to walk around by herself.

"Have you two met before?" Enea asked, surprised.

"We have. She used to belong to a Drow girl, one of the two that showed me the way to Master Jurg."

The lynx rubbed her body against my leg, then looked up at me, her gaze expectant and anxious.

Enea crouched next to her. "Are you lost, baby?"

Alpha scrambled out of the thorny undergrowth and scurried toward us, ready to defend his owner (he'd made two levels in these last few minutes). Then he reconsidered and stayed hovering in the background, showing a strange affiliation with the lynx.

"Where's your owner?" I asked.

The lynx emitted a short nervous growl and gave us another quizzical look. Then it turned round and trotted away.

"Sarah! Come back!" Enea called.

Reluctantly the lynx stopped and turned her head to us.

"If she's not marked as a pet, does that mean that her owner isn't here anymore?" Enea asked.

"In that case, her pet would have disappeared too."

"She knows her name. She didn't attack us. She recognized you, that's for sure. What can we do?"

"I don't know," I said. "Let's take her with us to see Jurg. He might know the answer."

"That's right! Sarah, come! Come with us!"

Reluctantly the lynx returned, looking expectantly at me as if she knew I was the one without a pet.

"This is weird," I said.

"I agree. Then again, we've seen lots of weird things just lately. Haven't we?"

"We have indeed," I reached down and rubbed the scruff of Sarah's neck. "Let's go, then."

We returned to the trail that led to the

blacksmith's hut. Contrary to our expectations, the lynx followed us at a respectful distance. Alpha too lagged behind, apparently curious about this new addition to our team.

Soon the path began to climb, snaking between the cliffs, until it finally took one last turn and started to descend.

The door of the smithy hung open.

Sarah emitted a nervous sniffle. I drew my sword. Enea cupped her flame-enveloped hands, readying an Inferno.

* * *

WE WALKED in. The place was in a state. It looked completely ransacked. All the chests and drawers were open, all the tools and ingots of metal gone. The fire was long dead, the old embers black and powdered with ash.

No sign of Master Jurg anywhere.

You could say I was upset. So was Enea.

"Let's take a look in the house," she suggested.

We checked every room, with zero results.

"No new quests?" I asked her.

"Nope. He's a quest character, isn't he? He can't just disappear."

I shook my head. "One possible explanation is that there's another quest concerning his disappearance, but we're not part of it."

The book was still in my inventory. I took it out and began leafing through it.

Quest alert: The Secret Alloy! Quest failed!

Oh, great. Clear as mud. *Failed*, just like that.

Bugger!

"Right, let's go," I said.

Alpha and Sarah were waiting for us outside. The former had climbed a nearby cliff and was hunting something. The lynx was basking in the sun, indifferent to everything around her.

"What are we going to do with her?" I asked. "Should we leave her here?"

"I suggest we take her with us," Enea said. "You can see she's not happy without her owner."

"But she's not a pet anymore."

"Does it really matter? You and your rules! Sarah, would you like to come with us?"

With a short nervous growl, the lynx scrambled up. Reluctantly she came over to me and rubbed her forehead against my knees.

"Okay," I stroked her back. "Come along."

* * *

IT WAS ALMOST sunset when we'd finally reached the Twin Watch Ravine.

Four dwarves awaited us by the foot of the giant statues.

"Enea, Alexatis, I'd like you to meet Grand Master Walmord of the Copperbeards, the Architects Clan," Mychior said. "And these are Masters Feligo and Swessbill."

The other three dwarves puffed their chests up. You could tell they belonged to a different ilk: they were slightly shorter and not as burly as Togien but just as dignified, with fiery-red beards braided with copper wire. Their clothes were made of quality leather.

"I'm pleased to meet you," I said. "I'm Alexatis; this is Enea. We're the founders of the Black Mantises Clan."

"We've heard a lot about you," Walmord boomed. "We'd like to see the castle."

As a sign of goodwill, all three made their stats public.

Holy hell! All three were level 170!

"What, just like that?" I said.

"Take us there," the dwarf interrupted me. I could already tell he was quite a handful.

"Very well. We'll discuss all the details once we're there. Come over here and keep as close as you can."

I turned to check on Enea. She grabbed
Sarah by the scruff of her neck. Alpha climbed on
the girl's shoulder and held on tight.

The teleport popped, sweeping us away. For
a brief moment, I didn't know where I was. Then
we were back in the Resurrection Hall of Rion
Castle.

The dwarves began looking around. Their
eyes glinted with genuine interest.

Enea let go of the lynx who immediately
wandered off to investigate the room, with an
indignant sniffle for the two Guards of Gloom.
She also gave Lethmiel a wide berth.

I turned to the dwarves. "We have rooms
ready for you."

"We the mountain folk don't mind the
dark," Walmord grumbled. "Torchlight is good
enough."

"Very well," I agreed, motioning them
toward the portal network.

A brief teleport took us to the outer defense
level where Togien and I had recently found a
runic stone while experimenting with his
Bricklaying skills.

Walmord immediately began inspecting the
stone. The other two followed him everywhere.
Walmord studied the destroyed part of the
parapet, then raised his gaze to take in the

surrounding panorama. With a chuckle, he returned his attention to the stonework.

"What cowboy builder did this?" he pointed at the part of the wall restored by Togien. Not waiting for the answer, he touched the rune cut into the stone and uttered a few words. The rune began to glow.

"These walls are still oozing the ancient magic," Walmord said. "Good. Which means it permeates them completely. Let's see if there's enough force around."

He froze. His gaze filled with a fathomless depth. With a screech, several blocks of stone rose into the air, raising small clouds of dust.

The two Copperbeard masters hurried toward them. In a few expert movements, they lay the stones in the wall and nodded, signaling to Walmord to complete his silent spell.

The wall trembled. A bright glow outlined the freshly-laid stones.

With a blissful smile, the Grand Master squeezed his eyes shut, meditating. When he finally opened his eyes, he pointed at the ruins of the barbican looming in the moonlight. "Take us there!"

"Think you can do it?" I asked Enea softly.

"Sure," she motioned the dwarves to come closer and laid her hands on their shoulders. They disappeared in a flash. I heard a soft popping sound coming from the barbican.

I ported, too.

"Let's have a look! Let's have a look!" Walmord stood cross-armed while his apprentices got busy setting up a system of hoists on the second floor. What a provident bunch. They'd brought everything they needed with them. They were yet to ask me or Enea for anything.

This time Walmord didn't do anything at all, just watched the other two do their jobs. They hooked up an impressive chunk of stone in the hoists, lifted, then placed it where they apparently thought it should belong. Having done that, they raised their torches and began searching for some missing part of the stonework.

They found several which looked like they might fit, then engaged in a heated argument, each defending his choice.

Finally Walmord had enough. "Shut up!" he snapped, then pointed at the one they should use.

The hoists creaked once more. The fragments of stonework screeched against each other as their ragged ends met with a flash. Perfect fit.

I couldn't believe my eyes. This part of the wall was perfectly restored. The repaired block of stone appeared whole: not a trace of the crack left!

The Grand Master looked pleased with his work. He seemed to like it here.

"How much will they charge us for *this*?" Enea whispered.

"I'm gonna find out," I said, climbing the rockfall. "So, Grand Master?"

Walmord bore a hole in me with his cunning frowned glare. The reflection of the torchlight danced in his eyes.

"What do you think?" I insisted. "You've seen the amount of damage. Do you need more time to make up your mind?"

"No, I don't," he said. "We will restore the castle."

"Then there're only your wages to discuss, aren't there?"

He heaved a sigh. I could see his inner struggle as the instinctive dwarven love of gold was wrestling with an equally strong creative impulse. "I could give you the price, I suppose. But I won't do that."

"Why not?"

"You have any idea how the castle was built?"

"Nope. There're no records left."

"The Founders used the power of the Elements," he said confidently. "That's how these walls were erected. Every stone here exudes the ancient magic. I can sense it. Feligo and Swessbill didn't even need my help to restore this part of the wall, and normally, it would be way outside their remit. I wouldn't be surprised if by the time they restored the barbican, both became Grand Masters. This citadel is absolutely permeated by the power of the Earth. But strangely enough, I can't sense any influence of the other three Elements. I wonder why?"

"Because their runic sequences are broken," I said.

The dwarf fingered his beard. "I appreciate your honesty. This is what I suggest: I can bring my whole clan here, to the last apprentice. We'll work until the most useless of them becomes a Master. We won't charge you. All I'm asking for is plenty of good beer as well as some food and lodgings."

"How many are you?"

"A hundred and fifty."

"What kind of lodgings do you need?"

Now it was my turn to fight temptation. If what he'd just said was true, it was actually him paying us for a unique profession-leveling opportunity. Once they'd finished restoring the castle, the Copperbeards could move on erecting new cities and castles, even setting up a proper Clan of their own. That would improve their standing among other dwarves no end. I was sure

Walmord realized that.

"Our requirements are quite modest," he said. "Enough double rooms to accommodate the workers. Their families should receive one gold a day. XP is fine but it doesn't fill the belly. I know what you're thinking," he squinted at me. "A hundred common workers have every chance of becoming Masters if they start shifting magic stones. Am I right?"

"You are," I replied. "But friendship is worth more."

"You're dead right there," the dwarf grinned, pleased with my answer. "Apart from restoring the walls, you'll need stone carvers, right? I have about fifty of those. I wouldn't say they're at the top of their profession, but... think you could hire them?"

Say yes, Enea messaged me.

"Very well," I said. On one condition. I need the donjon to be done first."

Walmord's eyes glinted with triumph. "If you say so."

There I was, standing and wondering whether I'd just made the right decision.

"That's settled, then," I said. "Bring your carvers over. I'll get a hundred double rooms ready."

"In that case, we'll be here tomorrow morning. We'll need a cargo portal to transport all the tools and personal stuff. They'll stay here for quite a while, you know."

"That's not a problem. I'll get a portal ready."

The dwarf offered me his strong hand.

It looked like the restoration of Rion was about to begin for real.

CHAPTER TEN

F INALLY, THINGS were looking up.

The castle bustled with life. We had so many newcomers I physically couldn't remember all the names. The dwarves worked double shifts, giving it their all. Togien and his team didn't leave the dungeons, gradually filling the clan storerooms with cratefuls of Spectral Dust, fragments of transformed matter and heaps of Snow Obsidian: the semi-precious stone which had accumulated the energy of the destroyed Altar of Chaos.

Archibald and Iskandar had formed combat groups which left every morning at daybreak for the moors where they'd discovered several decent farming locations.

Platinus and Raoul seemed to get on really well. I hired some NPC assistants to help them level up their skills. It was fun watching our two alchemists experimenting, creating new elixirs or trying to copy ancient potion recipes.

The donjon was gradually taking shape, looking more and more like the impregnable citadel it had once been. The dwarves worked tirelessly inside as well as outside, some repairing its walls and outer fortifications, others rebuilding the destroyed rooms and halls.

On the surrounding islands, the local fishermen, hunters and farmers were busy exploring and reclaiming new hunting grounds and farmlands.

I had relieved the two Guards of Gloom and the Elf ex-prisoners. They'd been pestering me for quite a while to let them go home and see their families who must have believed them dead. I didn't need them to swear an oath that they'd come back. They had promised to return, anyway, hopefully bringing their families along.

Dimian's new shop became the first structure built on the second defense level. He was doing good business there already while Enea took care of the finer points, representing him in his negotiations with the guild.

These days I spent a lot of time in the Hall

of the Elements as well as in the temple library. As it turned out, we couldn't take a single sheet of parchment out of the library so we had to hire some calligraphers to copy the ancient manuscripts.

To top it all, the Moor Goblins remained a constant threat. We hadn't yet discovered their totem and all attempts at negotiation had so far failed. After the defeat of their fleet by the castle walls, they didn't risk open confrontation but used every opportunity to hurt us in a thousand petty little ways, stealing fishermen's nets, scaring our herbalists or bringing a train of hydras to wreak havoc in the surrounding villages.

I wasn't going to start a war with them, not quite yet. Still, they needed a lesson. At the very least, we had to purge the nearby lands of them to stop them from impinging on our livelihood.

I had so many things to do I didn't even notice the time flying.

Every five days, Enea logged out to have her capsule supplies refilled and do a quick workout in the gym. She never lingered in real life, though, and hurried to return to Rion.

I hadn't seen much of Lethmiel lately: he was too busy running the household and only contacted me about really urgent things. Thanks to him, the castle was running like clockwork, leaving him no spare time at all.

* * *

ENEA LOOKED upset. She'd been like this all day since she'd logged back in: pensive and brooding but not in a hurry to share the bad news.

Enea and I did our best to visit the Practice Hall daily. Normally we went there just before lunchtime when it wasn't busy. Today, too, we were there alone apart from one of the newbs doing a bit of training in the far corner. His name was Astrum, if I remembered rightly. I nodded to him and turned to Enea.

"Today we'll do some shield work," I reached into the weapon stand for a practice sword which dealt virtually no damage.

Enea followed my example. On my sign she picked up a shield. She hadn't equipped the Bracelet of a Metamorph though: at our authenticity levels we had to really work on combat techniques, fine-tuning our reflexes and memorizing the blows and combos.

"Watch your physical energy levels," I said. "If it drops too low, you won't be able to attack and parry."

I tried a couple of lunges which Enea blocked with her shield. Predictably, she was spent.

"This won't do," I said. "Try to dodge my blows. Don't just stand there, keep moving, but always keep your eyes on your opponent."

She seemed to struggle with military skills.

"Let's do it again," I said.

"Sorry. I don't think I'm in the mood."

"Something happened?" I asked, attacking her again.

She dodged the blow. Much better!

"My father called," she said, lowering the shield.

"Did you talk to him?"

"Yeah. He apologized. He asked if he could come and see me."

"What's the problem? You can log out whenever you want."

"You don't understand me. He wants to come *here*. He wants to see the castle."

That rendered me speechless. Still, I quickly regained my composure. After all, why not?

"He can come if he wants," I said. "Although I don't think he'll appreciate the kind of life we live here."

She sighed. "That's the whole problem. He never does anything halfway. That's the way he is. He found out about the implant."

"Was he angry with you?"

"Not really. He just said that he'd ordered

one for himself. Apparently, Infosystems have already launched a limited series of them."

"Wait a sec. Say that again?"

I put the weapons away. Apparently, today's practice wasn't meant to happen.

"He bought an implant identical to mine," Enea repeated, "and had an in-mode capsule installed at his place. Now he wants to come and see us."

"Do you mean he wants to log in to the Crystal Sphere? Like an ordinary user?"

"Yep. He says he wants to see for himself. He's not going to actually *play*. He's not interested in quests or leveling. He just wants to get a taste of it. Do you mind?"

"No, I don't. I'm actually happy to hear that."

"Why?"

"Why do you think? It means he still loves you. Instead of ignoring you and blaming your stubborn character, he actually wants to see what it is that draws you here."

She perked up a little. "You really think so?"

"Of course. One thing I don't understand is how he did it. An implant and a capsule cost a king's ransom. And you can't just walk into a shop and buy them. Not yet, anyway."

"You don't know my father. When he wants

something, he goes for it. Trust me."

"So when is he coming?"

"In a couple of days' time. I didn't know how to tell you. Last time it wasn't very nice, was it?"

"Forget it. It's okay."

"I thought you were still angry with him."

"I was. '*Was*' being the operative word. Can't see why I should be angry with him now. Is he coming on his own?"

"Not really. He never goes out without at least two bodyguards."

"Why? What's the point? If they too register like regular users, they won't be much good to him. Two level-1 bodyguards! They won't be able to defend themselves, let alone anyone else."

"That's just the way he is."

"So that's how he wants it, then? Very well. That's not a problem."

"Why are you laughing?"

"He's just like I used to be. It took me some time to get rid of old habits. It's okay, don't worry. We'll give him a proper welcome. We can show him around the castle, then have a nice meal..."

"You're so cool," Enea gave me a kiss. She touched her Bracelet of a Metamorph, then raised her shield. "Let's get on with it!"

* * *

THE CRYSTAL SPHERE
TWO DAYS LATER

I WAS STILL half-asleep.

Enea awoke. She touched my shoulder gently with her lips so as not to wake me up, slid out of the bed and began getting dressed.

"Morning, sweetheart," I said.

"Oh," she turned to me. "It's still too early."

"Well, you shouldn't get up then, should you?"

The sleepy Alpha swayed on her shoulder, casting sideways glares at me. Last night he'd had to sleep alone in a chair.

"I'm a bit worried," she admitted. "My father knows nothing about the Crystal Sphere. And what with his implant-"

I really didn't feel like getting up but apparently, I had to. I hoped his visit would go without a glitch. Then again, I wasn't too sure. "Would you like me to accompany you to Agrion?"

"You don't need to. I can do it."

"Don't you want breakfast?"

"No. I won't enjoy lunch otherwise. Now, let's see. They arrive at nine. It's seven a.m. now. A bit too early but never mind, I can pop into the guild to sort out a few things... Alex? Why is it so quiet?"

"The dwarves are having a shift handover. Archibald has taken the rest on a Moor raid, don't you remember? There're not many people left in the castle at the moment."

"That's right."

"It'll be okay. Don't worry."

"I can't. I thought Dad had disowned me. And now look," she picked up an apple, bit into it, then laid it uneaten on the table. "I'm off, then. I have too many things to do."

She disappeared in the flash of a teleport.

I got up, equipped my gear and set off to check the guard posts. I just knew I wouldn't be able to do anything serious until they arrived.

I opened the chat. "*Lethmiel, is everything ready for our guests?*"

He took it as a personal offence. "*Absolutely, my lord. The table is laid in the Reception Hall. The stone cutters team finished it last night.*"

Just to give myself something to do, I went there and checked it. A ceremonial escort of several level-100 lancers lined the portal. Two knights towered by the freshly-restored double doors. Hiring all these top-level NPCs had cost me a pretty penny but they looked good. Impressive.

To while away the time, I walked out onto one of the outer fortifications to check on the dwarves' work. They'd already repaired all the breaches up to the level where the runic sequence of Air was supposed to start. Now the lower third of the donjon's walls looked brand new.

We couldn't move any further though as we'd run into a problem. The twelve runes of Air had been all but destroyed. We didn't have a single intact depiction of them. The dwarves had been forced to move on to work on the barbican and the outer walls — at least until we found the missing pictures which their carvers could use to copy the runes onto stone.

I rambled about the castle for a bit, enjoying the unusual silence. A few minutes before the appointed hour, I was back in the Reception hall.

At 9.05 a.m., the portal flashed open.

Out came Enea, alone. She looked pale and distressed. "Alex, they're gone!"

"Wait up. Take a deep breath. Good. Now tell me."

"They're not there! I looked for them. Some people told me about three newbs who logged in about half past eight. Their descriptions seem to fit."

"And? Where do you think they went?"

"I've no idea! They're marked as 'online'! I tried to contact them but their messaging is blocked!"

"Are they on your friend list?"

"Of course!"

"I want you to give me their coordinates. Do you remember how you once found me by checking your friend list?"

"Of course! Wait! So stupid of me!"

Three emerald dots lit up on my map, overlapping each other. Oh. Quite a hike. The Savage Lands, of all places. "Enea, I think they've been kidnapped."

"No! Why? How? Nobody knew!"

"I know, I know. Just give me a minute."

I activated several map-making apps at once. My Celebrated Pioneer status gave me access to some plugins which allowed me to locate both friends and incoming calls.

I changed the map mode to Local View. A moment later, a sketchy picture appeared, depicting a lopsided old hut sitting amid a forest glade next to a half-rotten barn and a crumbling water well.

A nice secluded place.

I contacted Archibald. "*I want you to hand over command to Iskandar and port immediately here. Use the scroll I gave you. Take Arwan and Highr with you. Do it!*"

I switched over to Togien,

"*I need you in the Resurrection hall, now!*

This is an emergency!"

Now the lab:

"Raoul and Platinus, grab all the combat elixirs you have and come here, quickly!"

It took them less than a minute to arrive. My choice of team was simple: these were those I could trust.

"What's up?" Togien demanded, taking in Enea's tearful eyes.

I explained the situation. "I'm afraid we've got a mole. A double-crosser. And I think I know who he is. We'll sort it out later. Now we need to rescue Enea's father."

"We can't just go there blindly," Archibald said. "We need to collect some intel first."

My interface flashed with an incoming call. I forwarded it to the combat chat for everyone to see and hear.

"This is Alexatis, I presume?" a rogue's avatar appeared in the box.

I wasn't in a hurry to reply. The map-making plugins took time to work.

"Are you dumb or just stupid?" the voice demanded.

His avatar looked vaguely familiar. Where might I have seen him?

"So, noob? Remember me?"

"Not really. Mind giving me a hint?" I said, purposefully provoking him because I'd already remembered who it was. Sarcastic nonchalance was the best tool against the likes of him.

"Shut your mouth, noob," he said, gulping non-stop. "We've got your noobs here."

Noob seemed to be his expletive of choice.

"I remember you," I said. "And your PK friends, too. How did you like our debuff? Or should I say, how did the mobs like you?"[2]

"You piece of-" he choked on his fury. "We're gonna cut them up and mail the bits to you!"

"Cut what up, their avatars? Please. The fact that their prisoner status prevents them from logging out doesn't mean anything."

"Oh yes it does! One of them is an old fart who used some artsy technology to log in. See, I know a few things about them. If I take my sword and poke him in the heart a few times, you really think he'll survive it back in real life?"

Enea turned pale as a sheet.

"Quit your bullshit," I said. "What is it you want?"

His face twisted with rage. It took him some time to get his wits together.

"Okay. If you're so smart, listen up. I offer a swap. I want those two dwarves who cast the debuff on us. You give them to me and I'll release

[2] Alexatis refers to the events described in The Crystal Sphere (The Neuro Book #1)

one of the three."

"How about the other two?"

"I could swap them for some cargonite. Say, two hundred pounds each? Good enough?"

"I think so. When do you want it?"

"Scared, aren't we? Good. You shouldn't mess with me, noob. You have sixty minutes. And time starts... now!"

"Not good. Not enough time to find the dwarves. Would you rather accept cargonite?"

"No, I wouldn't. That's your problem. Sixty minutes!"

The picture changed. Now I was looking at a well-equipped top-level orc:

"Don't you play no dirty tricks," he warned me. "If you file a complaint, we'll raze your castle to the ground. Is that clear?"

"Raze my castle to the ground, really? Now who might do that? Not you, surely?"

"Don't you get smart with me! Or I might come for real. Your moors won't stop me. There's no such thing as an undoable location. I want you to remember that. If you grass us up, you're toast."

* * *

TEARS WELLED in Enea's eyes. "Who are they?"

"Just some PKs. Togien and I crossed paths

with them in the past. The call was coming from the Ravens' castle. From what I heard, they took it from the Ravens during a recent raid."

"How do you know?" Archibald asked.

"I have a Celebrated Pioneer achievement and a map-making app that comes with it."

"We can't storm a castle," Togien mumbled.

"No. But the prisoners aren't there, anyway."

Enea began to shake.

"Get a grip," I told her. "In a few minutes, I'll need you as a team member. They're not gonna hurt him, trust me. They won't have time. The PKs may have buddied up with the Ravens but they know nothing about the teleport scrolls we have. They have no idea what I can do."

Archibald frowned. I could see the situation was out of his grasp. "How do you want to deal with them?"

"We keep the admins out of it. We can do it."

"Alex, are you sure?"

"This has nothing to do with the admins! Hostage taking is part of the gameplay. The PKs know it. Togien, I want you to find Gwain. I'll give him access in a moment. He needs to lie low for a while."

"Thanks. Will do."

"Why, what's the big deal?" Archibald

looked at us. "Don't you think you're going a bit over the top? What kind of threat is that? A bit of sword-tickling, so what? Enea, you don't need to be so upset! All your father needs to do is get up and walk away from the console."

I didn't have the time to tell him how neural implants worked. I had to limit myself to half-truths. "Enea's father uses one of those new-generation capsules. They're fitted with sensory gel responsible for the authenticity of the experience. Trust me, it'll hurt enough. I'm afraid, an emergency rescue mission is our only option. Thanks to my friend list and my map-making app, we know the prisoners' exact coordinates. We'll use a scroll to port there."

"Sounds good," Togien agreed. "It's not as if we're going to storm the Ravens' castle. I just wish we knew where we might land," he added, apparently remembering our first clumsy attempt to port to Rion.

I waved my hand, materializing a crystal screen, then forwarded the image to it.

Archibald studied the picture. "I see. I'm pretty sure they keep the prisoners in the hut. It's easier to defend. I'd say the PKs are about ten in total. There isn't enough place for them in the hut," he placed a few markers. "I'd say, two are inside, the rest are outside."

"How about the barn?" Platinus asked.

"It has no windows, does it? How are you going to survey the area? I don't think we're dealing with brainless dorks. I'm pretty sure they're outside and they keep their eyes peeled. It might take an hour or so for them to finally relax around the campfire."

"We don't have the time!" Enea cried out.

"Wait. This is the best-case scenario. There's another one which is also quite probable. Presuming the Ravens have indeed buddied up with some PKs and have even had the audacity to do some newb hunting, they must have had a very serious reason to do so. Two hundred pounds of cargonite sounds good, of course, now that people start to realize its value, but still gold is much more popular. And real-world money is even better because that way you don't risk exposing yourself by converting it. Alex, I don't think you're telling us everything. I can bet anything you want that the Ravens have their best warriors posted by that hut. The PKs with their stupid claims are only a smoke screen. In which case I just don't know what they want from us," he squinted at me. "What is it I don't know? Tell me."

Togien and I exchanged glances. The dwarf gave me a reluctant nod.

It looked like I might have to tell him about Gwain and his Humble Bow ability. Archibald was right: risking the admins' wrath just to lay their hands on some cargonite was a bit stupid. The PKs must have told the Ravens about Gwain's unique ability. So they wanted Gwain, then: getting hold of the monk was worth any amount of risk.

I gave everybody a quick rundown of the Ravens' possible motive.

"In which case they're anything but idiots," Archibald concluded. "They must have top players there. We can't go there blindly."

"What do you suggest?"

"I'll go there."

"What's the point?"

"The point is, we'll get some logs and screenshots. I'll need some gear. I'm not risking mine."

"Archibald, you don't have to do it!" Enea exclaimed.

"It's all right. As long as they don't cast control on me, I'll be okay. If I don't get killed soon, you'll have to play it by ear, I'm afraid."

Arwan stepped forward. "I have a better idea. I'll go instead."

"Sorry, man," Archibald said. "You can't do much against their top players. You'll be dead before you even know it."

"That's if I port directly to the clearing. Take a look," the Elf pointed at the map. "You see this small glade nearby? If I port there, no one will notice. I'll climb the tree and feed you the intel. Once you're there, I can cover you."

I paused, thinking. A sniper lurking in a tree! It sounded tempting.

I had to decide fast. "Right. You both can go. Arwan, you climb the tree and keep quiet. Archibald, you walk out into the opening. Tell them you're a hunter who got lost chasing a rabbit. They'll keep you there. If they cast control on you-"

"They won't. I'll play it rough if needs be. I like your plan. If we port right on top of them, they might get suspicious."

"Here's the scroll. I've entered the coordinates already."

* * *

THEY DISAPPEARED in the flash of a portal.

Time stood still. Archibald had to walk about fifty feet to the hut.

After a minute, he respawned in a green flash, minus weapons and gear.

"They smoked me!" he announced excitedly, hurrying to put on his backup gear. "Fifteen warriors and five wizards. All levels 50+. Don't think we can do it."

"At least we can try!" Enea snapped.

My point entirely. We couldn't wait much longer. I checked Archibald's logs. He'd been right. The enemy was nothing to sniff at. Still, I had a couple of surprises for them, especially for the wizards. With Arwan covering us, we just might rescue the prisoners and port out.

"I'll port us as close to the hut as I can," I said. "Raoul, you do the healing. Platinus, the moment you're there, attack them with Disintegration potions. If the door is locked, bring down its durability. Everybody else, try to distract the warriors while I cast the spell. After that, Archibald and Enea will rescue the prisoners."

"We're too few to tackle them," Archibald grumbled.

"That's exactly what I count on. The Ravens won't think much of us. Enea, take this. This is a backup teleport scroll. If they start smoking us, grab your dad and port him out."

Okay."

"Breaking the hut's door is our main objective. We need to do it fast. Archibald, you've got the biggest job: to barge in and kill the guards. Highr," I gave the kobold a stern look, "you stay out of it and don't budge."

He nodded, playing with his halberd.

"Remember, everyone: we rescue the prisoners and get the hell outta there!" That's it.

Raoul will buff us up now. Off we go!"

* * *

THE LANDING knocked our feet from under us. The coordinate teleport was akin to Russian roulette: it could kill you — but the surprise effect was worth it!

The Raven warriors were posted all around the clearing, controlling its perimeter. The arrival of our group at the center of their cozy little camp dumbfounded them. By the time they realized what had just happened, read our stats and had come up with a strategy, Enea had already struck with Inferno.

The grass caught fire. The moss started to smolder. A small haystack turned into a humming pillar of flames that raised clouds of acrid blue smoke, hindering visibility.

Platinus was busy hurling his vials right, left and center. A thick acid mist hung in the air, devouring the enemy armor's durability. Cussing, the Ravens recoiled. No wonder: their expensive shiny gear began to corrode, their precious clothes were falling apart and even the leather straps holding their armor together started snapping.

The air was blue with expletives and the stomping of feet. An orc with two one-handed swords was the first to lunge at is, taking in the situation as he ran. He went for Highr, probably thinking he'd found our weakest link.

The smoke had prevented the enemy wizards from reacting promptly. They were still lingering in search of a good position. Only one of them attacked us with SubZero, sending cascades of ice crystals to extinguish the flames.

The grass around us wilted, breathing steam. The spell crashed into our raid buff — all it did was nullify our additional defense. But the Aura of a Predator exuded by Enea's staff worked like a dream. It slowed the orc down just as he was about to make mincemeat of Highr, thereby breaching our ranks.

I mouthed a spell.

The ancient magic spread a circular shock wave of energy. The enemy casters froze, enshrouded with Muteness: a powerful debuff which lasted a whole ten seconds. Even more importantly, it affected all types of magic which meant that the enemy wouldn't be able to port the prisoners out.

The hut door cracked under pressure: that was Archibald and Platinus joining in.

Now we only had the warriors to tackle. Some of them were a good 3 or 4 levels above both me and Togien — but we still had more aces up our collective sleeves.

Alpha the Black Mantis flitted up Enea's shoulder and buried his sting in a Raven warrior's face. The warrior screamed and stumbled to the ground, dropping his weapons. His eyes glazed over with the bumper dose of the neurotoxin he'd just received. Alpha soared in the air, looking for a new target.

The orc did get to Highr, after all. He lunged onto the kobold, breaching his defense and halving his hp.

By then, Archibald had already barged into the hut and engaged with the two guards. Togien's battle hammer surging with lightning broke his opponent's shield, stunning him.

Raoul was busy healing the kobold. I blocked a combo and looked around me, searching for the Muteness-affected enemy wizards. Too late: Arwan had already smoked all five.

Excellent.

The spell expired. My interface blinked with the reactivated magic abilities icon.

Out of the corner of my eye I noticed Enea launch an Ice Spear. One of the warriors attacking Archibald staggered. A crit!

I lunged at another one, killed him, then rolled over the ground to get to yet another: a level-49 Paladin. His armor was in a bad way, its durability seriously affected by the Disintegration

Potion.

The crystals on my sword's hilt glowed, emitting a purple aura. I concentrated, activating one of them. The accumulated mental energy poured down the blade, activating the runes. I invested all my strength into a slashing blow impregnated with Mortal Allegiance. Still, the Paladin escaped unharmed, saved by a promptly cast Impregnability.

I activated another crystal. This enemy was too dangerous. I had to finish him off while his cooldown lasted. I promptly attacked the paladin with a combo, disrupting his healing attempt.

Everything was happening too fast. Three more warriors were running toward us from the opposite side of the clearing, right into Arwan's sights. The Elf began loosing off arrows at a frightening speed until his targets resembled porcupines. Their lives dropped dangerously low. Doubtful they'd ever reach us.

Another arrow landed in the paladin's shoulder. A crit! I shrank back a couple of paces to catch my breath.

Roaring, the orc lunged at me. Our swords met. I managed to parry his first blow but not the second one. Blood gushed from my slashed wrist. My mouth went dry. My heart raced.

Arrows kept coursing through the air. Arwan was doing his best. In the absence of a healer, two more Raven warriors died on the spot.

"Alex, we're done!" Archibald yelled.

My back felt the heat behind me. The hut was ablaze.

"Enea, port us out!" I croaked, struggling to fend off two more enemies. Despite Raoul's best efforts, my life kept dropping. I activated the last of the three crystals and went for the orc. He staggered and dropped to his knees. Still, the aura cast by the paladin prevented him from dying.

Very soon they'd overpower us.

"Serry ranks! Closer!" judging by the accompanying sounds, Enea had to enforce her order with a few hearty punches. "Good! Alex, Togien, back off!"

We retreated.

Arwan would have to fend for himself. He might have to get himself killed to get out. Still, there was no other way.

The teleport flashed open.

Rescue mission completed!

* * *

AT FIRST, none of us said a word.

We gasped. Our clothes and armor were soaked in blood. The game designers hadn't skimped on that particular feature.

So this was Mr. Friedrich White, then. The one who'd once done a fine job trying to "apply pressure" on me with the help from some high-level NPCs. *Infuriated* was the right word to describe him. He had a black eye; his hands were chained, his life halved, his lips smashed. His two bodyguards looked a sight, too.

"Raoul, would you please give our guests a heal and cast a Breaking of Shackles," I said, trying to sound as polite and hospitable as the circumstances allowed. "Gentlemen, please don't mind the blood. It'll disappear in a few moments. I have clean clothes for you to change into, if you wish."

"What the hell was that?" Mr. White demanded, furious.

"I'd say it was hostage taking for ransom. Which in prospective might have escalated to a new war, I suppose. We've just rescued you from the Ravens clan — currently the strongest and most powerful in the Crystal Sphere."

"How dared you let it happen!" Mr. White accused me.

Enea looked uncomfortable. "Dad! Please. I need a word with you. Sorry, Alex. We won't be a moment."

"That's okay," I said.

The respawn area flashed green, releasing Arwan. Without his gear he looked feeble. You wouldn't have thought this guy was capable of loosing off two arrows per second. I checked his stats. He'd gained three levels, excellent. He deserved it, too.

Not at all embarrassed, he waved his hand to us and hurried off to get his backup gear.

"Alex," Mr. White walked back to us, "I'm sorry for being so harsh," he proffered me his hand. "Can we try again?"

I didn't play hard to get. With a wink to Enea, I returned his handshake. "Let's go, then. I'd like you to see the castle. We can discuss everything at breakfast."

His two bodyguards — nicknamed Ylien and Stevenal — kept a low profile. Both looked around them with curiosity but refrained from asking any questions.

* * *

THE CASTLE had left a crushing and conflicting impression on our guests.

I could understand them. It can't be easy, stepping out of the 22nd century technosphere into the Dark Ages steeped in magic. The sheer realism of the experience provided by the neuroimplants must have affected them deeply. Besides, you could tell that Enea's dad was the VIP type not really used to having his ass kicked.

Judging by the state of his bloodied face, his kidnappers didn't make concessions for his untouchable standing.

All that porting up and down using the castle's portal system had given Stevenal a serious bout of motion sickness. Pale, he pressed his hand to his mouth and rushed out onto the open fortification platform. After a while he was back, looking subdued and embarrassed.

"Please come in," I swung open the doors of a room restored specially for this purpose.

Everybody took their places at the table. I pulled a heavy chair up for Enea. "It's gonna be okay," I whispered.

She gave me a barely perceptible nod.

"So," I raised my goblet. "Let's skip the niceties and talk like grown-up people. I have a few questions to ask you. Do you mind?"

Enea's father took a cautious sip of his wine and raised an eyebrow in surprise. The Tipsiness icon appeared in his name tag, detracting 1 pt. from both Agility and Intellect and giving him a Strength buff.

Ylien took a bite of his bread roll. "It's good," he said, watching in amazement as his health bar started filling and the shackle wounds on his wrists began to heal.

"My first question is, why did you have to take the risk, putting all our lives in danger?" I struggled to be polite, the combat adrenaline still coursing my veins. "A father worried about his daughter, I can buy that. But all this unnecessary character creating and neuroimplant capsule hiring sets my alarm bells ringing, to tell you the truth. What's wrong with a generic avatar on a white charger and an escort of top-level NPCs?" I asked, unable to resist alluding to our previous meeting.

"I wanted to see for myself," Mr. White leaned leisurely back in his chair. Still, his pompous bravado couldn't fool me. His cheek was twitching. The black eye may have disappeared but the memories were still there, competing for his attention. "I just couldn't work out what made her do it," he continued dryly. "Besides, there were quite a few red flags in the way the Infosystems management behaved just lately. So I decided to see for myself."

That came as a surprise. "Are you involved with the gaming industry?"

"Didn't you know?"

"No, I didn't."

Mr. White cast a reproachful glance at his daughter. "Stephen, you tell him."

Stevenal put his fork down. "What do you know of TransEnergy?" he asked me.

"A leading brand," I said. "They produce solar power batteries, don't they?"

"That's right. We had a standing contract with Infosystems..."

I choked. "Wait a sec. You work for TransEnergy?"

"I'm their head analyst," Stephen replied. "Ylien is our security chief. Mr. White is the owner."

Enea caught my eye and gave an inconspicuous shrug.

I took it well, even if I say so myself. I even smiled back. Virtual reality is rich in surprises. You take a walk by a pond in some local backwater, and the girl you meet there just happens to be the heiress to a financial empire.

"Recently we started having problems with them," Stephen continued. "The energy cells we produce are highly effective, reliable and low-maintenance. But for some reason, Infosystems have stopped buying them. They'd rather develop their own sources of power by using subterranean heat whose efficiency factor is known to be extremely low. At the same time they announced the advent of the so-called 'new digital era', advertising their neural implants and predicting that humanity is just one step away from moving over to cyberspace where they'll be able to work and live their lives to the full."

"Does that mean they're about to launch mass production of the implants?"

"Exactly," Mr. White replied. "And that's what worries me. I'm a down-to-earth person. I don't take anyone on their word. Infosystems have built the Crystal Sphere capable of receiving billions of simultaneous users. Recently they've had quite a few inexplicable technological breakthroughs. And now they're putting virtual property up for sale!"

"So that's why you wanted to see us," Enea's lips quivered. "Business as usual, isn't it? Nothing personal?"

"Enea, please. It's not like that," his voice betrayed fatherly notes. "I could have done it on my own without having to disturb either you or Alex."

Enea pursed her lips. She didn't say anything.

The tension between the father and daughter was so thick the air itself seemed to have electrified.

I decided to defuse the situation. Or maybe draw the proverbial fire on myself, I couldn't really tell. "How can we help you?"

"Excellent wine," Mr. White said, apparently happy with my intervention.

"Thank you. Our alchemist made it. He used his Instant Ageing recipe."

"I know. Enea told me. It's Platinus, right? The unrecognized genius?"

I nodded.

Stevenal perked up, joining the conversation. "How much would you pay for a bottle? Have you patented the recipe?"

"How much? I'd say, ten gold. At least. No, we haven't patented it yet. We didn't have the time. Things happen quickly here."

"Off the top of my head, that's about a million credits per year," Stevenal did a quick calculation of the profits we'd lost.

This felt like the arrival of several hardened sharks to our quiet waters.

"I had no idea what the experience was going to be like," Mr. White cast a quick glance at his daughter. "Now I know. This is a young dog-eat-dog world. I might actually stake a place for myself here. That's not a problem. Just now I have the opportunity to buy a server housing several of the Crystal Sphere's locations."

"Why would you want to do that?" Enea asked.

"To come and visit you, maybe? I'm a bit too old to train as a warrior — or even a wizard. A nice country estate, some trusty guards and a few bottles of *Chateau Rion...*"

For the first time during the conversation, a faint smile touched Enea's lips. "You're not cut out for the quiet life."

"How do you know?" her father's voice

warmed up too. "When everything feels so real, one can't help wondering about retirement. It was probably for the better, you know," he looked up at her again. "I had to get mugged and shackled to get a real feel for it all. I had to see you break down that hut's door. Having said that," he turned to me, "is it true that today's incident might trigger a clan war?"

"It's already started," I gave him a quick update of the situation the way I saw it.

He raised a quizzical eyebrow. "Never thought I might become a bargaining chip," he chuckled. "Are these dwarves so important?"

"Gwain has a unique ability," Enea explained, "which can decide the outcome of a big battle."

"I hope you've already taken care of his safety?" Ylien reacted instantly.

"We have," I said. "He's here in the castle."

"Are you serious about buying part of the Crystal Sphere?" Enea steered the conversation back to the subject which interested her the most.

"Absolutely," her father replied. "Today, I've seen many things in a totally different light. Now I know what Infosystems have to offer to their more affluent customers. People of my generation — those with money and at least an ounce of common sense — are bound to come here. But

I'm not going to interfere with your lives, I promise. I need to ask you about something though," he looked up at me. "Alex, can I have a word with you?"

We walked out onto the outer fortification platform.

"I think it's enough for one day," Mr. White looked around him, taking in the surrounding vista. "Do you think you can defend yourselves from a Ravens' raid?"

"Let them come — if they think they can cross the Moors first."

"Do you know how many clans there are in the Crystal Sphere?"

"Two."

Mr. White gave me a finger. "Two hundred and seventy-five! You didn't hear about them, did you? Once Infosystems connect all the clusters into a single network, then the place will be like a boiling cauldron. Now, let's do it this way. You're Alexatis, the clan leader and the owner of Rion Castle. And they," he nodded at Ylien and Stevenal, "they're your new volunteers. Agreed?"

"How about you?"

"I'm not staying. In any case," he squinted at me, "I have the capsule and the implant. I might come and visit you if you don't mind."

"Please do. We're always happy to see you."

"Promise me to take good care of her. And

yourself. I've seen everything I wanted to."

Mr. White shook my hand and returned to the Reception Hall. He walked over to Enea and gave her an awkward hug, whispering something in her ear.

Then he disappeared. Logged out, leaving me and Enea with two new clan members.

Ylien, level 1. Assassin
Stevenal, Level 1. Wizard

* * *

"HE SAID HE might come back in a couple of weeks," Enea gave me a long look. "Are you angry with me?"

"What, for not telling me who he was? No, not really."

The other two, Ylien and Stevenal, walked out onto the platform. They cast wary looks around themselves, taking in their new world.

"It might take you some time to get used to full immersion," I said. "It can be quite confusing. You'll have your share of blood, sweat and tears. But the opportunities are mind-boggling. A couple of months ago I was just as lost as you are now. Still, I survived."

"The only difference between the real and virtual worlds is the setting," Enea agreed. "All the rest is the same. Same emotions. Same money. I suggest you stay here for a week and try to get a feel for it. Do a bit of reading up. No need to get yourselves involved straight away. Just stick around for a bit, away from real life. Try to forget about it for a while."

"I'd rather get involved," Ylien said. "Steve and I have learned all the theory already. We need some practice now in order to figure out how it really works. We need to level up a bit too."

I liked his attitude. "That's not a problem."

"I'd start by looking into security," he continued. "You've got a mole. The Ravens had known about those dwarves for a while. The op was well thought out. They were waiting for the right moment to apply pressure."

"I think I know who the rat is. Archibald should be dealing with him right now. His nickname is Astrum."

"How sure are you?"

"He was the only one present in the Practice Hall when Enea told me about her father's visit."

"I need to think of some security measures against any leaks," Ylien promised.

"Don't bother. Here," I forwarded him the information about the Oathing Stone. "It's my fault. I should have sworn them in earlier. I thought the oathing ceremony might scare off some of the newbs."

My interface flashed with an incoming PM. I switched over to it. "What's up?"

"Astrum's gone," Archibald reported. "Sneaked away while on the raid with us. He's gonna perish on the moors, that's for sure. I suggest you tighten security by the respawn point. He might be there in a minute."

"I don't think so," I said. "He must have changed his respawn point. In which case he's already back wherever he came from. Continue with the raid as usual. Tell everyone we'll swear them in as soon as you're back. Say we're going to hold an Oathing Stone ceremony."

"Got it. I'll tell them and see if there're any more snoops trying to sneak away for a quick death on the moors."

"What do you want me to do?" Stevenal asked.

"You can start looking through the logs. I'll have all the necessary files for you in a moment. The analyst's job is to know the abilities of all the clan warriors and wizards, to be able to instantly calculate any mob's potential and deliver appropriate recommendations. Your voice in the battle chat should be loud and clear."

"Any non-combat-related activities?"

"The clan analyst is supposed to monitor its business dealings, keep an eye on the market and work out potential development strategies. The analyst decides on the best leveling scenarios for each player or group. For instance, a level-30 warrior has no business farming level-20 mobs which offer him or her no XP. It would be a total waste of time."

"I see. I'll look into it," Stevenal assured me.

A new system message popped up in my interface,

Warning! The Ravens clan has changed their Relationship status regarding your clan!

Current status: Animosity

From now on, all your clan members outside of safe city locations will be subject to the enemy clan's attacks who will receive no PK sanctions for any aggressive actions.

Recommendation: In order to avoid confrontation, try to improve your Relationship status by using whatever means are necessary to achieve this goal.

"The Ravens have just declared war on us," I said.

"You really think they might risk crossing the moors?" Ylien asked.

"They'll try," Enea said. "The news about a new war will encourage players' interest. We should expect a new surge of applicants in the next few days. Same for the Ravens."

"Do you mean they might call up an army?"

"Or a large raid at least."

"Is the castle defense-ready?"

"Not really," I replied. "We've managed to restore about 30% of its defense systems. Now we'll have to rebuild the rest ASAP. Enea and I might need to lock ourselves up in the library to study the manuscripts."

"Can't somebody else do that?" Ylien asked.

"No. These are the quest conditions. But don't worry: it'll be a few days before we face any serious threat."

"But what if the Ravens hire some top wizards to open a portal directly to the castle walls?" Ylien asked.

"They can't. The system deflects all incoming teleports to random swamp locations."

"Do the Ravens know that?" Ylien inquired.

"I think so. Which is why we might have a couple of weeks to get ready if we're lucky. You can go now. Have a look around. If you have any questions, I'll tell Archibald, Iskandar and Lethmiel to help you."

"You going already?" Stevenal asked.

"I'm afraid we have to," I said. "Time is an issue. If we manage to find the pictures of the missing runes, the Ravens can forget storming the castle. Besides, the dwarves are running out of things to do."

* * *

THE TEMPLE OF OBLIVION had changed a lot in our absence. A thick curtain of hydra skins shielded the entrance. The holes in the ceiling had been repaired. The temple was warm: Mossy Yorm made sure the fire never went out. Thanks to his frequent forays out on the moors, he had plenty of food and firewood.

The temple walls were lined with heaps of scrap cargonite: our clan's strategic supplies. After we'd redirected the ancient portal to Rion Castle, this isolated location was perfect for storing our vital supplies.

"Hi, Yorm," Enea said, waving to the troll.

"Hi to you too, Forest Nymph," Mossy Yorm replied, apparently happy to see us. "Alex! Come over to the fire. I'll make you some tea! I've got a nice big cauldron!"

"Thanks, man. Later, maybe. We need to see the library."

We walked through the rock tunnel until we came to the cave. The slab of stone covering the entrance had been dragged aside. A soft light illuminated the stone stairs.

The calligraphers I'd hired were busy copying the manuscripts.

"That's enough for today," I told them. "Go back to the castle and tell Lethmiel I've excused you."

"So where do we start?" Enea asked, walking along the shelves groaning with books. "We don't have much time. We need to come up with a search system."

"We can use our implants," I said.

"How do we do that?"

"We can connect them into a network. Do you remember what I told you about the mind expander?"

"I think so. I haven't used it yet."

"You don't have to. It's automatic. This is what we can do. Keep walking while focusing your eye on the books' spines, scanning the data. I'll process it. We both know what the word *'rune'* looks like so we can't miss the right book."

She liked the idea. "Are you ready?"

I nodded and closed my eyes. Enea started feeding me the data. My mental view filled with a sequence of fiery vertical inscriptions. I had to rotate each picture 90 degrees in order to read the titles horizontally and search through them.

My implant was a fast learner. After about a minute, I developed a light headache but I didn't have to turn each scanned spine anymore.

Most of the titles were impossible to translate. Familiar words were few. I opened two more windows in my interface: one with the Founders' alphabet and the other to copy all the titles into, creating a rough book database. We could use it in the future.

Gradually the process began to slow down as the implant started founding logical connections between the two windows, highlighting frequent combinations of letters. I tried to translate them but failed.

"I've finished the first row," Enea's voice barely reached my mind. "Want to take a break?"

"Keep going," I mouthed. I was in a strange state akin to a trance. I could sense the pressure on my mind growing, all the while sensing I was close to some mystery — a mystery that might have nothing to do with the purpose of our search but crucially important nonetheless.

"Alex,' Enea's voice trailed away. "There's something wrong with my eyes. I've got a headache, too."

"Take a seat," I mouthed. "Look away from the shelves."

"I'm sitting already. I've closed my eyes but it just won't stop!"

Indeed, the fiery titles continued to fill my mental view.

I tried to abort the process but couldn't. Now I could see the books' translucent outlines which began to merge, forming what looked like a massive database.

"What's going on?" Enea whispered, unable to shake off the implant's effect. "Alex, we can't stop this..."

Our minds went into overload. I was staring at the billions of symbols I absolutely had to read.

One after another, snippets of phrases left the gigantic lump of data and zoomed into view. Why so many numbers? Where were all the words?

Every new word was now followed by a long trail of digits. This is how it looked,

Steel Mist
3623 4863 0931 9846
2471 5092 6178 9326
3519 2074 8362 8934
... — ... — ... — ...
You've... studied... Steel Mist
... — ... — ... — ...

My consciousness was in meltdown, dissolving in all the data. I was struggling to keep my mind in control. My eyes were still moving, mechanically copying the words followed by the chains of numbers. The headache was now excruciating.

The runes... Enea...

What was happening to us?

A black flash exploded in my mind, scattering the numerical towers built with ancient symbols.

I was dropping to my death down a bottomless chasm.

Long plumes of digits trailed after my fading mind.

* * *

DARKNESS WASHED me awake.

The scattered remnants of my thoughts smoldered like fire-scorched ruins. I couldn't piece them together. Occasionally my mind exploded with visions of massive databases which resembled impossibly complex giant cities woven with the symbols of the Founders' language.

Everything around me was ephemeral, translucent, immaterial and intangible. I didn't feel my own body. The absence of time was confusing.

I heard a soft chuckle.

A shapeless glowing blob floated into my mental view, taking the form of a human figure, blurred and otherworldly.

"What did I tell you? They did drain you, didn't they? They did leave you to die."

I'd heard this voice before. The things it

said rang a few bells too. Last time I'd heard it, it was a certain Dietrich who'd said it: the ghost that used Altars of Chaos as portals.

"Dietrich? Is that you?"

"Who do you think? You're not easy to get through to these days," he sounded quite friendly this time. "Even the corporate rats can't monitor your mind anymore."

"Why can't they? Where am I? What's happened?"

"You won't believe me anyway. Have a look. See for yourself."

A blinding light assaulted my eyes.

I still didn't feel my body. Instinctively I tried to shut my eyes when I heard the familiar rustle of a surveillance camera's microdrives.

"Your mind is online. You don't have to believe me if you don't want to."

My vision momentarily lost focus, forwarded to the camera's lens. All I could see was some blurred spots around me. Still, Dietrich's presence must have somehow consolidated my consciousness, nudging it into action. I mustered enough mental effort to zoom in, changing the camera's focus.

I was looking down at a roomful of equipment: several medical machines, a few powerful neural computers and a couple of servers. There were also three unmanned control consoles, their empty seats facing holographic screens covered in some weird schemes.

I concentrated, willing the camera to turn. The servodrive creaked, forcing it into motion.

Two sarcophagus-like pieces of equipment were mounted on massive pedestals.

In-mode capsules.

They were connected to several transparent pipes and cables which reached out from the wall. Pumps were wheezing, sending fluids up and down the pipes.

The servodrive creaked again. Obeying my surge of emotion, the camera zoomed in. I peered through the tinted plastic at the face inside.

Enea.

She was pale, her eyes closed. Judging by the moving graphs on the medical monitors, she was alive.

Impossible. What was she doing here? Wasn't she supposed to be at home? I thought I knew the location of the equipment she used to log in!

Either this was one of Dietrich's dirty tricks, or... what if we were indeed in trouble? What if that's why they'd had to move her here?

The camera turned again, then refocused.

I peered through the lid of the other sarcophagus. That was me inside.

Time froze. My consciousness collapsed.

This wasn't what I'd signed up for! What kind of mind game was this? Enea and I were supposed to be in the Temple of Oblivion copying the ancient manuscripts!

Overcoming the shock, I zoomed in some more to focus on the inscription embossed on the pedestal,

Life support unit. Property of Earth's Military Space Forces.

Somewhere out of my view, pneumatic drives hissed. A door opened. I heard the sound of approaching footsteps.

A Corporation worker dressed in white coveralls walked in and took a seat at the central console. On his command, the screen filled with streams of data. He studied it for a while, then closed the windows.

The door hissed open again, letting in two more people. One was Mr. Borisov; the other, a Space Forces colonel.

"Are they okay?"

"Both are in medically induced coma on medicated support," the Corporation worker replied.

"How long is it going to last?" the Colonel asked with badly concealed irritation.

"That I can't tell you. Their mind expanders

went into simultaneous overdrive while processing the Temple library databases. Good job we noticed it in time. Their brains could have collapsed under the pressure."

"You shouldn't have done that!" the Colonel snapped.

"In that case we wouldn't have had anything at all."

"Why? Please explain. I know nothing about these things," the Colonel slumped into one of the seats. "We've given you the best equipment and plenty of time and money for your experiments! And what do you have to show for it? What prompted you to abort the process just as we started receiving the first transcripts of the Founders' technological codes?"

"These young people deserve better than having their minds scorched for the sake of your project," Mr. Borisov interrupted.

The Colonel's face turned crimson. His neck veins bulged. "The Phantom Server project is already launched! Welcome to the fucking future! If we fail to restore the Founders' space station, billions of people are going to die! The Earth is doomed, as you damn well know!"

"Not necessarily," Mr. Borisov raised his voice. "We shouldn't put all our eggs into one basket. We're sure more than ever that those who stay behind on Earth will have a chance of survival within the Crystal Sphere."

"Oh really? How would they do that?"

"Just like these two."

The Colonel sniffed his indignation. "You're a dreamer! I need the data! Do what you want! Split their skulls open if you have to!"

"I don't think it's gonna help," the corporate worker struggled to remain calm.

"Why not?"

"The technology you've shared with us is *alien*, for crissakes! It's not easily modifiable! Just as an example, we can't copy neurograms."

"That's bullshit! I know all about the Reapers! They somehow manage to obtain new neurograms for themselves, don't they?"

"The Founders' technology is based on the idea of identity matrix stored within the neural implant," the corporation worker said. "It's supposed to be immune to any external force. A person's neurograms can't be copied. The only way of obtaining them is by waiting till the person dies. Which is exactly what Dietrich did. He was our first test subject, if you remember. By killing several of our workers, he obtained snippets of their identities."

"Dietrich yes, but how about the NPCs? How did *they* manage to obtain neurograms?"

"Don't forget that the Crystal Sphere has been created specifically to test neural implants.

And all its NPCs, apart from the most primitive ones, are based on neurocomputers."

"Do you suggest that these incidents will persist?"

"No, they won't," Mr. Borisov replied firmly. "We've eliminated all of the defective mobs. Dietrich is dead. The Reapers are a thing of the past."

He rose, walked over to Enea's in-mode and checked the life support readings. "The Founders' technologies have an interesting peculiarity though. The person in possession of a neural implant has the option of sharing his or her neurograms. I think this is how those ancient alien beings exchanged their experiences, enriching each other's identities."

"Very well, then! In this case, would you *please* wake them up, explain the gravity of the situation and ask them to *kindly* forward us the deciphered data!"

"Why such a rush?"

"Because we can't continue the restoration of Argus station — the one in the Darg system — without having the Founders' codes!"

"I'm afraid we can't do that. A person suffering an information overload might not react as we expect them to," Mr. Borisov said. "I suggest we do it in a different way. Both Alex and Enea think that the data they've received is part of the Founders' magic. I'm sure they're going to copy it — or rather, their mind expanders will copy and consequently decipher the codes. All we need to do is access them without harming the hosts."

"When is that gonna happen?"

"We don't know yet. Their mind expanders are still busy processing the codes. The databases which we disguised as ancient manuscripts are absolutely enormous. The moment their mental loads drop to safe values, we'll wake them up and return them to the Crystal Sphere without stressing them out."

"Stressing them out! Don't you realize that once they're back to their castle, they'll realize they've been away for months or even years? How's that for stressing them out? Sorry, I can't wait much longer."

"I'm afraid you'll have to," Mr. Borisov said. "The data we already have is plenty to continue with the Phantom Server project. For the rest, you shouldn't worry about it. We've thought about everything. The entire Agrion cluster is about to be paused. They won't notice a thing once they're back."

"But how about other players?"

"All those close to them — both friend and foe — will be moved to cryo in-modes. They won't notice anything either. We knew of the experiments' potentially unpredictable nature. Which is why we only accepted single persons with anti-social tendencies."

"You don't mean you're capable of freezing a whole segment of the Crystal Sphere just for those two? Why?"

"Because they're our future. I'm not sure your Phantom Server project can guarantee humanity's survival. In the worst-case scenario, the Crystal Sphere might become their last refuge. Which is luckily out of your remit."

* * *

"ENOUGH," Dietrich disconnected me from the scene, once again submerging me into a darkness devoid of time and space.

"What do you want from me?"

"I showed you the truth. You should leave your body. You heard them. An identity matrix doesn't need a life-supported body in order to live in the Crystal Sphere!"

"No," I said unhesitantly.

"They've betrayed you! They used you! They basically killed you!"

"I don't believe you. You're a liar, Dietrich. It's not so difficult to fake a video. Go away!"

"You're gonna regret it. You're all gonna regret it!"

"We'll see."

"Whatever. I showed you the truth and offered you a solution. They don't understand! Can't you see? We don't have time!"

"What are you talking about?"

"I'm talking about the era of Black Sun!" he snapped. "They think they can do it! They can't! They don't have the time! I can fix it! All I need is some knowledge and a few neurograms!"

"Are you freaking mad? The era of Black Sun is a myth! It's a story made up by script writers!"

"Please help me!" Dietrich wheezed. "Leave this body! I'll take you to the testing grounds!"

"What do I want there?"

"Together we'll kill more researchers, you and I. We'll get their knowledge and their neurograms! We'll change everything here! The Crystal Sphere will belong to us!"

"You know you're a nutcase, don't you? The only truth about this is that you crave more neurograms! The rest is bullshit! Leave me alone!"

"Very well," he hissed. "I'm not strong enough yet to get you. You'll be back sooner or later. Then we'll see who's the nutcase here!"

His outline blurred, then disappeared completely.

My mind faded.

* * *

THE CRYSTAL SPHERE
THE LOST ISLAND. THE TEMPLE OF OBLIVION

"ALEX," Enea walked back into the library with a cup of tea. "You look completely exhausted. Did you fall asleep at the desk?"

"How long have I been asleep?"

"About half an hour. You're pale."

"I had a nightmare. Can we take a break? How are you feeling?"

"I feel excellent. So many interesting things happening. I'm already translating the runic sequences in the book. I even copied the pictures," she showed me her notes and drawings. "I just don't understand why there're so many numbers. Whole pages of them!"

I shrugged. Still, my body tensed up at the memory of the nightmare. "I'd rather we took a break. We can go back to the castle and give the pictures to the dwarves so they can start restoring the castle defenses."

Enea sighed. "What a shame we can't take the books with us. We are coming back here, aren't we? All this still needs to be read," she pointed at the shelfuls of manuscripts awaiting their turn.

"Of course we are," I said. "Now pick up

your notes, say goodbye to Yorm and off we go. We have too many things to do."

Enea rolled up the scrolls covered with her notes and drawings.

I couldn't stop thinking about the weird dream I'd just had.

As we walked over to the portal, my heart missed a beat. My nightmare had been too lifelike. Could it actually be true?

In a flash, we were transported thousands of miles back to Rion Castle.

My interface reacted with a standard message,

Your respawn point has been restored to its old value.

I looked around me. Nothing seemed to have changed. "Lethmiel?"

"Yes, my lord?" his voice was calm and unconcerned.

"Everything all right? How long have we been away?"

"A week, my lord. Slightly longer than usual."

"Nothing out of the ordinary happened?"

"No, sir. The dwarves had another drunken brawl in the tavern. They were at each other's beards. They're bored, my lord. They've already

---

restored the barracks and have nothing to do with their time."

"Good," I said. "They'll have loads to do now."

Enea glanced at the clock. "Jesus! I have an important meeting with the city hall in Agrion today! I'm late already!"

"Let me take you there."

"It's all right. I can manage."

"Please," I just couldn't shake off the weird dream. "I can check out the market while you're busy with the city hall. I've been meaning to do it for ages."

* * *

THE CRYSTAL SPHERE
THE CITY OF AGRION

THE MARKET was uncrowded. Not many players were online today.

"Alex, I won't be long."

"All right. I'll go check out the stalls."

Enea headed for the city hall's building. I stopped by a second-hand book stall like I always do. You never know when you might come across a rare scroll or antique manuscript.

As I sifted through the sheets of yellowed parchment, I heard the clatter of hooves coming from the town gate. A large cavalcade of mounted warriors rode onto the square.

They reined in their lathering horses by the tavern about a dozen feet away from me. The sharp odor of horse sweat hung in the air.

You could tell they'd come from afar. They must have had to battle through, judging by their dusty, tattered cloaks spotted with blood. Their richly decorated black armor was in a bad way too. The shields strapped to their saddles were chipped and dented, gaping with fresh crossbow bolt holes. The coats of arms painted upon them had faded.

The player leading the group dismounted and handed the reins to a tavern servant who'd hurried out to meet them. The tavern keeper walked out next, looking pretty frightened. I could understand him. It's not every day you meet a level-132 knight in Agrion!

I'd have loved to have known where they'd come from.

The tired warriors followed their commander's suit. I couldn't see their faces behind the lowered visors. Their gauntleted hands lay warily on their sword hilts as if they didn't trust this peaceful provincial town in the slightest.

"Jean, you have an hour's break. I'm going to find out how to get there."

"An hour, are you sure? Can't we take a day off? We need to sort out our gear."

"Shut your mouth! Let me worry about that. You'd better take care of the horses."

The tavern keeper awoke from his stupor. "How can I help the brave warriors?"

"Quit fussin'," the knight's voice boomed behind the visor. "I'm looking for a guide familiar with the Toxic Moors."

"The Toxic Moors, where exactly? It's a big place."

"Rion Castle. Ever heard about it?"

"Of course," the tavern owner replied, looking slightly lost. "The problem is, no one knows the route there."

The Dark knight pulled his helmet off and set it habitually into the crease of his arm. He ran a hand through his gray crew cut and added, unable to conceal his irritation,

"You don't understand me, peasant! I'm looking for my daughter. I haven't heard from her in three years. I'll go through your stinking little town with a fine-tooth comb if I have to! So you'd better do what I say. Go and find out how I can get to Rion. By water, by land or by magic — I don't care!"

His angry voice carried far in the air. A patrol of city guards beelined for the tavern to prevent a potential argument.

"Good morning, Sir Knight," their commander spoke politely, the way NPCs always begin their conversations. "How did you like our town? I hope your trip was uneventful?"

"Uneventful my ass! Reapers everywhere! They rob people in broad daylight! We had to battle our way here! The world is going to the dogs! Infosystems Corporation has lost the plot! If you call this uneventful-" he waved his own words away, remembering he was speaking to a cartoon.

Still, the exhaustion of the journey took the better of him. "What're you staring at?" he snapped, not at all impressed by the sight of three level-120 guards. "You want some problems?"

"My job is to preserve peace and order," the patrol commander replied impassively.

"Soon there'll be nothing to preserve," the stranger predicted.

He stood with his back to me. The level gap between us didn't allow me to read his stats. I had to activate my Neuro abilities.

Slowly his nickname floated into view,

Friedrich White

I startled.
Three years?

My back erupted in a shivery cold sweat. Three years? Reapers everywhere? The words circled my mind, freezing it solid.

I struggled to bring my shock under control. "I think I can help you."

He swung round.

A pale face. Puffy, baggy eyes. He'd changed a lot since our last meeting.

"Alex!" he stepped toward me and gave me a fatherly hug. "Is she alive? Tell me!"

I nodded. A freezing cold settled in my chest.

The city hall's door opened. Enea walked out.

Seeing her, Mr. White let go of me and stepped toward her. Gusts of wind tore at his tattered cloak. His armor glinted dimly.

Enea saw him too. "Dad? What's up? What're you doing here? How on earth did you level up so much?"

He threw his arms around her and froze, unable to speak.

END OF BOOK TWO

THE MC'S STATS AS OF THE SECOND BOOK'S END:

Alexatis. Level 44. Neuro

Life, 329.5/329.5 (Stamina, 275 + Gear, 32.5 + The Charm of the Sovereign bonus, 22)

Physical Energy, 170/170 (Strength, 155 + current abilities and the gear bonus, 15)

Mental Energy, 248/248 (Intellect, 180 + current abilities and the gear bonus, 68)

Physical Defense, 216.5 (Scaly Armor, 210 + Agility bonus, 6.5)

Physical Attack, 106,3 (Mysterious Sword at 50% Durability, 25 pt. + Strength, 13 + the gear bonus, 2 + Intense Training, 6 + character level, 44 + the Charm of the Sovereign bonus, 8.3)

Mental Defense, 89% (Self-Control + Spirit + the gear bonus + the Charm of the Sovereign bonus)

Elemental Defense, 40% (Spirit + the Scaly Breastplate + Elemental Control)

Mental Attack, 103.9 (spells studied, 50 + Unity of Schools, 2 + character level, 37 + the Charm of the Sovereign bonus, 8.9)

Mental Energy Regeneration, 18.34 pt./sec (Spirit divided by 2 = 7.5 + 0,84 bonus from Synergy, Power of Reason and Self-Control + the Charm of the Sovereign bonus, 10)

Strength, 15.5 (Secret Knowledge, 12+1 + the gear bonus, 0.5)

Intellect, 24.8 (Secret Knowledge, 18+1 + the gear bonus, 0.8 + the ring, 3 + the Exorcist bonus, 2)

Agility, 13 (12 + the gear bonus, 1)

Stamina, 27.5 (24 + the underwear kit bonus, 2 + the Charm of the Sovereign bonus, 2)

Spirit, 15 (13 + the Exorcist bonus, 2)

Main Professions, Require activation

ACHIEVEMENTS:

Celebrated Pioneer
A map-making app available

Clan Founder
+ 1,000 to Popularity, +1 to all Reputations

Exorcist
+2 to Intellect
+2 to Spirit

Centurion
Allows you to instantly summon any of the Cohort's legionnaires for the duration of 30 sec+3 sec. per level.

The Light of Passion
+1 to all stats whenever the person you love is with you.

Demon Slayer
+10% to any damage dealt to the forces of Inferno

First Amongst Equals
+10,000 to your Experience awarded for completing a unique dungeon;

+10,000 to your Experience for dealing a

critical hit to an enemy whose level is twice that of yours

Acclaimed Leader

Your influence on other players will keep growing with every new level you receive

THE NEURO DEVELOPMENT BRANCH:

Secret Knowledge, 1:
Observational Skills, 1
Spell Interception, 1
Unity of Schools, 1
Acquisition of Blows and Combos, 1
Reflex Optimization, 1
Unity of Origin, 1
Legacy, 1. Not activated. Requires level 45

Evolution, 1:
Intense Training, 3
Pain Threshold, 5
Synergy, 5
Crit, 3. Not activated. Requires level 45

Power of Reason, 1:
Insight, 1
Self-Control, 4
Enhanced Perception, 5
Energy Transfer, 1:

Elemental Control, 1 (activated ahead of schedule)

Secret Knowledge:

Eons ago, the Ancient Gods (sometimes also called the Founder Gods) tampered with our ancestors' evolution, endowing them with a number of abilities which are now almost completely extinct. Only occasionally do they resurface in certain individuals known as Neuros.

You're one of them. Both your body and mind harbor a potential yet unlocked.

+1 to Strength

+1 to Intellect

+1 to XP per each invested Ability pt.

Observational Skills:

You're highly perceptive. Whether reading ancient manuscripts or watching other people, you pay attention to every detail, immediately grasping the technique of a combat blow or a spell incantation. You can then enter the knowledge you thus receive into special books or dedicated parchment scrolls for further study.

Warning! The level of the blow or spell you intend to study cannot exceed that of your character.

Each Ability point invested gives +2% to your chances of studying the blow or the spell (regardless of whether the object of your study is an NPC or another player).

Spell Interception:

The fact that all spells are recited in the Founders' language combined with your ability to lip read allows you to learn any spell.

Warning! In order to successfully intercept a spell, the caster (observation target) should be located within your direct line of vision. At level 1, your lip-reading range is set at 30 feet.

Each Ability point invested adds 2 ft. to your lip-reading range.

Spell Interception does not preclude other possible ways of spell studying.

Acquisition of Blows and Combos:

You effortlessly memorize new movements while watching combat practice or live combat. Later, this allows you to make a drawing of the blow or even combo technique from memory, recreating both attack and defense maneuvers.

Requires Observational Skills and Intense Training.

Each Ability point invested adds +2% to your chances of studying a blow or a combo.

Unity of Origin:

According to legend, all living beings in the

Universe used to have a single ancestor. Some might snicker saying that an orc and a human being can't possibly share ancestry. Still, every legend harbors a grain of truth.

Each Ability point invested adds +2% to your chances of intercepting a spell or learning a new blow typical of other races, regardless of their affiliation (Light vs. Dark).

Unity of Schools:

Some time ago, you chanced upon an ancient book. As you struggled through it, trying to make sense of the faded writings on its crumbling pages, you were surprised to discover the writer's heretic ideas. According to the book's author, all types of magic and sorcery, including elemental and mind control, are firmly rooted in the long-forgotten school of Chaos.

Later, as you watched the effects produced by various schools of magic, your conclusions confirmed the ancient author's ideas. The powers of Chaos had been the foundation of all modern schools and practices.

Each Ability point invested adds +2% to the Range, Strength and Duration of every spell you study, as well as removes all bans and penalties for combining various kinds of magic and sorcery.

Reflex Optimization:

As you watch wildlife species (whose survival depends on their highest levels of ergonomics), you can learn and adopt their energy preservation skills. Your movements become more precise and calculated.

Each Ability point invested gives -2% to your mental and physical energy expenditures in combat.

Evolution:

The activation of this particular characteristic allows you to receive a small but continuous boost to your main stats, depending on the type of your daily activities. These changes will be visible as special boost bars situated opposite their respective characteristics in your character panel. For instance, if you read a lot you might notice the increase of your Intellect boost bar. Once the bar is full, you will receive +1 pt. to its respective characteristic.

The above boost does not cancel traditional characteristic leveling. Neither does it affect your items' bonuses.

Intense Training:

Each spell or blow you study requires constant perfecting. In order to improve your attack and defense skills, you need to practice a lot, creating your own combinations and turning new moves into reflexes.

Ability bonus: your damage, defense, mob control and aura range will improve. This only applies to the physical and magic skills you use on a regular basis, without affecting those you've learned but failed to apply.

Each Ability point invested adds +5% to attack strength.

Pain Threshold:

You learn to control pain. You might have already discovered, by extreme trial and error, that you don't experience pain as long as your Health is above 80%. As your HP dwindle, you start experiencing an increasing pain.

Each Ability point invested raises your pain threshold 3%. The maximum pain threshold allowed is 50% HP.

Synergy:

Everything in our world is interconnected. You can use various sources of energy, including elements, ancient artifacts and places of power marked by megalithic monuments. As you study them and listen intently to the world around you, you begin to tune in into various energy currents, allowing you to locate their sources and use them to restore your powers and even life.

Starting at level 20, you'll be able to trap and store any excess physical or mental energy within energy crystals.

+5% to your physical and mental energy regeneration speed.

Power of Reason:

A Neuro's intellect affects everything he or she does.

Every 30 pt. Intellect add +3% to both attack and defense and +5% to the XP received for successfully using the blows or spells you've learned from other characters. All such blows or spells will add +3% to your chances of dealing critical damage or, when used in defense, to your chances of reusing the blow or spell with decreased cooldown times and -50% of required energy expenditure.

+10% to your mental energy regeneration speed.

Insight:

You're constantly busy studying everything around you, analyzing the nature of all events and perfecting your abilities and skills. Your goal is to get to the bottom of everything trying to work out how things work instead of mindlessly using them, be it a spell, a blow or a professional skill.

Each Ability point invested gives -3% to

cooldown times and energy expenditure required for all types of physical and mental attack, defense and impact.

+2% to profession leveling speed for all farming and manufacturing professions.

Self-Control:

You have a natural 25% resistance to all kinds of magic and mind control. You can successfully resist mental attacks, preserving clarity of mind.

Each Ability point invested adds +2% to your chances of repelling a negative effect or boosting a positive one, be it a spell or your opponent's ability. +2% to your chances of successfully casting a spell when attacked. +3% to mental energy regeneration speed.

On reaching level 5, this ability will allow you to consciously control your mental energy distribution between several recipients — for instance, a magic artifact or an item of gear.

Enhanced Perception:

You learn with remarkable ease. Your outlook isn't limited by racial or class prejudices. You're free from all phobias and superstitions.

As a result, you see and notice a lot compared to others. Your night vision and reduced visibility navigation skills are considerably superior to theirs. At level 20, you will receive a new primary skill, Twilight Vision, which you can consequently level up and improve.

Enhanced Perception allows you to detect danger before others can. It also adds +20% to your chances of seeing a stealthed-up enemy stalking you. Each Ability point invested adds +1 to your Field of Vision Range.

Legacy:

From now on, you can control the ancient blood magic which exists in synergy with nature. The Founders' artifacts will reveal their secret properties to you alone.

Any acquired spells will be available 3 levels earlier than required.

-5% to Mental Energy required to cast a spell.

Crit:

+10% to your chances of dealing a critical hit. +5% to your chances of dealing damage with the Element of Chaos in a successful (i.e., not blocked by the enemy) attack. Every new level of the ability adds +3% to your chances of dealing elemental damage.

Energy Transfer:

You've learned to accumulate the

surrounding Elements' energy in order to transfer it to stones or charge up magic scrolls. Every new level of the ability adds +5% to both energy accumulation and energy transfer rates.

Elemental Control:

Activated ahead of schedule

+20 to Resistance to the Elements

Currently, in order to interact with the elements, you're required to use one of the Founders' artifacts built for that purpose. Direct interaction is available from level 10.

Requirements:

Intellect, 25

Willpower, 25

ALSO BY ANDREI LIVADNY

The Edge of Reality (Phantom Server Book #1)

He is a cyber dweller. A gamer who's grown up in the web of virtual illusion woven from hundreds of phantom worlds. His biggest dream is to dump the real world for good.

His desperate hunger of new experiences forces him to take a risk and become one of the first proud owners of a neuronet implant. The new gadget becomes part of him — but soon it's not enough. If only he could finally burn all his bridges and make a step beyond the real world!

He soon gets this opportunity. A new universe, overflowing with mystery and unimaginable, mind-blowing authenticity, opens up before him.

This is Phantom Server. The game of the future where your pursuit of an adrenaline rush soon turns into a battle for survival. But the most terrifying mystery lies ahead when you gradually start to realize: this is a road of no return. Your every decision may become your last. Your every step leads you further along the abyss between life and death.

The Outlaw (Phantom Server Book #2)

The Eurasia fleet has entered the Darg star system. The unsuspecting players look forward to the adventure of their lifetimes. Zander alone is now facing a harsh and unpredictable "alternative storyline".

The girl he loved is gone. His nervous system is impregnated with artificial neurons that contain fragments of ancient AIs and their identities. Zander's body is implanted with alien artifacts that allow him to survive in the deadly cyberspace of Phantom Server. But his unique development branch pushes him toward the edge of the precipice where his every step may become his last; where future itself is vague and uncertain.

Black Sun (Phantom Server Book #3)

Zander and his gamer friends used to face danger without fear, finding strength in the promise of a safe respawn. Nothing could harm or destroy them. This was only a game... or was it?

A game, played in an ancient hyperspace network. A game involving dozens of real-life alien civilizations. Earth is deserted. The fate of humanity is unknown.

The few human survivors are now stuck in

the Darg star system. All they can do is fight to the last. They must find the Phantom Server — the nucleus of the interstellar network created by the ancient civilization of the Founders. In order to live, they must solve its mystery or die trying.

The Crystal Sphere (The Neuro Book #1)

Alex is one of us. An office rat during daytime, he spends sleepless nights playing his favorite MMO game: a familiar, predictable world which is about to collapse. A new virtual universe arrives to replace it, aggressively devouring all others: the Crystal Sphere.

Alex gets involved in testing new technologies which promise to revolutionize gaming. Fitted out with a neuroimplant which provides a 100% authenticity of experience, he has to survive in the Crystal Sphere against all odds. What is he turning into? Will he become yet another expendable test subject — or the first player to transcend reality?

Humans have to deal with the treacherous nature of cyberspace in this powerful prequel to *Phantom Server*.

ABOUT THE AUTHOR

Andrei Livadny is a popular Russian science fiction author. Born on May 27 1969 in the city of Pskov, he was an avid reader from an early age. But it was the Russian translation of Robert A. Heinlein's *The Orphans of the Sky* that decided his choice of future occupation. The story has become a pivotal moment in the boy's life, leaving a lasting impression on him.

Andrei wrote his first book at the age of eight. Since then, he's never stopped working on new books. His passion for science fiction has gradually become his career.

In 1998, Andrei debuted in Russia's leading publishing house EKSMO with his novella *The Island of Hope*. Since then, he has penned over 90 books that have enjoyed a total of 153 editions.

Andrei has created several unique worlds, each unlike the previous. He wrote *A History of Our Galaxy* with humanity itself as a protagonist. This sixty-book series creates a history of our future civilization and its contacts with alien races, forming a convincing and logical picture of humanity's development for two millennia from now.

Besides hard science fiction, Andrei Livadny also works in cyberpunk genres which allow him to focus on human relationships and raise questions about artificial intelligence and identity uploading, describing cyberspace as humanity's future environment.

The English translation of *A History of Our Galaxy* will be available shortly.

Want to be the first to know about our latest LitRPG, sci fi and fantasy titles from your favorite authors?

Subscribe to our **NEW RELEASES** newsletter:
http://eepurl.com/b7niIL

Thank you for reading *The Curse of Rion Castle!*
If you like what you've read, check out other sci fi,
fantasy and LitRPG novels published by Magic Dome
Books!

Dark Paladin LitRPG series by Vasily Mahanenko:
The Beginning
The Quest

**The Dark Herbalist LitRPG series
by Michael Atamanov:**
Video Game Plotline Tester
Stay on the Wing

The Neuro LitRPG series by Andrei Livadny:
The Crystal Sphere
The Curse of Rion Castle

**The Way of the Shaman LitRPG series
by Vasily Mahanenko:**
Survival Quest
The Kartoss Gambit
The Secret of the Dark Forest
The Phantom Castle
The Karmadont Chess Set
The Hour of Pain (a bonus short story)

Galactogon LitRPG series by Vasily Mahanenko:
Start the Game!

Phantom Server LitRPG series by Andrei Livadny:
Edge of Reality
The Outlaw
Black Sun

**Perimeter Defense LitRPG series by Michael
Atamanov:**
Sector Eight
Beyond Death
New Contract

In order to have new books of the series translated faster, we need your help and support! Please consider leaving a review or spread the word by recommending *The Curse Of Rion Castle* to your friends and posting the link on social media. The more people buy the book, the sooner we'll be able to make new translations available.

Thank you!

Till next time!